# Caller Number Nine

CARRIE JACOBS

Copyright Notice

This is a work of fiction. Names, characters, places, and incidents are either the product of the author's imagination or are used fictitiously. Any resemblance to actual persons, living or dead, events, or locales is entirely coincidental.

Copyright © 2020 by Carrie Jacobs

ISBN: 978-1-7356311-0-3

All rights reserved. No part of this book may be reproduced or used in any manner, including for the training of generative artificial intelligence purposes, without written permission of the copyright owner except for the use of brief quotations in a book review. For more information, email carriejacobsauthor@gmail.com or visit carriejacobs.com.

Cover Design by Carrie Jacobs

Cover Art from Deposit Photos and/or Canva

First Edition 2020

Welcome to Hickory Hollow!

Each novel in the Hickory Hollow series is a stand-alone, and can be read in any order. There are some character appearances across books, so there may be some very minor spoilers if you read the books out of order.

<u>Hickory Hollow titles</u>:
Drunk on a Plane
Caller Number Nine
The Boy Next Door
Luck of the Draw
Cat Burglar
Mending Fences
Two Tickets to Paradise
Bad Advice
Where There's a Will (novella)

<u>Stand Alone titles</u>:
The Bucket List

For details about all of the Hickory Hollow books, visit my website at carriejacobs.com

For exclusive sneak peeks, behind-the-scenes information, and much more, sign up for my newsletter at carriejacobs.com.

*for Molly Jane*
*the goodest girl ever*

# Chapter One

Like it or not, Margo Lewis was on vacation.

A *camping* vacation.

"Who in their right mind does this for fun," she grumbled, shoving a suitcase in the back of her SUV. Since winning the contest, she'd come close to canceling a dozen times. The timing was awful. She'd just bought into a partnership at the Hickory Hollow Veterinary Clinic, but a week away from her stepmother's "Reunite Brad and Margo" campaign was the final temptation.

She'd given Brad's ring back six months ago, but neither he nor her stepmother seemed to have gotten the memo. Maybe being out of reach for a week would get it through their heads.

Besides, she reminded herself, it would be wasteful and kind of rude to *not* go on this vacation. Not only was she an unrepentant workaholic, she was an unapologetic trivia nerd, and the radio contest had been irresistible. She hadn't even considered the prize when she dialed the number. In fact, she hadn't given it a second thought until the prize packet arrived in the mail, detailing her all-inclusive trip to the Hickory Hollow Campground.

Margo started the engine, then fought the urge to turn it back off, take her suitcase inside, and go to work. *What is my problem? I've wanted a vacation for ages, and now that I'm getting one, I don't want it. Okay, not true. I do want it. I need it. Get it together, Margo.*

She squinted against the noontime June sun and tried to remember the last time she'd taken time off. She came up empty. Even back in college, she took courses year-round, and when she'd had school breaks, she'd worked extra hours to save money.

During the easy fifteen-minute drive to the Hickory Hollow Campground, she finally remembered her last real vacation. Disney. She'd been twelve and in the seventh grade. Twenty-two years ago. Her family had gone back to Disney when she was a junior in high school, but she hadn't wanted to take the time off work, so they'd gone without her. Her younger sister had been warned not to buy Margo any souvenirs since she didn't go along. Ashley bought her a Mickey Mouse t-shirt anyway.

Time off. What a concept.

She turned off the paved road and drove down a long gravel driveway. The tension – mostly self-inflicted – began draining from her shoulders as the lush green trees closed in behind the car, blocking out the real world. The road suddenly spilled out into a big square parking lot. At the far corner, bright red balloons gaily danced in the summer breeze, calling attention to colorful signs tacked to the fence row. The signs proclaimed, "Caller Number Nine Radio Contest Winner Parking!" with The Hollow 99's logo emblazoned on the bottom of each sign, complete with a cartoon picture of their mascot, Hollow Dog.

Margo pulled into a spot and sat for a few minutes, checking out her surroundings. A stone path led from the parking lot to the lodge – a three-story log home that belonged on the cover of a magazine. A massive wrap-around porch lined with rocking chairs was the focal point of the front of the building. To the left, a path led from the lodge to a children's playground and an area with several picnic pavilions. To the right, she could only see trees.

A little bubble of excitement welled up in her belly. She was truly on vacation. Vacation! She grabbed her purse and prize packet from the passenger seat and jumped out of the car. She heard water flowing but couldn't quite tell where the river was in relation to the parking lot. Bird songs and chirps filled the air.

Red balloons and arrows cheerfully marked the sloping path up to the lodge. She climbed the six or seven steps up to the big front porch and opened the heavy wooden door. Margo's eyes widened as she took in the room. The walls, floor, and ceiling were all wood plank, buffed to a shine, highlighting the wood's grain. A stone counter stood off to the right, and to the left was a waiting area with comfortable-looking leather furniture arranged around a massive stone fireplace.

"Hi, can I help you?"

Margo tore her eyes from the fireplace and smiled. "Hi. I'm Margo Lewis. I-"

The short blonde woman sped out from behind the counter and snatched Margo's hand, pumping it enthusiastically. A bright smile only emphasized the friendliness of the woman's face. "Of course! Margo. You're one of our contest winners." She let go of Margo's hand and returned to her spot behind the counter, talking the whole time. She patted the countertop. "Come on over here and I'll get you signed in. Welcome, welcome. I'm Bonnie Taylor. Not to be confused with Bonnie Tyler. I can't carry a tune in a bucket. Of course, you're probably too young to know who Bonnie Tyler is anyway. Doug tells me I should stop introducing myself that way because nobody gets it."

Margo chuckled. "Nice to meet you. And I *do* know who Bonnie Tyler is. 'Total Eclipse of the Heart' is one of my favorite songs."

Bonnie grinned. "Mine, too. Doug will be along in a few minutes. Oh. Doug's my husband. I don't think I said that. We're the owner-operators and we'll be taking care of you for the next week. He'll get your bags to your tent for you."

"Tent?" Margo had been hoping for a cabin.

Bonnie nodded vigorously. "Have you been camping before?"

"Summer camp a few times."

With a wink, Bonnie said, "You're in for a real treat, I promise."

A tent didn't sound like much of a treat. "About that tent. I... Do I have to assemble it or something? Roughing it really isn't my forte." Her shoulders deflated. This was a terrible idea. Why she thought she'd enjoy camping for an entire week was beyond her.

"Here comes Doug now. I think you'll be pleased with the accommodations." Bonnie winked and introduced Margo to her husband, who was very tall and dark-haired, a stark contrast to his wife.

"Right this way," he said, leading her back to the parking lot. A golf cart sat idling behind her car. "We'll get your bags to your tent and I'll show you where the facilities are, then you can look around a bit. We're having a welcome meeting for all the contest winners at the main lodge at four o'clock, followed by dinner."

Doug secured Margo's bags to the back of the golf cart. "Hop in." When she was seated and holding on, he drove down a path that took them behind the lodge and through a grove of trees. He waved to the right. "The cabins are over that direction."

"I was kind of hoping for a cabin. I didn't know what to expect, but I'm not too sure about roughing it."

Doug grinned but said nothing until they crested a hill and he jerked his chin toward their destination. "Tents are up ahead."

Two rows of tiny white buildings, five on each side of the path, rose in front of them. As they got closer, she saw they were constructed with thick canvas. Each "tent" was a canvas cabin set on a wooden platform large enough to serve as a floor inside and a little front porch outside. Each tent/cabin had two rocking chairs on its porch.

Doug rolled the cart to a stop in front of one of the cabins. "Here's your tent."

"This is a tent?" Margo took it in. The canvas front walls were tied open to reveal the inside of the building. A large bed - a real bed - took up the middle of the room. A small dresser and gas lamp sat beside the bed. Pieces of the canvas were rolled up on each wall, exposing mesh windows.

A wood picnic table was placed beside each tent, and each cabin had its own fire ring with a small stack of wood and a metal rack for cooking. The tent rows were staggered so the front porch of each tent faced the picnic table of the tent across the path, rather than having a direct view of the neighbors.

Doug watched her for a moment, grinning. "Yeah, most people don't mind roughing it when they see the tents."

"No, when I heard the word 'tent,' I was expecting something much more rustic."

"There's even one outlet behind the nightstand so you can charge your phone or tablet or whatever. If you want to rough it for real, we do have regular tents and sleeping bags in the storage room. I can bring one out for you."

"Nope, this'll do quite nicely."

He consulted a clipboard. "You're in number four. Tent number is right there." He pointed to a large wooden number four nailed to a fence post beside the tent's porch.

Margo looked around. "There are ten of these? Are all the contest winners going to be staying here? With regular campers?"

"Yes, yes, and no. Five of the tents will be occupied by contest winners, no other campers in this area this week. It's all reserved for you guys." Doug pointed to a log building at the end of a dirt path that ran through the little tent village. "Restroom and showers are in that building there. Ladies on the right, men on the left. The other areas have their own facilities, so you won't be bothered by too many other campers here." He pointed to the right side of the building. "The path that goes past the restrooms will take you to the river."

"Great, thanks."

Doug carried her bags into the tent and set them beside the bed. "If you need anything, you can come to the lodge or text us anytime." He handed her a card with their cell numbers.

"Thanks."

"Remember, welcome meeting at the main lodge at four." Doug hopped back into the golf cart and sped away, a trail of dust following him.

Margo watched him leave, then turned to investigate her tent. It was like a rustic hotel room, with a queen-size bed. She sat and gave it a little test bounce. It was exceedingly comfortable. Especially compared to the vision she'd had of sleeping on the ground in a sleeping bag when Bonnie said she'd be staying in a tent. The bed was covered with several layers of thin blankets, so no matter how warm or chilly the unpredictable June nights got, she'd never be too hot or too cold.

She marveled at how cozy the room was. The handcrafted nightstand was topped by an old-fashioned looking hurricane lamp that was actually electric, sitting on a delicate doily. The nightstand had one drawer, and just like in a hotel, a black Bible with silver foil letters rested inside.

Margo couldn't think of a single detail she'd change to improve the room. Except maybe add a bathroom. She was not looking forward to using a community bathroom for a week. Then again, it was definitely better than a port-a-potty. Or an outhouse. Bleh.

Margo leaned back against the fluffy pillows. Oh yeah, she could get used to this. She kicked her shoes off and swung her legs onto the bed. The air was full of chirping birds and the faint sound of the river flowing nearby. The melody of laughter floated from somewhere beyond the canvas walls of her tent. She considered getting up to close the door flaps, but she was just too comfortable. For the first time in probably ten years, Margo dozed off into a relaxing nap.

That relaxing nap came to a most un-relaxing, abrupt end when a large, furry, black body jumped onto the bed with her. Groggy and startled, Margo yelled, "Bear!" and half-rolled, half-fell out of the bed.

The "bear" barked and wagged his tail enthusiastically.

## *Chapter Two*

"Scout! Come!" Connor commanded, rushing onto his neighbor's little wooden porch.

The black Labrador jumped off the bed, bounded to Connor's side and dropped to sit, his tail thumping against the wooden floor.

"I'm so sorry about that. Are you okay?" Connor took a tentative step toward the woman standing beside the bed, her fists pressed to her hips. Her pretty hair caught his eye. Various shades of brown, blonde, and almost black came together in a long ponytail.

"Yeah, I'm fine. Holy crap." She turned her attention to the dog, pointing at him. "You scared me. Naughty dog."

Scout grinned, his tongue lolling out of his mouth. Clearly unashamed of his behavior, he went over to Margo and offered his head for scratches.

"Sorry again. He's usually much better about staying close…" Connor trailed off as he recognized the woman in front of him. His mouth went dry. His heart thumped faster in his chest. No. It couldn't be. Could it?

She was saying, "Yeah, labs can be pretty obedient, but all

bets are off when something catches their attention. No harm done." She reached down to rub the dog's ears.

"Margo?" His lips hadn't formed that word in seventeen years.

She jolted upright and warily studied him for a minute. He knew the second she made the connection. The friendly openness on her face vanished, replaced by a detached sort of professional expression and she took a step back. "Connor. I didn't recognize you." Ice. Her tone was pure ice.

He ran a hand over his thick beard. "I get that a lot. It's the whole lumberjack thing, I think." He gave a little laugh, which she didn't return. "I guess we're neighbors." He gestured to tent number six, next to hers.

"Great."

Connor could tell from her tight expression she most definitely did not think it was great. "Okay, well, I guess we'll see you around. C'mon, Scout."

"Bye, Scout." She turned and busied herself with something on the bedside table.

Connor stepped off her porch and waved a finger at Scout, who gave Margo another look before following Connor to their tent.

"You need to stay with me, dog. You can't be running off into other people's tents, and you definitely can't be jumping into their beds. I mean it."

Scout stared up at him, wagging his tail as if he understood but had no intention of listening.

"I'll explain later." Connor flopped his duffle bag onto his bed and unzipped it. The harder he tried not to think about Margo, the more insistent his brain was that he reexamine every detail of her. The years had been exceedingly kind to Margo. She'd be thirty-four now, same as him, and she was even more beautiful than she had been in high school. Her hair was longer, but her eyes were still the prettiest shade of chocolate brown he'd ever seen.

He remembered looking into those eyes. And he remembered those eyes filled with hurt, refusing to meet his. Of all the things he'd go back and do over if he could…

Connor zipped the duffel bag back up, then unzipped it again. "What was I doing with this, Scout?" Seeing Margo had thrown him for a loop. How many times over the years had he almost reached out to apologize but found a reason not to? It looked like his excuses had just run out.

Scout's tail thumped against the floor.

"Oh, yeah." He pulled a book out, set his bag on the floor beside the bed, then went out to sit on a rocking chair on his porch. Scout stood in front of him, then made a few circles before laying down with a loud huff.

"Big day, huh?" Connor reached over and scratched Scout's head. "Better rest up. We have a full evening ahead."

At a quarter 'til four, a dinner bell clanged from the direction of the lodge house. Connor closed his book and tossed it onto the bed. "You stay here."

Scout's eyebrows twitched, but he didn't bother moving.

As Connor stepped off his porch and onto the path, he discreetly watched Margo out of the corner of his eye. She walked ahead of him, moving fast. He guessed she was trying to make sure he didn't catch up and try to walk with her. He hung back, giving her space, wondering where her life had taken her since he'd last seen her.

A young couple passed him, holding hands. They both smiled and said hello, and he returned the greeting. He could hear a few more people chatting from behind him.

The campers gathered on the lodge's front porch, their group of eight forming a haphazard semicircle around Bonnie and Doug as they welcomed everyone and explained the VIP experience they'd created just for them, which included meals and activities like canoeing, hiking, nightly campfires, and a huge bonfire on the last evening.

He only half-listened. Margo was on the other side of the semicircle, directly in his line of vision. He studied her face until she caught him looking and he forced his eyes to the ground. When he glanced back up, her gaze darted away just as his had.

This was going to be a long week.

# Chapter Three

Margo crossed her arms over her chest, trying to pay attention to Bonnie's enthusiastic recitation of the activities that were planned for the group. Hiking, campfires, games, yada yada. Her attention wandered.

She looked at the rocking chairs neatly lined up on the lodge's porch, at the back of the head in front of her, at a bug on the window, at the wooden floor planks… anywhere but at Connor. Why was he here? Not just *here*-here, but in Hickory Hollow at all? Why did seeing him affect her after all this time? Her gaze flitted to him. He was looking at her. She jerked her head to the side, forcing herself to look at Doug, even as her face burned.

"Are there any questions?" Doug asked.

A guy standing near Connor raised his hand. "My wife wants to know the significance of the number nine."

Doug and Bonnie exchanged a glance and chuckled. She said, "You could say it's our lucky number. It was Doug's jersey number in high school for football and basketball."

"And baseball," he added.

Bonnie rolled her eyes with an affectionate smile. "Yes, heaven forbid I forget baseball. Our anniversary and both our sons' birthdays are in September, and this marks nine years since we took over the campground. We thought it would be fun to run the contest with our lucky number. Maybe it'll end up being lucky for all of you as well."

Margo doubted it, but she couldn't help but smile at their enthusiasm.

Bonnie continued, "Okay, we have the dining room set up for dinner. We're sure a lot of you want to go off on your own, but we thought it would be nice to get to know each other a little bit since it's the first night. If you'll follow Doug, he'll get you situated while I check on the food."

Margo stepped into a spot near the end of the line as the contest winners – and their guests – followed Doug. She felt out of place. There had been five winners, and she and Connor appeared to be the only ones who hadn't brought a guest along. Great.

In the dining room, which was more of a rustic-themed cafeteria, a round table was set up for them. Chatter filled the room as people grabbed chairs and sat with their partners, leaving only one open chair. Next to Connor. She fiddled with her napkin, devoting an incredible amount of attention to placing it on her lap and smoothing out every crease, real and imaginary.

Thankfully, he was talking with the couple on his left, so she shifted to her right and smiled at the woman next to her. Before they could strike up a conversation, though, Bonnie and Doug stood, waiting for everyone to quiet.

Behind them, two servers arranged bowls on a long buffet table. Bonnie reminded the contest winners of the hours the dining room would be open, that there would always be bottled water and cold cut sandwiches available in the attached kitchen, and ended with, "There's plenty of food, we hope you enjoy it."

Margo stood when the people beside her did and followed them to the buffet line. She was keenly aware of Connor right behind her. She tried to ignore his existence and focus on the tag sticking out of the pink tank top in front of her, but her mind refused to cooperate. Connor looked so different with a full beard and muscles filling out his plaid button-down shirt with the sleeves rolled up above his elbows to show off his solid forearms. Not that she'd noticed his forearms. Or the way his shirt strained across his shoulders. Or his full lips when he tentatively smiled at her. Nope. Hadn't noticed any of that.

The last time she'd seen him, he was tall and gangly with a baby-face. That had been a good look for him, but this? This was fantas- she cut herself off. Nope. No way. She'd be cordial, but he was still Connor. He was still the jerk who'd played with her heart. He'd lied. He'd used her. Just seeing him again dredged up old memories, and they stung. No matter how pretty he might be on the outside, a leopard rarely changed their spots on the inside.

She moved through the line, mentally arguing with herself that leopards probably didn't have spots on the inside as she piled her plate with spaghetti, garlic bread, meatballs, and topped it all off with a generous helping of parmesan cheese. Her stomach rumbled, reminding her she hadn't eaten since breakfast, and that had only been a sad granola bar on the go.

Back at the table, Margo readjusted her napkin in her lap and waited for the rest of the guests to settle back into their seats. From the corner of her eye, she watched Connor arrange his napkin. His hands were large, strong. A tiny white scar stood out on the tanned back of his right hand, near the knuckle of his ring finger. Not that she was paying attention. He leaned slightly toward her, his broad shoulder invading her peripheral vision. She caught the faint scent of his cologne. Or maybe detergent. She absolutely did not inhale slowly to determine that it was, in fact, detergent.

"What do you do these days?" Connor asked.

"Work, mostly." She glanced over and made the mistake of looking into the blue-gray eyes that had captured her fragile teenage heart so long ago.

"Still working with animals?"

He remembered? "Yes. I'm a veterinarian. I'm a partner now at the Hickory Hollow Veterinary Clinic."

His eyebrows rose. "That's great."

"And you?" She nodded at his plaid shirt. "Do you chop wood for a living?"

Crinkles appeared at the corner of his eyes as he smiled broadly. "Nah, lumberjacking is a hobby. I'm a structural engineer."

Margo caught the falter in his smile. "And what does a structural engineer do?"

"Inspect construction sites, make sure everything's up to code. Stuff like that."

"Ah. So you're the guy with the white hat and clipboard who watches everyone else do the actual work." She internally winced at how nasty that sounded.

Connor must not have taken it personally, since he grinned at her. "Exactly."

"Do you enjoy it?"

He shrugged. "Sure."

"Good." She looked around the table, studying her fellow campers as she picked at her food. Conversation slowed as everyone ate, then ramped up again as everyone finished.

Bonnie pushed her own empty plate away and said, "Alrighty, now that we're all fed, let's go around the table and tell us all a little bit about yourselves. Chandler?"

The pretty brunette next to Bonnie blushed slightly. Margo guessed she was in her early twenties. "Oh. Okay, um, I'm Chandler and this is my husband, Oren. We got married last month, so this is our honeymoon." Her hand curled around his upper arm as she gazed adoringly at him.

Everyone applauded and offered the young couple their congratulations. Oren put his arm across the back of Chandler's chair and gave a nod. "What she said. And thanks." He looked to the next person.

The man beside Oren took his turn. He was good-looking, fit, probably in his mid-thirties. He ran a hand over his short blondish hair as he leaned forward and put his elbows on the table. "Hi. I'm Tanner and this is my big sister, Sarah. I'm an ER doctor and I've been told I don't spend enough time with my family since I'm never away from the hospital. So here we are."

Sarah chuckled, revealing a smile identical to her brother's. "We're hoping to get through this togetherness without killing each other. I've been abroad for four years, so it's not Tanner's fault we haven't spent much time together. My husband is visiting his family in Colorado with our six kids, yes, I said six, so I'm going to enjoy every second of relaxation and quiet that I can."

When Sarah was finished, she looked at Margo to go next.

"Hi. I'm Margo." She gave a little wave. "I can sort of relate to Tanner. I'm a veterinarian, and I spend more time at the clinic than my own house. I haven't had an actual vacation since I was a kid, so my goal for this trip is to read an entire book, cover to cover. One without pictures of animal anatomy."

When the polite chuckling ended, Bonnie snapped her fingers and said, "Books, that's something I forgot to mention. There's a lending library in the lobby, right next to the fireplace. We have a good variety of books. You're all free to borrow anything you like during your stay. We do ask you to use the signout sheet. Sorry to interrupt."

After a beat, Connor added his introduction. "I'm Connor. Structural engineer. Grew up in Hickory Hollow, moved out to Oregon, and moved back just in time to catch the radio contest. My date for this vacation is my black lab, Scout."

The woman beside Connor patted his arm. "You seem really outdoorsy. This trip must be right up your alley."

"Yeah, I like the outdoors."

Margo saw him pull his arm off the table, away from the woman. And what a woman she was. All fake hair, fake tan, fake nails, fake boobs. Probably wanted everyone to get a look at the great job her surgeon did since they were barely covered. How lucky for Connor that they were right in his face. A little bubble of something suspiciously like jealousy flared. What? Oh, heck no. *That* was unexpected. And unacceptable.

The woman grinned and spoke to Connor more than anyone else in the group. "I'm Roxanne. I'm the CFO for a finance company based out of Pittsburgh. I'm here with my friend Shane. My goal is to have a really, *really* good time."

Margo couldn't contain her eyeroll. Could this woman be any more ridiculous? Or pathetic? Or obvious about coming on to Connor? Not that she cared, of course. She was only concerned about poor Shane, who winced when Roxanne called him her friend.

Shane cleared his throat. "Yeah, so, hi. I'm Shane. I teach high school math and accounting. I'm glad Roxy was able to take the time off for this vacation." He rested his arm on the back of her chair.

Roxanne leaned forward, her eyes still on Connor. "Me, too," she added.

Margo had never seen it, but she suspected lions pouncing on a wounded antelope had a more subtle approach than Roxanne. Sarah's eye roll suggested Margo wasn't alone in her opinions. Good, because that meant her own reaction was about Roxanne's absurdity. It had nothing to do with Connor. Nothing at all.

Doug lightly smacked his palm on the table. "Alrighty then. You already know Bonnie and I have had the campground for nine years. We inherited it from her parents, and hopefully at least one of our kids will want to run it someday. We ran this contest to try to bring in some more local folks who might not be aware of what all goes on here. For instance, a lot of folks don't realize our mini-golf course is open to the public."

Bonnie picked up as soon as Doug paused for breath. "At the end of your vacation, the local newspaper will be stopping by for a photo of the winners and to get your thoughts on the facilities. With your permission, of course." She stopped herself. "I'm probably boring you since this was all in your prize packet. Tomorrow we'll start with a grand tour of the entire grounds in the morning, then we have a hike planned. As always, all the activities we have planned are completely optional. If you want to do your own thing, please feel free. You won't offend us in the least, honest."

Roxanne lifted her glass to her lips and quietly said, "I can think of a few activities I'd like to do."

Connor jumped about a foot in the air, his legs knocking against the table. Margo saw Roxanne's hand slip back into her own lap. Connor's discomfort would have been more amusing if the whole situation wasn't so awkward for everyone.

Bonnie was on her feet in a flash. "Oh, my goodness, are you okay?"

"Yup, yes, I'm fine. I, um, I saw brownies. On the buffet. Over there." He took an awkward step away from the table.

Doug jumped up, too. "Sorry, we don't want to keep anyone from dessert. Please. Help yourself."

Margo stifled a laugh as Connor side-eyed Roxanne on his way to the buffet table. Taking pity on him, she wasn't sure why, she got up and followed him to the desserts before Roxanne could get behind him.

He piled his plate with brownies, cookies, and a scoop of ice cream that he drizzled with chocolate syrup.

Margo selected a brownie with peanut butter chips.

Back at the table, he said, "Thanks, I owe you one."

"You might want to booby trap your tent because I can't protect you there."

"I really hope that's not necessary." He shuddered and shoveled a spoonful of ice cream in his mouth. "This is really good. You should get some."

Margo picked at her brownie, wondering why she was giving Connor the time of day, let alone having an actual conversation with him. Maybe because they were the only two without partners? Her train of thought was interrupted when Connor jumped a little, surprised by Roxanne's red talons gripping his forearm. Margo's lips twitched. It was like being on the set of a really bad soap opera.

"You're right, Connor, this ice cream is to die for." Her eyes drifted shut in ecstasy.

Margo barely managed to not laugh out loud. No ice cream on Earth was *that* good.

Connor extracted his arm and wolfed down the rest of his dessert in silence while Margo finished her brownie. Roxanne kept making suggestive noises about her ice cream. It was absurd. It made Margo think of the boy-crazy girls in high school.

High school.

Every bit of amusement vanished as the last bit of half-chewed brownie in her mouth turned to a sinister tar. Bad memories mixed with the chocolaty lump, nearly choking her. Forcing herself to swallow the gummy mess, she fought the sudden nausea in her constricting throat and pushed the plate away.

"You okay?"

Her gaze darted up to meet Connor's concerned eyes. Afraid to speak lest she throw up, she simply nodded and faked a smile. She took tiny sips of water until the feeling passed and the last crumbs crawled down her throat.

The volume of conversation around them increased as people finished their desserts. Doug stood up and said, "Okay, guys, we'll be doing campfire and s'mores in the main field behind the lodge at full dark. Until then, you have a few hours on your own. Stay and get to know each other or explore the grounds. Or take a nap. Which is what I would do in your shoes." He finished with a laugh.

A few people stayed seated and chatting, and a few more got up and filed toward the door. Margo wanted nothing more than to get away from Roxanne and the memories that exhumed themselves over dinner. She put her trash in the designated bin and headed for the exit. Before she could stop herself, Margo took a couple of long strides and caught up with Connor, who'd just gone out the door. Outside, Margo breathed in the fresh air. The heat of the day was being gently carried away by the early evening breeze.

Despite a lingering discomfort, she kept her tone light. "You okay, or do you need me to escort you to your tent?"

He snorted. "Funny. I have the feeling I'm going to be looking over my shoulder for the rest of this vacation."

"I'm guessing Scout won't be much of a guard dog."

"Not even a little bit. He might knock somebody over or lick them to death, but that's about it."

"Wait. Are we talking about Scout or Roxanne?" Margo snickered.

"Stop, that's not funny." Connor grimaced, the crinkles at the edges of his eyes deepening. "Just no."

Margo burst out laughing. "Yes, it is. It's hilarious. You should see your face." At the word, she couldn't stop herself from taking in every detail – his thick eyelashes, those warm blue-gray eyes, smooth cheeks tanned from working outside above his meticulously groomed beard, and one stray freckle under his left eye. She nearly gave herself whiplash jerking her head to rip her gaze away.

They walked back to the tents where Scout was napping on Margo's bed.

"Apparently my tent's better than yours."

Connor sighed. "I'm sorry. I don't know why he's being like this. Scout! Down!"

Scout stretched all four legs straight out and rolled onto his back. His tail thumped against the mattress as he waited for a belly rub.

"Scout! Get down!"

The dog scooched his butt back and forth, his legs kicking at the air as he scratched his own back against the bed, ignoring Connor's demand.

Margo stepped up onto her tent's porch and snapped her fingers. "Down."

Scout immediately flipped over and jumped down onto the floor. He scampered over to her and flopped his butt down at her feet, leaned his body against her legs, and looked up at her, grinning his sweet doggy grin.

Margo scratched his head. "Good boy."

Scout's tail thumped harder, acknowledging that he was, in fact, a very good boy.

"What kind of black magic was that?" Connor stared at his dog in disbelief.

"He knew I meant business. He thought *you* were barking. Be firm, but don't raise your voice."

"Scout, come," Connor said. His eyebrows were pinched, his mouth pursed. Scout trotted to stand beside him.

Margo laughed. "You don't have to scowl. Be conversational. How long have you had him?"

"Just shy of six months."

"Is he a rescue?"

Connor grimaced. "Sort of. I took him when my brother got too sick to take care of him."

"Oh. I'm sorry." The question hung in the air, but she didn't want to give voice to it.

Fortunately, or unfortunately, Connor understood. "He passed away in March."

Margo reached out and touched his arm. Three months was still so fresh. She vaguely remembered Colin from high school. Three years ahead of her and Connor, she'd never had much interaction with him outside of theater club. They were never assigned to the same groups, but he'd always seemed nice enough. "I'm really sorry."

"Thanks."

"Do you know how old he is?"

He gave her a strange look. "He was thirty-eight." As soon as he finished the sentence, he squeezed his eyes shut and shook his head. "You mean Scout. Sorry. He's about five. Colin got him when he was a puppy."

"Sorry, I should have been more specific."

"No, that was all me. I was thinking about Colin and the train of thought kept heading that way." He shrugged slightly and looked around her tent, then reached down and focused all his attention on scratching Scout's head.

Connor still looked a little lost in his thoughts, so she tried to lighten the mood. "Do you need me to protect you at the bonfire?"

She wanted to yank the question back as soon as it was out. He'd been a jerk to her when she was at one of the lowest points in her life. Actually, he'd been the direct cause of one of the worst moments in her life, so why did she care if he was uncomfortable with Roxanne? It must be pity after learning he'd lost his brother so recently.

"That'd be awesome. Thanks." He glanced at his watch. "I might have enough time to finish my book before then."

Margo wanted to nod and send him on his way, but her mouth was uncooperative. "What are you reading?"

He paused and grinned. "I really want to say *War and Peace* or *Crime and Punishment* or some other highbrow example of literary genius."

"But?"

"I'm actually rereading *Harry Potter and the Half-Blood Prince*."

"You're kidding." That was not what she'd expected him to say.

He shifted and shoved his hands into his pockets like he was embarrassed. "Yeah, I know. It's a kid's book."

Margo didn't want him to think she was being judgmental about his choice in reading material. "No, no. I think it's great. Really. I've read the entire Harry Potter series three times, and I've seen all the movies a zillion times. Definitely qualifies as literary genius as far as I'm concerned."

He asked, "Which one's your favorite?"

"*Prisoner of Azkaban,* no question. You?"

"*Goblet of Fire.*"

"That's a good one, too. They're all good. Now I want to read them again." This was good. A nice, safe, generic topic they could discuss. She ignored the fact that it meant they had something in common.

"I only brought *The Half-Blood Prince.*"

Margo said, "I wonder if they're in the lodge library. I'll have to check later. Meanwhile, I'm halfway through some novel I can't even remember the name of."

"That good?"

"It's not bad. Just... forgettable. But it's probably not the book's fault. I can't remember the last time I sat down to read and wasn't interrupted by something."

"Did you see they have hammocks by the river?"

Margo perked up. She hadn't been to the river area yet to see what was there. Relaxing in a hammock and reading while the day drifted by sounded perfect. "Really?"

"Really. That's my plan for tomorrow. Book, hammock, iced tea."

"Sounds heavenly."

Scout stretched and walked a few steps away, then turned back to look expectantly at Connor.

Connor nodded at him. "I'm coming." He looked back at Margo. "I'll see you when it's time for the bonfire."

Margo gave him a nod, then went inside to get the book from her suitcase. She settled into the rocking chair on her porch. Chandler and Oren were laughing in their tent, making her smile. They seemed like a nice couple. She hoped this ended up being an amazing honeymoon for them and spent a moment hoping wonderful things for their whole marriage.

She opened the book, but her mind wandered immediately.

Leaning back in the rocking chair, she rocked and tried to figure Connor out. He obviously remembered her, but either he didn't remember any details, or he was hoping she didn't. She decided she would be cordial and friendly, but nothing more. They could talk about books and Scout, but nothing personal. She was drawing her line, and she'd stick to it.

# Chapter Four

Connor changed his mind about sitting down to read. Instead, he got one of Scout's tennis balls and played catch with him in the open space behind their tent. A warm breeze blew, helping to keep the humidity at bay.

"Good boy." Connor reached for the ball in Scout's mouth, but Scout danced away from his hand. "You know, if you want me to throw it, you have to give it to me."

Scout's tail wagged hard as he hunkered low, pretending he was going to hand the ball over.

Connor reached for it again as Scout bounced out of reach with a playful growl.

"Okay, let's see if Margo's magic works for this." He cleared his throat and stood upright. "Scout. Come."

The dog bounded over.

"Sit."

Scout sat.

"Drop it."

The ball fell from the dog's mouth and hit the ground. His ears perked forward and his front paws shifted back and forth excitedly as Connor picked up the ball.

"I can't believe that worked. Good boy." Connor threw the ball and Scout took off after it, puffs of dirt kicking up behind his paws as he ran.

Scout grabbed the ball and bounded back, waiting for Connor to toss it again.

"Drop it."

The ball dropped from Scout's mouth, the soggy felt picking up a fresh coating of dirt as it rolled toward Connor's feet.

"This is so gross." He threw it again and wiped his hand on his shorts.

Scout trotted back, stopping a few yards from Connor. The ball dropped from his mouth. His tail was down, slowly swinging back and forth. Definitely not his happy wag. He grabbed his ball again and laid down, his eyes fixed on something beyond Connor.

Connor frowned. "Whassamatter, boy?"

"*There* you are. I've been looking all over for you." Roxanne sauntered up and hooked her hand around his elbow.

He spun around at her voice and pulled his arm away from her grasp. "What's up?"

She looked him up and down and raised a drawn on eyebrow. "You tell me."

On a good day, Connor didn't have a lot of patience for people who played games. Or people who couldn't take a hint. Or people who were just plain obnoxious. Roxanne checked all three boxes, in a big way. It would be funny if it were happening to someone else.

"That's a nice dog."

"Yes, he is."

Roxanne bent forward and clapped her hands. "Come here, doggie."

Her voice grated worse than nails on a chalkboard. She

talked at Scout in some weird falsetto that suggested she'd never actually spent time with a real dog.

Scout tilted his head but didn't move.

Roxanne's mouth tightened and her tone dropped. "Doggie. Come here." She clapped to punctuate each word.

Scout looked back and forth between Roxanne and Connor. Connor could clearly read the *What the heck?* expression on Scout's face.

"Where's Shane?" Connor looked around, hoping to see Shane heading their way. No such luck.

"In the tent. He didn't want to go for a walk."

"Well, don't let me keep you from it. Let's go, Scout."

The dog trotted over, giving Roxanne a wide berth. She bent down and clapped her hands again. "Come here, dog. Come here." She clapped again. It seemed to Connor that she wasn't used to not getting her way, and she was not pleased about being ignored by a dog.

The sound was beyond Connor's last nerve. He could only imagine what Scout was thinking. "Yeah, he doesn't like that." *Neither do I.* Few people had the power to annoy him so thoroughly. If that was her goal, Roxanne was definitely bringing her A-game.

"I see." She straightened and gave him a fake smile. "How about we go somewhere and talk? Get to know each other better? That uptight chick – Mindy or Mary or whatever – you were stuck with at dinner can watch the dog or you can tie him to a tree or something."

"No." Irritation flared. Margo wasn't uptight. And even if she was, who did this woman think she was to insult her? And tie Scout to a tree? Really? Maybe someone should tie Roxanne to a tree. On second thought, she'd probably be into it.

Surprise lifted her penciled brows. "Why not?"

Connor wracked his brain for some way to get away from

her. "Look, I gotta go. I'll see you later." As soon as the words were out of his mouth, he regretted them.

Roxanne's face brightened. She reached out and squeezed his bicep. "Later, then." She winked and walked away, adding some obvious swing to her hips.

Connor shook his head. He took one step toward the tent, then thought better of it. Roxanne would probably take it as an invitation. He snapped his fingers to get Scout's attention and took a path that led past the bathrooms. He had no idea what lay in that direction, but it was in the opposite direction of Roxanne, so whatever lay ahead was an improvement. Scout bounded ahead of him, off the path, and through some bushes. A moment later, he heard a loud splash. He ran forward, the branches stinging his arms as he fought his way through the brush. He stepped through and his feet slipped on an uneven sandy surface.

The river lay directly in front of him. Scout sloshed around in chest-deep water, happily biting at twigs that floated past him. Every so often, he'd plunge his whole face down into the water.

"Where's your ball?"

Scout jerked his head up, water droplets flying from the tips of his ears, then splashed back to the shore where he'd abandoned his tennis ball. He dropped it at Connor's feet and looked up, looked at the river, then back at the ball, then up at Connor, then back at the river.

"Yeah, I get it. But I'm not throwing your ball in the river." He rubbed the dog's wet head with great affection. One of the last things Colin had said to him was, "Take care of Scout." He'd said it with a desperate urgency Connor hadn't understood at the time, but with every day he spent with the dog, he was getting it. Scout was a sweet boy, pure love and affection, wrapped up in fur. So much fur. Connor swore it covered every surface of his house. And car.

Scout shook himself, sending a spray of water in every direction.

"Thanks a lot." Connor wiped his face and flicked the water from his arms. He let Scout play in the water a while longer, enjoying the warm sun.

Scout finally tired himself out and trotted out of the river and rolled on the grass.

"Okay, buddy, let's go." He scooped the nasty tennis ball up into his hand and walked back through the bushes, Scout on his heels, hoping Roxanne didn't see them coming back to the tent.

Scout ran ahead, dirt from the path sticking to his wet paws. Roxanne stepped out of her tent and Scout skidded to a stop, his tail dropping straight down. He took a step sideways as Roxanne stepped off her porch toward him, holding her hand out. "Hello, doggie."

Connor, still at least twenty yards behind Scout, was just about to call the dog when he heard Margo's firm command.

"Scout, come."

The dog happily trotted over to Margo, who was rocking on her porch, holding a book in one hand.

"Sit."

Scout sat and his tail wagged, sweeping a rainbow of wetness onto the wooden flooring.

Roxanne scowled, standing ten or twelve feet from Margo and Scout. "What's its problem? I'm trying to be nice to it."

Connor reached them as Margo said, "Look, it could be anything. A good rule of thumb for dogs is to watch the tail. If it's straight down and they're standing stiffly, do not approach them. Ignore him and give him some space and maybe he'll make up to you."

Connor doubted it. In the time he'd had Scout, he'd never come across a person he didn't like. Scout had been out and about in every place imaginable, and like most Labradors, never had anything but love for everyone he came across.

Roxanne was not pleased. "I'm just happy his *owner* likes me. That's the important thing."

Frowning, Connor said, "Maybe just don't try getting close to him, okay?" It hadn't even been four full hours since he'd met her, and he was tired of her nonsense. Poor Shane.

She turned on a huge smile. "I'd rather be close to you, anyway."

Connor caught Margo's eye roll and managed not to roll his own.

"But if he bites me, we're going to have a problem." The smile was still on her face.

Margo put a protective hand on Scout's head. "Nobody wants that, Roxanne."

A stab of panic sliced through Connor's chest. Maybe he should have boarded the dog instead of bringing him along. The campground was pet-friendly, and he'd never imagined there might be the slightest possibility of Scout biting someone. Roxanne was an annoyance for him, but she could be a real problem for Scout. And poor Scout had had enough upheaval in his life lately.

"I'll keep him close, so you won't have to worry."

Roxanne frowned. "I'll see you later." She turned on her heel and walked back to her tent. Shane appeared in the doorway and his face lit up when he saw her approaching.

Margo watched her go. "Keep your eye on that one, Connor. She's bad news."

"Yeah, I get that." He'd made mistakes in his life, and let people down, but he'd do anything to protect Scout.

"And keep your eye on Scout. He's a good boy." Scout's tail

thumped in agreement. "But any dog can bite. And a dog his size could really do substantial damage."

"I know." He looked at Scout, who was leaning his wet body against Margo's leg. "Thanks. And sorry about the wet fur. Scout found the river."

She scratched his head again. "Yeah, I figured that out. Silly boy. You like the water, don't you?"

He thumped his tail again. Yes, yes, he did like the water. Any kind of water, but preferably dirty. The dirtier the better. And if there were fish and other smelly critters in it, that was hitting the jackpot.

The sun had lowered, sending ribbons of orange and red across the sky.

It warmed his heart that Margo was looking out for Scout. At least she wasn't punishing his dog for his old sins. It gave him a little hope that maybe she'd hear him out and accept his apology. All he had to do was gather up the courage to give it to her. Maybe she'd forgive him. Maybe her obvious affection for Scout would rub off on him, too.

He mentally smacked himself upside the head. Get carried away much? He needed to focus on convincing Margo he wasn't the same idiot who'd hurt her. Period. Nothing more.

"Come, Scout." He looked at Margo. "Are you sure you still want to be my buffer at the bonfire?"

"No problem. I've dealt with way worse than her."

"If you're sure." Now he was curious about the people she'd dealt with that were worse than Roxanne.

"Trust me. She scares you *way* more than she scares me."

"If I'm being completely honest, you're kind of scaring me right now, too."

Margo's long ponytail swung as she tilted her head back and laughed. "Good."

Connor and Scout went next door to their own tent. Scout jumped up on the bed and started licking his paws.

"Down!"

Scout huffed at the offense and slunk off the side of the bed. He cast a longing look at it, then flopped onto the rug and resumed his licking. A Scout-shaped wet spot soaked the comforter.

"I guess I know which side of the bed is yours," Connor muttered.

Scout ignored him and kept licking.

# Chapter Five

The bright moon lit the path to the bonfire. Stars popped out across the entire sky. Crickets chirped and the occasional owl hooted. Walking beside Connor, Margo could hear the logs crackling on the fire as they approached. In the trees, fireflies blinked off and on. It was a little unnerving, walking beside him. If someone had told her this morning that she'd be spending the evening with Connor, and that his company was tolerable, she'd have laughed until she peed herself.

Lawn chairs circled the perimeter of the bonfire. Margo picked the seats farthest away from Roxanne and Shane, separating them by twenty-odd feet and a blazing fire. Scout flopped down beside Connor's chair and promptly went to sleep. The flickering orange glow illuminated Roxanne's contemptuous glare while Shane tried to get her attention.

Margo was over Roxanne's middle school mean girl act already. She grumbled, "If she doesn't knock it off, I'm going to bite her myself."

Connor laughed. "You probably don't want to do that unless all your shots are up to date."

"Excellent point."

Bonnie flitted around the group, handing out plastic trays covered with ingredients for s'mores and long sticks that had already been stripped of bark and were ready for the marshmallows.

She paused in front of Margo and fidgeted with the last tray. "Here you go... Do you two mind sharing? I mean, I know you're not together, but... Oh, goodness, never mind. I can make up another tray. I shouldn't have even thought..."

Margo reached for the tray. "It's not a problem."

"I'm... well, a little embarrassed. Most of the activities are set up for two people. Like partners. If that's not okay, we can change some things around. I wasn't even thinking when I put the trays together. Oh, dear."

"It's fine, Bonnie, really." Margo smiled and gave a little nod to signal an end to the conversation.

Connor took the sticks from Bonnie and agreed. "If it's okay with her, it's okay with me."

Bonnie looked relieved but didn't move away. "I mean, we aren't trying to force you two together or anything, not that you two being together would be a bad thing, you make a cute couple. We just don't want you to be uncomfortable."

That particular ship had sailed. Margo held the tray over to Connor. "Truly. It's fine. We don't mind." He selected two marshmallows and slid them onto the sticks.

"Okay, if you're sure," Bonnie said uncertainly.

"We're sure." Margo punctuated her words with a wide smile, hoping Bonnie would take the hint, stop talking, and move on. And if that didn't happen, maybe the earth would do her a favor, open up, and swallow her whole, putting an end to this whole awkward conversation.

Bonnie finally nodded, then smiled back. "Okay, wonderful! Great! If you need *s'more s'mores*, let me know." She walked away, glancing back at them every few steps until she reached her own lawn chair next to Doug.

Margo felt bad about being even mildly annoyed with Bonnie. She'd worked so hard to put together an amazing vacation for all of them. She took a deep breath and let the feeling go. Bonnie's intentions were good.

Connor held his stick into the fire and pulled it back out a second later.

"You didn't even let your marshmallow get warm. No way you'll be able to squish it."

He stuck it back into the fire. "You're an expert on s'mores?"

Margo put her own stick into the flames. "Pfft. I'm an expert on darn near everything," she joked.

"That must come in handy."

"Absolutely." She pulled her flaming marshmallow out of the fire and blew it out, then smooshed the charred goo between the chocolate and graham cracker. "See? This is as good as it gets."

"Nope, *this* is--" Connor pulled his stick out of the fire, but there was no marshmallow. Just an empty tip with a little flaming residue. He blew it out.

"You were saying? Should I just start calling you Chef Gordon Ramsay now, or would you prefer I wait until you actually assemble a s'more? Assuming, of course, you ever do." She bit into her s'more. The crunchy graham cracker coated with melted chocolate and marshmallow was camping perfection.

"Very funny." He grabbed another marshmallow, shoved it onto the stick, and held it into the fire. He watched it intently, then pulled it back and blew the fire out. "See?" He twirled the stick around. "Every side of it is perfectly done."

"You're getting cocky. And taking too long. It's going to be too hard to smoosh if you let it cool."

He wrestled with his chocolate and graham cracker, then finally smeared his marshmallow onto it, making a mess.

"Harder than it looks, isn't it, Gordon?" Margo laughed as she licked melted chocolate off her fingertips.

"I'm trying not to show you up." Connor's graham cracker snapped in half. He barely managed to keep it from falling.

Okay, she didn't have to like him to appreciate that he didn't take himself too seriously. Her ex-fiancé had zero ability to laugh at himself, and it had been exhausting. She teased, "You're doing an outstanding job."

Connor held up his mess of a s'more in triumph. "See? Perfect."

"Nice." She made herself another treat.

"Why do you burn your marshmallow like that?"

"To obtain the perfect balance between a crispy outside and gooey inside. It's all about nailing the ratio of crisp to goo."

"I see."

"Have you ever had s'mores? You seem like a s'more newbie." She drew back and gasped in mock horror, pressing fingertips to her throat. "Or do you just… not *like* them?"

"Um…" He gave her a thumbs up and an exaggerated grin. "They're great. The best thing I've ever eaten in my whole entire life. Ever." A few graham cracker crumbs dotted his beard. If it wasn't Connor, it might have almost been adorable.

She clicked her tongue in disapproval. "Tsk, tsk. You do realize that's camping blasphemy, right? You're legally obligated to enjoy s'mores if you're camping."

A twig cracked behind them. "He's a grown man. He doesn't have to like anything."

Margo heaved a labored sigh. "Whatever you say." She'd been ignoring her so successfully that she hadn't noticed Roxanne leaving her chair.

"*Some* women don't feel the need to tell their man what he

can and can't do. *Real* women. Ones who aren't insecure." Roxanne struck a pose, splaying her hands on her hips, cocking an eyebrow, smirking.

"Come on," Connor muttered.

Margo finished the last bite of her s'more and deliberately licked the chocolate off her fingers, then looked Roxanne in the eye. Connor was irrelevant. Margo had no intention of backing down from this idiot. Hopefully, when she got the message that Margo wasn't playing her stupid games, she'd go away. "*Some* women don't string decent men along for a free vacation and spend their time hitting on other men. You know. *Real* women. Ones with integrity and common decency."

Roxanne snorted. "Whatever."

"Good comeback," Margo muttered to her retreating back.

After Roxanne took her seat beside Shane, she glared at Margo through the flames.

Margo's irritation turned to amusement at the absurdity of Roxanne's behavior. It reminded her of the morons on Jerry Springer's show, screaming and throwing punches, usually over some man.

"Whoa." Connor stared at Margo. "I thought you guys were going to end up fighting."

"Don't be expecting some kind of floofy pillow fight. Because if I end up in an altercation with her, there's going to be blood."

He still stared. "Sooo, it would be wrong of me to think that would be really hot?"

"Yes."

"Um… alrighty then. Not hot. Not hot at all. Got it." He had a ridiculous half-smile on his face.

Margo wanted to smack it off him. "Not funny." That was a lie. The whole situation was totally amusing.

"False. It's at least a little bit funny. Besides, it's your fault I now have this whole bikini pillow fight thing in my head."

"Where did the bikinis come from?" Margo rolled her eyes and glared at him but couldn't keep her lips from twitching. "Never mind. Now you're being a chauvinist pig."

"Ouch." He pressed his hand to his chest. "You wound me."

She pointed her stick at him. "When I wound you, you'll know it."

Connor leaned back in his chair. "You really are scaring me now."

Margo laughed. "You're such a wuss."

Scout lifted his head up, huffed, and stretched out in the dew-covered grass.

They watched the fire for a few minutes until Connor leaned over and quietly said, "I'm going to the restroom. I'll be right back."

Margo smiled to herself when Scout perked up, then looked at her and decided to stay where he was. She reached down and scratched his hind leg. His tail thumped. Someday soon she'd have a dog of her own. Maybe even a lovable lab like Scout.

She leaned back, watching the orange licks of flame glowing on the logs. The crackling was steady and rhythmic and relaxing. Her hand trailed over the side of her chair, resting on Scout. She wondered what Connor's life had been like since she last saw him. He seemed like a decent man, which was hard to reconcile with her memories. Granted, even she could admit that he probably wasn't entirely the horrible villain she remembered.

Roxanne still glared through the flames. Margo was sorely tempted to give her the finger, but she resisted the impulse. Chalk one up for maturity.

Scout lifted his head and his tail thumped as Connor

walked back to his chair. He'd brought a blanket with him and spread it over their laps.

Margo straightened her side of the blanket and said, "Have you told this woman in plain English that you aren't interested in her?"

"No. But I'm gonna have to. I'm afraid she'll take it as a challenge."

Margo snickered.

"What?"

"You'll hate me."

"Oh, geez, what?"

"I was just thinking that you might want to move to a different tent or see if you can get a tent that locks. I'd be afraid she'll pee on you to mark her territory."

Connor turned his head, giving her an expression that was bewilderment, disgust, and annoyance. "Surely not."

"Hopefully Shane's a light sleeper."

"Promise me something."

"What?"

"If you hear me screaming like a little girl, come rescue me."

Margo laughed. "Yeah, tough guy, I'll come save you."

Connor reached over and took Margo's hand. Her heart skipped a beat before she gave herself a mental shake and mentally chanted, *It's all for show. It's all for show. It's all for show.* That's the only reason she laced her fingers with his. Because it was all for show to annoy Roxanne.

Laughter from the other side of the fire filled the air. Margo looked around at the faces she could see. Everyone – except Roxanne – was talking, laughing, and making more s'mores. Even Shane was chatting with Tanner and Sarah. Bonnie and Doug relaxed at the far end, a little away from the group, but close enough in case anyone needed anything.

The night was cool. Margo's face was warm from the fire,

but her back was getting chilly. She snuck a glance at Connor. His face was relaxed, the light from the fire reflecting in his eyes. The moment was so peaceful she couldn't muster up the will to be mad at him.

Connor squeezed her hand. "It's getting late."

"Yeah. Let's head back." She didn't get up.

"You're not moving."

"Neither are you." She checked her watch in the dimming firelight. "It's after midnight."

"I don't really want to get up."

She chuckled. "Me, either."

Beside them, Chandler and Oren got up and headed toward the tents.

"Okay, if they can do it, we can do it. Ready?"

"Ready." Margo whisked the blanket off their laps and stood up. She haphazardly folded it and held her hand out to Connor. "Come on, you can do it."

He grabbed her hand and heaved himself out of the chair. "Who knew lawn chairs could be so comfortable. Scout, let's go."

The dog stood up and stretched his back legs out behind him, then shook himself. He looked up at Connor and wagged his tail.

Connor's fingers squeezed hers lightly. She pulled her hand away and refolded the blanket. She tucked her hands under it as they walked back to the tents. Suddenly, she just wanted to be away from him so she could think. Holding hands had taken things too far. It was too familiar, too easy. It wasn't a road she wanted to go down.

Scout stopped to sniff a fence post, then peed on it.

# Chapter Six

Connor relished the feeling of holding Margo's hand, brief as it was. He'd been surprised she'd even offered it to him. He wondered if she knew how much he'd loved holding her hand back when they were kids. Things were so different then. *They* were so different then. And he'd do things a lot differently if he had the chance.

The air was thick with moisture and the sound of crickets and frogs. The moon lit the path with a milky glow.

He cleared his throat, trying to think of something to say. "Sounds like tomorrow's going to be a busy day."

"Yeah, hopefully there will be time after the hike to just relax by the river."

He tentatively suggested, "Maybe after dinner we can try to snag some hammocks?"

"That'd be great." Margo kicked a stone off the path.

He let out a relieved breath. Being near her made him feel like an inexperienced seventeen-year-old again, afraid of being shot down and rejected. "I might check out the lodge library if you want to see what they have."

They reached Margo's tent. "Sounds good. I'll see you at breakfast then."

Connor was glad the darkness hid the grin that spread across his face. He didn't want her to see how eager he was to spend time with her.

Margo handed the blanket to him. "Good night. Scream if you need me," she laughed.

"Not funny." Connor chuckled. "See you in the morning."

Scout stood on Margo's porch, wagging his tail. She bent down to scratch his head. "Good night, Scout."

"Let's go," Connor said to the dog.

After a moment of indecision, Scout followed Connor back to their tent.

Connor stepped up onto his porch while Scout looked back toward Margo's. "Hey, pal, let's try to remember that you're *my* dog, okay?"

Scout wagged his tail.

Inside his tent, Connor turned on the antique-looking but very modern lamp on the bedside table. The soft glow from the LED light illuminated the whole room. He grabbed his toiletries and robe and headed for the showers. He half expected Roxanne to make an appearance, but he made it through his shower and back to his tent unscathed.

Scout jumped up onto the bed and turned in a circle before flopping down with a yawn. He rolled onto his back and stretched his paws into the air, then relaxed.

"You're hogging three-quarters of the bed."

Scout's tail swept back and forth.

Connor untied the "doors" of the tent and zipped them closed, then climbed into the sliver of bed that remained for him. He heard the muffled sounds of other campers making their way back to their tents, then nothing but the chirps of crickets and an occasional owl hoot.

His plan was to go to sleep, but he stared into the unfamiliar darkness and thought about Margo instead. He knew she was conflicted about him, and he'd need to apologize and explain everything to her sooner than later. Seeing her again had brought back so much – the guilt, but also the good things. The sweet awkwardness of being close to her, the rush of pride when he earned a smile or a laugh, the pounding in his chest at her touch…

Tomorrow. He'd wait for a calm, quiet moment and explain everything.

The sun was barely nudging the horizon when Scout jumped off the bed and stood with his nose inches from Connor's face. He whined. Loudly. While simultaneously beating his tail against the mattress.

Connor blinked and reached out to scratch Scout's head. "I hear ya. Hang on." He reluctantly climbed out of the warm bed into the chilly room. He unzipped the tent and stood on the porch while Scout ran behind the tent to take care of business. He wondered if there was coffee in the dining room.

He debated crawling back into bed but got dressed instead. He went to the bathrooms and when he came out, Margo was leaving the women's side of the building carrying a tote bag. A towel was wrapped around her hair. She wore a plain gray t-shirt and jean shorts, the very definition of casual and effortless, and he couldn't take his eyes off her.

"How'd you sleep?" he asked, keeping his voice low. The rest of the tents were still closed, with no signs of life yet.

She matched his quiet tone and gave him a brilliant smile. "Excellent. I'd prepared myself for an entire week in a sleeping bag or a rickety cot instead of a real bed. You?"

"Good, although I probably would have had more room in a sleeping bag."

"Scout's a snuggler, huh?"

"If that's a nice way of saying 'bed hog,' then yes. He's a snuggler."

Margo chuckled. "How bad can it be? He's only, what, eighty pounds?"

"Eighty-five, and he sprawls. And rolls. And snores. And runs in his sleep. He's worse than my ex-wife." Oops. Didn't mean to bring that up.

"I didn't know you had one of those."

They strolled back toward the tents.

"When my brother got sick, I was living in Oregon. I mentioned to Sherri that we might have to move back home for a while. Colin was to the point where he couldn't drive, and his ex-wife worked a lot, so I wanted to help him see the boys as much as he could. She told me if I left, I'd be going alone. I told her that if geography was more important than our marriage, we could be done right then. She left."

"That seems abrupt."

"She always said she'd never leave Portland, but I assumed a temporary move back east so I could be with my dying brother would be an exception." He shrugged. "I was wrong."

"I'm sorry. Maybe she couldn't move because of her career?"

He managed not to laugh at the idea of Sherri with a career. Her job was picking up the phone to ask her daddy for money. "No, I'm pretty sure she just didn't love me. I didn't realize it at the time, of course, but I was a rebound after she broke up with her last ex."

"Did she tell you that?"

"Not in so many words, but they got back together and got married like thirty seconds after our divorce was final."

"Do you think…" she trailed off. "Never mind. Sorry."

"What, do I think she was cheating?" He considered the question, as he had many times since he'd left Portland. "No. I don't think she was. Even looking back, I can't think of one thing that should have made me suspicious."

"I wasn't suggesting that you should have been. And I shouldn't have even hinted at such a question. I was just curious if you had some great epiphany. It seems like everyone has this amazing rush of clarity when they break up, but I didn't."

"Recent?"

"We split up in January."

Six months. Hopefully, that had given her time to get over the ex. "Was *he* cheating?"

They arrived in front of Connor's tent, so they stopped walking. Scout jumped off the bed and ran over to Margo for some attention.

She bent and scratched Scout's ears. "No. We were polar opposites in a lot of things that really mattered to me. So I broke up with him. Unfortunately, most of my family didn't. Which makes things super awkward."

"Your family stayed in contact with your ex?" He hoped that didn't mean she was open to getting back together with him.

The towel slipped from Margo's hair. She pulled it down and rubbed at her wet locks. "They not only stayed in contact, they invited him for Easter dinner. Which I found out when I walked into the kitchen and saw him carving the ham." She sounded annoyed.

"We' stay in touch with Colin's ex for the kids, of course, but your situation is a whole other level."

"Yeah. It was brutal."

Around them, other campers emerged from their tents with polite greetings and made their way to the restrooms.

"He didn't think it was at all strange to come to a family holiday?"

"In his defense, he thought I knew and was okay with it. Supposedly." She flung the towel over her shoulder. "I can only imagine what Jean – my stepmom – told him."

He remembered exactly who Jean was. She'd despised him on sight, for reasons he still didn't know. "Your family's as over-involved as ever, huh?" Connor felt a pang of annoyance that her family got invested in this guy, when they'd written him off as trash. He gave himself a mental shake. *It was almost twenty years ago.*

"That's putting it mildly. Ashley – she's my younger sister – tries to run interference for me, but she doesn't carry any more weight than I do since she's the baby of the family. And Heidi – my older sister – is always in complete agreement with Jean. They're so similar you'd swear Jean was her biological mom."

She straightened and gave him a brilliant smile. "But I'm not worrying about them this week. It's all about relaxing and having some Margo time. I'll be ready in ten minutes if you want to walk to breakfast." She headed for her tent.

"Just holler when you're ready." He watched her turn, certain that the image of her walking away in those shorts was something he wouldn't soon forget.

# Chapter Seven

In her tent, Margo draped the wet towels over the back of the chair. The morning was still chilly, and she had goosebumps from talking outside with Connor for so long. She'd meant what she told him. She was resolved to have some much-needed Margo time. It appeared they were stuck together for Bonnie's activities, so she'd swallow her misgivings, ignore the past, and tolerate him. She shook out her damp hair and flipped a piece upwards to examine it, frowning at the split ends. It was way past time to get a trim. She pulled it all back, tying it into a messy half-bun half-ponytail. Tugging a hoodie on, she wished she'd known there would be electricity for her hair-dryer when she was packing. She kicked off her sandals and put socks and sneakers on, assuming they'd be sufficient for today's hike.

Margo stepped outside and zipped closed the tent flaps serving as her front door. It wasn't much in the way of security, but she didn't suppose there was much to worry about, since anything valuable was locked in her car.

For the millionth time, she second-guessed her decision to spend time with Connor. As if it were a sign directly from

Heaven, a dirty tennis ball landed at her feet as she stepped off her little porch. Maybe she'd look at it as spending time with Scout. Time with Connor was an unfortunate consequence.

"Good morning, handsome," she said to Scout, then picked up the ball and tossed it lightly. Scout watched it roll away.

"Go get it," she said.

Scout wagged his tail and gave her his best doggy grin.

"Fine, then don't, you goofball." She scratched his head and followed him to Connor's porch. She peered in through the open door flaps. Yeah, it didn't feel so unfortunate watching his broad shoulders stretch his tshirt as he adjusted his pillows. Staring at his butt in those shorts wasn't much of a hardship, either. He might be the last man on Earth she'd consider dating, but he sure was fun to look at. "You ready for breakfast?"

Connor finished straightening his bed. "Ready." He stepped out of the tent and gave her a smile.

Margo tried to ignore the little skip her heart took. Okay, fine, she could admit he was attractive. Even if she didn't normally like beards. Or *ever* like beards. But on him, it worked. Whatever. He was still Connor, so he was off-limits. You are now entering the Friend Zone, where you will stay. Permanently.

They walked to the lodge house, where a buffet was laid out for them. The room was full of campground guests in addition to the contest winners, so it was easy to avoid Roxanne.

Margo filled her plate with scrambled eggs and fruit chunks. "Everything looks so good."

"You're not kidding," Connor answered as he popped a piece of bacon in his mouth.

"You can't wait until we sit down?" Margo laughed.

He shook his head as he chewed. "Bacon."

She rolled her eyes and carried her plate to an open table. "How long do you think the hike will be?"

"Probably a couple of hours."

"You know, I've lived here my entire life and never gone hiking locally. I didn't realize there were so many trails and stuff."

"It's funny how we don't notice the things all around us."

She thought about that for a moment. "Very profound."

"You're making fun of me."

Shaking her head, she said, "No, it really is profound. That whole 'smell the roses' thing. It's a good reminder. I tend to work too much and forget I actually have a life outside of that." The admission slipped out. Too often, she let the weeks turn into months without pausing for breath.

They watched their fellow campers as they ate without conversation. Everyone seemed to be in good spirits, laughing and talking and eating. When she and Connor finished their breakfast, they put their dirty silverware and plates in the designated bins and walked out to the front porch where their group was congregating for the hike.

Margo fanned her face with her hands. "It warmed up faster than I expected. I'm going to run my hoodie back to the tent. Hopefully I don't miss anything important."

"I'll fill you in."

She paused on the top step. "Is Scout joining us?"

"Probably. He likes two things. Sleeping and socializing. If he's awake, he'll tag along. Go put your hoodie away. I'll make sure we don't leave without you."

Margo quickly walked to the tents and tossed her sweatshirt on the bed. She poked her head into Connor's tent. Scout was lying on the bed, belly up, fast asleep. "Hey, sleepy head. Wanna come?"

Scout's tail whipped back and forth. He flipped over and

jumped off the bed. After a big stretch, he came to Margo's side and looked up at her as if to say, "Let's go." He trotted beside Margo as she headed back toward the group.

When they got back to the lodge, she answered Connor's smile with, "I picked up a hitchhiker on the way."

"I see that." He scratched Scout's head. "You better be a good boy."

Scout's tail whacked Connor's leg.

"Ow, hey, bruising me isn't the best way to demonstrate how good you are."

*Whack. Whack. Whack.* Scout turned so his back leaned against Connor's leg, a not-so-subtle request for scratches.

"Fine. I'll scratch your back." He looked up at Margo with a grin. "He's so demanding."

She laughed as Doug led the group away from the lodge, down a gravel path into a copse of trees. The perfect tour guide, Doug talked the whole way, then stopped and patted the trunk of a tree. "If you don't know, this big guy here is a bitternut hickory tree. They're plentiful in this area, which, obviously, is how Hickory Hollow got its name. If you notice the nuts here," he nudged the ground with his foot, "the squirrels love them. They're too bitter for us to eat, but they're the reason we have delicious hickory smoked ham and bacon."

"Yay, bacon!" Someone yelled at the front of the group.

Margo nudged Connor. "I think we just met your new BFF."

"Bacon friends forever?"

She laughed. "That works."

They walked through the trees and met up with an established trail. Doug stopped the group and listed the dangers they could possibly face. "Bears do live in the area. You probably won't see one, but on the off chance you do, make a bunch of noise and they'll most likely take off."

Connor snorted. "'Most likely.' That's reassuring."

"What, mister lumberjack can't take on a couple of bears?" Margo couldn't help but laugh.

"Me? One-handed." He curled his arm to make a muscle. "I was worried about the rest of you."

Margo squeezed his impressive bicep before she could curb the impulse. "Why worry about us if you can protect us all?" She yanked her hand back, cursing whatever had possessed her to touch him. The feel of his warm flesh clung to her palm.

He put his arm down and shook his head. "Oh, heck no. You're on your own. All you'll see from me is a cloud of dust. "

She laughed. "And they say chivalry is dead."

Connor shrugged with mock seriousness. "Better chivalry than me."

"I guess I can't argue with that. Just one problem with your plan."

"What's that?" He raised one eyebrow as if contemplating the possibility of a flaw in his plan.

Margo pointed down to her pink sneakers. "I guarantee I can run faster than you. So you better hope some of these other people can't."

Connor narrowed his eyes and stroked his beard as he surveyed the group. "No problem. You don't have to be the fastest, you just have to be faster than a few of 'em. There's at least three I can outrun, guaranteed."

She giggled, thoroughly enjoying the silly conversation. "Even if they're properly motivated?"

"Yup. My adrenaline rush will be just as strong, the playing field is pretty level."

"You've given this a lot of thought."

"More than I need to, for sure."

As the group moved, it naturally separated. Margo and Connor were near the end of the pack, walking leisurely while Scout weaved back and forth over the trail, sniffing at everything. Doug was up ahead with the front of the pack, pointing out various trees and flowers.

Connor said, "Can I ask a personal question?"

"You can ask whatever you want. That doesn't mean I'll answer you."

"Fair enough. When you said about your ex fitting in so well with your family... it's important to have a partner that fits in, so why'd you end up breaking up?"

Margo sighed. She'd had to defend her decision to break up with Brad ad nauseam over the past six months. "My family thinks my reasons are stupid. He was a nice guy and checked all the boxes. But like I said, we had some diametrically opposed viewpoints. We got along well, but the big problem was that he doesn't like animals. I had no idea, until one day he told me that he'd never allow pets in his home. I know that sounds like a stupid reason to break up, but there it is." She waited for his reaction. Not that it mattered. She certainly didn't care what he thought about it. Not at all.

Connor frowned. "Um, you're a veterinarian. Liking animals and wanting pets seems to be a pretty reasonable standard requirement in a partner."

She agreed. "I thought so. And I don't know why he never bothered telling me that he doesn't like animals. I mean, if he was a sommelier, I would have mentioned early on if I didn't drink wine." Ugh, wine. Brad had dragged her to a million fancy dinner parties with the driest of expensive wines and the driest of expensive people.

"Right."

"I'd even plainly said – on more than one occasion – that once my life was more settled, I was going to get a dog and a cat. Probably two cats, since they do well in pairs. And not a peep. It was after we were engaged and planning this stupid wedding that I didn't even want that he just casually mentions that he'll 'never allow' an animal in 'his' house."

Connor's eyebrows climbed his forehead. "'Allow?'"

"Exactly." She talkedwith her hands. "I mean, seriously. We had put an offer on a house, for crying out loud. I was adamant about having a fenced in yard for a dog. He could have said something then. Or any of the millions of times I came home from work talking about whatever animal I'd had that day that I wanted to bring home. But whatever. It was more than the animals, too."

Connor grabbed her arm. "Watch out." He pointed to a root sticking out of the ground.

"Thank you." Margo scanned the ground in front of her. His fingers slid down her arm. She pulled away before he could touch her hand and one part of her brain loudly explained that she did *not* want to hold his hand. Other parts weren't quite convinced."Tripping would not have been fun."

"Maybe not for you."

"Ha, ha. Smartass."

"So what else was it?"

There were a million reasons in hindsight, so it was easy for her to pick one. "The wedding. He was driving me crazy. He wanted this huge elaborate thing with four hundred guests at some country club. Blech."

"What did you want?"

"Something small. Simple. That didn't cost more than a house. His idea of compromising was cutting the guest list to three hundred." She stepped over another root and they waited while Scout investigated a tree. "I think the wedding should be about the marriage and the guests should *matter* to the bride and groom. I don't care about my dad's business partners. I've never even met most of them. Why would I invite them to my wedding? It's just stupid. I want a small, intimate wedding, surrounded by people I love, who love me."

"That's beautiful."

"Have you ever thought about what kind of – oh. Sorry. What kind of wedding *did* you have?"

They started walking again. Connor said, "The fancy hotel, the limo, four hundred guests, the whole nine yards."

Oops. She hoped her tirade about big weddings hadn't offended him. "Was it what you wanted?"

"I didn't care, really. She had her heart set on a big wedding, and I was just along for the ride."

"You didn't get a say? Or did you truly not care?" Brad had been so involved she'd eventually abdicated all of the planning to him. He'd even wanted to "help" pick out her dress.

Connor shrugged. "Like I said, I was fine with whatever she wanted. She asked my opinion on a few things, but I pretty much stayed out of the way. I would have given my input if there was something I didn't like."

"Would she have compromised?"

"Probably."

"So, the only thing she wouldn't compromise on was living in Portland?"

"I can't say. That was the biggest issue we'd had. It's possible she would have drawn a hard line on other important things, too, but that was the thing that derailed us, so I'll never know."

"You didn't talk about the important things before you got married?"

"We did. But the things that were important before we got married were different than the things that turned out to be important after we got married."

"Hmm. That's insightful." She slowed to watch two squirrels chase each other up a tree. "Do you miss her?" She didn't miss Brad at all, but she felt like she was supposed to.

Connor gave her a long look.

For a minute, she thought she'd gone too far. "That's too personal. Sorry. None of my business."

"No, it's fine. Sometimes I miss her, but I think I miss the *idea* of her more."

Bingo. That summed up exactly how she felt. "That's a great way to put it. I miss a lot of the relationship part, but I don't really miss Brad so much." She hadn't said that out loud to anyone, not even Ashley.

Connor shook his head. "It sounds really awful that way. She's not a bad person. It just didn't work out."

"No, I agree. Brad's a decent guy. Mostly. Just not for me."

"Or your future animals."

"Exactly."

"So you already have your future pets picked out. What about kids?"

Margo smirked. "Goats? Probably not, unless I can get a big place outside of town."

He looked confused for a second. "Goats? Oh. Never mind. Kids. I'll give you that one."

"Of course you will. That was comedic gold."

"Definitely not gold." He pretended to consider it seriously. "Maybe stainless steel."

"Not even bronze?"

"What comes after bronze?"

She tried to think of the Olympic medals. "I have no idea. Is there anything after bronze?"

"Pretty sure it's just a ribbon."

"Huh. I should at least get a ribbon."

"For a goat joke? No, ma'am. You don't get credit for a joke that lame. You might even say it was just plain *b-a-a-a-a-a-a-d*."

She couldn't help but laugh. "You're a tough judge."

"The toughest."

"Do you judge your own stupid jokes as harshly?"

"I'm too biased to judge my own work. But I'm sure you'll let me know if any of my jokes fall flat."

"If? Pretty sure you mean when. Because they will. And I'll be sure to let you know." This was entirely new, a teasing conversation with a guy who wasn't looking for a reason to be offended.

"I have no doubt."

They walked along in companionable silence for a while, looking at the trees and watching Scout weave back and forth around bushes and rocks, sniffing whatever caught his attention.

Margo asked, "What about you? Do you want goats?"

Connor smiled. "No, but I think I'd like to have my own kids someday."

"Think? Someday? That's pretty vague."

"There's not a lot of point in putting a hard timeline on it until I find the right woman."

"You could always adopt a couple of kids on your own if you really wanted to."

"I don't. I'd rather not be a single parent on purpose."

"What if you meet the right woman and she can't have kids? Or doesn't want them? What then?"

Connor stepped to the side, allowing Scout to run between them as he chased a butterfly.

"Then we won't have kids. Or we'll adopt. Whatever. I'll deal. I'm not against adoption by any means, but it's not my first choice. And now I'll just point out that you never answered the question at all."

"I don't know the answer. I don't know if I have room in my life for kids. And like you said, I don't want to be a single parent on purpose." She repeated his words. An image of some sort of life with Connor formed in her mind too easily and she immediately shut it down. This was getting too deep. Too personal. Something inside slammed shut, reminding her of the nights she lay in her bed sobbing because of him.

"Right now, Scout's enough of a kid." Connor gestured toward the dog, who was running ahead. "And I regularly spend time with my nephews now that I'm back home."

"You seem to have changed a lot since high school."

"How so? You mean this?" He grabbed his beard.

"No. I mean you were kind of a jerk."

His eyebrows shot up. "To who? You?"

Margo stopped short and jammed her hands on her hips. "You don't remember, do you? You know what? Forget it. Just forget it. Oh, wait, you already did." She turned and strode ahead.

Connor matched her speed and grabbed her elbow. "Margo, wait."

She yanked her arm from his grasp. "Don't." She glared at his bewildered expression. "Just don't." She turned and walked in the opposite direction, back toward her tent.

"Margo?"

Margo practically ran back to the tent village. Once there, she sat on the edge of her bed and put her head in her hands. This was ridiculous. He'd used her and ghosted her *seventeen years ago*. They had been kids, for crying out loud, and Connor probably had no idea how he'd affected her back then. She felt bad about her outburst, quite certain she wouldn't want someone pointing out her long-ago transgressions.

The unpleasant – and unwelcome – realization that she lashed out because she was finding herself enjoying his company and she wanted to keep him at arm's length frustrated her. It wasn't her style. No, she was more likely to keep everything bottled inside until it went away.

She needed to apologize.

And if there was one thing she hated more than letting her emotions get the best of her, it was apologizing.

With a sigh, she stood up and walked back toward the hiking trail. A couple of campers she didn't know were already heading back out of the woods. She smiled and exchanged pleasantries but kept moving until she spotted Scout with his face in a bush. Connor stood with his back to her, his hands in the pockets of his shorts.

"Hey." Margo reached him and tentatively spoke.

"Hey."

"Look, I'm sorry about that. It's been seventeen years since high school. I'm not who I was. Obviously. And—"

His brow furrowed. "Margo, I'm sorry about what happened."

"You know what I'm talking about?" She was skeptical.

"Senior Prom."

"So you *do* remember." Partly. It wasn't just about the prom.

"Of course I do. And I'm sorry I was a jerk."

That's it? Sorry for being a jerk? "No, I get it. Your friends made it abundantly clear that it was all a joke. It's okay. I'm over it. Well, obviously I still have some residual resentment, but I'll deal with it." She resigned herself to the fact that nothing he said would bring her the kind of closure she needed. It hadn't mattered to him then, and it barely mattered now.

"A joke? What are you talking about?" His brows pinched together, puzzled.

She cocked her head. "Come on. Charlie and Twizzler and Pack? After you stood me up for prom, all I heard every time they saw me was *Moogo* and *Cargo Margo*. The stupid cow who thought she had a boyfriend." She made air quotes around the insults. Repeating them still cut.

Connor grimaced and shoved his hands deeper in his pockets. "My friends were assholes. And for the record, I never participated in that crap. I'm sorry I never defended you. I should have. But I was seventeen and stupid and kind of an idiot myself, and I had my own issues at home. Not that any of that's an excuse."

There was no excuse. They started walking again, following Scout's curious nose until they had looped back around toward the campground.

She could feel Connor looking at her. Without turning her head, she said, "You know it was more than that, Connor. You didn't have to pretend you liked me. That was an awful thing to do. Especially after we – never mind."

He stopped short; his brows furrowed. "Margo, it was never fake. I should have talked to you. Explained. But I was embarrassed, and I just couldn't. I'm uncomfortable talking about it now."

She was dangerously close to telling him how she'd cried herself to sleep in her prom gown to make him understand how he'd hurt her. Or how she'd been grounded for three months and called a slut because Jean had found the open pack of condoms in her purse. But that was too much. It was all too much emotion being exhumed when it was better staying buried. "Then let's not. It was a long time ago. I'm sorry I brought it all up in the first place and then flipped out. Let's talk about something else." Margo held her hands up. "Please."

Connor looked as if he was going to say something, but instead, he gave his head a shake and said, "Okay."

Scout bounded over with a stick in his mouth. Margo took it and threw it.

"My mother went into the hospital that day." Connor kicked a stone off the path.

"I had no idea." She held her breath for a beat. It was the last thing she'd expected to hear.

"Nobody did. We weren't supposed to talk about it. Colin didn't even know until a week later when he came home from college."

"Why the secrecy? I mean, if she was sick…"

Connor blew out a huff of air. "It wasn't that kind of sick."

"Oh." Margo wanted to ask more questions, but she had the feeling Connor had told her all he was willing to share, at least for the time being.

He abruptly stopped and looked at her. "Margo, I'm sorry."

Her heart lodged somewhere in her throat as she stared at him, unable to think of a single thing to say. All she could do was blink and pray she didn't cry. She didn't doubt his sincerity for a second.

Tanner and Sarah came out of the woods, shattering the moment.

Connor changed the subject. "Do you want to go to the lodge and check out the library?"

"Sure."

They walked back through the tent village, an odd sort of tension pinging back and forth between them. Scout abandoned them there, opting to jump up on Margo's bed and go to sleep while they continued toward the lodge.

The lodge library was a huge six-shelf bookcase on a wall at the far end of the lobby. Built next to the fireplace, the heavy wooden shelves were home to at least two hundred books.

"Oh, I wish I had the gumption to organize my shelves like this," Margo said to break the silence. She wanted to test the waters and see if maybe they could get back to the easy place they'd been in.

Connor nodded. "I don't keep too many books. I usually get them from the library or read them on my iPad."

Relieved that his tone sounded back to normal, she said, "I've read a few on my phone, but usually just when I'm stuck in line somewhere. Or in the bathroom," she added with a laugh.

Connor chuckled. "That's where I get caught up on my magazine reading."

"Not newspaper reading?"

"Who reads newspapers anymore?"

"I do. We get the *Hickory Times* at the clinic and I read it every week. Who reads magazines anymore?"

"I do. I'll have you know *Lumberjack Magazine* has a huge subscriber base."

Some of the tightness in her chest loosened as he teased. "What, like two dozen?"

"Four." He held up four fingers for emphasis.

"I stand corrected. But the newspaper is better for, you know, *news*."

"I read the news on my phone. No more trouble with all the folding and unfolding. Everything stays neat."

"Oh, you're one of *those* people," Margo teased.

"What people?"

"People who can't stand to have papers folded wonky. It has to be crisp and none of the pages sticking out."

"Of course. What kind of person just flops a newspaper any which way? It's anarchy."

She pointed at herself with both index fingers. "I kind of do."

Connor gave her a hard look. "At least tell me you don't dogear the pages of books to mark your place."

Margo put her hand over her heart. "Please. I'm not a monster."

"I was starting to wonder. So let's just make a deal right now."

"What?"

"If we ever have occasion to share a newspaper, I get to read it first."

Her belly fluttered. She tried not to read too much into his comment and pretended to consider it for a moment. "I can live with that, but only if you don't mess around. I'm not waiting until mid-afternoon to read the paper."

"Deal. I read the news first thing in the morning." He held out his hand for her to shake. "Hopefully any future negotiations will be as easy and productive as this one."

Margo shook his hand and laughed. She turned to the bookshelf. "Let's see what we've got here." She tilted her head to the side to read the spines. "Oh, I haven't read this one yet."

"What is it?"

"The newest Stephanie Plum."

"Excellent choice for reading in a hammock."

"You've read them?"

"A couple of the earliest ones, but they weren't my thing. I like my mysteries more on the serious side."

"Like this?" Margo pulled out a John Grisham novel.

"Already read that one."

She slid it back into its spot. "I usually stick with lighter reads. I can't seem to focus on anything too deep these days."

Connor reached around her and tugged a book from its spot. "Jackpot. There are only two of Sandford's Prey books that I haven't read, and this is one of them."

The scent of his detergent wafted over her shoulder. She totally did not take a deep breath. "Awesome. Let's go stake out our hammocks."

Checking his watch, Connor said, "Now, or after lunch?"

Margo looked at her smart watch. The screen stayed black. She tapped it, tapped it again, then grabbed Connor's wrist to check the time. "It's only eleven. Hammock for an hour, then lunch and potty break, then hammock some more?"

"Brilliant. I'll grab some bottles of water." He went through the doorway to the dining hall while Margo wrote their names and book titles on the library sign out sheet. He reappeared a minute later with two bottles of water.

"Great." Margo took a bottle and handed him his book as they left the lodge.

They walked back past the tents. Scout lifted his head when Connor called his name, thought about it for a minute, then jumped down and followed them along the path to the river.

"What's the worst animal to deal with in your practice?"

Margo didn't hesitate. "Humans. Without question."

"I suppose I should have guessed that, huh?"

"It sounds awful, but it's true."

The path wound through a break in a thick row of shrubbery, then ended at a grassy lawn area that led to the river's edge. Six hammocks on stands were positioned at various locations – some closer to the water than others. All but one of the hammocks had already been claimed by relaxing campers.

Connor scratched his head. "It looks like options are limited if we want to talk."

"The big one is open." Margo wanted to snatch the words back as soon as she said them. She was beginning to question her mental health. One minute, she's yelling at him for something he did nearly twenty years ago, and the next minute, she's offering to get close and share a hammock. What was wrong with her? Before she could take it back, Connor walked to the hammock and grabbed the edge of the striped fabric.

Scout watched them for a moment, then dashed into the water, snapping at twigs and little fish.

"After you."

Margo kicked off her flip flops and gingerly sat on the edge. She leaned back, swinging her legs up, then scooted closer to the middle.

Connor held the hammock steady and mirrored her actions, ending up so they lounged opposite each other. "If my feet bug you, let me know."

Margo laughed. "If they bug me, I'll just push you off the hammock."

"Suit yourself, but you'll be coming with me." He wiggled, rocking the hammock for emphasis.

She grabbed the edge of the fabric and considered his words. "You're probably right."

"Okay, tell me – what was your worst human experience? Besides me," he added with a tentative smile.

Wow. He must be testing the waters, too. Margo playfully smacked his leg with her book. "We had a woman come in and wanted her puppy put down. The dog appeared to be healthy. Friendly little guy. When we asked her why she wanted him euthanized, it turned out the dog belonged to her husband. Apparently, they had had a huge fight, so she decided to get back at him by killing his dog."

Connor's mouth dropped open. "That's…" His hands flailed. "I don't even have a word."

"I know, right? We had her fill out the paperwork and she just turned around and walked away. Needless to say, we did *not* euthanize the puppy."

"What did you do?"

"Erica, our amazing office manager, tracked down the husband through the puppy's microchip. He came and picked the dog up and swore up and down he had no idea his wife was crazy, and that he'd take care of the dog."

"Did he?"

Margo shrugged. "I wish I knew. They weren't clients of ours."

"I can't imagine someone would put a pet down for something like that."

"You'd be shocked at the reasons we hear. Thank God we can refuse convenience euthanasia at our practice. 'We're going on vacation.' 'We're having too much company over the holidays.' 'She peed outside the litterbox.' 'We didn't expect a freaking Great Dane to get so big.' Crap reasons like that." Margo could feel her blood pressure rising. Her hands clenched the edges of her book.

"That's horrible."

"It is. We refuse them and know they probably go somewhere else that'll do it, but I like to think that every once in a while, our refusal makes someone think twice and reconsider."

Connor looked over to where Scout was happily lying in the sun, kicking his wet legs into the air and scrooching his back against the dirt. "I just can't understand how a person can treat an animal as disposable."

"I don't get it, either. Then again, I might not be the best judge of assigning an appropriate place to animals, since I called off a marriage because he didn't want any pets."

"He didn't have to be an axe-murderer to make him wrong for you."

"To hear my family talk, *I'm* the axe-murderer."

# Chapter Eight

Connor chuckled. "I'm sure you're exaggerating."

"Okay, maybe not an axe-murderer." She shrugged. "But I'm not exaggerating by much. They definitely think I'm an idiot for breaking up with Brad, so they feel justified in staying close to him and constantly reminding me how stupid I was. I've known my family my whole life. Literally nothing they do surprises me."

"I'm sure they could come up with something."

"Pffft, doubtful. It's almost like Ashley and I got all our genes from Mom, and Heidi got all hers from Dad."

"Does your mom live around here?"

"If you count a permanent storage unit, yes. She's still with Doctors International, so she's only home for a few months a year. Right now, she's in Haiti and loving every minute of it."

"Does it bother you? Her being so far away? That was the worst thing about being in Portland for me – being away from my mom and the rest of the family."

"It does and it doesn't. It's just always been this way. Yeah, I wish she'd been here more while we were growing up, but it's kind of cool when your mom's literally out saving the world.

And with technology, we talk every few days. I talk to her a lot more than I talk to my dad or Jean, and they only live five minutes away." She flipped her book open.

Connor followed suit and began to read. Soon the sounds of the river faded, and he was deep into the story.

It was well past the hour they'd agreed on when Scout barked, rousing them both from their books.

Connor checked his watch. "I bet we missed the lunch buffet. I hope they kept a plate for us." His stomach rumbled in agreement.

"I hope so. I didn't realize how hungry I was until now."

Scout stood at attention, focused on the tree line, wagging his tail. A moment later, the object of his interest walked through the trees.

Doug waved to them and walked over, pausing to scratch Scout's head. "Oren said I might find you here." He rubbed the back of his neck, looking slightly uncomfortable. "Um, Margo, would you mind coming up to the lodge? I hate to bother you, but there are, ah, some visitors to see you."

Connor watched the confusion cross her face.

She asked, "Who is it?"

"I'm not exactly sure. Bonnie got me on the walkie and asked me to find you." His tone was indecipherable.

Margo slid her legs off the hammock and held it steady while Connor got out the other side. He put on his sandals while Margo slipped into her flip flops.

He didn't like Doug's elusiveness, nor the trepidation on Margo's face. This was supposed to be her vacation. Who would be bothering her here? His brow scrunched. Could it be the ex? Maybe he came to his senses and wanted her back. Connor hated the idea more than he cared to admit. He gave himself a mental smack. What if it was an emergency? Maybe someone was sick or hurt, and he was worried it might be some other guy?

After they cleared the tree line, he reached out to grab her hand and gave it a squeeze. "Hey, relax. How bad can it be?"

She returned the squeeze before dropping his hand. She chewed her bottom lip, her eyes wide and wary as they walked through the tent village like she expected something to jump out at them. Connor slowed as they approached his tent.

Margo looked up at him. "You coming? We can get lunch after… whatever this is."

"No problem. Scout, stay." Well, this was unexpected. In a good way. He'd appreciated the truce she'd made with him, but for her to want him with her to face something unknown was more than he could have hoped for.

The dog pranced into the tent and jumped on the bed. Connor could practically feel Margo's anxiety. She walked stiffly, her face expressionless, her hands clenching and unclenching her book, her eyes darting around.

They turned the corner that would take them to the lodge. Her pace slowed. "It's not on fire, so that's a good sign, right?"

"Right." He nudged her back to a quicker pace. "Get it over with. Just like a band-aid."

They followed Doug up the lodge steps and across the comfortable wooden porch, with its line of rocking chairs. Voices spilled out of the lodge as Doug opened the door.

Margo stepped through the door and came to a dead stop. Which Connor realized when he ran smack into her. The room was full of people. Connor had just made the connection when a few of them threw their arms in the air and yelled, "Surprise!"

She tried to take a step back, but Connor was behind her. He put his hand on her back to steady her. "It's okay," he said quietly.

Her voice trembled. "Wh- what are you guys doing here?"

Margo's stepmother stepped out from the group, grinning from ear to ear. "We knew you wouldn't want to spend a week all by yourself, so we arranged it so we could all vacation with you."

"Why?" She leaned close to him, so he let his hand rest on her back.

Doug and Bonnie were off to the side, giving each other a concerned look.

The oldest sister came to stand beside their stepmother. "Just think how much fun this'll be. We haven't had a real family vacation in years. Are you totally surprised?"

Margo nodded.

Connor looked at the assembled faces. How could these people not see how uncomfortable she was? She white-knuckled her book like a lifeline.

The sister spoke again. "Jean worked hard to plan this in such a short time frame. Those contests don't give you much time to prepare, but she made it happen. Isn't this great?"

Finally, Margo spoke. "Sure." He didn't hear anything vaguely resembling "great" in her tone, only defeat and resignation.

Her shoulders practically wilted in front of his eyes, and it pissed him off. This family clearly had no concept of boundaries. And her father, engrossed in his phone, didn't seem to have any concept of his surroundings.

Doug cleared his throat. "Well, folks, let's get you, um, checked in."

"We'll stay wherever Margo is," the stepmother declared.

Bonnie flashed a brilliant smile. "Oh, I'm so sorry, there are no spots vacant in that area since it's reserved for the contest winners. But we can put you over here in the cabins." Her fingernail tapped the glass panel on the counter, which covered a colorful map of the grounds. "There's plenty of room for all of you."

"Margo, you can move to the cabins with us," the sister said.

That finally snapped Margo to action. Too loud, she said, "No. Can't. Against the rules. We have to stay in the contest winner area."

"Surely they'll make an exception," said the stepmother, with a dismissive wave of her hand.

Connor was glad Bonnie caught on. She gave a sorrowful, "Oh," and put on a sympathetic smile. "I'm so sorry, but Margo is correct. The contest winners have to stay in the winners' village. It's part of the prize agreement. No changes allowed."

She was so convincing Connor tried to remember if there *was* such an agreement. He really should have read through his prize packet.

Bonnie continued, "Unfortunately, we have a full schedule for our contest winners. But don't you worry, we'll have you all so busy you'll hardly even notice Margo's off with the contest group. Doug, why don't you get their bags gathered up and as soon as I confirm the payment, you can show them to their cabins."

Margo's relief was tangible. As for himself, he felt invisible. No one in her family had acknowledged him or even looked directly at him. Which was fine. Weird, but fine.

Finally, his invisibility wore out. Margo's stepmother looked him up and down with a disgusted sneer. "Who's this?"

Margo held her book tighter. "Connor Anderson. Connor, my dad's wife, Jean Lewis."

Connor was impressed with the way Jean was able to make him feel like a pile of dog crap with only a look, like she was a super villain in a low budget superhero movie. Did that make him Dog Crap Man? He didn't bother trying to hide the smirk as he gave her a nod. "Jean, nice to meet you."

She didn't smile. "Anderson. We've met." She turned to Margo. "Why is he here? He was a louse years ago, and I'm sure he still is."

Margo's back stiffened even more against his hand. He nodded toward Jean. "Yes, ma'am, that's me," he said mildly.

Bonnie cleared her throat. "Um, Mrs. Lewis? We're all done with the paperwork. Doug's ready to show you all to your cabins. We hope you enjoy your stay." She flashed a friendly customer-service smile. "Margo, Connor, your lunch is in the fridge."

"Thanks," Margo said.

Jean shot Connor another filthy look before addressing Margo. "I assume that means you won't be joining us?"

"Not right now, we're getting lunch."

Jean blinked a couple of times. It was probably disapproval in Morse code. She walked outside without another word.

As soon as the door clicked shut, Margo sagged against him. "I guess I was wrong."

"Huh?"

"Thinking they couldn't surprise me. This sure did."

"Are you okay?"

She ran a hand over her hair. "Of course. I'm fine. I'm always fine." Her chin quivered.

Guessing she was trying not to cry, Connor didn't push. Instead, he said, "Let's go see about that lunch, okay?"

Margo wiped her hand down her face. After a deep breath, she said, "Yeah," then led the way to the empty dining hall. They put their books on the table closest to the door to the large commercial kitchen. Margo flipped on the kitchen's light and stopped short. "Which fridge? There are three of them."

She went to the first one and read over the sign taped to the door.

Connor tapped a sticky note on the third stainless steel door. "'Contest Winners Only.' That's us." He took two plates from the fridge. Big oval paper plates were piled with a sandwich, macaroni salad, baked beans, chips, pickles, and a brownie. He handed a plate to Margo and they sat down to pull the plastic wrap off their plates.

Margo wolfed down her sandwich and the macaroni salad then shoved the plate away. "No," she said under her breath.

"No what?" Connor was taken aback by her sudden shift. "Not good?"

"No, I mean I can't do this. I can't let them get under my skin. I've come way too far."

He was curious but didn't ask what she meant. Instead, he made a mental note to talk to her later when she wasn't still feeling blindsided by her family. They all seemed oblivious to Margo's discomfort. Except the younger sister. She'd given Margo a look – sympathy, maybe? – and reached out to squeeze her arm when they had walked out of the lodge. He finished his brownie and looked at Margo's plate, still untouched after she'd pushed it away. "Are you going to eat that?"

"No." She slid the plate toward him.

He took the brownie. No sense letting it go to waste. "Do you want to go back to the river?"

She let out a heavy sigh. "I'm going to be lousy company, there's no way I'll be able to concentrate on my book, and I don't want to ruin your afternoon. Maybe I'll just sit in my tent and wait for them to find me," she finished darkly, glaring so hard into the tablecloth he wouldn't have been surprised to see it ignite.

Connor raised an eyebrow. The idea of her sitting in her

tent, miserable, didn't sit well with him. He tried to cheer her up. "Let's go back to the river. The sound of running water will help your nerves, and you always have the option of swimming away if we spot them in the distance."

"I can't swim," she grumbled.

"No problem. We'll go with Plan B - steal a kayak and escape that way."

She cracked a smile. "I'm sorry. I told you I was lousy company."

Connor picked up their plates and dumped them in the trash. He put the dirty silverware in the bin. "You're great company, Margo."

She stood and pushed her chair in and picked up their books. "You should get out more."

"Probably." He grinned at her. "Let's see if you pass the ultimate test."

"What's that?"

He pushed the door open and followed her across the porch and down the stairs. Scout was snoozing in the grass. When he saw them, he stretched and ran over to Margo, his tail wagging.

"That was the test. Scout says you passed with flying colors."

"His bar's set a little low, don't you think?" She leaned down and scratched the dog's ears.

"Roxanne couldn't get over it, soooo…" Connor shrugged.

"Wow." She laughed.

Connor was glad to see her smiling. "You can't argue with that, can you?"

"I suppose not."

"River?" He hoped he could make her feel a little better. Maybe that'd be a point in his favor and she'd decide he might be worth keeping around.

"Fine."

Connor smiled and put his arm around Margo's shoulders. "That's the spirit."

She mock-glared at him but put her arm around his waist. "Whatever," she grumbled. "You're too persistent. I can't fight you in my weakened mental state."

Connor laughed. "I'll file that away for future reference." He relished the heat of her arm through his thin t-shirt. He had to be careful, or he'd get used to this.

"Jerk."

They turned the corner of the lodge and took the path back through the tent village. A couple of the tents were closed up, but most were open and empty. As they passed the restrooms and reached the brush, Connor swept his arm to the side to move branches that encroached over the narrow path for her to go through ahead of him. "Hammock again, or do you want to sit near the water?"

She kicked off her flip flops and set her book on top of them. She walked toward the water's edge. A tree that probably should have died when it was knocked over, grew horizontally with half the roots exposed. Its trunk ran parallel to the water's edge, but healthy, leafy branches reached for the sky. The tree's strange position created the perfect seat to sit with their feet dangling into the water. Margo perched on it, the water rippling around her ankles.

Connor watched her for a moment, then joined her on the fallen tree, the water cool on his feet. Scout bounded out into the river until he was chest-deep, biting at twigs and bugs floating by, and dunked his entire head to snap at the tiny fish that swam near his legs.

After a few minutes, Connor felt Margo relax while she watched Scout's antics. "You almost had it," she said, pointing. "There's one, right there."

Scout wagged his sopping tail and splashed to the general area Margo pointed at, scaring away any fish that might have been there a moment earlier.

Connor wondered what was going on in her head. He remembered her family as over-involved way back when they were kids. When he'd asked her to prom, she'd said yes, but worried what her family would say. But she was an adult now. A strong, successful one at that. Shaking his head, he turned his attention to Scout. It wasn't his place to critique her relationship with her family. He certainly wouldn't appreciate someone criticizing his mother, despite her sizeable faults and flaws.

The afternoon stretched out in front of them as they laughed at Scout and talked about safe things. Books, work, food… anything other than Margo's family.

Eventually, Scout got tired of the water and trotted onto the grass, where he shook himself, launching water droplets in every direction. Margo got up from the log, swished her toes in the water, and stepped onto the grass. They made their way back to the hammock, where they both picked up their books, but never cracked them open.

Connor watched Margo watching the water for the better part of half an hour.

She groaned. "I suppose I should go find my family." She got out of the hammock and put her flip flops back on.

"I'll walk along back if you don't mind. If I don't get Scout out of the river, he's liable to turn into a fish."

Margo held out her hand to him. He scrambled out of the hammock, nearly tripping and making a fool of himself to take it. She gave him a half-smile that made his heart do a little skip.

On impulse, he kissed her knuckles. "My offer stands. If you want to steal a kayak, just say the word."

Her smile was genuine this time and it made him feel like a million bucks. "I'll pass. For now, anyway. I reserve the right to change my mind."

He laced his fingers through hers and whistled to Scout. "Just promise that if you change your mind, you'll let me know. Don't leave me here to fend for myself with Roxanne."

"Deal."

# Chapter Nine

Margo reluctantly let go of his hand when they got to the tent village. "I'll see you for dinner."

"Want me to take your book?"

"Sure." She handed it to him and sighed heavily at the thought of seeing her family. They were exhausting. Margo could never relax when everyone was together. Instead, she had to watch what she said and always be prepared for verbal grenades lobbed in her direction.

"You look like you're being marched to your execution." He sounded concerned.

"I'll put my happy face on when I make the turn." She gave him an exaggerated smile with wide eyes and pointed to her face. "How's this?"

"Terrifying."

Margo laughed and waved at him as she walked to the path. At least she could count on Connor to cheer her up after the inevitable disaster that awaited her at the cabins. She took a deep breath and forced the tension from her face. She tried to think of the positives. Her family wanted to be near her. That was a good thing, right?

Okay, Ashley, Elliott, and Livvie were a definite positive. Heidi's kids were mostly a positive. There. She'd focus on the nieces and nephews just like she did on holidays. Auntie Margo, always the fun aunt who got on the ground to play with them... the kids didn't have to know they were a welcome buffer.

She left the tent village and turned onto the path that would take her to the cabin area. It was set up much like the tent area, with ten cabins, five on each side of a dirt lane, staggered so the front doors didn't face each other.

Her twelve-year-old niece Jeanette sat on a cabin's step, looking forlorn and miserable. Jordan and Jonathan, her nephews, came barreling at her full speed from around the corner. Margo put her arms out and bent over to grab them in a hug. "Hey, hey, slow down, munchkins."

Jordan giggled. "Munchkin, munchkin, munchkin," he chanted, poking at his brother. Apparently, when you're five, "munchkin" is a hilarious word.

"Knock it off, munchkin," Jonathan answered with his know-it-all seven-year-old big-brother irritated tone.

"Munchkin!" Jordan shrieked, running away.

Heidi appeared in the doorway of her cabin, frowning. "Is that really a word you should be teaching them?"

Margo straightened, her hand still resting on Jonathan's shoulder. "What?"

Jonathan's eyes were huge. "Is 'munchkin' a swear?" He clapped his hand over his mouth.

"No, it's not," Margo said. She had a wicked impulse to teach him the F word.

Heidi's lips pressed into a thin line. "It's inappropriate. Jonathan, go play with Jordan."

Margo debated asking about the stick lodged in her sister's rectum, but settled on, "Whatever." Margo rolled her eyes and walked past Heidi and Greg's cabin. Ashley, her younger sister, must have heard her voice. She came out of her cabin to the little porch and smiled.

"Auntie!" Ashley's four-year-old sprinted at her from the side of the cabin, a tornado of dirt and love.

"Livvie!" Margo held out her arms for Olivia to jump into. "Hey, sweet girl."

Olivia launched herself into Margo's arms and pressed a loud, sticky kiss to her cheek. "Mommy letted me play in the dirt."

"I see that." She wiped her cheek. "Thanks for sharing."

Olivia giggled, then wriggled to be set down. She scampered off to where the boys were playing with Matchbox cars. Margo watched her skip away, loudly singing a Sesame Street song about sharing.

As soon as she was out of earshot, Margo turned on her sister. "Really, Ashley, not even a heads up? A text? Something?"

"Sorry." Ashley furtively glanced around and lowered her voice. "I knew you were going to hate this, and honestly? I didn't want to ruin your day yesterday because if I'd have told you, you would have been freaking out the whole time."

"Bull. How long did you know about this?"

Ashley came down off the porch to stand with Margo. "Okay, fine. You know how Jean is. She complained that you didn't want to go on the family vacation this year."

"I haven't gone on a family vacation in over a decade." Little wonder why.

"You haven't gone on any vacation at all. So as soon as she found out about this trip, she started making plans to turn *this* into our family vacation. We'd have been here yesterday, but it didn't suit Heidi's clan."

"How *did* she find out? It's not like she'd do anything as plebian as listen to the radio."

Ashley promised, "It did not come from me. If I had to guess, she heard it from Brad."

Margo clenched her teeth and made a frustrated growl. "Always Brad! Does it not occur to her that I didn't want to go on the 'family vacation' this year because she was planning to invite Brad?" She was so sick of hearing his name.

Something close to guilt crossed Ashley's face.

Margo took a step back, shaking her head. "What? No. She didn't. Did she? Oh, no, she did, didn't she?" She ran her hands over her hair, tugging on her ponytail.

Ashley's expression was pained. She looked around again, then said, "She *invited* him, but he said he couldn't come on short notice."

"You have got to be kidding me." She felt the blood boiling its way up her neck into her face until it pounded against her eardrums with a steady whooshing beat.

"Psst." Ashley slightly nodded her head to a spot behind Margo. "Incoming," she whispered without moving her lips, a trick they'd perfected over the years.

"There you are, dear. I was starting to think you were planning to avoid us the entire trip." Her tone was accusing.

"Tempting," Margo snapped. She needed a moment to deal with the fact that Jean had – again – invited her ex into her space.

"Don't be fresh. I see you got rid of that awful Anderson boy. Good riddance."

Impotent frustration clenched Margo's jaw. "Don't start."

Ignoring her, Jean reached out and swept Margo's ponytail off her shoulder. "Why do you have all these different colors in your hair? Your natural color would be much prettier."

"They're highlights. I like them."

"Hmm. Does... er, did Brad like them? I should think a professional man would want his future wife to be more presentable."

Margo jerked her head back, away from her stepmother's hand. Ashley said, "Oh, for crying out loud, stop worrying about her hair."

"I can't imagine why anyone over thirty would want something like that," Heidi chimed in from her cabin porch. "And it's much too long." Heidi touched her own stylish chin-length bob. Identical to Jean's.

Margo took a step back, the need to flee stronger with each passing second. "I have to get back for the next activity, but I'm sure I'll see you guys at dinner."

"They should plan these activities for everyone," Jean said. "We would have had activities if we'd have gone on a cruise like your dad wanted to."

Ashley rolled her eyes. "Then there'd be no perks for the contest winners."

"Well. It was a silly contest anyway." Her squinty eyes focused on Margo. "You always did spend too much time with your nose in a book. I'm not sure how you ever found the time to meet Brad, let alone get engaged."

Margo's neck tightened. "You keep forgetting I also found the time to break up with him."

Jean waved her hand, dismissing the notion. "It was a spat, and you overreacted like you always do. Hopefully, you'll come to your senses before Brad moves on. Although why he still waits around is a mystery to me."

Turning on her heel, Margo knew any more words would be wasted. She faked a smile and blew kisses to the kids on her way back to the path. Once she turned the corner, she practically ran back to her tent. Thankfully, she didn't see anyone along the way. She stood in the tent's doorway, her fists pressed to her hips, emotions swirling together like some internal storm of chaos and negativity.

She picked up her sweatshirt that was laying on the floor and flung it onto the bed, then picked it back up and flung it toward the chair. Flopping on the bed, she groaned and rubbed her face with her hands.

Why did they have to come here? It was bad enough she was dealing with all sorts of Connor-related emotions. She felt drained and suddenly tired all the way to the bone. So much for a relaxing, restorative vacation.

The bed jostled beside her. She jerked her hands off her eyes and was met with Scout's doggy smile. He slurped the side of her face. Laughing, she wiped her cheek. "You're as bad as Olivia." He took it as a compliment and stretched out alongside her. She rolled onto her side and flung her arm over the dog.

"This whole thing is ridiculous. Maybe they should adopt Brad or something since they think he's so great. He's not, though. He's a jerk. Did you know he doesn't even want to have a dog? What kind of person wouldn't want a dog, right? I knew it was stupid to think this would be a nice, relaxing vacation." She sighed and blinked back tears.

He lay his head down on her pillow and huffed in solidarity, then closed his eyes.

"At least I got to meet you. That's pretty awesome. And Connor's okay, I guess," she chuckled. "You're such a good boy."

His eyebrows danced, but his eyes stayed closed.

Margo scratched his ears, the feel of his soft fur helping her to calm.

He snuffled his face closer to her and let out a long breath.

She could feel the tension melting away. Her jaw and shoulders relaxed. "See? This is exactly why I can't marry someone who won't 'allow' a dog in his house. 'His' house. That's bull, too. I make more than he does. It's like my stupid family thinks being a veterinarian is a cute little job to pass the time until I can be a housewife. Just because that's right for Jean and Heidi doesn't mean it's right for me. Heck, I don't even know if I want kids. Sacrilege, I know. What kind of woman wouldn't want kids? This kind, that's who." Margo sighed and snuggled closer to Scout. It felt good to talk it out, even to someone who couldn't offer any advice. Maybe that was better anyway. She'd had enough advice for one day. "Thanks for listening. You're a good boy."

Scout's tail thumped twice against the mattress.

Margo smiled against his dark fur and dozed off.

# Chapter Ten

Connor closed his book and reached down to pet Scout, but instead of fur, his fingers brushed against the wood of the deck. "Where the heck did he go?" he muttered.

The hair on the back of his neck stood at attention. He looked around and saw Roxanne staring at him. When she saw him looking, she leaned back, pushing her chest out. Seriously? Connor turned his head so fast he could have gotten whiplash. As a rule, he tried not to make snap judgments about people, but Roxanne's over the top act made it hard to believe there was a genuine person inside.

Inside the tent, his bed was empty. He set his book on the nightstand and walked to the restroom. On his way back, he walked past his own tent and peeked into Margo's, where he guessed Scout had gone.

He had to laugh.

Scout lay on his back, all four paws in the air, with Margo's arm slung across his chest, both of them dozing. He unlocked his phone and almost snapped a picture to show her later. As he aimed the camera, he wasn't sure if she'd find it sweet or creepy, so he slid his phone back into his pocket without the photo.

He watched them for a few minutes, half jealous of Scout, and half jealous that Margo and the dog had bonded so fast. It had taken him months before Scout started trusting him. Then again, he couldn't make Scout understand why both Colin and his home were suddenly gone, and he was stuck with Connor.

Margo's ponytail trailed over her pillow and off the edge of the bed. He imagined running his fingers through it, then tried to stop the image because it wasn't appropriate. Granted, he didn't try too hard.

Margo stirred, stretching, and grinned at the dog. She scratched his chest and snuggled her face against his neck.

Connor cleared his throat and stepped up onto her porch. "Hey, I wondered where he got to."

"Oh, hey." She sat up, blushing. "I wasn't planning on taking a nap, but Scout convinced me it was a great idea."

"He's a bad influence." Connor hoped a little Scout therapy and a nap had helped Margo feel better.

Scout stretched his legs straight up until they quaked, then rolled over and slid off the bed in another elaborate stretch.

Margo laughed and took her hair out of the elastic band. "Terrible influence. I could have read half my book." She ran her fingers through her hair and tied it back up in a ponytail.

"That's what I was doing when I realized he was gone. I figured he was probably here. How was your family?"

Her smile faltered. "About how I expected. Jean insulted everything from dumping Brad to my awful hair, and my older sister agreed with her."

Connor frowned. "What's wrong with your hair? I think it's pretty." *Ooops, didn't mean to say that out loud.* Her hair was long, thick, and wavy, several dark shades underneath, with chunks of various blondes throughout. Not that Connor was any kind of hair expert, but it looked good to him.

"You do?"

He shrugged, hoping he appeared nonchalant. "Sure. Not as pretty as mine, but still." He stroked his beard for emphasis.

"Yes, Connor, you're very pretty."

He batted his eyelashes. "Thanks for noticing." Yeah, she'd been teasing, but wouldn't it be great if she actually *did* find him attractive? He tried to ignore the little flutter in his belly. It was way too soon for thoughts like that.

"What's on the agenda for the afternoon?" Her voice broke his train of thought.

It took him a second to remember. "Uh, geocaching."

"What?" She crossed her legs under her, a puzzled expression on her face.

"Geocaching. It's like a little treasure hunt. Didn't you read about it in your prize packet?" he teased.

"Touché." She laughed. "Are we too late?"

Her laughter was like a ray of sunshine straight to his heart. "No, I think that's an activity on our own sort of thing."

"Good. I need to stop at the restroom and then we can go." She got off the bed and put her flip flops on, then stopped short. "Oh. Um, I mean, if you wanted to. If not, it's okay. I guess I shouldn't just assume."

"Not much of an assumption, since I'm standing here in your doorway, right?" As far as he was concerned, Margo could assume she was welcome to be with him anytime. He hoped this meant they were becoming friends, and maybe she'd even forgive him.

"Looking for your dog."

Scout's ears perked up at the word "dog."

"Eh, where else would he go?" He stepped back off the porch and turned toward the restrooms. "Shall we?"

Margo joined him. As they walked toward the restrooms, she asked, "How do we do the geocaching?"

He was glad to know the answer. Maybe it'd impress her in some small way. Or maybe that was just wishful thinking. "It uses GPS. I have the app on my phone. We just follow the coordinates and then try to find the cache. It looks like it's usually a plastic container with a logbook you sign."

"There's an app for everything these days, isn't there?"

"Yes, thank goodness. I can't imagine how much stuff I'd be losing if I had to keep track of my phone, a calendar, a GPS, an MP3 player, an alarm clock…"

"Okay, okay, you made your point." She went into the restroom and when she came back out, Connor was waiting nearby.

He held up his phone and continued with a smirk, "A handheld game system, a pedometer, a camera…"

Margo shot him a look. "Dude. Seriously."

He laughed loud. "Dude? I can't believe you just called me that."

"Can we just go?" She rolled her eyes, exasperated with him.

"Have you ever done this?"

"Obviously not, since I didn't even know what it was."

He tapped at his phone. "Okay, pick one."

Margo looked at the map on his phone and selected one of the dots indicating nearby caches. They walked in the general direction of the coordinates.

Connor asked, "Are you feeling better? About them being here, I mean?"

"No. But I'll get over it. I always do."

He hated the defeat in her voice and tried to come up with a silver lining. "It's nice your family wants to spend time with you."

"I suppose that's one way to look at it. The problem is that they don't want to spend time with *me*. They don't know me. They want to spend time with the person they think I should be."

"Are you sure that's accurate?" He held back, afraid the question would offend her. It made no sense that they couldn't know her inside and out. In the last day, he'd gotten a pretty good sense of who she is. Thirty-four years should be plenty.

"I know how it sounds. But when every interaction is a commentary on how I'm doing everything wrong, and how perfect – no, how *correct* – my life would be if only I would do things the way I 'should,' then yes, I think it's accurate. You'll see."

That sounded a little ominous. "What do you mean?"

"At dinner. I bet you five dollars I'm called out for doing at least three things wrong during dinner." She turned and held out her hand for him to shake.

"Is this from everyone or just Jean?"

"Hmm. Your call."

"Okay, I'll give you the advantage and say overall. Five bucks." He'd be happy to lose this bet.

They shook hands to seal the deal.

After they walked into the woods for a few minutes, Margo said, "I'm sorry I'm being such a downer. I think I'm just going to go back to the tent and read for a bit before dinner. I'm too aggravated to enjoy myself."

"Hang on. I'll go back with you." He looked around and whistled. A bush rustled and Scout jumped out, proudly carrying a stick.

They followed his bouncing form back to the tents. Connor stopped to grab his book and sat on the rocking chair beside Margo's. They opened their books. Connor stared at the pages, but his mind wandered. He wanted to say something to make Margo feel better, but he had no idea what that might be.

He understood family issues and touchy subjects. He'd borne the brunt of his mother's wrath and hateful words more times than he cared to remember. In his case, his mother had a lot of issues that contributed to her actions. He suspected Jean was just a jerk.

As his mind wandered, he noticed the pages of Margo's book weren't turning, either, even though she was staring at them. He reached over and put his hand over hers, wrapping his fingers around hers. She turned her palm up without lifting her eyes from the page. Nothing had ever felt more right than touching her. It occurred to him that there was a good chance he might be the one to end up with a broken heart this time.

Just before dinnertime, the other contest winners returned loudly from their geocaching excursion, laughing and talking. Except Roxanne, who glared at Connor and Margo on her way past. As usual. Even if he had, on any planet, been remotely interested in her, he wouldn't be after witnessing her ugly attitude and penchant for drama. No thanks.

He couldn't figure out why Shane was chasing after her like an adoring puppy. Literally. He was right behind her. "Roxy? Roxy. Did you have fun? That was so nice, wasn't it? What would you like to do later? Do you want to go to the bonfire? Or would you rather we just stay in tonight? Roxy?" They reminded him of Spike the bulldog and Chester the terrier on Looney Tunes, with the terrier yapping incessantly until the bulldog punched him in the nose and sent him hurtling into a fence, but Chester always bounced right back over for more punishment. It wasn't much of a stretch to imagine Roxanne punching Shane. Or to imagine Shane bounding right back over to her. The image might be funny if it weren't so darn sad.

Margo squeezed his fingers. "Shall we follow the crowd to dinner?"

"Sure." He set their books on Margo's bed, where Scout was sleeping, and walked with her to the lodge. Looking at the inviting building, he said, "I don't think we're getting a real sense of roughing it on this trip."

She seemed to be glad for the light topic. "Suits me fine. Until now, I defined roughing it as staying in a *two*-star hotel."

"I think our accommodations are better than a two star hotel."

"Mostly. But even two-star hotels have a bathroom in every room."

He couldn't argue that fact, but he did anyway. "I suppose if you're picky about such things, that could matter."

"I suppose when you can pee behind a tree, it wouldn't."

"Totally depends on the size of the tree."

"Oh, brother."

Connor laughed as he followed her up the steps and across the porch. The dining room was already full with the other campers.

"Margo! We saved you a seat." Her sister Ashley waved and pointed to an empty chair near her.

"We need a spot for Connor, too," Margo said.

Ashley grinned. "Jean's going to love this."

Margo tilted her head and gave her sister a look, but Ashley was busy shifting seats at the table.

"You don't have to sit with me," Margo said.

Connor put his hand on her back. "It'll be fine."

"No, really. I'm starting to question your sanity."

"I never claimed to be sane." He nudged her toward the dinner buffet. "Margo, seriously. It's okay. Maybe Jean will focus on me and I'll take your five bucks." He hoped so.

"Don't count on it. She's got enough venom to go around."

He didn't doubt it. They filled their plates. Well, he filled his plate. Margo put a few tiny scoops of food on hers. He assumed she was too nervous to eat much. That wasn't something that ever seemed to afflict him. He could eat his way through anything.

He followed Margo to the table. Her family was already sitting down, their plates untouched.

"Hurry up, Margo, the food's getting cold."

"We're coming. Geez." Margo said.

"Are you going to eat all of that? You know the metabolism slows down after thirty and you have to watch what you eat." Jean took a roll off her own plate and set it on Margo's. Connor couldn't quite grasp the irony of that ridiculous maneuver.

John, Margo's father, sat tapping on his phone, oblivious to everything around him. It was obnoxious enough on its own, but he had the sound turned on, and up, so every letter he typed was accompanied by a loud click. *Click click click click click click*, pause, *click click click, click, click.* He didn't even look up to acknowledge his family.

Connor sat down and put his hand on Margo's knee, giving it a squeeze. Her hand covered his, squeezing his fingers twice, then she let go. As much as he wanted to keep his hand on her leg, he thought it might be too much, too soon for her, so he moved it.

"Margo, say grace."

"No."

Jean gave her a filthy look, and Margo relented and mumbled a fast prayer.

Ashley's husband, Elliott, sat directly across from him. He said, "Connor, I went to school with a Colin Anderson. Any relation?"

"My brother."

Elliott smiled. "Really. Is he still in the area? I should give him a call."

"Uh, he passed away a few months ago."

He felt Margo's hand on his leg.

The smile dropped from Elliott's face. "I'm so sorry. I had no idea."

"No, it's okay. Cancer," he added. Everyone always wanted to know how, but no one wanted to ask. It was easier to just volunteer the information.

An awkward silence covered the table for a moment until Connor asked Elliott what he did for a living.

"I'm a structural engineer."

"No kidding. Me, too." Elliott's smile seemed genuine. "Where are you working?"

"Nowhere at the moment."

Beside Ashley, catty-cornered from him, Jean snorted and rolled her eyes, giving a meaningful look at Margo.

Connor continued. "I just moved back to Hickory Hollow. I'll be starting at Hansen next month."

Elliott's brows rose. "Hansen? That's where I'm at. You must be the hotshot from Oregon I've been hearing so many rumors about."

Connor deflected the compliment. "Hotshot? I wouldn't go that far."

Jean snorted again and raised her eyebrows at Margo.

Margo's fingers dug into his knee. "Problem?"

"Nope." Jean sipped at her water.

Ashley sighed and changed the subject. "If you just got back, how'd you hear about the contest?"

"I've been back about three months."

Jean leaned back in her chair. "And don't have a job until next month? Must be nice to have so many friends you can depend on."

Connor had no idea what she was talking about. "What

friends?"

"I assume you're staying with friends." She made air quotes. "Couch surfing? Isn't that what they call it?"

"I'm not."

"Sleeping in your car, then? This trip must be heaven for you." She waved a regal hand, encompassing the campground.

Connor felt the heat spreading up his neck, and if she wasn't Margo's stepmother, he'd have a lot to say. He settled for a mild, "I live in my house. No, it's not cardboard, and no, it's not under a bridge. Parts of this vacation have been wonderful. Other parts, not so much."

Jean glared. "Who helped you win the contest? I can scarcely imagine you're literate enough on your own."

"Jean!" Margo was on her feet.

"Seriously? What the hell?" Ashley added.

"You said 'hell,'" Olivia said.

"You just said 'hell,' too," Jordan said to Olivia.

Jeanette smacked Jordan.

Jonathan yelled at Jeanette, "You're hitting. Mom, she's hitting."

John looked up from his phone and bellowed, "Knock it off!"

Silence descended over the entire dining room for a moment as campers looked around to see what was going on. Conversation quickly resumed, but it was the hushed murmur of juicy gossip.

Jean glared up at Margo. "Sit down. You're making a scene. And you watch your language," she said to Ashley.

Margo stepped back from the table and pushed her chair in. "Until you apologize, stay away from me."

Heidi said, "There's no need to overreact. Mom was a little harsh, but –"

"Shut up," Margo snapped and spun around, leaving the

dining hall.

"'Shut up' is bad words!" Jordan yelled.

John's phone *click-click-clicked*.

Connor grabbed their plates and put them in the bin, then followed Margo outside. She was walking across the porch, down the steps, and onto the path back to the tents. He jogged to catch up with her then matched her pace, walking in silence until they reached her tent, where Scout was still sleeping.

Margo paced the wooden floor, agitated and upset.

"Hey." He wasn't sure if he should reach out, and he had no idea what to say to make her stop hurting.

She spun on her heel and looked at him. Tears shimmered in her eyes. She opened her mouth, waved her hands, and snapped her mouth shut. "I'm so sorry."

He was across the floor before the tears spilled down her cheeks, pulling her tight against him. "Don't."

"I'm so sorry," she sobbed against his shoulder. Her arms went around his neck, holding on tight. Her body shook against him.

He felt a bizarre combination of relief that he hadn't caused her to be upset this time, anger at the people who had, and pleasure that she was letting him comfort her. "Don't you dare apologize for her." He rubbed her back while she cried, knowing she was letting out a lot more than the disaster at dinner.

Scout jumped off the bed and leaned against Margo's legs. He whined, his chocolate eyes looking up at his favorite person.

Margo's tears slowed and she reached down to scratch Scout's head. "I don't understand. I swear, if I knew she'd be like that I never would have made you sit there. I mean, I expected some bullcrap, but that... That was just over the top."

"I know."

"She's not usually that bad. I don't understand."

"I don't know." He smoothed her hair back from her wet face, his thumbs wiping the tears from her cheeks. "Thank you for standing up for me. I know it wasn't easy."

"I couldn't just let her talk to you that way. I... I truly don't understand. I've never heard her be so hateful. Well, to anyone outside the family, anyway."

Connor kissed her forehead. He hated that she was feeling bad, so he leaned back and grinned. "I know what it is."

"What?" She looked up at him, her wet eyes earnestly searching for some answers.

"It's the beard. It's like a magnet. Jean probably found herself so uncontrollably attracted to me that she couldn't help but hate herself, so she was lashing out. Perfectly natural."

Margo stared at him for a moment, wide-eyed, then burst out laughing. She laughed hard, leaning against him for support, clutching handfuls of his shirt. "Oh my gosh, you're crazy."

Success! He was going for a smile, but a hearty laugh was even better. "If by 'crazy,' you mean 'magnificent,' then I totally agree."

Margo's laughter subsided and she stood back and wiped her face. "Thank you."

"For what?"

"For being amazing."

Her words went straight to his ego. Mental note: *Whatever you're doing, keep doing it.* "Oh, that. I can hardly take credit for something that comes so naturally."

She giggled again. It was quickly becoming his favorite sound in the world. He didn't want to think too much about that. His mind, traitorous jerk that it was, instead decided to ponder what might have happened if things had ended differently so many years ago. If he hadn't just ghosted. If he had called her to explain why he'd stood her up on prom night. If he hadn't let her spend years thinking he was an unfeeling jerk who'd used her.

Would they still be together? Would they have had a family? Would either of them have gone to college and created successful careers? Would they have survived the relentless assault of her family?

Margo snapped her fingers, pulling him back to the present. "Hey, where'd you go?" She waved her hand in front of his face. "Earth to Connor."

"Sorry. I was just thinking about how awesome I am." He wiggled his eyebrows.

Margo rolled her eyes. "I'd ask you if you're joking, but I'm kind of afraid of the answer."

Connor gave her a wink, then changed the subject. "Kidding. I was thinking about the five bucks you owe me. They didn't pick on you at all." He chuckled at her surprised gasp. "You're welcome. Now, are we going to the bonfire tonight?"

"Maybe. I'm a little hesitant because I don't know if my family is going. I really don't want to deal with any more drama. I *hate* drama. I avoid it at all costs and now look at me. Surrounded by drama. Everyone in the dining room was watching that whole scene. I looked ridiculous."

"They looked ridiculous. *You* looked amazing. Like Wonder Woman."

"Oh, brother."

Connor grinned. "I'll be back to walk you to the bonfire. It'll be fine."

"Fine." She jerked her head toward the bed, where Scout had resumed his position. "Take your bed hog with you."

"Scout!"

The dog yawned in protest, slunk off the bed, and followed Connor to his tent.

# Chapter Eleven

Margo approached the bonfire warily, searching the fire-lit faces for her family. She was glad for Connor's calm presence beside her, and for his strong hand holding hers. How strange was that? A day ago, she wanted him to go away, and now she was glad when he was close. Heidi and Greg sat at the far side of the fire with their three kids and Jean. John wasn't present. No surprise there. On the opposite path, Ashley, Elliott, and Olivia walked toward the fire. Ashley nudged Elliott and walked around to Margo's side.

She grabbed Margo's arm and leaned close to her ear. "You are never going to believe this. Never in a million years." Her eyes shone with mischief and excitement.

"What?"

She whispered so no one else could hear. "I found out why Jean can't stand Connor."

Margo's fingers tightened around his. "What? How? Why?"

Ashley grabbed Margo's arm. "We have to go someplace private."

Margo glanced at Connor, who shrugged and said, "I'll save you a seat."

"Let's go back to my tent," She said to Ashley, turning back to the path.

Margo and Ashley hurried to the tent. Margo zipped the front door and windows shut. The suspense was driving her nuts. "Spill it."

They sat on the bed, cross-legged, just like they'd done a million times over the years.

Ashley leaned toward her, her voice low. "I couldn't figure out why Jean was freaking out and being so evil to Connor. She's not normally… well, you know. Not so obvious. So after the whole fiasco at dinner, I locked myself in the car and called Grandma."

"You didn't." Margo should have thought of that. Grandma knew everyone and everything that ever happened in Hickory Hollow.

Ashley talked with her hands, gesturing intensely. "Well, I called Mom first, but you know she'll never say a bad word about Jean even if she deserves it, and she wouldn't tell me anything, but I think she knew. I called Grandma, and as soon as I said Connor's name, she did her 'Hmmm' thing and –"

Margo wanted to shake her. "Get to the point!"

"I'm getting there!" She lowered her voice. "Jean used to date Connor's dad."

Margo's mouth dropped open. Did not expect *that*. "What?"

"I know, right? Apparently, they dated all through high school, then broke up when they went to college. Jean thought they were on a break, he thought they were done."

"Wow."

"That's not all."

"Come on, you're killing me." Margo leaned close, anxious to hear what other gossip her sister had uncovered.

"She objected at their wedding." Ashley squealed and clapped her hands together.

Margo gasped. "What? No way."

Ashley continued, practically breathless. "Yes, way. She wasn't invited. But she showed up at the church anyway and when the preacher asked for objections, she stood up and said that he was in love with *her*. I guess Connor's dad tried to take her aside to talk to her, but she wouldn't go with him, so in front of the whole church, he told her he didn't love her anymore, that it had been over since they broke up before college. Grandma said he tried to be gentle, like he didn't want to embarrass her, but she slapped him across the face and ran out. And he got married."

"Holy crap."

"Yeah, the last little piece of the puzzle?"

"There can't be more." Margo was reeling from what she'd heard. Anything more was unthinkable.

"Apparently, Connor is the spitting image of his father. So that just sent her off the deep end."

"Does Dad have any idea about any of this?" She doubted it. A juggler on a unicycle with flaming chainsaws probably wouldn't get his attention.

Ashley shrugged. "No clue. I'm sure he knows they dated, but I don't know if they ever met that he would know Connor looks like him. Freaky, huh?"

"Holy crap," Margo repeated. She wondered how Connor would react to this development. For a moment, she considered not telling him, but she didn't want him to find out some other way. She sighed, and because she couldn't think of anything else to say, she said, "Holy freaking crap."

Ashley sat back, giving Margo a hard look. "You really like him."

"He's a good guy. Despite what happened..." she waved her hand as if to gesture to the past in general, "...way back."

Ashley had been the one to lay beside her and threaten bodily harm on him as Margo sobbed and eventually cried herself to sleep. She had also been the one to help Margo ceremonially burn her prom dress. In fact, it had been Ashley's idea.

"Have you forgiven him? And a better question – does he deserve to be forgiven? Because I'm still willing to strangle him if that's what you want."

Margo gave Ashley a quick hug. How miserable her life would be without her sister in her corner. "I don't know. It almost seems like I'm not dealing with the same person and I can't quite reconcile it in my head. Like there's Past Connor and Present Connor."

"I mean, there kind of is, right? You're not the same person you were back then, are you?" Ashley patted her knee.

Margo lifted a shoulder. "I don't know. We're stuck together as partners for most of the activities planned for the contest winners. We're friendly, and we're going to have a good time together. And of course all this family drama muddies the water, so I'm leaving it at that. A good time for a week."

"And after vacation?"

"We'll go our separate ways." The words didn't sit right on her tongue.

Ashley's eyebrows scrunched up. "Why?"

Leave it to Ash to make her go deeper than she wanted to about Connor. "I'm not looking for a relationship. I don't need to be married and start squirting out kids. Sorry." Margo held up a hand in surrender. "I don't mean—"

Ashley cut her off. "Of course you don't. I know that you liked being in a relationship when you were with Brad."

"And we see how that turned out."

"Because he wasn't the right guy for you."

Margo sat up straight and bored her gaze directly into her

sister's. "Do *you* believe that?" It mattered. So many people seemed to think she was crazy to break up with a catch like Brad that she second-guessed herself. Even though in her heart of hearts, she knew she'd made the right decision.

Ashley reached over and put her hand over Margo's. "I absolutely believe that. You did the right thing by ending it with him, and getting married to him would have been an unmitigated disaster."

"Why didn't you tell me that when I was in it?"

"Would you have listened?"

"Probably not," Margo admitted.

Grinning, Ashley said, "Like when you tried to warn me about Ronnie the Drummer?"

"Oh, gosh, I'd forgotten all about him. And his beat-up Camaro and horrid reputation. Eeew. What did you ever see in him?" Margo laughed. Ashley had dated some oddballs when she was young.

"Mom hated him. Dad hated him. Jean hated him. Instantly made him a thousand times more appealing."

"That always does."

"Tell me you wouldn't love to see Jean's face if you told her you and Connor had eloped this morning."

Margo imagined it. "Yeah, that is pretty spectacular."

"Her entire head would explode." Ashley touched her head and shoved her hands outward, miming the explosion.

"Sort of like it did when you and Elliott eloped?"

Ashley laughed at the memory. "I've never seen her turn so many shades of red."

"Why'd you decide to do it that way?" Margo wondered why she didn't know the answer. She and Ashley had always been close.

Ashley grew serious and took a minute to gather her

thoughts. "I couldn't take it anymore. From the second we announced the engagement, she tried talking me out of it. Told me Elliott was the kind of man you dated, not the kind of man you married, whatever that meant. The last straw was when she called his parents and told them the rehearsal dinner would be at the country club and they would have to pay. Elliott's mom called him crying and then his dad said they might be able to cash out part of their retirement if that's what we wanted."

"What? You never told me this."

Ashley looked down at her hands. "It was one of the worst moments of my life, realizing that Elliott's parents loved him – and me – so much that they were willing to do every single thing they could to make us happy. Mom was out of the country, so I didn't feel like I should burden her. Meanwhile, my own father and his wife were doing everything in their power to tear us apart. Which almost worked. Elliott was so furious. I'd never seen him so angry, and hope I never do again."

"How did you know he was worth it?" Margo was happy her sister had found Elliott. What they had was special, and she hoped to have a love like theirs someday.

"It sounds stupid, but I just knew. The way he treated me, the way he looked at me, the way he'd be talking to someone else and just reach over and touch me without even looking. Little things like that. And after the whole rehearsal dinner thing, I knew without a shadow of a doubt that I'd rather live in my car with Elliott than in a mansion without him."

"That's so cheesy."

"You'll be cheesy, too."

"I was never cheesy about Brad." She wasn't sure what she *was* with Brad. Looking back, their entire relationship was superficial. It was never deep. Probably never real at all.

Ashley gave her a small smile. "I know."

"Come on. Cheesy isn't an indicator of a good relationship."

"No, but you deserve better than what you had going with Brad."

"He would have been a good husband." Margo wasn't sure why she was defending him. Or maybe she was defending her choice to be in the relationship with him.

"He would have been a good roommate."

"Jean seems to tolerate Elliott well enough now, so I guess that worked out."

Ashley shifted and looked away.

Margo knew there was more. "What? Ash?"

"When I told her I was pregnant, she handed me a business card for a divorce lawyer. I tore it up and told her that if she and Dad ever wanted to see my children, she would treat my husband with respect and never, ever suggest anything like that again. Dad said he was standing with Jean. I called their bluff, and neither of them met Livvie until she was three months old."

"Ash, how did I not know any of this?"

"You were building your career and didn't have time to breathe, let alone deal with stepmama drama."

"I'm sorry I wasn't there for you."

Ashley lightly tapped Margo's cheek. "You were never 'not there' for me. You would have dropped everything to come home and rescue me. I know that. Anyway, we better get back to the bonfire and make sure Jean hasn't tried to tie Connor to a stake in the middle of it."

Margo grimaced. "I hope she stayed on her side of the fire the whole time."

Ashley jumped up and unzipped the door. As they walked back toward the bonfire, she said, "I don't hear any screaming."

"So either everything's okay, or we're too late." Margo hoped it was the former.

"Can you see anything?"

Margo stood on her tiptoes. "Everything looks okay. People sitting around the fire. Doesn't look like anybody's really talking."

"Excellent."

Margo and Ashley sat in the empty chairs between Connor and Elliott, who were both staring into the flames.

"Everything okay?" she asked.

Connor gave a curt nod. "Yup."

That was less than convincing. Margo decided she'd hold her tongue for now and ask him what happened later. She had no doubt Jean had made some snide comments, and she also had no doubt that Connor hadn't taken her bait. Which would have only further infuriated her stepmother. She sighed. Some vacation. She would have been better off working instead, because the whole idea of taking time off to relax... well, that wasn't in the cards unless her family packed up their crap and went back out the way they'd come in.

Which wasn't likely to happen. She sighed again.

Connor leaned over to her ear. "I'm going to head back to my tent for the night."

She pulled back and looked in his eyes, trying to read his expression.

He added, "I'll see you in the morning."

She put her hand on his arm. "Connor?"

He planted a quick kiss on her forehead. "Good night, Margo." His tone left little room for discussion.

"Okay." She let go of his arm.

He stood up and snapped for Scout, who wagged his tail and stood for a minute, waiting for Margo to stand up. When she didn't, he cocked his head, but followed Connor. When they were out of sight, Margo leaned over Ashley and asked Elliott, "What the heck happened?"

"Saint Jean. Helpfully explaining why he'll never be good enough. Like me." He glared through the flames. One of the logs crackled and shifted, sending a spray of sparks into the sky as if directed by his gaze. He looked at Ashley, his mouth a firm line. "Never again. No more vacations or trips or long weekends or anything with this bunch. Ever."

Ashley wrapped her arm around his back and buried her face in his neck. "Sorry, baby. I always hope it'll be okay."

He kissed the top of her head. "It's not your fault. But now we can safely say your eternal optimism is completely unfounded."

"I suppose so."

Margo put her arm around Ashley and leaned her head on her shoulder, linking the three of them together. "I don't know what I'd do without you guys."

Elliott looked at her over Ashley's head. "You'd be gone. Saving animals out west somewhere. Or south. Maybe on a tropical island. Rolling beached whales back into the ocean."

Margo laughed, causing heads to swivel in their direction. "That sounds wonderful."

Ashley grinned and nudged her husband. "Speaking of wonderful, what do you think of Connor?"

Elliott shrugged. "Jean hates him, so he can be my new BFF." He glanced at the group on the other side of the fire. "His brother and I were friends back in the day. He's a good guy. We'll see if he can put up with the bullcrap."

Ashley squeezed her husband tighter. "I think he's perfect for Margo. They seem really good together."

"What's Margo think?"

Margo leaned back and smiled. "I like him. He's pretty great."

A voice came from behind them. "Talking about me?"

Margo spun around on her chair and nearly tipped it over. "Oh, no. How?"

Brad's eyebrow rose. "I pictured you jumping into my arms. This isn't quite the reaction I expected."

"Why are you here?" She bit the words out. Jump into his arms? Was he crazy?

He took a step toward her, but someone came rushing at him from the side.

"Bradley!" Jean threw her arms around him. "What a wonderful surprise."

"Oh, please," Margo spat. "Surprise, my ass."

"You don't need to be crude. And I *am* surprised." She patted Brad's chest. "I didn't think you'd be able to make it."

"Why did you invite him?" The other campers were looking but trying to look like they weren't looking. Margo was beyond caring about the scenes they were making. At least they were giving everyone else a fun vacation story to tell when they got home.

Brad looked confused. He leaned away from Jean, who was still clutching his arm, and said, "I thought you knew."

Margo stood up and took a step toward the path. No way. She was over hearing that gaslighting line from him. "Did you really? No, Brad, I didn't know. Just like I didn't know you were coming for Easter. Or Jeanette's recital. Or Jonathan's kindergarten graduation. No clue you were going to be at any of *my family's* events. But here you are."

He held up his hands, palms toward her. "Hey, I'm sorry. Jean said you were glad I was coming."

"Jean is a liar. Which you are well aware of."

"Margo!" Jean snapped.

"Oh, save it." Margo stalked to the path and jogged back to the tents, looking behind her to make sure no one followed.

She walked to Connor's tent, but the door was zipped shut. She heard snoring but couldn't tell if it was Connor or Scout. She hesitated, wanting to talk to him. Then again, he probably didn't want to hear her venting about her family after he'd had his own run-in with her wicked stepmother.

With a sigh, she went to her own tent. The night was warm, so she unzipped the windows before zipping the door shut. She changed into her pajamas and climbed into bed. Maybe tomorrow she'd pack up and leave. She already had the time off work, maybe she'd get in the car and just drive somewhere else without telling anyone where she was.

She drifted to sleep with her childhood warnings coming to life – if she went off alone, she'd end up lying in a ditch somewhere, unable to call for help, and no one would know where she was. Sometime in the night, the crickets and frogs soothed the nightmares away and lulled her into a peaceful sleep.

Morning came and she smiled at the weight on the bed behind her and the warm breath on her neck. She reached back to pet Scout and encountered a decidedly unhairy not dog. As her groggy brain struggled to make sense of the situation, it decided it was probably Connor. No... he would never... She turned and two things happened simultaneously. One, her brain came completely awake and informed her that the man in her bed was not Connor. Two, a blood-curdling scream flew from her throat.

Immediately following this, Margo's knee connected solidly with Brad's crotch as she scrambled away from him and out of the bed. He grunted and half-rolled, half-fell out of the bed onto the floor as the zipper on the door wrenched open and the canvas yanked aside. Connor crossed the room in two steps, hauling Brad to his feet by his neck.

Brad shrieked, lifting one hand to protect his face. His other was still cradling his injured crotch through silk boxers.

Margo ran around the bed and grabbed Connor's arm. "Connor!"

He glanced at her, breathing hard, hand fisted, back tense, ready to swing.

Scout barked wildly in the doorway.

"Let him go."

"Who is this guy?" He let go of Brad's neck and the man crumpled to the floor, still holding himself and groaning miserably.

"This is Brad."

"Brad? Ex-Brad? What is going on?" His gaze fixed on Margo.

His accusing expression cut. And it pissed her off. "Don't look at *me* like that. I went to bed alone. That's why I screamed. I didn't expect to wake up *not* alone."

Connor's glare swung back to Brad. "What kind of pathetic piece of garbage are you that you need to sneak into a woman's bed?"

Brad was still on the floor, glowering at them both. "None of your business," he wheezed.

"Are we calling the cops?"

Margo shook her head and put a hand on Connor's arm. "No. Brad, get up and get out."

Brad gingerly got to his feet. When he was upright, he touched his neck. "I'm the one who should call the cops. You assaulted me."

"Shut up," Margo yelled.

Scout's barking quieted to an uneasy growl as he assessed the situation.

"Get your dog away from me."

"Don't worry about my dog."

Brad crossed his arms over his bare chest. "Animal control can worry about it."

Disgusted, Margo spied Brad's clothes neatly folded beside the bed. She kicked the pile at him. "Get dressed."

He shot her a filthy look, then scrambled into his khaki shorts and yanked his shirt over his head. "What's going on between you two, anyway?"

"Are you kidding me?" Margo felt like her head was going to explode with incredulity. She pressed her palms to the sides of her head. "Get out."

"Are you dating? Sleeping together?"

She felt Connor tense beside her.

"None of your business, Brad. Get out, and don't ever pull another stunt like that. Stay away from me."

He actually smirked as he tucked his shirt into his shorts. "It's not like I haven't been in your bed plenty of times before."

She took a step forward, her fist drawn and ready to blacken his eye, but she stopped herself. Barely. He flinched, though, and that was victory enough for now.

Scout, sensing a new tension, resumed his growling. The hair stood up along his spine.

"Scout, sit," Connor commanded.

Scout's butt dropped to the floor, but he still growled low in his throat.

"I'm calling animal control." Brad pointed at the dog.

Margo's fist was still clenched. "Stop being ridiculous. This is all your fault."

"*My* fault? It's yours, with your mixed signals."

Margo's jaw dropped. "Mixed signals? You're out of your mind. We broke up. Over. Done. Finished. I want you out of my life. Gone. Forever. I cannot possibly be any clearer. I don't want to be with you, I don't want to be anywhere near you, and I don't want you crawling into my bed!"

"You're just saying that now because this bozo is standing

here. You might not have said it in so many words, but I could tell you were glad to see me last night."

What freaking planet was he from? "I wasn't. I'm not."

Brad shoved his feet into his sandals and shouldered past Connor.

Margo kept a tight hold on Connor's arm. "Scout, come."

The dog sprang to her side, his tail hanging straight down.

She reached down and scratched his head. "Good boy."

Brad paused in the doorway. "We'll talk later. When we don't have an audience."

Connor glared. "Start walking, pal, unless you want your mouth busted open."

Before Brad could respond, Margo said, "Leave. Now."

He shot one last glare at Connor, then walked away.

When she couldn't hear his footsteps scuffling along the dirt path anymore, she let go of Connor's arm. Her words spilled out in a rapid jumble. "He showed up last night at the bonfire. Ashley told me Jean had invited him, but he couldn't come. I thought that was the end of it. I was talking to Ashley and Elliott after you left and boom, here comes Brad. Jean acted all surprised and jumps up to hug him. He asked if I was happy to see him. I said no, and I left. I wanted to talk to you, but your door was closed. So I went to bed, and woke up this morning to find Brad."

Connor let out a deep breath and ran his hand down over his face. His hand stopped, absently stroking his beard. "I don't even know what to say. This whole situation is messed up."

"It's too much drama. I get it." She crossed her arms, hugging herself, mad and sad and disgusted and defeated all at once. "I'm sorry. About all of this." She didn't know why she was apologizing when she hadn't done anything wrong. She turned and picked up her toiletry bag and clothes. "I'm going to get a shower." She needed to scrub Brad's nearness away.

"Okay."

She petted Scout's head on her way past him but didn't look up at Connor. She didn't want to see the finality in his expression.

At least this time she knew what went wrong between them.

# Chapter Twelve

Connor watched Margo walk toward the shower rooms. It took all his strength not to follow her, but he didn't want to be the one to tell her the things her stepmother had said. That woman seriously had a screw loose somewhere.

He and Scout walked back to their tent. He gathered his things and went to the men's shower room.

Oren was brushing his teeth. He spat into the sink and said, "Hey, man, everything okay? We heard Margo scream so we ran out, but it looked like it was under control by then."

"Yeah. Just a big misunderstanding." Why did it seem like everything around them was a misunderstanding?

Oren's eyebrow rose, but he simply nodded. "So Margo's family showed up out of the blue?"

Connor snorted. "Yup."

"Huh. They're an… interesting bunch."

"That's an understatement."

"If there's anything Chandler and I can do to help, just let me know."

Connor had no idea how they could help, so he simply

said, "Thanks." He turned the corner and went into a shower stall and closed the door.

The hot water felt good on his aching neck and back. When had he gotten so invested in Margo? He put his forehead against the cold tile wall. High school, that's when. The day she'd dropped her books in the stairwell and her papers had flown everywhere, and he'd stopped to help her. She'd looked up at him with those beautiful eyes and smiled, and he was lost. It had taken him almost two months to work up the nerve to ask her out. When she'd said yes, he could hardly believe it.

For a few weeks, everything had been perfect.

Then everything went to crap.

He finished showering and toweled off, then dressed. On his way back to the tent, he heard footsteps crunch on the gravel close behind him.

"Trouble in paradise?" Roxanne caught up to him and put her hand on his back.

"Nothing you need to worry about." He twisted to the side to dislodge her hand, not bothering to be subtle.

"It's funny. I didn't take you for the kind of guy who'd be okay being sloppy seconds." She tapped her nail against her bottom lip.

Connor gritted his teeth but kept walking.

"I was surprised, the way she was all over him at the bonfire right after you left. I didn't think she'd be the type to bounce from guy to guy. Of course, with such delicious options, why not, right? And they have such recent history. Must be hard to let go. Maybe it was just a roll in the sack for old times' sake. I'm sure it didn't mean anything."

Speeding up, he focused on his front porch. At least Roxanne had done him one favor – convinced him beyond all doubt that Margo was telling the truth. He wouldn't believe

Roxanne's version if it came notarized, signed in blood on virgin lambskin, hand-delivered by angels.

She said, "If you need a little company to soothe your bruised ego, you know where to find me," then turned to her own tent.

He'd rather walk barefoot on rusty nails with an expired tetanus vaccine. Connor let the flap of his door down and sat on the bed beside Scout. "What is with these people? They're all insane."

Scout flopped onto his back for a belly rub. Human drama didn't mean the belly rubs had to stop.

"What's on the agenda for today?" He checked the day's schedule with one hand while scratching Scout with the other. "Canoeing. That could be fun. At least it'll be winners only. No family drama, and we won't be stuck with Roxanne."

He got up and walked over to Margo's tent. She was sitting in the middle of her bed, holding a magazine, but it was closed. Her face was red, as if she'd been crying. Scout jumped up beside her and licked her cheek, earning a tired smile and a head scratch.

"Hey."

She looked up. "Hey."

"Canoeing today. You up for it?"

Her brows rose in surprise. "Together?"

"Of course." He felt like an idiot. She must have thought he put some of the blame on her for Brad's stunt. "Unless you'd rather go with Roxanne." His joke fell flat.

"I don't like the water."

He sat down on the edge of the bed. "What are you talking about? You love the water."

"I love being *by* the water. Not on it."

"Do you get seasick?"

"I don't think so. I mean, I don't know. It just freaks me out.

I already told you I can't swim." She tossed the magazine to the far side of the bed and hugged her knees to her chest.

"You don't need to. The river's calm, you'll have a life jacket, and besides, Doug was saying the river's pretty low right now. You'd be able to touch the bottom pretty much everywhere." Connor wasn't sure if this was really about canoeing.

"What if the boat tips over?"

"It's not going to tip over. They're a lot more stable than you think."

"But it's not impossible."

"I suppose it's *possible*, but extremely unlikely."

"But what if it does happen?"

He heard the fear in her question. "That's what the life jacket's for. It keeps you upright. But we don't have to go if you don't want to." Sure, he'd like to go canoeing, but if he went alone, he'd only be thinking about her the whole time anyway.

"You want to go. I don't want to keep you from going. You don't need to stay here because of me. We're not even here together."

He reached over and took her hand. "I'd rather spend the day with you. We can do the geocaching we missed yesterday, or we could do mini-golf."

"She needs to spend time with her family," Heidi said from the doorway. She turned her gaze to Margo. "We came here to be with you."

All her soft vulnerability vanished. A door slammed shut behind her eyes. Her expression hardened, her spine stiffened, and her tone went cold. "I didn't ask you to."

Heidi crossed her arms and clucked her tongue, annoyed. "You're so ungrateful. Mom put a lot of thought into this trip for you."

Connor watched a range of emotions cross Margo's face

before she spoke. "*Jean* didn't do any of this for me. You can't possibly say that with a straight face. It was for her. Period."

He rubbed his thumb across her knuckles.

Heidi sighed and snapped her fingers. Scout jerked his head in her direction. "Get ready. We're taking the kids for a hike."

"I can't. We're canoeing with the group. The activities are mandatory."

Connor kept his face neutral. *Hey, thanks, Heidi, I owe you one.*

"Fine. What time will you be back?"

"I don't know."

"Well, when you get back, you need to spend some time with your family. You know, the people you belong with."

"Heidi, stop it." Margo sounded tired.

"And while you're at it, maybe use this time on the canoe ride to think about how you're going to apologize to Brad. You could have seriously injured him."

Oh, please. Brad was lucky he didn't have a broken nose and a fresh police record.

Connor nearly yelped as Margo's fingernails dug deep into his hand. "We should get going." Her words came through clenched teeth.

Margo let go of his hand and climbed off the bed. Scout watched her for a second, then jumped down to stand beside her, wagging his tail. She pulled her old sneakers on and took her time tying them. She finally stood and grabbed his hand. "Let's go." She glanced at her sister. "I'll see you sometime this afternoon."

"I'll let Brad know."

Connor's fingers suffered another crunch in Margo's grasp.

"Why would you even say that? Brad doesn't need to know anything."

Heidi was undeterred. "You're making a mistake. He's not going to wait forever for you to come to your senses."

Connor shook his head. Yep, these people were crazy.

Margo hesitated, like she wanted to say something else, but she just tugged his hand. "We don't want to hold everyone up."

They walked to the parking lot, where a large 15-passenger van with the campground's logo emblazoned across the side waited for them. Oren and Chandler, Tanner and Sarah, along with six campers from the main grounds assembled for the ride to the canoe launch site. Scout trotted over to Chandler, who bent down to give him kisses and rubs.

Connor stopped short of joining the rest of the group and gently tugged Margo's hand to get her attention. "I know you don't want to do this. We don't have to."

Margo gave him a smile that looked more like a grimace. "My options are limited. At this point, I'd rather drown."

"I hate to disappoint you, but the odds of you drowning aren't good."

"What about getting lost?"

"Sorry, there aren't any tributaries."

"Darn."

He didn't want her to get on the river if she really didn't want to. "We can go back, Margo. There's plenty to do. Lots of hiding places."

She shook her head, determined. "No. I want some guaranteed away time. Even if you won't help me disappear."

Doug called to the group, "All aboard!"

"Hey, there's always the possibility of an alien abduction."

That earned him a smile. "Don't get my hopes up." She nudged his arm. "Let's go canoeing."

Connor opened the door to the van. "After you."

Margo climbed into the far back row. Scout jumped in and took the spot next to her, leaving Connor on the edge of the seat. The other canoers filled in the rest of the seats. Thankfully, Shane and Roxanne had opted out of the activity, saving them from awkwardness and discomfort on that front. Doug drove the van, while Bonnie occupied the passenger front seat.

Bonnie spoke into a tour bus microphone as the bus bumped several miles along a back road. "Yeah, I know the PA system is a bit much, but I want to make sure you can all hear me." She went over safety information. "Go at your own pace. We've been checking water levels and currents, and you're going to have a pretty mellow ride. Life vests are mandatory for everyone for the entire float, even for Scout."

Upon hearing his name, he perked his ears up and gave a mild "boof."

A few minutes later, they pulled into the boat launch area and the guys helped Doug unload the canoes from the trailer.

# Chapter Thirteen

Connor got Scout in his doggy life vest and grinned at Margo. He was excited she wanted to – well, was willing to – do the canoeing trip with him. He held back, letting the other teams get their canoes launched. He helped her tighten the straps on her vest, then adjusted his own. His job for the next several hours was making sure Margo was comfortable. Piece of cake, right? He held the side of their canoe, sliding it into the water. "We're going to wade out just a little bit, then get in."

Margo inched into the river, having second thoughts as the water skimmed over her ankles, filling her shoes. "Are you sure this is safe?"

"Yes."

"You're not going to let me drown, are you?"

His laugh rumbled in his throat. "Earlier you said you wanted to drown. You'll have to make up your mind."

She took another step, water swirling around her calves. "Yeah, I don't think I want to drown today after all."

"Good choice."

Scout bounded into the water, happy as could be.

Connor pushed the boat farther into the water until its

bottom no longer scraped the ground.

"Ready?"

Margo took another step. "Um, I don't know about this." Her heart pounded. She looked out over the calm water. Visions of awful things lurking below the surface filled her mind. Tentacles, murky depths, being sucked into a pitch-black watery grave... A tiny fish grazed along her leg. She shrieked and jumped, nearly losing her balance.

Connor grabbed her arm until she steadied. "You okay?"

She managed to laugh at herself. "Just got sideswiped by a sea serpent."

"You mean one of those?" He pointed into the water at a school of minnows.

"No. It was this big." She held her hands at least four feet apart. "And fangs like this." She held her thumb and forefinger to demonstrate five or six inches. "I think I scared it away, so, you're welcome."

He grinned. "You're a natural fisherman."

The other teams were already in their canoes, halfway out into the water. Doug hollered from the van, "Everything okay?"

Margo nodded to Connor.

"We're good," Connor yelled back.

Doug gave them a thumbs up.

"Scout, in." Connor pointed to the middle of the boat. Scout ran over and jumped up into the boat, then shook the water off his coat. He turned his head and snapped at the life vest as if it was annoying him.

"You ready?"

The water was cool on her calves. "I don't know. Where should I sit?"

"Right here at the front." He patted the seat. "You can help paddle, and I'll steer from the back."

"Okay." She bit her bottom lip. The shiny aluminum bench seat seemed to be waiting for her to decide what to do. She put her hands on the edge of the boat. It rocked slightly.

"I've got it." His voice was reassuring but didn't do much to calm her.

She lifted her right leg up and over the side of the boat and leaned her butt toward the seat.

"Almost there."

Her rear hit the seat and she pulled her other leg into the boat. It rocked with her movement. "I don't think I like this."

"Do you want to get out? We can ride back with Doug and Bonnie." He looked at her, patiently waiting.

She felt better simply knowing he was willing to pull the boat back onto the shore. It was nice to be around someone who was willing to compromise. Besides, being on the river meant being away from her ridiculous family. A few hours floating down the river could be fun. "No, it's okay. We can go."

"Are you sure?"

"Yes."

"Okay, I'm climbing in, so it'll rock a little bit. Ready?"

"Ready." She held the paddle across her lap, clutching it tightly when the boat rocked as Connor took his seat. She blew out a breath. The best way to face a fear was head on, right? She considered worst-case scenarios, then balanced them against what was likely. This was going to be fine. In fact, she was only nervous because it was something new. The chance of real danger was minuscule. She gave her head a resolved nod. Yes, this was going to be fine. The weather was perfect. Sunny with enough clouds to keep it from being too harsh. Hot, but with a nice breeze over the water. "I want to do this."

"Here we go. You good?"

"Yup." She gripped the sides of the canoe, steeling herself

until the rocking motion stopped.

"We'll go pretty much straight until we're in the middle of the river, then we'll head downstream."

"Okay." She appreciated his play by play commentary.

"I can't see your face. Are you freaking out?"

"Little bit, yeah." Her muscles were still tense, but she was calming down. Her heart rate was mostly normal. She bet in a few minutes she might even relax. Maybe.

The canoe sped up, slicing through the water. Margo could hear Scout panting behind her.

"Should I be paddling?" she called over her shoulder.

"You can if you want to, but you don't have to yet."

"So it's okay if I sit here and don't move?"

"Yup."

"Okay." She could do that.

They turned slightly, the nose of the canoe pointing toward the direction the river was flowing. Margo kept a death grip on the paddle.

"You doing okay?"

"Uh huh." She was glad he couldn't see her face. Her eyes darted from one side of the boat to the other, trying to guess how deep the water was under them. For a moment, she considered asking but decided some things were better left unknown.

The other boats were far ahead of them, dots in the distance.

"Hey, Margo. If you look down to the right, you can see some fish."

She turned her head and leaned slightly to see better. Her stomach lurched, expecting the boat to capsize, but it stayed steady. Her stomach appreciated that fact and settled. A school of spotted fish darted around, red stripes running down their sides.

"What are they? I'm afraid my animal expertise ends at the shoreline."

"Rainbow trout. They're delicious."

She risked a glance back and had to laugh at Scout's ears, perked up as he stared down into the water.

"They're pretty."

The bottom of the river was an alien landscape, covered with rocks and little clouds of dirt stirred up by creatures either leaving or darting into hiding places. Clumps of long grassy seaweed swayed with the current. The sunlight refracted and mottled, casting odd shadows and pinpoints of bright light under the water.

A slight breeze blew across the river, playing with Margo's hair. Ahead, something splashed. Connor's paddle made a slight noise as he raised it out of the water. She heard a mild *sploop* as it entered the water on the other side of the boat.

This wasn't so bad.

She heard Scout scramble to his feet. He *boofed* low and quiet, not quite a bark, but not a growl. Turning her head in the direction he was looking, she pointed. "Oh, look, a great blue heron."

The large grayish-white bird swooped down from beyond the treetops and settled its long flamingo-like legs onto a tiny grassy island poking up through the water. Its long neck stretched, parallel to the water, and its beak sliced into the surface, neatly grabbing a small fish. Songbirds' melodies carried from the tree-lined shores, and the almost-tropical-sounding *ee-ee-ee-ee-ee-ee-ee* of a woodpecker echoed through the valley.

Connor stopped paddling, so they simply drifted, watching the heron toss his lunch upward and inch it back toward its throat.

"Do you see a lot of birds in your practice?"

Margo shook her head. "We do as a clinic, but I don't personally. I don't work on birds or the little rodents or exotic pets like turtles or lizards or snakes. We have two vets who are more specialized. I mainly deal with your traditional pets like cats and dogs, some ferrets, animals like that. I also go out and help with some farm animals like pigs and goats. I'm not as comfortable with the horses and cows, but sometimes I'll assist Dr. Murphy when he goes out."

"You do house calls?"

The heron finished his lunch and gracefully swooped up into the air, away from the humans that had disturbed his peaceful meal.

"Farm calls. Last March we had to go out in the middle of the night, in a snowstorm, of course, to assist a cow with complications birthing her calves. She was having triplets. See, cows usually only carry one calf at a time. Twins are a little rare, and triplets are something you just don't see, like, hardly ever. So Dr. Murphy called me to go with him. I got to help turn one of the breech calves so it could be born. It was one of the coolest things I've ever done." It had been a proud moment when the calf bleated, and prouder still when all three calves stood on their wobbly legs and hungrily fed from their tired mama.

"It sounds interesting."

Margo laughed a little, suddenly self-conscious. "Sorry, I know most people don't think being shoulder-deep in a cow would be much fun." She straightened, facing forward, feeling stupid for rambling on and on about helping a cow give birth. How many times had Brad – or Jean, or Heidi – told her nobody but her coworkers wanted to hear those kinds of stories?

Connor said, "Don't keep me in suspense. Were the calves and the mother all okay?"

"Yeah. They were pretty small, but she ended up being a good mama and they all survived." She abbreviated the end of the story to humor him humoring her.

After a beat, he asked, "Is that unusual? For triplets to survive?"

Okay, so maybe he actually was interested. "Very. We honestly didn't expect live births for all three of them, so that was miraculous in and of itself. And with their low birth weights, we kind of figured at least one of them would die within a few days. But they were fine. The owners decided not to breed the heifer again, since one multiple birth means a greater likelihood of future multiples, and it wasn't a risk they wanted to take with her."

"Doesn't the male cow kind of decide who breeds?"

"Oh, no. They're artificially inseminated."

"Seriously? I kind of thought the male cow picked."

"Bull."

"No, really."

Margo chuckled. "No, the male cow is called a bull."

"Oh. So I thought the bull would go out into the field and, um, have, um, *relations* with whatever female he picked."

"Nope."

"Huh. Well, you taught me something today."

She didn't read any sarcasm, but then again, she couldn't see his face to tell if he was teasing. "I'm sure you're thrilled with your new knowledge."

"It's actually pretty fascinating. Did you have your whole arm up *inside* the cow?"

"Yup. Had to get all the way in there to grab the calf's legs and get him turned the right way."

"Weren't you afraid she'd kick you?"

"No. At that point, she was exhausted and beyond fighting." Margo could relate.

"I'm impressed."

"Okay. Now you're teasing." She rolled the paddle over her legs, embarrassed again.

"Not at all, I'm serious. If the calf would have died during birth, what would have happened to the cow?" He sounded sincere.

"Any number of things, but in that situation, it was life or death for her as well."

"Wow. So you literally had the power to save her right in your hands. That's a big responsibility."

Scout turned awkwardly and curled up on the bottom of the boat, laying his head down with a huff.

She changed the subject away from herself. "What about your job? There's a lot of responsibility in that, too."

He was quiet for a moment. She thought maybe he hadn't heard her until he answered, "There is."

"Why'd you leave Portland? Was it all because of Colin?"

"No."

She felt the change in his tone. "I'm not trying to pry."

He was quick to respond. "No, I know. It's just not something I've really talked to anyone about."

She cautiously half-turned so she could look back at him. "If you do want to talk about it, I want to listen, okay?" His vague response only served to ramp up her curiosity. It'd be nice to talk about something other than her drama for a change.

He gave her a smile. "Okay."

"I think we're catching up to the group." Margo pointed up ahead.

"Yeah, it looks like they're stopped. I wonder why."

"Are they out of the boat?" Margo's voice rose an octave and her nails dug into the paddle. "Did someone fall out?" Her heart pounded. The anticipation of seeing her worst fears playing out in front of her made it almost impossible to breathe.

As soon as they were close enough, Connor yelled, "Everybody okay up there?"

Chandler's laughing voice returned, "Super. We found a swimming hole the guys wanted to check out."

Margo swallowed hard as relief crashed over her like a wave. "I… I don't want to get out of the boat." What she really meant was that she didn't want either of them getting out of the boat, but that sounded needy and controlling.

"I wouldn't ask you to."

"Do you want…" She shook her head, not bothering to finish the sentence.

There was a long pause. "No. I don't want to get out with them. If that's what you were wondering."

A little sheepish, she said, "It was. I mean, I don't want to hold you back." It was silly, really. If he wanted to hop out and swim, she'd be fine. He'd be fine. She was worrying for nothing, and she relaxed more as they approached the group and saw they were all having a good time. No tentacles in sight.

He laughed. "Chill, Margo. I'm good. If I wanted to get out and swim, I'd tell you."

"Okay, okay."

"Hey." His voice was soft.

"What?"

"I'm really glad you decided to do this. I'm having fun."

Margo nodded, glad he couldn't see her blush. "Me, too. Do you want me to paddle?"

"Sure."

"Which side?" She gripped the paddle, ready to put it in the water.

"Doesn't matter."

"How can it not matter?"

"The front paddle helps with moving forward. The back steers."

"Huh. I still think I could make us go in circles."

"I could just counter whatever you do up front and keep us going straight."

Margo teased, "Unless I knock you out of the boat."

"Yeah, but then you're just as screwed as I am."

"That's probably true."

Scout jumped to his feet, rocking the boat slightly. Margo let go of her paddle and clutched the sides of the boat. The paddle slid off her leg, heading straight for the water. She let out a little shriek, let go of the boat, and grabbed the paddle.

Connor laughed, long and loud. He pulled his own paddle out of the water, laughing until he was bent over.

"You suck," Margo grumbled.

"That was priceless."

"Hey, guys!" Oren bobbed beside his boat.

Scout barked and pranced a little bit, wanting to get in the water.

They drifted alongside the other canoes. Margo relaxed even more, watching the other campers splashing around. They didn't seem to be in any mortal danger, or worried about drowning. There was no way she'd be getting out of the boat, but the knots in her stomach loosened, and she felt mostly secure, even surrounded by water of unknown depth.

They parked for a little bit, chatting with the group until they all loaded back into their canoes and began paddling toward camp.

This time, Margo and Connor stayed with the group, next to Chandler and Oren's canoe.

Chandler was at the front of her canoe, too. She looked over, concerned. "Everything okay after all that drama with your ex this morning?"

Embarrassment flooded her cheeks. She'd known other people had witnessed the scene but was hoping no one would bring it up. "It was... I guess a sort of misunderstanding."

"Misunderstanding? The creep climbed into your bed while you were asleep."

Yeah, not much to misunderstand there. "I know. It's complicated. I mean, we were engaged." It sounded so lame out loud.

Chandler's sour-lemon expression made it clear she wasn't giving an inch. "*Were.* He had no business going into your tent, let alone getting in your bed. None."

"I know."

"Don't make excuses for him. It was creepy and wrong and a total violation. I was at the bonfire. I know you didn't give him any encouragement, so he's a creep *and* a liar. And even if you *had* been glad to see him..." She waved her hand. "Don't make excuses for his behavior. Eew."

"I'm not trying to make excuses. The whole thing is really embarrassing." As was being lectured by a new friend, even though she knew Chandler's heart was in the right place.

"He should be embarrassed, not you. He should be glad you didn't call the cops. I guess I know why you broke up. The guy's a creep. I'm sorry, not really, but I was glad to see him scuttling along like the cockroach he is after you kneed him. What a jerk."

How on earth did everyone know all the details?

Chandler kept talking, saving her the trouble of thinking of a response, then abruptly asked, "Why did you guys break up anyway? I mean, besides him being a creep and a jerk and a liar."

Margo took a deep breath. It was one thing to tell Connor the real reason. He was more apt to be on her side, no matter how ridiculous the reason. But it was what it was, so she said, "He didn't want any pets."

"Like, ever?"

"Ever." Margo swished her paddle in the water, more for something to do than to actually help move the boat.

Chandler scrunched up her face. "But... you're a veterinarian, right? Isn't it kind of a given that you'd have pets?"

"You don't think that's a stupid reason to break up?"

"Are you kidding? I love my cats. I told Oren when we started dating that they were non-negotiable, and after they die, there will be others. If he had allergies, he'd have to get drugs, because the cats are staying. Period. No discussion."

"He was okay with that?"

Chandler grinned. "Didn't matter. That was my deal-breaker. The pet discussion is just a couple steps down from kids, I think. You have to be on the same page."

"My family thinks I'm crazy for breaking up over it."

"No offense, but from what I've seen of your family, I wouldn't put a lot of stock in what they think." She glanced over her shoulder, then lowered her voice. "Especially when it comes to Connor. He's a great guy. Much better than Creepy McCreeper."

Margo laughed. "We're just friends, though."

"You never know what the future holds. And I'd take a friend like that over the creepy other guy any day of the week."

"Me, too." She meant it. Even if her relationship with Connor never went past this easy friendship they'd settled into over this trip, she wouldn't risk it to preserve Brad's feelings, regardless of the respect she felt she owed him due to their history. A thought hit her like a ton of bricks. She worried about not being disrespectful of him or their past, even though he didn't afford her the same courtesy.

"Huh."

"What?"

Margo looked up, startled. "Oh. I didn't realize that was out loud."

"Ha, I do that all the time. What's up?"

She took a minute to put the feeling into words. "I was just thinking that I spend so much time worrying about being respectful or nice or accommodating to people who don't care how they treat me. That's really messed up."

"It kind of is. But I think you'd feel horribly guilty if you were mean just because someone was mean to you." Chandler winked. "Doesn't mean you shouldn't stand up for yourself. You should."

"True." Funny how that worked. In some areas of her life, she had no problem standing her ground. In others... well, it was like her spine melted or something. It was time to change that.

The guys' voices from the back of the canoes rose and fell as they chatted and laughed. It was comfortable, hearing Connor's voice.

They rounded a bend and the dock came into view. They paddled over to it and Connor and Oren jumped out of the boats to pull them toward the shore. Scout jumped out and splashed around in the water while the rest of the boats arrived and were loaded onto shore, where Bonnie and Doug were waiting.

Margo and Chandler stepped out and helped pull the boats up the bank. Margo took Scout's life jacket off, then helped Bonnie fold the vests and stow them in the trailer.

Chandler said, "Let me know if you guys want to hang out later."

"I'll see what Connor wants to do. We were talking about

going geocaching since we didn't really get a chance yesterday."

"We only found two before we decided to have our own activity." Chandler giggled and blushed.

"Say no more. Please. Really. No more." Margo laughed along with her.

"We'd totally be up for going along. If you want us to, I mean."

"I'll let you know." She looked forward to spending more time with Chandler and Oren.

"I hope there's some lunch somewhere. I'm starving."

Until Chandler had said it, Margo hadn't noticed she was hungry. "Me, too."

Connor came up alongside her and took her hand as Chandler walked away to where Oren was standing.

"Well? Are you glad you went?"

"Definitely. That was a lot more fun than I expected. I probably should have put more sunscreen on, though. My face feels pink."

Connor leaned back and studied her face. "Maybe a little bit. Right here." He tapped the tip of her nose with his finger.

"If that spot peels, I'm blaming you."

"Deal. Do you suppose there's food somewhere?"

Before Margo could answer, a cold spray of water coated her back. She shrieked. "Scout! Holy crap!"

The dog wagged his tail, proud of his accomplishment, then dashed off to roll in the grass.

"What a brat," she laughed.

"Thanks for covering me. I didn't get hit at all."

She poked his chest. "Keep it up and I'll toss you in the river."

# Chapter Fourteen

"Really?" In one smooth motion, Connor bent and picked Margo up around the middle, slinging her over his shoulder.

"What the heck- no, no you are not! Connor! Put me down!" Margo clutched the back of his shirt, squirming and kicking her feet.

He kept a solid hold on her and marched into the water until it was knee-deep. "What were you saying? You're going to what?"

Scout bounded into the water ahead of him, barking and wagging his tail, then busying himself with sticking his face in the water.

"Stop it, you freaking Neanderthal. Put me down." Laughter mixed with her squeals.

"What? You want me to put you down?"

"On the shore! Connor!" She pinched his back.

He twisted. "Ouch, what did you do that for?"

"Because you're being a jerk. Put me down." She pinched him again.

The other campers were on the shoreline, watching and laughing.

"Ow, stop that." He swatted behind himself.

She pinched him again.

"One more time and I'm dropping you in the water."

"Put me down."

"That's the idea." He grabbed her hips and pulled her down into the water, but kept ahold of her so she didn't fall over.

She squealed as her legs hit the water and clutched his shoulders. "Jerk."

He grinned down at her. "I could have dropped you."

"That would have been a mistake." She poked his chest.

"Big talk. I could still do it." He rather enjoyed having her glare up at him, her eyes bright with amusement.

"Yeah, and it'd be the last thing you ever did."

Connor picked her up again. "What? What were you saying?"

Her arms went around his neck, nearly strangling him. "Stop," she laughed, locking her legs around his waist.

He turned around and carried her out of the water and set her on the ground. "Here you are, Your Highness." His hands slid down her arms, and he took her hand.

"You're lucky I'm not really royalty. I'd have your head on a stake."

Connor laughed. "You'd miss me."

"Nope, I'd have it shrunken and then wear it as a necklace."

"Wow, that's kind of romantic in a totally creepy way."

It was Margo's turn to laugh. "Romantic? Only you would think chopping off your head and shrinking it for jewelry would be romantic."

He noticed she hadn't let go of his hand. Good. For a minute, he'd been afraid he'd made her mad for real. Or worse, scared her. He'd forgotten about her fear of the river until they were already standing in it. Luckily for him, his assumption that her fear was actually of the deep water must have been mostly correct. Still, it wasn't a mistake he'd make again. She had enough people in her life who didn't respect her boundaries.

The group split up, heading in different directions. Connor and Margo walked toward the tents, with Scout zig-zagging around them, sniffing every possible thing he could find and peeing every two seconds.

"Chandler said she and Oren wouldn't mind going geocaching if we were going to do that this afternoon," Margo said.

"Sounds good. Is that what you want to do?"

"Yeah. It looks fun, but the last time was kind of a train wreck. Sorry."

"Stop apologizing. We'll go and have fun. But first, we need to find some food. I'm starving." He rubbed his stomach, which growled on cue.

"Me, too."

They passed the tents, where Scout gave up and jumped onto Margo's bed.

"Great. I'm going to have to sleep in a dog-sized wet spot."

Connor grinned. "I'm starting to see the advantages of him liking you better."

Margo giggled and covered her mouth.

"What?"

"I was just thinking it would have been awesome if Brad had tried his little stunt with a giant wet puddle from Scout on the bed. He sure wouldn't have been able to be so sneaky."

He kept his expression neutral, even as his jaw clenched. Being reminded of Brad getting in her bed immediately pissed him off. Yeah, Brad crawling into a wet spot would be great – if he'd drown in it.

Margo must have read his expression. "Okay, I guess that's not really funny."

"He's an idiot, and I'd rather not think about him," he said mildly. It wasn't worth letting her know how irritated he was.

"Sorry. Humor is my go-to for dealing with uncomfortable situations. If I let myself be as pissed off about it as I really am, it'd be ugly."

"The whole situation was ugly."

"Agreed."

Connor opened his mouth to say more, but instead, changed the subject entirely. "If we have chips with lunch, I hope they're not stale. The ones yesterday were kind of stale."

Margo side-eyed him for a moment, then squeezed his hand. "Yeah, they were."

The rest of the canoers were ahead of them, heading into the lodge, along with another group of campers.

"Something sure smells good."

Margo sniffed. "Mmm. Barbecue. I hope it's our lunch."

"Me, too. I could eat a nice juicy steak." At this point, he actually didn't care if it was steak or a plain, bunless, ketchup-less hot dog, he just wanted to eat.

"I hope it's chicken."

They passed through the lodge's common room. The smoky-sweet smell intensified as they got closer to the dining room. Servers filled the buffet table with trays of barbecued chicken and baked potatoes. Dishes with all the fixings to load the potatoes were strategically placed so they could be reached from either side of the buffet table.

Connor's stomach growled. "Oh, man, I'm going to gain twenty pounds on this trip."

Margo's expression was unreadable. "The food is definitely good here."

"I wonder if it's normally like this, or if it's special for the contest."

"Both," a voice answered behind them.

They turned and Bonnie smiled at them. "We do catering for special events, and we also offer camping packages that are all-inclusive."

Connor had expected the campground to be just that – camping. Sitting out in the woods, surrounded by nature. He hadn't realized there could be more to it. Then again, he hadn't ever given camping much thought. "Do you get a lot of campers who just want to throw a sleeping bag in the woods?"

"Lots of people do that. We like to offer a wide range of options. We really believe camping is for everyone. We should all get back to connecting with nature, whether or not we want to hunt for our own dinner." Someone called her name from across the room. "Sorry, I'll talk to you again later." She parted with a cheerful smile.

Connor picked up his plate. "I have a feeling I should have known everything she just said."

"Well, it *is* outlined in our packets. You did read your packet, didn't you?" She smirked.

"Of course I did. Speaking of reading, I think I'm going to spend the rest of the afternoon in a hammock. Join me?"

"Sounds heavenly. Count me in."

They filled their plates and sat down across from each other at a table. They were eating in comfortable silence when Connor saw Brad come in, square his shoulders, and head toward Margo.

"Incoming," he growled.

She looked up and immediately looked unhappy. "Oh geez," she said under her breath.

Brad didn't glance at Connor. "Margo, when you're done, can we please talk? I have some things I need to say."

Margo pulled her napkin from her lap and wiped her mouth. She sat back against the chair. "I don't want to hear a bunch of bullcrap."

Brad held his palms up. "I know." This time his eyes did flick in Connor's direction. "I won't take up much of your time. I know you're busy. Please?"

Connor picked up their empty plates and carried them to the bins to give her a moment to answer Brad. He took his time scraping the food residue into the trash and piling the plates neatly before going back to the table.

Margo was standing, arms crossed. When Connor reached her side, she put her hand on his arm. "I'll meet you at the hammocks, okay?"

"No problem." Connor resisted the urge to get up in Brad's face and threaten him. Not that he'd ever been the confrontational sort, but something about Brad's smarmy face made him want to punch it. Instead, he completely ignored him. He lightly touched Margo's hip, gave her a smile, and walked out of the lodge without a glance back.

Part of him was concerned that Brad would be able to sweet-talk his way back into Margo's good graces, but another part of him knew she wasn't willing to compromise on the pet issue. Yet another part reminded him it really wasn't any of his business.

He reached the tents and whistled for Scout.

The dog bounded out of the brush behind the tents, excitedly wagging his whole backside as he leaned up against Connor.

"Good boy. Let's grab a book and go to the river."

Scout agreed wholeheartedly with the plan.

Connor stepped into his tent and grabbed his book. "Okay, Sandford, you better distract me."

The author's photo seemed to nod.

The hammocks were deserted, but several people were swimming in the river. Scout dashed over and jumped into the water. Connor watched to make sure he wasn't bothering anyone before settling into the big hammock in the hopes Margo would join him. He leaned back, watching Scout jumping up and down, shoving his head into the water, then coming back up with a stick.

After a few minutes of watching the dog, he opened his book and started reading, trying not to think about what Brad might be saying to Margo.

# Chapter Fifteen

Margo turned on her heel and walked out of the lodge, toward the empty playground at the side. She didn't want anyone overhearing any more of her business. In fact, *she* didn't want to hear any more of her business. "What do you want to say?"

"First of all, I'm sorry. That's the main thing. For this morning, for insulting your friend… he is just a friend, right?"

The comment grated on her last nerve. "If you mean Connor, that's not any of your business."

"You know I mean Connor. Anyway. I'm sorry for coming into your tent. I really thought you'd be happy to see me when you woke up."

Margo didn't bother trying to keep the annoyance and disbelief off her face. "Are you really that ridiculous? We broke up. Done. Over. And you thought it would be okay to sneak into my bed without my consent?"

"I thought it would be romantic." He shrugged.

"Romantic." She bit the word out. "It was creepy and wrong and offensive and a complete violation." Did he actually believe she'd think it was romantic?

"Yeah, I get that now." He ran a hand through his hair. "It

seemed like a good idea at the time. Like one of those stupid Hallmark movies you like to watch. Where they break up, but they're really meant to be together, so he does this grand romantic gesture and she falls back in love with him. I'm sorry."

His apology seemed sincere but lacked a little something when he felt the need to insult her choice of movies. Cheesy? Yes. Stupid? No. Just one more thing she'd compromised over their relationship – only watching her favorite shows when Brad wasn't around but suffering through countless hours of droning programs about wise financial investments. Ugh. "I accept your apology. But don't ever, ever, ever do anything like that ever again. To anyone. It's not okay."

"I know. I won't."

Good. She hoped he was done, and she could move on now. "Was that all?" They'd reached the playground and stopped in front of the swings.

"No." He took a deep breath, then turned to face her. "I'm sorry for the way things ended. No, wait. I'm sorry *that* things ended between us. I miss you. I was an ass, and I'm sorry. I didn't listen to you, and I didn't realize how important it was to you that I'd allow pets in the future." He shoved his hands deep in the pockets of his khaki shorts. "It was a stupid line to draw in the sand, Margo. If you want to fill my house full of dogs and cats, that's okay with me."

This was what she'd wanted to hear. Well, what she *thought* she'd wanted to hear. He still had an issue with the whole "allowing" thing, didn't he? And "his" house? Oh, brother. His whole speech was much too little, much too late.

He continued, "I don't have any excuses. Or expectations. I just want you to know I'm sorry and I hope you'll forgive me."

Margo should have just accepted it and walked away, but she heard herself asking, "Why the sudden change of heart?"

Brad ran a hand through his hair and looked to the ground. "Well, since we're being honest… it's the guy. The way he looks at you."

Margo hadn't expected that. "When he came to my defense because you scared me?"

"Kinda. I should be the man coming to your rescue."

"When strange men climb into my bed."

"It seemed like such a good idea." His brow furrowed as if he was still confused that his plan hadn't turned out so well.

"Brad, your jealousy isn't a good enough reason for us to get back together."

"It's not jealousy. It's that I realized that you're amazing and I was an idiot to let you go over some stupid dog. Or cat. I thought… well, I thought if I let you go, you'd realize you were being unreasonable, and you'd be back. I didn't expect someone else to come into the picture."

*Wait, what? Let's get this straight…* "You thought you could just wait it out and I'd come crawling back." This conversation sucked, but at least it provided solid, final confirmation that breaking up was the right decision.

"I didn't think you'd have other options."

The words were like a sucker punch. Had his opinion of her always been so low? Then why did he bother with her in the first place? "Wow. So if you waited long enough, I'd get desperate because what other man would possibly want me?"

"Margo, come on. You're beautiful. Of course other men would want you. That's not the problem with you."

She blinked rapidly. She *really* should walk away now, but morbid curiosity was in charge. "Please. Enlighten me." It was fascinating, in a detached sort of way that confirmed once and for all that she was over him and had zero interest in his opinion.

He missed her deadpan tone and took her words at face

value. "Well, for one, your schedule is crazy. You work late nights and weekends. It makes it hard to plan anything."

Margo raised an eyebrow, but said nothing, waiting for him to fill the silence. He did not disappoint.

"I know it's your job, but you talk about stuff that should stay at work. You know, with other people who understand. Most people don't want to hear about dogs having surgery or animals being put to sleep."

"I didn't realize my topics of conversation bothered you." She did know, thanks to his not-so-subtle gripes, but he'd never come right out and said it.

"A little bit goes a long way."

"I never complained about your inane blathering about stock options."

He looked confused, as though everyone should be thrilled with such conversation. "Stock options don't get incisions or ooze. And it's interesting."

*Oh, contraire.* "Okay, my schedule and my conversation. What else?"

"Your relationship with Jean is too strained. You should make more effort to see her side of things. Many times, she's right. She hasn't had an easy time being a mother to you and your sisters."

"*Step*mother, since we already have a mother, but please, do go on." At this point, Margo couldn't even be mad. Relieved maybe, that she hadn't fallen for the 'you can get a dog' crap when he started talking. Or more to the point, relieved that she'd broken up with him six months ago. Hopefully now he'd accepted that fact and would leave her alone.

"Heidi, too. They just want what's best for you. Some of your friends aren't the most... appropriate people to be spending your limited free time with. Sometimes they encourage some of your ideas that a real friend wouldn't."

This one was new. What bad ideas? "Such as?"

"Your belly button piercing for one thing. Your hair for another."

She protectively touched the braid that hung over her shoulder. "I happen to like my hair. And I like my belly ring." She'd worked so hard to get to a point where she was confident enough to have her navel pierced, and Brad knew that.

"Yeah, those things are fine if you're a teenager. But once you get past thirty, you should make some different choices." He moved his arms as he talked, getting more and more comfortable with picking her apart.

Ugh, he sounded like Jean. "Why?"

He looked surprised. "Because grown-ups don't need to do things like that for attention. They let their careers and mature lives speak for them."

"Brad, you're such an idiot. I'm a grown woman. I have a wonderful career. I own my own home. I put myself through college and veterinary school. I've worked my butt off my entire life. I love my belly ring and I love my hair, and I don't care if nobody else in the world likes it, because I did it for me."

"Sometimes you need to compromise when you're in a relationship."

"Compromise *what*, exactly? My hair?"

"Your appearance reflects on your partner. You have to take that into consideration." He was definitely taking lines out of Jean's playbook.

Margo stared at him, trying to find something, anything, to remind herself what she'd ever seen in him. How had they gotten involved in the first place? What had she been thinking? "Nope. No. Compromise is going out for Chinese when you're actually hungry for Mexican because it's your partner's turn to choose. You know what? I'm awesome." She waved her hands, gesturing from her head to her feet. "And I'm not changing to suit some man whose balls are so tiny he thinks a woman who can take care of herself is a threat to his masculinity."

"That's a recipe for being alone, Margo."

"If those are the options, I'll take being alone every time."

"I hope you mean that. Your lumberjack friend isn't going to want a woman he can't control, either. It's cute on vacation, but he'll get tired of you, too, and it'll be too late to call me."

*Control? Really?* Margo's shoulders relaxed and she smiled. This may be vacation, and she may not know him well, but she would confidently bet Connor had no need to control his partner. "Take care of yourself, Brad."

"What's that mean? Oh, so I'm honest with you and you can't handle it."

"No, it means that we were right to break up. Our goals in life are diametrically opposed." She wanted a partner. He wanted a puppet.

He looked baffled. "How so?"

"You want a wife who will be what you want. I want a husband who wants me for who I am."

"I *do* want you for who you are."

How could he say that with a straight face? "With a few tweaks and improvements."

He shrugged. "Well… I mean, nobody's perfect. I don't get it, Margo. It's just hair."

"If it's just hair, why do you keep harping on it? Never mind. It's irrelevant. But let's carry your point through, shall we? What will you change – oh, I mean what will you *compromise*, Brad? Would you volunteer at the shelter a few hours a month? Maybe try spiking your hair a bit on the weekends? Watch some football with my friends? Go to an actual game?"

"Margo, come on. That's ridiculous."

"So that's a no. You're not willing to 'compromise,'" she made air quotes, "but I have to make a few changes. Got it."

"You're making this a bigger deal than it has to be."

"I promise you, it's not a big deal at all." She sighed. "Because this conversation is pointless. We're done, it's a good thing we're done, and I wish you well."

"You're making a mistake." His tone was confused, as if he had no clue this could have been the outcome.

Turning toward the path, she didn't respond. The first time they met, he'd been so charming. Why couldn't people just be themselves and save everyone a lot of time?

Brad called after her, "I'm serious. If you walk away from me, that's it. Don't call me when you change your mind."

"Okay." She kept walking.

"I mean it. That's it. Last chance."

She waved over her shoulder and was a little bit proud that she didn't give him the finger he so richly deserved.

He wasn't done. "You made your choice, Margo, now you have to live with it."

She'd love to live with her choice. Maybe now he'd get the message and go away. She stopped at her tent and grabbed her book. Nothing in the world would be better than climbing into the hammock with Connor and losing herself in Stephanie Plum's antics.

Right after she filled Ashley in.

# Chapter Sixteen

Connor looked up to check that Scout still wasn't annoying anyone. It took a minute to spot him, occupying himself with a stick near the bank.

"Just so you know," Brad's voice instantly set him on edge. "Margo and I are getting back together. I told her she can save some mutt, and she's happy as can be."

"Congrats." The words stung for half a second, but when Connor met Brad's eyes, the other man shifted and faltered, obviously lying. "I'll be sure to tell Margo I'm happy for you guys."

"That's why I'm here. To tell you to stay away from her. She doesn't want to talk to you."

"And she sent… you… to tell me that." Liar, liar, pants on fire. Connor managed not to laugh, but he couldn't control the smirk. This guy was such a tool.

"She's busy. I'm here as a courtesy. Man to man."

Connor bit back a retort. "Okay, *Brad*. I'll see you around." He turned his attention back down to his book.

"She doesn't want you." Brad was getting more snivelly with each word.

"So you've said."

"She's too good for you."

Connor squinted up at him. "Can't argue with you there." Margo was amazing. And yes, probably too good for him.

The muscle in Brad's jaw tensed, but he said nothing.

Connor said, "But she's *way* too good for you."

Brad snorted. "Just stay away from her."

"I don't force my company on women who don't want it. That's your department." His little dig hit the mark. Brad's mouth pursed and his nose scrunched while his brows folded inward. It was not an attractive look.

"Screw you."

Connor grinned and reopened his book. He was rather enjoying getting under Brad's skin.

Brad looked like he was going to say something else, but he just shook his head and walked away.

The river was a good visual distraction. The water streaming by made a smooth path for Connor's thoughts. Doubt crept in. Was Brad lying? It certainly seemed like he was. But where was Margo? His rational side immediately offered several plausible options. Bathroom. With her sister. Trapped by her stepmother. Napping after her conversation with Brad. Talking to Chandler. She could be anywhere, for a million reasons that had nothing to do with a reconciliation. Or him.

Maybe she needed to cool down after Brad said something stupid. Now *that* was almost certainly the case. He relaxed a bit. Yeah. He'd give her an hour or so and then go see if she wanted some company. He flipped back a page to pick up where his attention had wandered.

Half a page later, a voice broke into the story.

"This spot taken?"

His head jerked up and his heart skipped a little as he

gauged her mood. "Hey." He held her book while she gingerly slid onto the hammock. When she was settled, he asked, "How was your talk with Romeo?"

She rolled her eyes and grunted. "Ugh. He's delusional."

Connor's shoulders relaxed. Good start. "How so?" *Let me count the ways*, he thought.

"He started out being all sweet and telling me he'd made a huge mistake and he wanted me to have pets and he was sooooooo sorry he'd been unreasonable, and that he was willing to compromise on that." She rolled her eyes so hard she probably saw her own brain.

Connor understood the feeling. "Huh."

"Yeah." She snorted. "While he was talking, I realized it wasn't just the pet thing, it was everything. We just wouldn't work. Before I could say anything, he then decided to share with me all the ways that I could compromise and be a better partner."

He could feel the irritation radiating from her. He wasn't sure if it was contagious, or if his own was lingering from his earlier interaction with the moron. "How?"

"Well. In return for his *gracious* concession of *allowing* me to have a pet in *his* house, I would-" she held up a finger for each item, "-take out my belly ring. Dye my hair back to its natural color. Not *too* natural, though, it should be stylish but not trendy. Cut my hours and not work evenings or weekends. Stop talking about work. Stop talking about animals. Beg Jean's forgiveness for all the things I've done to ruin our relationship. Be nicer to my older sister. Drop my unacceptable friends. Impress his boss and colleagues, but certainly not with my own accomplishments. Because after all, I'm just a woman with a cute little job."

"You pierced your belly button?" Yeah, so he was stuck back on the first item.

Margo glared at him. "That's what you heard. From everything I just said."

He grinned. "No. I heard Brad's an asswipe, but I already knew that. I want to know more about your belly ring." He hadn't expected that. Ever. Margo had her belly button pierced? That shot to the top of the list of things Connor wanted to see, edging out Alaska by a mile.

She shook her head, clearly exasperated. "Honestly. I'm trying to rant here."

"Rant away. Then I want to talk about your belly button."

She giggled and he knew he had nothing to worry about. Not from Brad or anyone else. For whatever reason, for whatever wonderful thing he must have done in some past life, Margo was giving him a chance.

"He tried telling me he wanted me back, but when I said I wasn't going to dye my hair for anybody, he said I needed to make sure my choices didn't embarrass my partner."

"What is it with those people and your hair?" What an odd thing for them to fixate on.

"I know, right?"

"Let me guess. Ashley likes your hair just fine, but Heidi doesn't."

"Oh, how'd you know?" She laid her head back against the hammock's little pillow. "I like my hair."

"I like your hair."

"Thanks."

"I'd probably like your belly ring, too." Speaking of fixating...

"Probably?"

"Eh, it could be weird. I mean, you might have a skull and crossbones or a monster truck or something." She relaxed back into the hammock, comfortable with him. His chest tightened with a little rush of pride that she was choosing his company and enjoying it.

"No, the skull and crossbones is my tattoo."

"Ah. I would have thought you'd have a giant eagle spanning your shoulders."

"I do. Duh. With a giant American flag in his beak that trails the whole way down my back."

"Obviously. So the skull and crossbones is what, on your hip?"

"Yup."

"Classic."

She tapped the pocket of her jean shorts. "And Mickey Mouse on this hip."

"That goes without saying."

She giggled. "You're a goofball."

"At your service."

She reached down and pulled the hem of her shirt to just above her belly button.

Connor's breath caught. He swallowed, then turned his gaze to the tiny silver piercing. *Don't act weird, don't act weird, don't act weird.* There was a little silver ball atop her belly button, anchoring a tiny dangling diamond pawprint. Without thinking it through, he reached over and ran the tip of his finger over it. He felt the muscles in her belly tense at his touch. *Don't be weird, don't be weird.*

Although he didn't particularly want to, he pulled his hand away and turned his gaze back to her eyes. She was watching him, serious, as she flicked her wrist and her shirt covered her belly again.

He cleared his throat. "Well. If you're taking votes, I say keep it."

"You don't think it's silly?"

"It doesn't matter what I think. But since you asked, I think it's sexy and cute and fun. It's very… you. And I wouldn't change a thing." Okay, he'd change one thing, in that he'd still be touching her.

"Thanks." Her voice was quiet.

He watched her for a minute. "How's the book?" He couldn't care less about the book, but he wanted to keep her talking and make her laugh again.

"No idea. I haven't been able to get back into it."

"Now's your chance."

"I hope so. I wanted a vacation so I could relax. You know, try something new, since relaxing isn't in my vocabulary."

"Yeah, this hasn't been very relaxing for you, has it?"

"Pshht, me or anyone around me." She casually rested her hand on his calf, oblivious to the rush of warmth her touch sent everywhere. "I'm glad the drama hasn't scared you off. Your company is the only thing keeping me sane."

He tapped his fingers to his forehead in a salute. "Don't worry. At some point, I'll be the thing driving you insane."

"And I'll return the favor."

"Wouldn't have it any other way."

He mirrored her position, resting his arm over her calves, balancing his book on his belly. It took a few minutes before he was able to drag his attention away from the warmth of her smooth skin against his forearm and focus on the words on the page.

# Chapter Seventeen

Margo closed her book and glanced up at Connor. His eyes zipped back and forth across the page, his brow furrowed. A moment later, his eyes widened in surprise. Margo stifled a laugh as she watched the story play out over his face.

A few minutes passed before Connor looked up and had to blink a few times to come back to reality.

"Good book?" she asked.

"Excellent. I did not expect that ending."

"I love it when that happens."

"Me, too."

She stretched and closed her own book. "I think I'm going to go see what Ashley and Elliott are up to and then catch up with you at dinner?"

He seemed reluctant to say, "Yeah, about that. I don't want to sit with them again, so I can have dinner with Oren and Chandler if you want to be with your family."

No way was she subjecting him to that nonsensical drama again. Or herself. "Ugh, no, I don't. We'll figure something out." She gingerly sat up and pulled her legs off the side of the hammock, trying not to flip it.

Connor held the fabric taut until she was out, then he hopped out his side, much more gracefully than she had. She watched the fabric of his shirt stretch across his broad shoulders as he bent to get his shoes on. She hadn't minded holding onto those shoulders as he pretended to throw her in the river. She also hadn't minded casually touching his leg while they lay in the hammock, although she did have to keep reminding herself not to start rubbing his calf. He probably wouldn't have minded.

Nearby, Scout stretched and rolled his back against the grass, then jumped to his feet to follow them. He was the sweetest boy and gave Margo all kinds of desire to adopt a dog. The upside? She could take her dog along to work with her, so those offensively long, crazy hours wouldn't matter. Back at the tent, Connor gave her a wave and turned to his tent. Impulsively, Margo grabbed his arm to turn him back. She went up on her tiptoes and planted a kiss on his cheek. "See you later."

He grinned and nodded.

Before he could say anything, she walked away, unable to wipe the smile from her face. She took her book back to the lodge library, then went down the opposite path to the cabin area.

"I'm glad to see you finally stop by to see us."

"Hey, Jean." Margo kept her voice light, but she was wary, waiting for something to happen. What, she never knew.

"Brad's packing his bags." Jean sounded sad and disappointed.

Margo was not. "Good. He shouldn't have been here in the first place."

Irritated, Jean's voice was sharp. "You don't get to decide who we spend our time with. Especially since you're never around."

"Okay." She wanted to remind her that they'd ambushed her vacation.

"He's trying to win you back, and you're not even giving him a chance. He's a wonderful catch. You're going to regret letting him go."

"Can we not do this?" Brad, Brad, Brad. It stung that her stepmother cared more about Brad and appearances than she did about Margo.

Jean shrugged. "It's your loss, I suppose. Brad's really going places."

Margo sighed. She'd be happy for Brad to go places. As in, any place but here.

Jean made a face as if she'd just sucked a lemon. "Unlike that foul miscreant you've been spending time with."

"I have to wonder. If Brad's so great, why would you want him stuck with someone like me?"

Jean ignored her completely. "And Brad doesn't have anything he's hiding." She wore an I-know-something-you-don't smirk.

"Okay."

"Your little friend can't say that." She practically radiated malevolent glee. No wonder wicked stepmothers were a stereotype.

"Okay."

"Do you really have your head so far in the sand that you don't even want to know that his actions nearly killed some *children*? Or doesn't that matter to you since they're just *people* and not dogs?"

Margo's teeth were on edge, and her patience was all but gone. "Yes, Jean. I was hoping to find a guy who blew up a busload of orphans and nuns but I couldn't find one here, so I'm stuck with Connor."

"Everything's a joke to you. But what he did isn't funny to

those children or their families." She pressed her lips together and shook her head, clucking in disapproval.

"What are you talking about?" She regretted asking before the word "you," was out because she knew it was ripping the lid off a whole can of worms.

"That's why he had to leave Portland. He blew up a building with people inside. A dozen children were seriously injured. Almost *died*."

"Okay." She assumed there was half a grain of truth somewhere in the story, but she doubted Connor intentionally blew up a building. She'd ask him about it later.

"He got run out of Portland. He only left to get out of jail time."

Nope, didn't believe that part. "I don't think it works that way."

"You don't know anything about it."

"I'm sure you don't know the whole story." Probably not even a quarter of it.

"Stop being so naïve. This is exactly why you need Brad. So he can help you see how things are."

Margo barked out a laugh. "Wow. You really do think I'm stupid." Her jaw ached from clenching it during this absurd round and round.

"Of course I don't. But any woman who leaves a perfectly good man over a *dog* has a lot of growing up to do."

Red. She saw red. "Growing up? Are you kidding me? I'm a grown woman with a career and a home and a whole life, and I built it all by myself."

Jean snorted. "By yourself. Your father and I handed you everything."

Margo couldn't formulate a response to her stepmother's obvious delusion. Her eye started twitching. Margo had worked hard and earned scholarships and taken out soul-crushing loans to pay for the rest. Her mother helped with books and meals. Her father and Jean had contributed exactly zero dollars to her education. Unless you counted the money they'd given her for birthdays and Christmases. Which they undoubtedly did.

"You're making a mistake letting Brad go. You need to fix things with him before it's too late. He already told you he'd allow you to keep a pet. He's been trying to get through to you."

Margo knew she should just walk away, but her irritation moved her mouth. "By crawling into my bed in the middle of the night?"

"Oh come on, Margo. You're engaged. I'm sure you spent plenty of nights together."

"We're *not engaged.* Just because he was allowed in my bed at one time doesn't mean he has lifetime access! How do you not get that that was not okay? It was a complete violation. It. Was. Not. Okay."

Heidi appeared in Margo's peripheral vision. "Mom, she's right, that wasn't right."

Jean pressed her lips tightly together.

Margo might have fallen over, shocked at her sister's words, had Heidi not kept talking.

"But Mom's right that you're overreacting. Brad's a great guy. He's good for you. He's trying to get you to be the best version of yourself. And you're good for him. I don't think that one lapse in judgment should be enough to end the relationship."

The best version of herself? What the heck? "What do you people not understand? There's no relationship. We broke up six months ago." Her last words were loud, but she couldn't muster the energy to care who witnessed this ongoing drama.

Heidi gave her a smile that looked eerily like Jean's.

"Honey, we just want what's best for you. Brad told us he was going to talk to you. He's okay with you getting a dog or a cat, and he said he wouldn't even ask you to cut back your hours."

Margo looked up and down the path, her chest constricting as the air closed in around her. "How generous."

Her sarcasm was lost on her sister. "I know. He's very open to compromise."

"Do you see this?" She held up her wrist and pointed to her smartwatch. "They don't have these in 1952, or whatever alternate universe you're from. Here on Earth, in the twenty-first century, we womenfolk get to keep our own careers if we want to. We can even wear *pants* if we want to."

Again with the Stepford smile that looked just like Jean's. "When you have children, you'll change your mind. Brad will be a great father, and you'll be happy to have his support when you want to only work part-time or stay home with the kids."

Margo knew she'd have better luck talking to the fencepost. "Where's Ashley?"

Jean rolled her eyes. "Oh, we're not good enough to talk with?"

"Whatever." She turned to walk away and spied Olivia playing at the edge of the clearing. Where Olivia was, Ashley wouldn't be too far away. "I'll see you later."

"We'll save you a seat at dinner," Jean said, as though nothing had just happened.

"Don't bother. I'll be sitting with Connor."

The distaste on Jean's face was clear.

As she turned away, she heard Jean mutter to Heidi, "I have no idea why Brad puts up with her."

She hurried to her niece. "Hey, Livvie girl." Instantly, her favorite girl helped her tense muscles relax.

Olivia beamed, holding up toy cars covered in dirt. "Auntie! Come look."

Margo hunkered down for a closer look at Olivia's piles of dirt. "What's all this?"

"This is a house and this is a store and this is where a animal doctor is." She pointed to mounds of dirt, connected by tire tracks left from the toy cars. "This is the daddy's car and this is the mommy's car."

"Awesome. Where's the river?"

Olivia contemplated for a moment, then put her hand palm down in the dirt and swished a wide arc. "There it is."

"Cool beans." She accepted the dirt-caked car Livvie held out to her and made zooming car noises as she moved it from the store to the animal doctor, making Livvie squeal with laughter.

"Do animal doctors give lollipops?"

Margo chuckled. "Nope, just people doctors."

Olivia looked up at her, her blue eyes wide and serious. "Mommy's doctor didn't give her a lollipop." She looked seriously affronted.

"I think it's mostly kid doctors."

Olivia scowled. "That's stupid." She clamped her dusty hand over her mouth and stage whispered, "That's a bad word. Don't tell mommy."

Margo whispered back, "I won't tell."

"Everybody should get lollipops."

"I agree. Where's your mom?"

Ashley's voice came from behind them. "Here I am. I figured you needed a few minutes of private Livvie therapy."

Her sister knew her so well. "Thanks."

"I was in the cabin. With the window open." Ashley hunkered down beside them and drew some lines in the dirt with a stick.

"Ah. You heard that conversation, huh?"

"Every ridiculous word." Ashley shook her head. "I don't

get it. I mean, yes, Brad's a decent guy, but holy crap, that's some next-level bullsh—baloney going on."

Margo laughed at Ashley almost saying "the s word" in front of Olivia, then quickly sobered. "How can they defend him for sneaking into my bed? It's so gross."

"I have no idea. That was creepy and so far out of line, I don't even know how to respond to it."

"Why are you guys even here? No offense. I'm so glad you and Elliott and Livvie are here, but what was the point?" Hot tears unexpectedly stung the backs of her eyes. She squeezed them shut until the sensation passed. "I need a break before I lose my freaking mind."

"Hey, don't get upset. It'll be fine."

Olivia reached over and patted her leg, leaving a dirt mark. Margo managed a smile and tapped Livvie's nose with her fingertip, earning a giggle. This girl was her heart.

Ashley continued. "I think Brad's leaving, and you have Connor, so there's that."

"I have to keep looking over my shoulder. What was Jean talking about with the building in Portland?"

"I don't know. Something Brad showed her on his phone. I do think something happened, which makes sense as to why he'd stay here after his brother died instead of moving back, but I don't know any details, and I wasn't about to ask any of them."

"I'll have to ask him, which will be completely awkward. How do I ask him about it when he hasn't mentioned it, without sounding like I'm accusing him of something, or like I went digging for dirt?"

"I like dirt," Olivia offered.

"Beats me, but you should bring it up sooner rather than later. I can just imagine one of the clan members shouting something about it over dinner."

Margo groaned, visualizing the scenario. "I can see that. Okay, I'll go talk to him now before the shit gets any closer to the fan."

"What's shit?"

"Oops." Margo grimaced.

Ashley gave her a hard stare and said to Olivia, "That's a bad word."

"Why'd Auntie say it?"

Margo groaned again. "Sorry, Livvie. Auntie shouldn't have said that."

Olivia dropped her cars and stood. She put one fist on her hip and pointed at Margo with her other filthy hand. "We don't say bad words. It's not nice."

Margo tried not to laugh at her stern expression. "You're right. I'm sorry."

"Make better choices."

She couldn't help but laugh at that. "Oh geez, you are your mother's mini-me, aren't you?"

Olivia's dirty face scrunched. "What's that?"

Ashley laughed as she scooped Olivia up. "It means we need to get you cleaned up before dinner. Auntie has to go talk to Connor."

"He's nice. How come he has all that hair on his face?"

Margo laughed and made a mental note to share Livvie's comment with Connor. Unlike most of the comments from her family, he'd enjoy hearing that one.

## Chapter Eighteen

"You again?" Connor leaned back in his rocking chair. Scout abandoned his nap and sat up.

Brad smirked as he approached. He crossed his arms and propped one foot onto Connor's porch. "I just wanted to let you know that Margo knows all about your *troubles* in Portland. She was quite distressed to learn you were responsible for those poor injured children. And she was so fond of you, too."

"What's your point, douchebag?" Connor ignored the way his neck tightened, and the voice in his head warning him that he should have come clean with Margo already.

"Oh, no point, really. I just wanted to see your face when you realized that your chances with Margo were over."

Connor wouldn't give this jerk the satisfaction of seeing him sweat. "Which is what you said earlier. Seems to me you don't speak for her, and you should probably stop trying. You're just making yourself look like a jealous fool."

"Jealous? I wouldn't take Margo back if she begged me. She had her chance."

Connor laughed. "Wow. You're even stupider than I thought. And that's really saying something."

The muscle in Brad's jaw jumped. "You're starting to piss me off."

The feeling was mutual. "Easy solution. Stay away from me."

"Gladly."

"Why are you still here?"

"To give you a warning."

"Shove your warning straight up your ass." Connor stood up and snapped for Scout to follow him. He stepped down beside Brad and paused, his face inches from Brad's. "Don't approach me again."

"Or what?"

"Or I'll have Margo bust your other nut."

Brad flinched. "Threats? I could have you prosecuted. I know people."

"Good luck. You've been stalking and harassing me." Connor shook his head. This engagement was foolish and it was time to end it. He glanced down to make sure Scout was with him and walked away, toward the river. Maybe he'd find some peace there.

Scout trotted ahead of him, glancing back every so often to make sure Connor was still on the same path.

The hammocks were occupied, so he walked to the edge of the water and threw a stick in for Scout. The dog bounded after it, his tail wagging as he got himself soaked.

Connor sat on a patch of grass on the bank. Scout brought the stick back, shaking water all over him. Laughing, he tossed the stick again. Inside, he wasn't laughing at all. He'd known Margo would have to know about Portland at some point. But he'd assumed it would come from him. Who knew what stories they'd told her.

He waited a few minutes, trying to muster the strength to go find Margo and have a hard conversation. Maybe he'd punch Brad the next time he saw him, just on principle. The guy was a troublemaker.

Just as he was about to call Scout and stand, Margo plopped down beside him, cross-legged. "Hey." She didn't sound upset or wary, so that was good.

"You must be psychic. I was just going to come looking for you."

"I knew that. I sensed a disturbance in the force and was compelled to come here." She wiggled her fingers to demonstrate the disturbance.

"Excellent. My Jedi mind tricks are working." He wondered if he could Jedi mind trick this conversation away.

She picked at a blade of grass and flicked it.

"Have you ever done this?" Connor plucked a blade and pressed it between his thumbs. He lifted it to his mouth and blew. A loud whistly screeching sound came out, causing Scout to jump to attention and run over. His ears perked up as he looked around for the source of the noise. Connor blew again and Scout barked.

Margo laughed. "That's a horrible noise. How do you do it?"

Connor pulled a thick piece of grass and demonstrated. Margo copied his actions and made her own awful noise as they laughed. Scout bounced back and forth between them, barking every time they blew on the grass.

Finally, they both dropped their blades of grass. It was a quick distraction, but Connor knew he had to tell her about Portland. He heard Margo take a deep breath and blow it out. His stomach clenched. He tried to think of how to start telling his story since there was no way of knowing what she'd heard.

Margo said, "There's no pleasant way to ask you this question, but I don't want to make any assumptions. You know Jean is on a campaign to keep me away from you."

"She is? Gosh, it's been so subtle I hadn't noticed." Jean wouldn't be more obvious if she carried a blazing neon sign that said, "I hate Connor."

Margo gave him a half-grin. "Yeah, I know. They were telling me that the reason you left Portland was because there was an accident and some kids got hurt." She picked at the grass beside her knee. "And that you were responsible and you only left Portland to avoid going to jail. I'm sorry. I feel stupid repeating it."

Connor reached over and took her hand. He lifted it to his mouth and kissed her fingers, then let go, trying to organize his thoughts. He was kind of glad she'd brought it up. At least her tone reassured him that she was open to hearing him out. "First of all, thank you for not making assumptions. Second of all, it's partly true. Maybe even mostly true. Third, no, I wasn't facing jail time."

"What happened? I mean, you don't have to tell me. I suppose if you had wanted me to know you would have already told me."

A little twinge of guilt poked his insides. He could have brought it up when they talked about Sherri and his coming back home. Should have, even. "Yes and no. I've been planning to tell you about it, but it's not exactly a fun topic to bring up."

"If you're not ready to talk about it, you don't have to. I don't want to force you to share something with me if you don't want to. We can put it on the shelf for another time."

Part of the weight lifted from his shoulders. He couldn't even articulate how relieved he was that Margo was showing him such grace and respect. He'd return the favor by laying it all out on the table. "Now's as good a time as any. Unless you don't really want to hear about it." He partly wanted to avoid the topic, and partly wanted to get it over with because if there was anything real between them, he'd have to tell her everything anyway.

"I do. But like I said, I don't want to pressure you into talking."

Her gentle approach warmed his heart. "You're not." With a sigh, he jumped into his explanation and hoped she didn't judge him too harshly. "Here goes. You know I was basically a safety inspector. We were doing demolition on a building site and we'd gone through and approved the placement of the explosives and had everything ready to go. We imploded the first part of the building, but then somebody from the city came and stopped the work before the whole thing was down. The permit only listed one address, which was the only *mailing* address, but because of the size of the building, it actually covered three lots, with three separate property addresses."

Margo nodded, understanding the difference. "An easy detail to miss, I would imagine."

He shrugged one shoulder. "We should have caught it early on. We went back and forth all day, trying to get the permit issue resolved. It got late and we sent the demo team home." He swallowed hard. "I got a call in the middle of the night. A bunch of teenagers snuck through a gate and were screwing around in the partially collapsed building." The memories rushed back, the sound of the phone vibrating, looking at the clock, hearing the frantic words…

"Oh, no."

… arriving on-site with the chaos and flashing trucks and emergency personnel rushing everywhere, talking to the police, unrolling the blueprints on the hood of the police car to help guess where the kids might have been… "Yeah. Another section fell and trapped two of the kids. One kid called 9-1-1, and two others ran off. It took nineteen hours to get the kids out. One of the kids' dad was a retired judge. So, of course, there was a massive investigation." It felt like he'd talked to a hundred lawyers.

"But you didn't do anything wrong."

"I did. I didn't make sure the site was secured before everyone left. I was on the phone off and on all day with Colin and my wife. The night before, she had told me she was filing for divorce. I was distracted and by the end of the day, I just wanted to get home and talk to Sherri and check in on Colin, and I wasn't careful enough. "

"You can't blame yourself. It –"

His chin jutted forward, determined. "Yes, I can. It was my responsibility to make sure the site was secure before I left. That's the bottom line. I screwed up and people got hurt."

"But Connor," Margo started.

He'd love to cut himself some slack and stop shouldering this guilt, but the truth was… he screwed up, and people got hurt. "But nothing. It's not like I gave them onion rings instead of French fries. They could have died. All five of them."

"They didn't." Her voice was soft.

"Do you think that makes it better?"

"Of course it makes it better. Are you saying it wouldn't be any worse if they had?"

Connor ran his hand over his face and scratched his beard. "No. Obviously that would be worse. But it's little comfort. One of the kids was in the hospital for three weeks."

"And the other one?"

"Overnight."

"You couldn't anticipate –"

He held up a hand. "Stop, please. I *should have* anticipated it. That was my job. To anticipate every possible obvious issue and mitigate the risk. Instead, I didn't check the side gates and I didn't make sure my men did, either. I can't excuse what I did. What I didn't do." It was a strange feeling, arguing with her when she was on his side and he wasn't.

She seemed to take that in for a moment. "What happened after?"

He let out a long breath. "I spent a lot of time cooperating with the investigation, in between begging Sherri to stop packing and waiting for my brother to die on the other side of the country. My company suspended me and once the investigation was complete, they fired me. That was a lousy day, let me tell you. They called me into the main office to hand me my personal effects and a check to keep my mouth shut, and by the time I got home, Sherri was gone. Mid-afternoon, Colin was in hospice. He was at Mom's house and nurses came in around the clock."

"Oh, Connor." She reached over and took his hand.

He leaned into the comfort she offered. "There was nothing left in Portland, so I packed the car with as much as I could and started driving. I got home and had a few weeks with Colin before he died." He'd be forever grateful that Colin was still able to talk. Connor picked up Colin's boys every morning and his ex-wife brought dinner and picked them up every evening. They made their peace with each other. Connor took care of Scout and talked with his brother long into the nights, until the last one. The boys had just gone home, and their mom had just gone to bed. Colin had smiled and told Connor, "Tonight's the night I meet Jesus." Those were his final words, and Connor was honored to be the one to hear them.

"I'm sure your family was grateful to have you home, especially then." Her voice brought him back out of his own head.

He nodded. "Yeah, I'm glad I had that time with him."

"I'm sure he was glad, too."

"He was."

Long moments passed as Connor watched Scout. He could

feel Margo looking at him. She finally said, "What happened with Sherri?"

"I called to tell her Colin died and some guy answered the phone and told me not to bother her. It was after midnight there, so I drew my own conclusions."

"Ouch."

Connor sat for a minute, just looking at their hands linked together, feeling the warmth in Margo's patient presence beside him. How different would things have been if they had stayed connected way back?

"They took my mom to a mental hospital. Prom night. That's why I didn't show up." The words were out before he could think too much about saying them.

"Connor." Her voice was barely more than a breath.

This sucked, wading through such dark memories, but he needed her to understand he hadn't intended to hurt her. "She had a lot of problems that were exacerbated by her drinking. She drank to handle her problems, which created bigger problems, which led to her drinking more. It was a horrible cycle. We didn't know it back then, but she's bipolar. Nobody looked deeper than the drinking, so she didn't get the help she needed until just a few years ago."

"How is she now?"

"Good. Really good, actually. She's been sober for about six years and treating her bipolar disorder for the last four. She had a hard time with Colin's death, of course, but I'm really proud of her. She didn't drink at all." He couldn't call it a silver lining, but their mother had drawn on strength she hadn't believed she possessed during Colin's decline and death. The pride welled in his chest.

"That's great. I'm glad she's better." She squeezed his hand, pulling it onto her lap, and leaned her head on his shoulder.

"Thanks." He looked out over the river, not quite sure

which was more calming – it, or her. The conversation had gone better than he'd expected. He wasn't sure what he'd anticipated. Margo wasn't likely to be cruel, no matter what he'd done in Portland. Or in the past.

"Margo." One last thing he had to admit.

"Yeah?"

"You were my first, too."

She sat up straight and stared at him.

"It wasn't... I didn't..." He looked out over the river, not sure what words to use. He ran a hand over his face and tugged at his beard until he gathered the courage to look at her again. "I just... I'm trying to say it was a big deal for me, too, being with you. I know I was so wrong standing you up for prom and never explaining. I don't think I can ever put how sorry I am into words. You deserved so much better."

She let go of his hand and for a second, he was sure she was going to get up and walk away. Then she reached over and touched his cheek. She didn't say a word, but he looked into those unforgettable brown eyes and knew he'd just been forgiven. A gift he didn't deserve, but one he was beyond grateful for.

Scout chose that moment to launch into a barking frenzy, heralding the arrival of a pair of ducks across the river. The ducks ignored him and, as usual, it only took a few seconds for something else to capture his attention.

Connor huffed a little laugh. "I think that covers everything. The past, the job, the divorce..." He was tired. The conversation, though liberating, was draining.

"Doesn't it take a while for a divorce to be final?"

"It was faster and simpler than I thought it would be. It only took about a month to have everything done."

She considered this. "It seems like it should be more complicated."

He agreed. It felt much too easy. "I imagine it is if you own property or have kids. But I know what you mean. Marriage shouldn't be so... disposable. No, that's not quite the word I want."

"Insignificant? Unimportant?"

"That's better. I never expected to be divorced. Marriage is supposed to be for life, but a couple of signatures and a FedEx envelope later, it was over."

"Are you okay?"

He was. "Sometimes I think I haven't dealt with it because of Colin, but then I think I put one foot out the door when Colin first got sick and she didn't even want to come back home with me to visit, so maybe I started dealing with it before it was officially over."

"That makes sense."

"What about you? Are you really done with Brad? Or is there still something there?"

Margo looked at him, her dark eyes boring into his. "I'm done. I've been done. It hurt when it ended, but that doesn't mean it was wrong for it to be over."

"What if he had changed his mind right away on the pet thing? Do you think you would have ended up getting married?" He wasn't sure he wanted to know the answer. If she said yes...

She sighed and looked out over the river.

Connor rubbed his thumb over her knuckles and waited.

"I think it would have delayed the breakup. But I don't think it would have lasted much longer anyway." She ended with a shrug.

"Well," Connor said, "not with hair like that."

The intense mood broke and Margo laughed. "Exactly."

Connor let go of her hand and put his arm around her back, twisting the ends of her colorful hair around his fingers.

She put her head back on his shoulder and he breathed in the clean scent of her shampoo.

"I do wish either my family would respect me enough to stop acting like Brad's still part of the family, or that Brad would have the decency to cut ties with them." She sighed. "I suppose it's not nice or realistic to dictate who my family can have relationships with, but I feel like there should be some kind of loyalty. I mean, sure, be nice to him if you bump into him in public, send him Christmas cards if you want, but don't invite him to dinner. It's not like we have kids. I could see it then. If he was the father of their grandchildren, it would make sense to maintain a close relationship. But he's not."

"I'd feel the same way. I guess it's a good thing Sherri never really got close to my family. At least I don't have to worry about walking into my mom's house and seeing my ex-wife." Perish the thought.

"Yeah, it's not fun."

They sat in comfortable silence for a long while, watching Scout splash in the water and then roll around in the grass and eventually fall asleep.

Little by little, the other campers left until they were alone. The sun stretched across the sky, touching the tops of the trees. Long shadows formed across the surface of the river.

Scout finished his nap and came over to them, wagging his tail. They both rubbed him and scratched his ears. Connor caught her eye over Scout's head. "Dinner?"

"Yep."

Connor jumped up and held his hand out to help Margo up. Scout ran to the edge of the water. Connor whistled for him, so he skidded to a stop and procured a stick to carry with him, then trotted back to where they stood.

Holding Margo's hand as they walked, Connor couldn't name the feelings swirling around him except relief. He was relieved to have everything out in the open, relieved the Brad issue had resolved itself, relieved Margo was still at his side.

As usual, Scout stopped at the tent, letting them go on without him.

"Don't be getting my bed wet," Margo warned.

Connor laughed. "You know you're wasting your breath."

"I know. He's lucky he's so cute."

"Just like me, huh?" He wiggled his eyebrows at her while she looked heavenward and groaned.

At the lodge, they filled their plates and found a table at the opposite side of the room from her family. And Brad. Connor sat with his back to them. "You okay?"

"I'm good. Just baffled."

"At?"

She set her fork down and leaned toward him. "When I saw them earlier, Jean said Brad was packing. I thought he would have been gone by now."

The sooner he left, the better. "Maybe he wanted to eat first."

"Maybe." She didn't look convinced.

Connor looked around the full dining room. "I don't see Ashley and Elliott."

"Hmm. Maybe they ate earlier, or maybe they got smart and are eating somewhere else."

Connor raised an eyebrow and leaned in. "We could do that, you know."

"Do what?"

"Eat somewhere else. We're not hostages."

Her eyes widened. "We could, couldn't we?"

"Tomorrow for dinner, we'll escape to the outside world."

Margo grinned. "Okay. It's a date."

If he were a little less smooth, he might jump up and down at those words. "Perfect."

"Where should we go?" she asked.

He hadn't thought that far ahead. "Do we have to decide now?"

"No, but if you pick someplace crappy, I have a whole day to fake being sick."

Connor set his fork down to laugh. "You don't think I'll be suspicious now?"

"Nope." She coughed delicately into her napkin. "I'm very convincing."

"Hmmm. Not half as convincing as you think you are. How about BBQ Palace? Then we don't have to worry about finding nice clothes. How's that cough?"

Margo sipped her water. "Much better, thank you so much for asking."

"You're not coming down with something?"

She tapped her chin with her index finger and looked up at the ceiling. "No, I seem to be feeling quite well."

"Hopefully you don't have a relapse tomorrow."

"Let's hope not." She winked at him, and he laughed again.

Holy crap, he was taking Margo on a date.

# Chapter Nineteen

The meal ended without a single hint of drama from Margo's family. If she were being completely honest, she knew Jean's insistence on ignoring her was a form of drama, but she refused to engage in it. It was a nice change from the nasty comments. Who decided the silent treatment was punishment?

Later that night, Brad was absent from the bonfire, so Margo assumed he'd gone. Until she went to the restroom and on her way back, Shane cornered her.

"Margo."

"Oh!" She jumped, startled. "Shane, you scared me." She pressed a hand to her pounding chest.

"Sorry, I didn't mean to." He put his hands up and took a step back. Even in the dim light, Margo could see he was apologetic.

She said, "It's okay, I didn't realize anyone was out here. Good thing you're not a bear, huh?"

"Good thing for both of us."

Margo laughed, even though it didn't quite make sense. She'd gotten the impression over the past few days that Shane wasn't overly skilled in small talk. "Are you heading to the bonfire? I'm on my way back."

"I wasn't… yeah, I guess. Can I walk with you?"

"Of course."

They took a few steps when Shane cleared his throat. Loudly. "So. Margo. I keep hearing that you and Connor are just friends, even though you spend all your time together."

"That's true." Where was this going?

"So he wouldn't be jealous if I told you that I think you're… very beautiful." His voice cracked.

Margo paused in the pool of milky light from one of the overhead lamps. What was he doing? She kept her voice measured. "Shane. Thank you for the compliment."

Laughter came from one of the tents, and voices, followed by movement Margo couldn't quite make out in the darkness. Shane stared in that direction. A moment later, he turned back to Margo.

"I… I really like you." He leaned toward her.

Margo stepped back, putting her hand up. At the same moment, Roxanne and Brad appeared, pulling luggage out of Shane and Roxanne's tent. She put her hand on Shane's chest, preventing him from coming closer. "Stop it." She kept her voice low, not wanting to embarrass him.

He looked crestfallen.

"Shane. I get what you're doing. You want to make her jealous."

A look of relief crossed his face and he nodded, then leaned again.

She pushed on his chest. "Stop. First of all, I'm not participating in this. Second, it'll never work. Third, she doesn't deserve you."

"I love her." He sounded like a wounded animal.

"This isn't love."

Roxanne and Brad strolled next to them and stopped. Roxanne slithered closer to Brad, wrapping her arms around his middle and fixing Margo with a triumphant gaze. "Gosh, I hope this doesn't bother you. You know what they say, though. Finders keepers, losers *weepers*."

Brad looked slightly embarrassed, while Shane looked like he was going to vomit. Margo felt nothing except disgust at the way Roxanne was destroying Shane.

"It doesn't bother me at all. You two should have a lot in common."

"What's that supposed to mean?" Roxanne snapped.

"You're both in finance. You'll have plenty to talk about." And they were both jerks, but Margo left that unsaid.

"Sorry, Margo." Brad said.

She answered, "I have a feeling you'll be much sorrier later. Good luck."

Shane's face paled. "Roxy…" he pleaded.

Roxanne didn't even glance his direction. "We have to go."

Shane took a step toward her, then wilted as she walked away with Brad, her rolling suitcase leaving track marks in the dust.

"Why is she doing this to me?"

Margo patted his arm. "Because she can. She's a viper and an opportunist. You deserve better."

"Someone like you?" he asked hopefully.

He definitely needed to work on social cues. "I already told you I'm not interested."

He gave a little laugh. "If you change your mind…"

"I won't." Shane was definitely not her type.

"Because of Connor."

Annoyance flared, but she tempered her response. "Because

I'm not. I don't have to justify my interest or lack thereof to anyone."

"Oh."

"I have to get back to the bonfire. Are you going that way?"

"No, I think I'm going to pack." Shane walked away, surrounded by a palpable cloud of sadness.

She watched him for a few seconds, then turned and went back to the bonfire. She dropped into her spot beside Connor and leaned into the arm he'd immediately put around her.

He put his chin on her shoulder and spoke low in her ear, amused. "I heard you and Shane were making out in the woods."

Margo rolled her eyes. "Good grief."

A log shifted on the fire, sending a spray of sparks into the air.

"He *did* try to kiss me."

Connor's eyebrows rose and his beard shifted as he smiled. "No kidding. He's got more guts than I gave him credit for."

"I felt bad for him. He was trying to make Roxanne jealous."

"Poor guy. Maybe someday he'll meet a nice girl and be happy."

Margo doubted it. "Or Roxanne will get bored and order him to crawl back."

"So cynical. Maybe he learned something from this."

"Maybe."

His breath was warm on her ear. "I know I did."

Margo leaned back against his shoulder, curious. "What might that be?"

"That I should probably try to kiss you before you think I don't want to. I'd hate for someone better to come along and succeed."

A rush of pleasure fluttered in her belly at the thought of

kissing Connor. "Oh, and you think if you kiss me first that I'll be ruined for all other men?"

"Absolutely."

"Because of your magical beard." She reached over and gently tugged on it.

"Yes, ma'am."

"Let me guess. I'll fall hopelessly in love with you and never even be able to look at another man." She teased, but, whoa. That thought was a lot less crazy than it would have been forty-eight hours ago.

"Pretty much."

"How do you handle wielding such tremendous power? It must be tempting to enslave the entire female population." *Keep it light, just keep it… oh my goodness he smells good.*

His breath tickled her neck as he chuckled. "Tempting, yes. But I'm not interested in the entire female population."

"How fortunate for womankind." She joked, but noticed she sounded a little breathless.

He laughed again.

Margo relaxed against him, watching the flames curl around the logs. Across the fire, Heidi glared through the flames at her. For what, she had no idea. Not that it mattered, but it brought Margo's mood down and made her think of her family. She didn't want to think of them, she wanted to think about Connor.

"I'm ready to head back to my tent," she said.

"Any particular reason?"

"Two. First, the filthy looks from across the way are getting on my nerves. Second, I want to see if you actually work up the courage to try to kiss me." A walk in the dark, through the trees, the opportunities were endless.

"Wow, no pressure, huh?" He stood and reached for her hands to pull her out of her chair.

"Pressure?" She grinned at him and deliberately leaned against him when she got to her feet. "You have the almighty beard on your side. I'm merely a helpless woman, subject to your whims."

"True. But I don't like to be so in your face about it." His hands let go of hers and rested on her sides.

"Because you're so modest."

"Yes. And let's not forget humble."

"As if I could." She stepped around the chair and tugged Connor's hand toward the path.

Scout jumped up from his spot behind their chairs and led the way to the tents.

They walked slowly, their entwined hands swinging easily between them.

They were out of sight of the bonfire when Connor broke the silence. "You know, Brad was right about one thing."

"What's that?"

"You're too good for me."

She rolled her eyes. "Come on."

"I'm serious. You deserve some filthy rich prince with a giant castle who slays dragons for you and lays the world at your feet. Someone who comes from a long line of brave warriors."

Margo stopped walking to face him and pulled his arms around her back until he was against her. She looked up at him and took a hold of his beard, forcing his eyes to hers. "Castles are drafty and princes only give the orders to slay dragons. They never do their own dirty work. I'd rather have the knight who saves the dragon from the prince and understands that I can rescue myself." She let go of his beard and paused. "Unless I could have Prince William. But he gave up waiting on me and got married, so that ship has sailed. Unfortunately."

Connor's face was closer to hers. "Prince William doesn't even have a beard."

"No, but he's got a British accent."

"He's kinda skinny."

"British accent."

"He's going bald."

"British accent."

"Is that really a thing?"

"Absolutely. A British accent multiplies a man's attractiveness exponentially." Although even Prince William probably couldn't drag her away from Connor at this point.

"*Heah, wot aboot thees?*"

Margo laughed. "Please don't. That wasn't British."

"What was it?"

"Irish Canadian with an Alabama background, living in Transylvania."

"That bad?"

"Worse, I was being kind."

"Ouch."

"Maybe you should stop talking."

He leaned closer. "*That,* I can do."

A second later, their lips met. Margo's fingers tightened on his shoulders as his spread over her back and pulled her closer to him. The sounds of the night fell away until all Margo was aware of was the feel of his breath, the taste of his mouth, and her pounding heart.

The kiss lasted both forever and no time at all. Margo wasn't sure who pulled back, or if both of them did, or if neither of them did. Their surroundings gradually filtered back into her awareness, the crickets, and occasional hoot of an owl, but they still barely competed with the feel of his arms around her, his breath warm against her mouth.

At last, she let her eyes open to find him looking at her,

seemingly as entranced as she was. She felt his hand leave her back, then he reached up with the lightest touch and brushed a stray hair back from her forehead and tucked it behind her ear.

She breathed, "Wow."

A slow, gentle smile spread across Connor's face. He whispered back, "Wow."

They stared at each other for another long moment before finally parting and walking the rest of the way to Margo's tent. Her mind and her heart were racing.

Scout was already curled up in Margo's bed. Connor snapped and pointed to the ground. Scout huffed, then slunk down and trotted to his own tent.

"So," Connor began.

"So."

"I'll see you in the morning."

"Yup."

"Um… yeah. So morning then."

Margo laughed softly. "I guess your magical beard doesn't give you great command of the English language, huh?"

"Apparently not."

"Ah. So its powers are limited after all."

"Yeah, I think I got it all wrong. I'm pretty sure you're the one with all the magical powers."

Margo laughed again. "Impossible. I don't even have a beard."

He kissed her again, sweet and quick. "Maybe it's the belly ring."

"I hadn't considered that." She kissed him. "Would a magical belly ring trump a magical beard? I'm not sure what the hierarchy is."

"That makes total sense, though."

"It does?"

"Sure. You have a diamond in yours. I bet that makes all the difference."

"When you show up tomorrow with diamonds in your beard, I shouldn't be surprised, right?"

"Probably not. If I can regain the upper hand, I might try anything."

"Assuming you *could* regain the upper hand."

"Hey, allow me the illusion, okay? Even if we both know better."

She wound her hands in his hair and kissed him again, slow and deep.

"Never mind."

"Never mind what?" she asked.

His beard tickled her chin. "If you keep kissing me, I don't care if I ever get the upper hand back."

She chuckled against his mouth. "Back? As if you had it in the first place."

"Shhh, illusion."

"*Delusion.*"

"Whichever."

After one more kiss, he finally took a step backward, his hands trailing along her hips as he let go. "Good night, Margo."

"Good night, Connor."

She stepped up on her porch and into the tent, then watched Connor walk to his tent. His whistling brought a smile to her face. She pressed her fingertips to her lips, not wanting the tingling to stop. Maybe there was some truth to his magical beard theory because she had never been kissed like that. Best first kiss ever. Or second first kiss. Whatever.

Even though she didn't want to, she couldn't help the comparison to Brad from springing to mind. Brad had always been adequate, but he never made her knees weak. She'd always thought that was the ridiculous stuff of fairy tales and romance novels, but here she was, her belly fluttering and her toes tingling from Connor's touch.

If there had been a shred of doubt left in her mind about whether she was developing feelings for Connor, it was gone.

She curled up and went to sleep, unable to stop smiling.

# Chapter Twenty

Scout woofed in his sleep and woke himself up, which, in turn, woke Connor up. The stars were fading in the deep blue of the early morning. Scout did his business while Connor went to the showers and took care of his.

The agenda for the day was open. There weren't any scheduled activities until wine tasting and karaoke in the evening. Connor planned to have a great deal of wine before even considering karaoke. Much more than that, he was looking forward to taking Margo out for dinner. And kissing her again. He couldn't help but smile at the way his lips tingled at the new memory.

Until then, they had an entire day of possibilities. He rubbed a towel over his hair and slicked it back with his fingers.

Scout waited for him outside the facilities. He jumped up, his tail wagging a mile a minute while Connor scratched his head. "What do you think about fishing? Does that sound like fun?"

Scout was very enthusiastic about the idea. Connor was

sure Margo wouldn't be quite as excited about it, but she would probably be game for something quiet and relaxing.

He went back to his tent and sat on the bed with Scout, playing games on his phone until the sun came up. He stretched and listened to the sound of movement from Margo's tent.

A few minutes later, she stepped up onto his porch and peeked through the open door flaps. "Knock, knock."

"Hey. Good morning." The sight of her was even better than the image in his mind. Plain white shorts, plain gray t-shirt, hair in a ponytail, no makeup – she was perfect.

"I'm heading to the bathroom then to breakfast. You in?"

"You had me at breakfast." *You had me years ago.* He scratched Scout's head. "Ready when you are."

She gave him a dazzling smile, then went on her way.

Fifteen minutes later, Connor held the dining-room door open for her to pass through. They filled their plates at the buffet and picked their seats. As they sat down, Jean and Heidi came in and sat across from Margo with their breakfast.

Jean shot Connor a filthy look, then dismissed his presence altogether. "Are you sure you should be eating that many carbs?" She gave a pointed look at the pancake on Margo's plate.

Connor's blood boiled as he watched Margo put her fork down and push the plate away. "What do you want?" he snapped.

"Nothing that concerns *you*."

Margo put her hand on his arm. "Can we not do this? Please?"

Connor immediately forced himself to sit back and focus on his breakfast. He should have kept his mouth shut. It wasn't his place to question these people, no matter how absurd they were. Margo peeled a banana.

"We need to do something about Brad," Jean began.

Heidi nodded in agreement, primly taking bites of a muffin.

Jean said, "Surely you saw him last night, leaving with that *woman*."

Around a mouthful of banana, Margo said, "Yeah. So?"

Heidi leaned forward, her brows furrowed. "You... you honestly don't care, do you?"

Margo said, "I do not."

Jean's lips pressed into a thin line. "Of course she cares. She's just not admitting it because *he's* sitting right here. She's probably afraid he'll threaten to hit her like he threatened Brad."

Margo was on her feet. "I'm done."

Before Connor could get up, Heidi put her hand on Jean's arm. "You can't say things like that. We don't have to like him, but it's not okay to suggest he'd be abusive."

*How generous.*

Jean sniffed. "He screamed in Brad's face and said he'd punch him."

"Brad's a man. And he was... where he shouldn't have been."

Connor raised an eyebrow. It was almost amusing that Heidi was defending him in spite of her obvious dislike of him. Almost. It was far less amusing that Heidi minimized Brad crawling into Margo's bed uninvited.

Margo was still standing. "Are you going to apologize or not?"

Jean glared. "I'm not."

Margo picked up her plate and walked away. Connor cast a longing look at his half-eaten breakfast. It was a doggone good pancake, too.

"You're ruining her," Jean spat through clenched teeth.

Nope, not engaging with a psychopath. He picked up his plate and followed Margo to the trash cans. They put their dishes in the proper bin and left the dining room. *I hope we have pancakes again tomorrow.* Once they were outside, she kicked a stone and watched it skip across the sidewalk and land next to the fencepost. "I can't do this."

Connor waited until she looked up at him, her eyes full of worry and frustration. He put his arms around her waist.

"I'm going to pack up and go home." She looked so defeated. "I feel horrible. This is such a wonderful trip and Bonnie and Doug have worked so hard to put it together, and Shane already left."

Connor didn't even want to entertain the thought of Margo leaving. He suggested, "What if we just stop eating in the dining room? They never venture over to our tents, so if we stay to our side of the campground and eat somewhere else, that could solve most of the problem."

"The problem is they're here at all. Pretending they're not doesn't make them any less here."

He pulled her closer. "Or we could leave."

"We?" She relaxed a fraction and slipped her arms around his middle.

He leaned his chin against the top of her head. "Scout would be miserable here without you."

He felt her smile against his chest. "That's something to take into consideration."

Footsteps thumped across the lodge porch and down the wooden steps.

"Margo." Jean's tone was clipped. "If this is how you're going to treat us, we're going to leave. Is that what you want?"

"Yes, actually."

"Someday you'll regret turning your back on your family."

Margo's fingers tightened on his t-shirt, then she let go and turned away from everyone and walked away.

Connor fought the urge to say what he was thinking. Instead, he shook his head at Heidi. To her credit, she shrugged, looking uncomfortable and perhaps a little regretful. He didn't bother looking at Jean. She didn't deserve any acknowledgment.

"This is all your fault," she hissed as he passed her.

He hesitated but kept walking. No good could come from confronting her, and he wouldn't do anything to make things worse for Margo.

"Mom, stop." Heidi pleaded.

"Stop what? He's trash. He's ruined everything and turned Margo against us."

Connor shook his head again, a humorless smile playing across his face. If only he had that kind of power to influence people.

He caught up with Margo near the tents. She walked past her own and sat on the step of his porch, where Scout was lying. She leaned down and put her forehead against the dog's. Scout stayed still, except for his thumping tail. Margo scratched his ears and spoke low to him.

Connor sat beside her and put his hand on her back. She scratched the dog for a few more minutes, then sat up and leaned into him.

He kissed her forehead. "Your stepmother thinks I'm the devil."

She snorted. "You have no idea."

# Chapter Twenty-One

"What do you mean?" he asked.

Margo took a deep breath. This was going to be awkward. "I didn't get a chance to talk to you about it after I talked to Ashley. We found out why she can't stand you."

"Ah, so it *is* me."

"Yes and no."

"I'm intrigued." He also sounded wary, not that she blamed him. This could be leading anywhere, knowing her crazy family.

She bit the bullet and just said it. "Did you know that your dad used to date Jean back in high school?"

His eyes widened almost comically. "What?"

"Yeah. Apparently, they were fairly serious." Margo wasn't quite sure how to tell the rest of the story.

"I had no idea."

She hurried to add, "It was way before he met your mom." No sense adding more crazy to the fire.

He nodded. "Sure. He met Mom in college. Come to think of it, he never really talked about anyone he dated. Then again, neither did Mom. I don't know if she was ever serious with anyone else."

Cautiously, Margo asked, "Did they ever talk about their wedding?"

"Yeah. They always joked how they were the only couple they knew who had someone actually object..." He laughed then abruptly stopped. He stilled and pulled back to look at her. "It wasn't..."

Margo swallowed hard. "It was."

"You're not serious."

Her heart drummed in her chest. She couldn't read his expression beyond the obvious incredulity. This conversation was harder than she'd thought it was going to be. "From what I understand, they took a 'break' when they went off to college. While they were on said break, your dad met your mom and fell in love. He came back home and told Jean and she refused to believe he was serious, until he was getting married."

"Why would they invite her to the wedding?" Connor spoke softly, more to himself than to Margo.

"They didn't. Ash called our grandma to find out if there was something we didn't know, and boy did she fill us in. I guess my grandma used to be in the same card club with your grandma, so she was actually at your parents' wedding. She said Jean crashed the wedding, stood up right when the preacher asked for objections, and she had a whole speech. Your dad tried to take her outside to talk, and when she refused, he had to tell her it was over in front of everyone. Jean ran out of the church and your parents got married."

"Wow."

"Yeah. And from what my grandmother says, you're the spitting image of your dad. Which is apparently what's sent Jean off the deep end."

"Wow," he repeated.

Margo could only guess at what must be running through his head. "I'm sorry." If she were him, she'd walk away and not look back. Okay, maybe not, but she'd seriously consider it.

"Nothing to be sorry for. It's all history." He took a long breath and blew it out. "I guess that explains a lot. Still doesn't have anything to do with the way they treat you, but at least I can see where the venom comes from for me."

"It's not fair, though." Even if it was a good reason, which it wasn't, Jean had no right to treat Connor so poorly.

He gave her the lopsided grin she was growing very fond of. "Life isn't fair."

"Very wise."

"Stick with me, grasshopper, you'll learn a great many things."

"*That,* I believe."

He wound his arm around her back and rested his head on her shoulder. "But you're going to have to do something with that hair." He chuckled into her neck, his beard tickling her and sending a tingle all the way down her spine.

"And take out my belly ring that no one ever sees anyway?"

"I saw it."

She had the feeling he'd be seeing it again. "Yeah, well, you're the exception."

"I like the sound of that." He planted a kiss on her neck.

She put her hand on his knee. "I am sorry there's a whole mess and history and whatever with my family. It sucks."

"It's okay. I mean, it's not *okay,* but it's not like I'm going to judge you for what your family does. Or says." He kissed her cheek, then her forehead. "Let's go fishing."

*Huh?* Margo sat back. "That was rather abrupt."

"Sorry, what's the appropriate transition between horrible families and fishing?"

She laughed. "I have no idea. I mean, they're both kind of

slimy, but that's not much of a segue." Nodding, she agreed. "Fine. We'll go fishing. Wait. You don't mean in a boat, do you?"

"Nope. We'll fish from the bank."

"Okay." She stood and held her hand down to him.

He grabbed it and stood. "Doug said the gear's in the shed behind the lodge."

A few minutes later, they had signed out fishing poles, a tackle box, and gotten a styrofoam bowl full of nightcrawlers from Doug, and were walking down the path to the river. Scout followed behind, sniffing at everything.

Margo said, "I haven't been fishing in years."

"Me, either. My dad used to take me and Colin fishing all the time when we were kids."

"My grandpa took me. Dad was always too busy working to take us. And he thought it was one of those things girls shouldn't do."

"Ah. And what should girls do?"

Margo made a face. They'd had so many ridiculous dos and don'ts growing up. "According to my dad? Be prim and proper and land a 'good' husband. Which includes doctors, lawyers, and a select few financial jobs. That was the whole point of college education for his girls. To meet a potential spouse and get a degree in an approved field. Otherwise, we had to pay for it ourselves."

"Wow."

"Yep." It sounded terrible out loud, even glossing over the details to make it more palatable.

"I'm guessing the veterinary field wasn't on the list."

"Nope. Although..." she put her fingertip on her chin and looked to the sky. "If I had met a man studying to be a veterinarian, he would have been acceptable."

"Just not becoming one yourself."

"Right. A veterinary assistant would have been fine, but wanting to be an actual vet was a bridge too far. 'A pointless waste of money' was the verdict, since the goal was to meet a husband and never actually use my degree."

"That's messed up."

"What's messed up is that Heidi got a business degree, and after she graduated, dad and Jean gave her a big fat check to reimburse her for everything she laid out for school."

"What?"

"Yup. Then there's me. Not a penny. Which is fine. I earned everything I have. But Ashley, who has a degree in business management similar to Heidi, didn't choose the right husband, so she also got nothing."

"You're kidding."

"I wish I was."

They reached the edge of the river. No one else was in the area, so they had the place to themselves. Scout dashed out into the water, happily entertaining himself a safe distance away from their hooks and fishing line.

"Money is a reward for toeing the line?" Connor opened the tackle box.

"And a punishment for stepping outside the line."

"You've inspired me."

"How?"

"I'm going to set up college accounts for my nephews."

She looked at him, puzzled. "How did you make that connection?"

"It might make things simpler for them if someone tries to hold their education hostage. Not that they'd ever have the same situation, but at the very least, it'd make it easier to get an education. I know Colin left them some money, but who knows what college will cost when they get there."

"That's very thoughtful."

"I'm pretty fantastic that way."

She loved the way he could steer a conversation up out of the deep. "Ha, ha. Give me a worm."

Connor handed her the Styrofoam container full of nightcrawlers.

Margo picked out a fat worm and impaled him on the hook. "Sorry, buddy. Snag me a big fish, okay?" She cast the worm out toward the middle of the river.

Connor followed suit, casting his worm upstream from hers.

"Should we make a wager?"

She laughed. "About who catches the most fish? *I* should make that wager. *You* shouldn't."

"Oooh, trash talk."

She shrugged. "I don't want to bruise your ego."

He made a noncommittal grunt and focused on his line. It jerked and held tight as he reeled it in. "You were saying?"

Margo watched him wrestle with the line, reeling it in and letting it run back out a bit, then reeling it in a bit more. He walked into the water, his full concentration on the fish at the end of his line.

"Must be a big one," he said. "You sure you don't wanna bet?"

"No, I'm good."

He grappled with the line for a full ten minutes and finally had it close enough that he reached out and grabbed the line, triumphantly lifting his prize into the air. "And that's how it's done."

A sopping clump of seaweed and sticks dripped water.

"Wow. That's… impressive."

Connor stared at the offending wad of junk, then set to freeing his hook. "You're just jealous."

"Yup. Green with envy."

"I knew it."

Her line tugged. She yanked it and reeled the line in.

Connor stood watching while she pulled in a rainbow trout. She grabbed it and yanked the hook out in one smooth motion, then pulled her phone out of her pocket and snapped a selfie before dropping the fish back into the water.

"Show off."

"No, no, please, remind me how it's done."

"I bow to your superior fishing skills."

"As you should. Remind me, what did we wager?"

"I'm pretty sure we didn't end up wagering anything."

"Pity."

"Don't get so cocky. There's plenty of time for you to lose."

"I suppose that's true." She baited her hook and cast it. "Although you should probably get a line in the water if you intend to win."

He cast his line. "Bossy."

She did a little shimmy. "Boss lady to you." She would never have picked fishing, but being here with him, she couldn't think of a single better way to spend the day. She hoped her thoughts weren't written all over her face, because she kept imagining scenarios just like this – hanging out with Connor at home watching movies, going on trips with Connor, waking up next to Connor…

Scout barked at something across the river, pulling her from her daydream. Mission accomplished, he trotted onto the bank and rolled around in the grass.

Connor pulled in two fish in a row. "Hmm. I can't help but notice you've hit a bit of a dry spell."

Margo laughed. "It's because I was trash talking. This is my punishment."

"It seems fair."

"Not really. You were trash-talking, too, and now you're catching my fish." Margo finally reeled in another fish.

Connor cheered. "Now it's a tie. Shall we call it while we're both winners?"

Margo cast a sideways glance at the river, then at Connor. "Sure. But only because I don't want to show you up."

He laughed as he wound his line in. "Except that you already did."

They packed up the gear and whistled for Scout. He sat up abruptly, his nap interrupted. After a yawn and a stretch, he moseyed over to where they stood and put his forehead against Connor's leg for a scratch.

"Shall we actually try the geocaching this afternoon?" Margo asked.

Connor picked up the tacklebox in one hand and took the poles in his other. "Yes. Let's clean up and do that. Then we can make plans for dinner."

"Sounds good." She stopped walking. "Just one thing."

Connor stopped and raised an eyebrow, waiting for her. "What?"

Margo took his face in her hands and kissed him.

When she pulled back, he sighed. "No fair. My hands are full."

"I know," she laughed. "That was kind of the point."

"What, taking advantage of me when I was helpless?"

"Something like that." She smiled up at him. "I'll warn you, though, I might do it again."

"I'm okay with that."

*Chapter Twenty-Two*

Late in the afternoon, Connor took his time in the shower, wishing he was at home so he could primp and preen to be more presentable for taking Margo out on a real date. A real date. He whistled as he lathered his hair and rinsed. He turned the water off and dried off, then wrapped the towel around his waist.

"Geez, somebody's in a good mood." Oren stood at the sink, washing his hands. He smirked. "Margo's family leave or something?"

Wouldn't that be nice. "They threatened to, but I won't believe it until I see them drive away."

"Wise. I saw what's-his-face hooked up with Roxanne and they left together. That was convenient."

Connor grinned and spit out a mouthful of toothpaste. "Yeah, I couldn't have planned that better myself. Feel bad for Shane, though. Poor sap."

"No kidding. Chandler kept asking him why he put up with that nonsense and all he'd ever say was that he loved her. I love my wife, too, but if she was handing out her goodies to everybody that walked by, I wouldn't be sticking around to see if I could get the leftovers."

Connor leaned close to the mirror to trim his beard.

"Big plans?"

"I'm taking Margo to dinner."

"Busting out, huh?"

"Exactly."

"That explains the whistling." Oren gave him an approving nod. "It's probably the best thing for Margo. Get her away from her relatives and somewhere she can relax without looking over her shoulder."

Connor's hand paused in midair. "Do you have issues with Chandler's family?"

Oren shrugged. "Every now and then. It's all good now, but it wasn't always. Her mom didn't like me much at first. I'd just hang back and keep my mouth shut. My parents didn't care for Chandler, either."

Connor's eyebrows rose in surprise. "Why on earth not?" She was so personable he couldn't imagine they didn't like her immediately.

"They liked my ex better. I met Chandler right after we broke up and they decided that she was somehow responsible. She wasn't."

"Ah. The sainted ex." He was getting a taste of that himself.

"Yeah. And she definitely wasn't. They don't know the half of it. But they're slowly coming around. Chandler does the same thing. Keep quiet, grin and bear it until we get home. So where are you taking her?"

"BBQ Palace."

"Nice. Not too pricey, not too cheap." He gave another approving nod. "Have a good time."

"Thanks."

Connor trimmed the last spot on his beard and got dressed.

He couldn't remember the last time he'd looked so forward to a date.

Scout was sitting, waiting for him outside the building, his dark fur coated in light brown dirt.

"What the heck were you into?"

Scout wagged his tail, kicking up a small cloud of dust, but didn't reveal his source.

"Never mind. Let's go."

Bouncing to his feet, Scout dashed ahead to the tents.

Connor glanced down to make sure Scout hadn't gotten dust on his dark jeans.

Back at the tent, Scout had found a patch of grass to roll in.

Connor frantically searched for his wallet, and after he'd taken everything out of his bags, he remembered he'd locked it in the car for safekeeping. Shoving his clothes back in the bag, he made a mental note to check before they actually left the campground.

"Don't you look spiffy!"

Connor turned to Doug's smiling face as he climbed off the golf cart. "Hey. Yeah, I'm taking Margo out for dinner." He hoped it didn't offend his host.

"Oooh, nice. You'll be back for karaoke, though, right?"

"Wouldn't miss it."

"Excellent. I just stopped by to check in with everyone and make sure you're enjoying your stay."

"It's been great. You and Bonnie have done a great job. It's great." *Hey, genius, can you say great again?*

Doug didn't notice. "Glad to hear it! If you need anything, let us know."

"Thanks."

Doug hesitated before heading over to talk to Tanner and Sarah. "I feel terrible for Margo. Bonnie and I have been wracking our brains to think of some way we can make it a better experience for her, but we're at a loss. Short of kicking people out, that is."

Connor grinned. *If only.* "Too bad that's not an option, huh?"

"Yeah, we would have used it more than once over the years."

"I have no doubt." Probably more than once this season.

"We're glad you're spending time together. You make a nice couple."

Connor held his hand up. "Let's not get ahead of ourselves." Even though he might have been thinking the same thing himself.

Doug gave him a guilty grin. "Sorry. You guys enjoy your dinner. And if you think of anything we can do to help... well, just let us know."

"Thanks. We'll be back for karaoke."

"See you then." Doug walked away.

Connor tugged at the hem of his shirt and gave Scout a treat. "Okay, buddy, I'll see you in a couple of hours. Stay out of trouble."

Scout wagged his tail and jumped up on the bed.

Suddenly nervous, Connor walked over to Margo's tent. He knocked on the porch railing as he stepped up. His greeting stuck in his throat as he took in Margo's simple sundress and sandals. Her hair was loose around her shoulders, dark and light streaks winding around each other in loose curls.

"You look great." *Word of the day, huh?* He mentally kicked himself for the lame compliment.

Her dazzling smile added more than any diamond jewelry ever could. "Thanks. You look pretty spectacular yourself."

His ego stood up straight, primping and preening in his head. He held out his hand. "Shall we?"

"We shall." Margo took his hand and laced her fingers with his as they walked to the parking lot.

His brain misfired, unable to come up with any sort of conversation. He ended up mumbling, "I'm pretty sure my wallet is in the glove compartment. I have to check."

"Is that a warning I'll be buying dinner?" she joked. "Thanks for the heads up, I guess."

His tongue loosened. Joking. He could handle that. "Noooo, that would be a total jerk move."

"Yes. It would be."

"If I was going to do that, I wouldn't tell you ahead of time."

"Oh, it'd be a restaurant surprise."

"After lobster and an expensive dessert, of course."

"I'll be sure to carry extra cash if we go to a seafood place."

They reached his car. Connor hit the button, unlocking the doors, and leaned in the passenger side to open the glove compartment. He pulled out his wallet and held it out triumphantly. "See? I wasn't lying."

She shrugged. "Doesn't mean there's anything *in* it."

He stepped back and held the door while she got in. "You're so suspicious," he said as he got in his side and closed the door.

"After some of the nightmare dates I've been on, a 'forgotten' wallet doesn't even rank in the top ten."

"Seriously?" Now he wanted to know about all of her nightmare dates.

"You have no idea. I think half the dates I've been on have ended up being married or engaged."

He asked, "Have you dated a lot?" He certainly hadn't. First dates were a whole level of awkward he didn't care to experience too often.

"I did go on a lot of dates after Brad and I broke up. I

wasn't looking for anything serious, but it was good to get out. Sometimes it was nice. Other times, not so much."

"Any second dates?"

She snorted. "Not a single one. Let's see. Aside from the married and engaged men, there was a guy who literally lived in his mother's basement and hadn't had a job, like ever. He told me he wanted to marry a doctor and be a househusband, and even though I wasn't a doctor, a veterinarian would do, but he'd need to see my last five tax returns to make sure I was stable enough to keep him in the lifestyle to which he'd become accustomed."

He couldn't contain the laughter. "Holy crap."

"Yup. Then we have the guy with *three* wives. He was looking to 'add to the family,' as he put it. No thanks. Who else… oh, yeah. There was the guy who was perfectly nice and normal. Right up until he took me home, I thought we'd have a second date. At that point, he brought up the cost of my dinner and said it might not be enough for sex, but it had surely earned him a kiss. And he didn't mean on the lips."

"What a disgusting pig." Connor wanted to believe she was exaggerating, but he'd heard enough stories from his female friends to know there were some real pigs out there.

"Yeah. The world is full of creeps."

"Where'd you meet them all?"

"Everywhere. Online, in person, fixed up by friends."

"Sheesh."

"And in case you're wondering, yes, I've lived through more than one forgotten wallet story, so I always have enough cash on me to cover dinner so I don't have to wait for them to run my credit card."

"Smart."

"Except today. I've only got my card, so if you turn out to

be a cheap date, I'm stuck for a bit." She reached over and patted his leg. "Maybe we should stop at the ATM."

He barked a laugh, then promised, "I'll try not to be a lousy date."

"Even if you are, I can't imagine you'd land in my top ten Hall of Shame."

He put on his turn signal and waited for the line of traffic to clear before pulling into the parking lot. "I'd really like to not place anywhere on that list. How do I break the top five in best dates Hall of Fame?"

Margo snorted. "You're assuming I've had five dates good enough to warrant making a list."

"Now you're just being cynical."

"Maybe a little. I did have a great date one time. He picked me up on time, brought me flowers, and took me to a play. Then we had dinner and it was really nice."

"Nice? That's the bar I have to hurdle to make the greatest list? Challenge accepted."

"You're already behind. No flowers."

"Maybe I just haven't given them to you yet."

She cocked her head and raised an eyebrow.

"Okay, no flowers. But I still think I've got a shot."

"We'll see."

Connor parked the car and jogged around the back to get to Margo's door, but she already had it open and was stepping out.

"I was going to open that for you."

She batted her eyes and faked an innocent expression. "But you didn't, did you? No points for intent."

Oh, this was going to be a fun evening. "Ouch. Can I at least see the scorecard so I know what categories I'm being judged in?"

Margo laughed. "All of them, Connor."

He pulled open the door to the restaurant. The smell of barbequed foods floated out and enveloped them.

"Mmm, that smells amazing."

Connor nodded his agreement. "I get a point for picking this place, right?"

"Maybe."

The hostess led them to a table in the back of the restaurant. Connor watched Margo over the top of his menu, while she read the selections. One curl hung over her shoulder and bounced when she moved her head. He wanted to reach over and touch it. After a few minutes, she lowered her menu. He looked away before she could catch him staring.

"Know what you're getting?" she asked.

He looked at his menu for the first time. "I'm not quite sure yet." The words on the page didn't make a lot of sense. The only thing his brain would focus on was how to make her happy. How to give her the kind of evening she wanted. Deserved.

The waitress came with their drinks. Margo ordered a combo platter. Combo of what, Connor had no idea. He handed his menu over and said, "I'll have the same."

She was looking around the mostly-full restaurant. "I haven't been here in ages. Most of my meals are crockpot or take-out."

"Or the occasional lousy date."

Grinning, she said, "I remembered another one that cracked the top three worst dates ever."

"Do tell."

"No food. For a lunch date."

Connor stopped with his cup halfway to his mouth. "Really?"

"No. Food. None. No restaurant, no picnic, no nothing. He took me to this really pretty cottage that had these pretty gardens all around the property. There were people all over the place doing yoga and meditating. We stopped in this one garden and he wanted to meditate and see if our spirits aligned."

"That's... interesting."

"So we're sitting cross-legged on the ground in the middle of this rose garden and he tells me that our auras match because we're both yellow and we're completely compatible. He was super nice, so at that point, I was still leaning toward quirky and eccentric instead of weird and insane. I went along with it and after an hour or so of sitting in this garden – in complete silence, mind you – I mentioned that I was getting hungry."

"Uh-oh."

She made a face. "Yeah. He tells me that he's fasting and that I need to start fasting to cleanse my spirit and that I need to transcend my physical desires in order to become my most authentic self. When I suggested that my most authentic self wanted a burger, he made this horrified expression and went off on a thirty-minute monologue about meat being murder."

"Nice."

"I asked him to take me home, and this transcended, evolved, I-am-love 'nice guy' said he couldn't be around me any longer now that he knew I was an animal murderer. He said I had faked my aura, and I should call a cab."

"What?"

"Yeah. I ordered an Uber and got out of there."

"That's crazy."

"The craziest part is that he called me the next day to give me the opportunity to apologize and redeem myself."

"No way."

"Needless to say, I did not. And right after I hung up, he

filed a complaint with my bosses saying there was no possible way I could be compassionate with my patients if I ate meat."

Connor's mouth dropped open. "That's insane."

"I thought so. Fortunately, so did my bosses. They told me about it right away, so I threatened to get a restraining order and blocked his number."

"I hope he left you alone after that."

"Thankfully, yes. My poor friend Sandy, who fixed us up, was mortified. She had no idea he was so zealous. In fact, she had no idea he was vegetarian since the last she'd seen him was at a barbecue a few months prior." She rolled her eyes.

"Ah. What do they say? There's no convert like a new convert."

"Exactly. Your turn. Dating horror story."

"Mine are all so boring compared to yours." Even if they weren't, he wasn't half the storyteller Margo was. The dates had to have been torture, but hearing her tell the stories was pure entertainment.

"Come on, there has to be something."

Connor thought for a minute until one woman came to mind. "Oh, yeah. There was this one date. I picked her up at her house and everything seemed fine until we were halfway through dinner and she says, 'What do you think of Tyler and Elizabeth?' and I said I didn't know Tyler and Elizabeth. She laughs and says, 'No, silly, I meant to name our babies.'"

Margo's eyes widened. Her cup stopped halfway to her mouth. "No way."

"Way. I just kind of stuttered and stammered and said something about it being a little soon to discuss kids."

"Holy cow." He could see the corners of her lips twitch as she tried not to laugh.

"At which point she burst into tears and everyone is staring at us and she's really loud and says, 'Why don't you want to have children with me?' and now everyone's glaring at me like I'm some kind of monster to bring her out in public and break this news. I really wanted to stand up and yell that it was only our first date, but I didn't." He shuddered a little at the memory.

Margo was still trying not to laugh and not being very successful. "What did you do?"

"She ran out, so I paid the bill. She was waiting by the car, so we left, and then she asked me why I was taking her home so early. I think I just mumbled something about being tired. I walked her to her door, and she tried to kiss me, and then asked when we were going out again."

That did it. Margo laughed. And laughed. "Yikes."

It made him laugh, too. "I did the typical jerk move and told her I'd call her. She called me four times before I made it home, so I blocked her number as soon as I pulled in my driveway."

"That's awesome." Margo's eyes were bright with laughter.

"It wasn't awesome at the time, I can tell you that." He was glad he didn't have nearly as many first date horror stories as Margo. *What if this is the last first date for both of us?* He almost choked on his soda. Whoa.

"The white sauce on this chicken is fantastic. Most places go too light on the horseradish." Her comment was so casual, like he hadn't just had a heart-pounding revelation.

It took a second for Connor to bring himself back to normal. He shoveled a bite into his mouth. "Agreed," he said, even though he didn't really taste his food.

"I'm not overly impressed with the macaroni and cheese, though. I think it's overdone."

*Say something about the food.* "I haven't tried mine yet."

"It's not bad at all, just not terrific."

Connor nodded and they ate in comfortable silence until he asked, "What are you singing tonight?"

"Me? Nothing. I don't sing in front of people."

"Why not?"

She squirmed a little under his gaze, piquing his curiosity. "I guess it's just another one of those things I was told I should keep to myself."

He waited, knowing there was more to the story.

"In junior high, I had a solo in the Christmas program. My teachers and friends all raved, and when I got home, Jean just gave me *that* smile and said, 'Well, you didn't completely embarrass yourself.'"

Connor thought he couldn't dislike the woman any more than he already did, but apparently, he could. "That's vile."

"Yup. So I never did that again. The next year, they offered me a part, but I worked on the stage crew instead."

"Margo..." He wasn't sure what he wanted to say. There really wasn't anything he could do to go back to the girl she'd been and make her feel better.

"And more recently, Brad told me not to sing in the shower anymore. So I haven't."

"Screw him."

Margo shrugged. "Maybe there's something to it."

His head ached with the kind of frustration that had no outlet. He couldn't time-travel back and knock some sense into these people. "For Pete's sake. If finger painting stick people makes you happy, you don't stop painting just because it's not a freaking Rembrandt." He didn't get it. Margo was an amazing woman. How different would she be if she'd had unconditional love and support?

"Yeah, but I wouldn't try hanging them in a gallery."

"Maybe not, but you can put them all over your own fridge." The level of anger he felt was probably irrational. He recognized that and tried to let it dissolve. He didn't even know who he was mad at. Jean for being herself? Brad for being a douche? Margo, for accepting their lies as truth? Or himself for letting her go?

"It's not a big deal."

"Okay." He let out a breath.

"What are you singing?"

He lifted a shoulder in a half-shrug. "I haven't decided yet."

"Something lumberjacky?" She smirked.

"What exactly would that sound like?"

"I have no idea. Maybe something raspy and countryish?"

"With a hint of chainsaw?"

"Oh, heavens no. Ax noises. Maybe falling trees or the occasional shout of 'Timber!'"

"I was thinking more of a ballad."

"Ooh. Something unexpected."

"Maybe I'll sing 'Angie' by the Stones."

"I love that song."

"Or… do a duet with me."

She nearly spit out her mouthful of soda. "You have no idea what you're asking."

"What's the worst that could happen? It's a campground in the middle of nowhere. Nobody's going to know."

"Ugh. I'll think about it."

He took it as a positive and didn't push any more. "You're right about the mac and cheese. I think the cheese is too mild."

"That could be it."

"I use a lot of sharp cheddar in mine."

Margo raised an eyebrow. "You make your own?"

Huh. Jerkface Brad must not have cooked, either. Another point for Connor. "Of course. If I want it, I have to make it, right?"

"I never get around to making mac and cheese. I just order in restaurants and hope it's good. I should, though."

"I'll make you some." As soon as the words were out of his mouth, he wondered if she was going to assign some greater meaning to them. Or if they did mean more than he intended.

"Sounds good." She began working on pulling the meat from the ribs.

So what did *that* mean? Was she open to something after this trip, or was she just keeping the conversation light? Who knew? He decided to just roll with it. "What else should I make? Meatloaf?"

"Depends. Is your meatloaf any good?"

"You wound me, madam." He clutched his heart, which made her laugh.

"Okay. I'll tell you what. You make dinner and I'll bring dessert."

"Perfect. Wait. 'Bring' dessert? Like store-bought? After I've slaved all day over your meatloaf and mac and cheese?" He didn't care if she brought an expired pack of stale crackers if this was about a real date. Was it?

"I didn't specify. There will be a dessert, and I will bring it. Whether it's store-bought or homemade is to be determined at a future time."

*Is she serious? She's serious, isn't she? Are we planning a date? Play it cool, Connor!* "Fine. You're in charge of dessert."

"And you are hereby forbidden from complaint, snarky facial expressions, snide comments, or other expressions of disapproval."

"What if it's covered in coconut? Can I complain about that?"

"You don't like coconut?"

"Nope." One of the very few food items he didn't care for.

"Good to know. What else don't you like?"

"Dessert-wise? That's about it. What about you? Any food you don't like?"

"Onions."

*Well, she had to have* some *flaws, right?* "I'm glad you said that. I put a ton of onions in my meatloaf."

She made a face. "Eew, why would you ruin a perfectly good meatloaf like that?"

"Hey. I won't insult your dessert, you don't insult my onions."

"Onions are the devil. Why would you enjoy a food that makes people cry, unless you're some kind of sadist?"

He shrugged. "I like onions. I can relate."

Margo rolled her eyes. "All the layers?"

"Exactly. Layers and layers. I'm a puzzle."

"And just what kind of puzzle are you, Connor?"

He thought about it for a minute. "Maybe a maze. You have to take a lot of twists and turns to get to the prize."

"I thought the beard was the prize."

He chuckled and stroked his cheeks. "No, no, the beard is the Venus fly-trap. Draws you in and then you're caught."

"Oh. So you're like one of those creepy hedge mazes that looks like fun, but you wander into and then get all turned around and can't get back out so you're trapped and you end up losing your mind or starving to death." She snickered at him over her glass.

His fork stalled halfway to his mouth.

"I really don't even know what to say to that." He set his fork back down and shook his head, not sure why the comparison bothered him.

She must have seen it wasn't sitting well with him. "Okay, okay. You're not a creepy hedge maze. You're a completely un-creepy hedge maze."

"With clearly marked exits. Because if someone doesn't want to be there, I don't want them sticking around, either."

Her expression turned from teasing to contemplative. "Point taken."

He pushed his empty plate back. "Dessert?" He thought she'd refuse. She'd been weird about eating too much ever since her family came to the campground.

"I've heard the brownie sundaes are fantastic."

"Sounds good."

The waitress cleared their plates and took their dessert order. A few minutes later, she returned with a gigantic bowl and two spoons.

Connor shook his head. "That's ridiculous."

"It is, isn't it?" She grabbed her spoon and wrangled the perfect combination of brownie and ice cream. "Mmmmm."

Connor dug in and was happy to see her enjoying it, too. "Wow, that's delicious."

A bit later, they both eyed the half-empty bowl and sat back.

Margo dropped her spoon. "Uncle."

"Ditto. Not even one more bite."

"Nope."

The waitress came and set the bill on the table. Connor grabbed it, then patted his pocket. "Ah, geez, I forgot my wallet."

Margo laughed. "Brat."

He laughed with her and counted out some cash. He over-tipped by a lot, handing the waitress the money and saying, "No change, thanks."

Her eyes skimmed over the bills and she smiled broadly. "Thanks! Have a great evening."

In the parking lot, Margo teased him. "The waitress seemed pretty impressed by you. Big tipper?"

He pulled open her car door and winked at her. "No tip. In fact, I shorted the bill. I get away with it because of the beard."

She rolled her eyes and got in the car. "Liar."

As he put the key in the ignition, he nodded. "My mom was a waitress. It's a tough job, so I tend to be pretty generous when I tip."

"Me, too. I waited tables in high school and a little bit in college, so I know the crap they put up with."

"I'm sure you have some stories." His mom certainly did. People could be amazing. And they could be disgusting.

"Ugh. They're worse than the date stories. Or at least as bad. There was one guy who laid a stack of one-dollar bills on the edge of the table and when his glass was empty, he made a big show of taking a dollar away. Now mind you, he finished his drink as I was walking to the table."

"What a jerk."

"Yeah. But then he put a couple of quarters on the stack when I brought them extra bread."

"Quarters. How generous."

"Yeah. And people wonder why I prefer working with animals." She laughed.

Connor carefully followed the speed limits back to the campground, wanting to prolong their time out as long as possible. "I delivered pizza in college. Definitely not as bad as waiting tables, but there are some real weirdos out there."

"I need examples."

This was easier than coming up with date experiences. "We had one guy who ordered five large pizzas every Friday night at five forty-five, like clockwork. One cheese, two pepperoni, two supreme, no anchovy. He always wanted the pizzas left on a chair right beside the door, where he'd leave an envelope of cash for us. He'd watch us through the curtains until we pulled out, then he'd whip the door open, grab the pizzas, and slam the door shut."

"That's sad."

"It was. A few years later, though, he didn't order his pizzas one Friday, so the manager, Blake, actually called but he didn't answer. Blake went out to his place and the guy had had a heart attack or something, so he called the ambulance and it saved the guy's life."

"Wow. Kudos to Blake for checking on him."

"Yeah, he was a great guy." Connor cleared his throat. "As to other examples, I'll just say this. The whole delivery boy fantasy? Apparently, that's a real thing."

"What?! No." Margo squealed with delight and covered her gaping mouth with her hand.

"Oh, yes. It happened more than once that I'd get to a place and someone would open the door in lingerie. It's very disconcerting."

"And tempting?"

He shuddered, not wanting to remember any of the details. No, please no. "Ah, no. I mean, I'm sure it *could* have been, in the right scenario, but not the way it happened in reality."

Margo laughed. "You look like you're sucking a lemon."

"Yeah, some of those old memories are just unpleasant."

"Let's talk about good ones, then. One year on Christmas Eve, we had this guy come in and he secretly paid the checks for everyone in the whole restaurant and gave all the employees hundred-dollar tips."

"That's awesome."

"Yup. He did it to honor his wife after she passed away. Rumor was he'd do something like that every year on Christmas and her birthday. It was so sweet. He didn't want to broadcast who he was, but people tried to figure it out. There was even a reporter for the local paper trying to out him one year for a feel-good story, but we never breathed a word. I don't think anyone really wanted to know, it would have taken the spirit out of it."

"That's a great story." He was disappointed when the turnoff to the campground appeared. "I guess we're back."

Margo looked straight out the windshield. She sounded a little disappointed when she said, "I guess so."

He parked and turned off the car, then sat for a minute before he said, "I hate to get out."

"Me, too."

He was surprised when she reached over and touched his face, then leaned over to kiss him. Connor hesitated, then wound his hand around the back of her head, his fingers tangling gently in her hair, letting her lead.

# Chapter Twenty-Three

Margo was breathless when the kiss ended. She was pretty sure she could be content to come home from work every night and do nothing but kiss Connor. Judging from his ragged breath and the way his thumb stroked her jaw, he was equally happy to be kissing her.

She kissed him again, then sat back in her seat. "Shall we?"

"Must we?" he returned.

She laughed softly. "We probably must."

He sighed. "You're probably right." As he pulled his hand away, he ran his fingertips across her cheek, pausing ever so slightly to touch her lips. He got out of the car, then came around the front and opened her door.

Once she stepped out, he closed the door and pushed the button on his key to lock the doors. They took a step away from the car when he stopped and let go of her hand. She looked at him, questioning, and after a second of hesitation, he put his hands on her waist and pulled her close to him, his mouth covering hers. Her hands went to his shoulders, then wound into his hair as he backed her against the car.

They kissed until she was breathless again. She hoped

desperately that she wouldn't see her family and have them burst this lovely bubble she was in. *Why are you thinking about them? Stop it!*

Finally, he stepped back and planted a small kiss on her forehead. "Sorry, I probably got the back of your dress dirty."

She turned so he could check, not that the dim lights overhead offered much light.

"It's not as bad as I expected," he said as he brushed his hand across her back. "I haven't washed the car in forever."

"I couldn't tell you the last time my poor car got washed." She thought it might have been in March after the last snow of the year.

"I try to keep mine washed, but I've been busy lately. I don't usually go through the automatic wash. I like to do it by hand."

"Not me. Automatic all the way."

"It misses too many spots to suit me."

Who knew he was so fussy? She definitely wasn't. "Well, la dee dah. I only wash mine when I stop being able to recognize it in parking lots. Then I go through the automatic wash and voila, I can tell what color it is again."

"At least you have a strategy. I'm not judging, by the way. I'm just particular about my car."

"Of course you are. It's a chick magnet, just like your magical beard," she teased. No, his Chevy sedan was nice enough, but not a chick magnet by any stretch.

He laughed. "If that's the case, I need to get it fixed because it's not working." He raised an eyebrow and brought her hand to his lips to plant a kiss on it. "Or maybe it is."

"It's not," she answered drily, with narrowed eyes, then laughed. "That's kind of an unfair advantage, isn't it? Double whammy with the beard *and* the super clean car?"

"I'm just hedging my bets."

"You're incorrigible."

He pulled out his phone.

"What are you doing?"

"I have to look that up. You're using your magical language skills to keep me off my game and insult me." He tapped on his phone. "Wow. 'Beyond reform. Impervious to correction. Unruly. Naughty.' Hmm, okay, maybe you're not too far off base, so I can no longer claim to be insulted."

She slipped her arms around his middle and looked up at him. "You won a contest by correctly answering a literary question. Don't act like you don't have a command of language."

Connor barked a laugh. "Mine was easy. I would have never gotten yours. A telegram? Who knows that stuff?"

She pressed a finger to her lips. "Shh, I'll tell you a secret." She whispered, "I only knew it because I did an essay on Margaret Mitchell in high school."

"Still. You had to know it in the first place, *and* remember it all these years later."

"I guess. It was a fun contest. I heard the exposure really helped the library with their fundraising campaign."

She pulled him down for another kiss, then they reluctantly walked back toward the tent village.

"That's great. I haven't been in the library for ages. I need to get set up here. I still borrow ebooks from my library back in Portland."

"I was so excited when our library got hooked up with the ebook lending. I have a wish list a mile long and I forget what I have, so it's like a little Christmas present when I get an email telling me I have a book waiting."

Scout bounded out of Margo's tent and raced over to greet them. Connor scratched Scout's head and nodded. "Almost as good as finding out you've been selected by a Nigerian prince to collect three million dollars."

She laughed. "All you have to do is provide your banking information so they can deposit it for you."

"So convenient."

She told him about her most recent bit of spam. "The last one I got was from Bill Gate. Not Gates, Gate. He wanted to send me ten million dollars so I could 'have happy life.' I would have been happy with a new laptop, but I guess I shouldn't complain."

Connor made a little groaning noise. "That reminds me. I need to replace my laptop sooner than later. It keeps shutting off randomly. I'm pretty sure one of these days it's not going to come back on."

She gave him a serious look. "I hope you have everything important backed up."

"Yes, ma'am."

A bang caught their attention. It turned out to be a drum intro to whatever song was playing over at the stage area.

He asked, "Are you ready for karaoke?"

If she hadn't told Bonnie earlier in the day that she'd go, she'd beg off. "I'm ready to go see what's going on. No promises about whether I'll participate."

"Deal." He squeezed her hand and led her toward the makeshift stage that had been set up in a field beyond the bonfire area.

Chandler and Oren waved them over to where they were sitting, next to Ashley and Elliott. Scout dashed over and happily let Olivia rub his belly. He rolled over and she patted his head. He licked her face, making her giggle.

Margo scrunched her nose. "Eew."

Ashley watched the dog and her daughter for a minute,

then shrugged. "That's not even close to the most disgusting thing she's been into today."

"Where's the rest of the clan?"

Looking around, Ashley gave a slow shrug. "I assumed they'd be here."

"They didn't leave?" Margo couldn't disguise her disappointment.

"Are you kidding? You know Jean's the queen of idle threats."

"Someday she'll make good on one of them," Margo grumbled.

Chandler was flipping through a binder when she suddenly looked up and nodded vigorously. "Oh, yeah. We're gonna rock this song, girls."

On stage, a camper Margo didn't recognize was belting out a decent version of Eye of the Tiger. She found herself humming along.

"I'm signing us in." Chandler was up and heading to the DJ before Margo could protest.

She looked at Ashley. "What did she mean, 'us'?"

"Beats me. I guess we'll find out."

A moment later, Chandler bounced over, whipping her hair around in some kind of dance. "Okay, girls, we're on the list."

Margo groaned. Singing was the last thing she wanted to do. Hopefully, they'd be up soon so they could at least get it over with.

"Oh, stop. It'll be awesome."

As the minutes ticked by, the crowd grew until Margo was sure every single person staying at the campground was there. Blankets were laid out and lawn chairs set up like an outdoor concert.

Their little group cheered when Tanner took the stage. Even with Connor beside her, Margo couldn't help but stare.

Tanner's white t-shirt and dark jeans clung to him like he was being prepped for a photo-shoot.

Connor nudged her arm. "Careful or you'll drool all over your dress."

Margo's face heated. A twinge of guilt flared until she saw Connor's teasing smirk. This was new. Brad, and every other man she'd ever dated, really, was jealous and insulted if she noticed other men. Connor was definitely one of a kind.

"You're not offended?"

Tanner opened his mouth and began to sing. Horribly. His words were not in sync with the song, and if there was no music playing, Margo wouldn't have been able to identify the song.

Connor snorted. "Nope."

"Don't be mean."

"Hey, he's still pretty."

Margo laughed. "And that doesn't bother you at all."

"Should it?" He looked genuinely curious.

She studied his face. "Nope." She felt kind of stupid that it was a revelation to learn that Connor wasn't threatened by other men. It was silly, really. Margo was surrounded by beautiful women and it didn't bother her. She supposed it had more to do with who was sitting beside her. Brad openly ogled other women on a regular basis, and although Margo didn't doubt his faithfulness, it made her feel inadequate. Probably because Brad had never loved her for how – or who – she was.

Tanner finished caterwauling and took a bow to raucous applause. A woman she didn't recognize took the stage. The shoe was immediately on the other foot as Margo took in the short shorts and low-cut tank top. She reached over and put her fingers under Connor's jaw. With a laugh, she said, "Don't drool into your beard."

"Touché." He grabbed her hand and pressed it to his mouth

for a kiss. Suddenly, he grinned and jumped up, making his way to the DJ. He flipped through the binder and wrote something on a clipboard.

He flopped back onto his chair.

"What did you do?"

"I picked my song."

Before she could say anything else, Chandler was on her feet, pulling at her and Ashley. "It's our turn. Let's go, let's go!"

They walked up to the stage. Margo watched the screen, waiting to see what song Chandler had chosen. She burst out laughing when "It's Raining Men" popped up. Margo, Ashley, and Chandler shared the microphone, all of them belting out the song. Their voices complemented each other nicely, and they managed to stay pretty much on tune.

When the last line of the chorus rang out, the crowd whistled and cheered while the women laughed and held onto each other to take a bow.

They made their way back to their seats. Margo practically collapsed into her chair, laughing hard and holding her belly. "Oh, my goodness, that was awesome." It wasn't the horrible torture she'd imagined. Dare she even say… it was *fun*.

Connor was laughing, too. "That *was* awesome. Good job. You sounded great."

They listened to several more songs, good and bad, before Connor's turn came.

Margo sat forward, waiting to see what song he'd chosen. Her breath caught in her throat as the first strains of "I Only Have Eyes for You" played through the speakers. Connor's eyes went back and forth from the screen to her. The crowd and all the noise melted away.

"Dang," Ashley said.

From the corner of her eye, she saw Ashley nudge Elliott. He just shook his head.

Chandler and Oren gazed at each other while Oren sang along.

Margo swayed a little in her chair, unable to wipe the grin from her face. Holy crap, Connor was singing to her in front of a hundred people. If that wasn't making his intentions clear, she didn't know what was.

When the song ended and Connor took his bow, the audience was full of applause and a chorus of "aww." And a few catcalls.

He came back to his spot, but instead of sitting down, he leaned over, took Margo's face in his hands, and kissed her. Another round of applause and plenty of hooting and hollering rose from the crowd. The loudest of all came from Ashley, Elliott, Chandler, and Oren. Olivia slept through it all. Margo laughed against Connor's mouth, overwhelmed by the absolute perfection of the moment. She wanted to hang onto this feeling of being surrounded by friends and the man she was falling for. Yup, she was falling for Connor.

A scream pierced the night.

The DJ abruptly stopped the music. A low murmur ripped through the crowd when the scream came again, this time the word, "Help!" clear and unmistakable.

Movement on one of the paths drew everyone's attention. Bonnie sprinted down the path toward them, her face a mask of fear. She gasped, "9-1-1! Someone call an ambulance! Please! Call 9-1-1!"

Tanner leaped to his feet, racing toward Bonnie. He yelled something and gestured to his sister, Sarah, who took off at a full sprint down the path to the tents. Bonnie and Tanner disappeared down the path while Connor called 9-1-1.

Margo grabbed Connor's arm and pulled him toward the path while he talked with the dispatcher. They jogged in that direction until they spotted light from a flashlight and people low to the ground. Oren and Chandler were right behind them.

"At least ten minutes for the ambulance," Connor said.

Oren said, "I'll direct them in," then sprinted toward the parking lot.

They reached Bonnie and Tanner at the same time Sarah did. There was someone on the ground. Sarah handed Tanner his medical bag and gently pulled a hysterical Bonnie back from the man on the ground. The only word that was intelligible through her sobbing was, "Bees."

Margo gasped. She would never have known it was Doug. His face was swollen beyond recognition. The monstrous wheezing sound coming from him as he tried to breathe was heartbreaking. Even nature was silent around them as if it waited to see the outcome.

Tanner pulled an EpiPen out of his bag. He yanked the cap off, tossing it aside, and jammed the needle into Doug's thigh. A moment later, Doug was able to pull in a real breath. Tanner pressed his fingers to Doug's wrist and fished his stethoscope out of his bag with his other hand.

Margo knelt on the other side of Doug and said to Tanner, "Tell me what you need."

Tanner passed her the stethoscope without looking up. "Lungs."

As she did with her non-human patients, Margo slipped into Professional Dr. Lewis. She stopped seeing the whole being in front of her and focused on the individual parts that needed attention.

She listened to the air, concern mounting. "The epinephrine is wearing off."

Tanner checked his watch and cursed under his breath. "Thirty more seconds?"

Margo listened and shook her head. "No."

Tanner pulled another EpiPen out of his bag and injected Doug. Again, his breathing improved within seconds, but the progress was short-lived.

The entire world beyond Doug and Tanner faded into the background. Margo and Tanner functioned as a team, as if they'd worked side by side forever. With a nod, they stripped Doug's shirt and rolled him to the side so Tanner could assess the situation. Even he, a seasoned ER doctor, did a double-take at Doug's back.

Margo shifted up on her knees so she could see. Angry red welts covered Doug's back, sting on top of sting on top of sting. Two large dead hornets lay under him. Margo flicked them away and they rolled Doug back onto his back.

She repositioned the stethoscope.

Tanner checked his watch. "He needs a trach."

She pulled the stethoscope out of her ears and listened intently. "No sirens yet."

Connor's voice broke into their world like a voice-over narrator in a movie. "Dispatch says they're still six minutes out."

Tanner cursed again and pulled his bag close, shining the flashlight into it and pulling items into his hand. "Connor."

Immediately, Connor knelt beside them, above Doug's head, and Tanner gave him the flashlight

"Shine the light right here." Tanner motioned to Doug's neck. "Keep it steady. Margo, you ready?"

"Ready." She took the Betadine wipe from Tanner's hand and wiped Doug's neck. She didn't have human patients, but she agreed with Tanner's course of action. They couldn't wait six minutes, or five, or four. Doug needed air or he was going to die.

"What are you doing?" Bonnie screeched.

"Sarah." Tanner said only the one word and Sarah held

tight to Bonnie, keeping her out of the way. Chandler took Bonnie's other side, murmuring soothing words.

Connor put the dispatcher on speaker and shifted the phone so Tanner could talk to her.

Tanner identified himself and gave the dispatcher quick details while he wiped the blade of his scalpel with a sterilizing wipe.

He nodded to Margo and she tilted Doug's head back, exposing as much of his grotesquely swollen throat as she could. Her fingers felt like they were sinking into dough.

Tanner felt around Doug's neck with his fingers, exchanged a glance with Margo, took a deep breath, then in a quick motion, pressed the blade into Doug's neck, creating an opening. Instantly, his chest rose with the desperately needed air filling his lungs.

Ripping the wrapper off a small plastic tube, Margo handed it to Tanner to be inserted into the new incision in Doug's neck. After a long moment of intense observation, Tanner relaxed a fraction and gave Margo a nod.

Margo scooted to the side to give Bonnie room to settle next to her husband. She clutched Doug's hand. Now that the most critical moment was over, the surroundings began to filter back into Margo's consciousness. The cooling night air, the murmuring crowd, the tiny rocks digging into her bare knees. She gave Bonnie's shoulder a squeeze while she watched Doug's chest, counting as it rose and fell.

The last two minutes before they heard the siren felt like forever. Long moments later, blinding LED lights from the ambulance sliced through the darkness as it roared toward them. The vehicle came to a stop and two EMTs and Oren jumped out.

Chandler and Sarah helped Bonnie to her feet and stood with her as the EMTs lifted Doug to the stretcher and loaded him into the back of the ambulance. One of the EMTs climbed into the back and told Bonnie she could ride along to the hospital. She jumped into the back, the harsh lighting magnifying the terror on her pale face.

The door slammed shut and the ambulance sped away, small stones and dirt kicking up as it raced back toward the main road, the shrill siren deafening.

Nobody moved or spoke until the last wail of the siren faded into the distance. Finally, Tanner breathed a sigh of relief and reached over to give Margo a hug. She stepped into his arms and hugged him tightly.

He let her go and nodded. "Great work, Dr. Lewis."

"You too, Dr. Brenneman. Nice working with you, but I don't ever want to do it again." She managed a little laugh. The edge of adrenaline started to wear off.

"Yeah, I'd be happy if I never have a repeat of that."

Connor's voice was awed. "You guys saved his life."

Tanner gave a modest shrug. "Just did what anybody would have done. I'll follow up with the hospital in a while to see if we can get an update." He picked up his medical bag and let Sarah fuss over him.

Margo snapped to attention. "We need to find out how to contact the family."

By this time, a small crowd had gathered. Chandler rubbed Margo's arm. "Let's check the office for an address book or something."

Tanner offered, "We'll go back to the stage and give everybody an update."

"Good idea." Margo reached for Connor's hand, grateful for his quiet strength. They walked alongside Chandler and Oren toward the lodge while Tanner and Sarah went back to the assembled crowd.

As they reached the lodge steps, they heard the faint strains of music from the field.

"Good," Chandler said. "Get the guests relaxed and having a good time again."

In the lodge, Margo hesitated before turning the knob to the office door. "I feel like we're doing something wrong." She pushed and the door swung open. Flipping on the light, she walked to the large desk and checked a drawer. Chandler checked the opposite side of the desk. "Bingo. Here's an address book."

"Thank goodness they still have some old-fashioned habits," Margo said.

Chandler picked up the phone and called one of Bonnie and Doug's sons. Thankfully, he answered on the first ring and promised to call the rest of the family. She was quiet for a moment, nodding, then hung up. "He said there's a 'closed' sign for the lodge door and asked if we would lock up for the night."

They left the office as they found it, closing the door behind them. Chandler found the sign under the counter in the lobby and hung it in the door window as they left.

# Chapter Twenty-Four

Connor was quiet as they walked back toward the stage area, hoping to meet up with Tanner and decide who was going to the hospital. They found him hanging back at the edge of the crowd, which seemed to have gotten back into the vacation state of mind. Tanner smiled as they approached. "Hey. Doug's stabilized. It sounds like everything's under control."

"That's wonderful."

Connor mashed down the sudden ping of jealousy as Margo touched Tanner's arm. She was still holding his hand, and it was nothing more than a friendly gesture. He tried not to solidify the vague notion that he might be measuring himself against life-saving-hero Tanner and coming up short. Or life-saving-hero Margo and not being worthy. He pushed thoughts of the building collapse away and tried to focus on the conversation about Doug. Doug. It was all about Doug right now, not him.

"We shouldn't take a whole group to the hospital."

Oren said, "Tanner and Margo should go. They're the ones who saved his life."

Connor forced himself to nod. "Yeah. You guys should go."

Margo hugged Chandler, then wrapped her arms around Connor's middle and lay her head on his chest. He hugged her tight and kissed the top of her head. "Let me know when you get back. I don't care what time it is."

She nodded against him but didn't speak.

Tanner handed his medical bag to Sarah. "Thanks, sis." He kissed her cheek, then he and Margo walked away.

Connor felt like an idiot for being jealous as he watched them leave.

Chandler bumped his arm with her elbow. "Hey. He still can't carry a tune in a bucket."

He couldn't help but laugh. "Thanks. I feel so much better now."

She cocked her head and squinted a little. "Seriously, Connor. You have nothing to worry about." Was he so transparent?

He shrugged. "I'm not worried." He saw her skepticism. "Not *really*. It's just hard not to start measuring yourself against the hero of the hour."

Chandler smirked. "Tanner? Or Margo?"

"When you put it that way - either one," he answered with a laugh.

Oren clapped his back. "Relax, dude. It's not like he's serenading her on the way to the hospital."

Connor snorted. "I kind of hope he is."

They laughed until a small group approached them. Margo's family. Ashley reached out and grasped Connor's forearm. "What happened? We heard the sirens and now we can't find Margo."

Connor felt bad not even thinking to let Ashley know what was happening. "She's okay. Everything's okay. Doug got stung by a bunch of bees and had a bad reaction. Margo and Tanner saved his life."

"Margo?" Jean sounded skeptical. "She's not a *doctor*."

Ashley's fingers tightened on his arm. If she had spit fire at Jean, he would not have been surprised.

Connor decided to ignore Jean and focus his answers and attention on Ashley alone. "She and Tanner went to the hospital to check on Bonnie and see how Doug's doing."

Ashley nodded, tears in her eyes. "I was just so worried when I couldn't find her to see what was going on."

To her credit, Jean also looked like she might have been concerned.

Connor gave Ashley a quick hug. "She's fine. Good. Great. You should have seen her. She was amazing. They looked like they performed surgery on people on the ground all the time, like it was no big deal. Totally calm and just getting it done."

Ashley smiled. "She's always been like that, able to turn off her emotions and do what she needs to do, and then after it's all over is when she breaks down if she needs to."

"I'm sure that makes her a great vet."

"The best."

Jean chimed in with, "The best? I'm sure she's adequate, but there's no need for hyperbole."

Teeth clenched, the word amplified through his mind. *Adequate.* He wanted to throttle Jean where she stood. Even Heidi, her clone, stood behind her, not endorsing the comments, but not incensed like Ashley was. Probably she was so used to it that the comments barely registered as insulting.

Ashley, however, looked up at Elliott, who had his hand on her back, undoubtedly helping calm her, judging from the unspoken conversation that was going between them. He held a sleeping Olivia in his other arm.

Connor spoke through gritted teeth. "I'm going to my tent. I'll see you tomorrow."

Ashley nodded and she and Elliott walked away.

Chandler and Oren still stood beside Connor, quietly waiting for the drama to end before leaving Connor alone.

Heidi spoke first. "Thanks for letting us know what –"

"He didn't let us know anything. We had to go searching and try to find him."

"--happened with Doug. If there's anything we can do, let us know."

Connor gave her a curt nod. "Thanks. I think it's covered. We got ahold of their son, so their family is on the way to the hospital."

Jean gave an annoyed half-surprised gasp, half-irritated snort. "I don't know why Margo insists on making a nuisance of herself. I'm sure Dr. Tanner didn't need her help, and their family certainly won't want her there bothering them."

Heidi put her hand on Jean's shoulder. "Mom. Stop."

"Stop what?"

Connor held up a hand, done with her. D-O-N-E, done. "Good night."

He turned and walked away, Chandler and Oren flanking him. When they passed the crowd in front of the stage, Oren patted his shoulder. "You're a freaking saint, man."

Chandler's voice spit nails. "I wanted to deck her. Margo is freaking awesome, and that *woman* has no freaking clue. How is that even possible? She's beyond ridiculous."

Their words were confirmation he didn't need, that Margo was an amazing woman, but he felt the tension in his shoulders relax a little with the commiseration. They'd only met her a few days earlier and had quickly bonded with her. Her stepmother had had most of a lifetime and apparently missed something along the way.

He felt a brief twinge of pity. Jean was missing out. He quickly tamped it down. He wouldn't waste charitable feelings on someone so wholly undeserving of them.

Parting company at the tents, Connor lay back on his bed. Scout must have sensed his emotional turmoil, because he jumped up and cuddled next to him, nuzzling his snout into Connor's neck.

"She'll be back soon, buddy."

Scout licked the side of his face and thumped his tail once.

"Exactly." He stared up at the canvas ceiling for what felt like hours. He didn't realize he'd dozed off until Scout jerked, his lethal tail whacking his side before he jumped down. The scratching sound of the door zipper being slowly opened must have woken the dog.

"Hey." Margo's voice was soft at his doorway. She gave Scout a scratch, then zipped the door shut.

"Hey. Did you just get back?" He checked his watch. It was nearly three a.m.

"Yeah." She sounded exhausted.

"Do you want to sit down?"

Instead of answering, she crawled into bed beside him. Scout jumped up on her other side, sandwiching her in the middle.

"Doug okay?" Connor wondered if she could feel his heart pounding under her hand on his chest.

"Yeah." She burst into tears.

Connor held her tight. He hadn't thought it possible to admire her more, but he did. How strong did a person have to be to get the job done, see it all through, and only let the emotions out when the coast was clear? Stronger than he was, he knew.

When her shuddering subsided, he asked, "You okay?"

She nodded vigorously against his shoulder. "Yeah." The word was barely audible.

"That's what matters. That's all that matters."

Her crying eventually faded to sniffles. Connor wouldn't have moved for anything in the world. At some point, she drifted to sleep. When her breathing was steady and deep, he let himself drift away, too.

# Chapter Twenty-Five

Her nose was itchy and stuffed when she woke up, slowly becoming aware of her surroundings. Instead of her pillow, her head was nestled against Connor's shoulder, his arm protectively around her, his t-shirt smooth on her cheek. She felt the edge of her skirt, much higher on her thigh than she would have liked.

Scout's back pressed tight against hers. She relaxed into the cocoon they created, debating whether to move her arm from Connor's middle to scratch her nose.

As the seconds ticked by, the itching became intolerable. She moved slowly, not wanting to disturb him, and scratched the offending itch. *Much better.*

She lay her arm back down across him, and his other hand came up from his side to rest on her arm. His fingertips lightly traced the back of her hand, letting her know he was mostly awake but in no hurry to move.

She turned her hand into his, their fingers lacing together.

"You okay?" he asked.

She nodded against his shoulder. "Yeah. Just a long night."

His hand left her shoulder and went to the back of her

head, playing with her hair. "If you want, we can go to the hospital and check on Doug."

"And Bonnie."

"How was she doing?"

"About as well as can be expected. I can't imagine she got any rest."

Scout stretched and turned, snuffling at the back of Margo's neck.

She scrunched down with a giggle. "That tickles."

Connor gently swatted at Scout.

Deeply offended, Scout jumped down and lay in front of the door.

"What time is it?"

Connor turned his wrist without letting go of Margo's hand. "Not quite six."

"It seems later." She paused. "Is it awful that I'm wondering what's happening with breakfast?" Saying it out loud made her feel guilty. Bonnie was probably starving.

"I hope not because I had the same thought."

"I'm not cut out for roughing it."

He dismissed the notion. "We're practical. We can channel our ancestors and utilize the resources they would have if they were faced with this dire situation."

She raised an eyebrow. "What resources?"

"The diner for food, followed by high octane from Caretti's Coffee Shop."

"Our ancestors would be proud."

"I think they would."

Margo stretched. "I suppose that means we should get up."

"I suppose it does."

"It's nice and cozy, though. I hate to move." It was a little too easy to imagine laying with him like this on a much more regular basis.

"Me, too. Even though I can't feel my arm. It is still attached, isn't it?"

"Don't worry, you'll feel it in a minute." She sat up and ran her fingers through her hair.

Connor's hand lingered on her back. She hated to move and break the connection, but she slid off the bed and straightened her dress. "I'm going to change and hit the showers."

He sat up and grimaced, rubbing his shoulder. "Sounds good. We'll meet back up and figure out what we're doing."

Margo leaned back across the bed and kissed his cheek before walking back to her own tent and getting her clothes, towels, and toiletries. Glad to see she was the only one in the shower room so she didn't have to talk, she took her time conditioning her hair. The events of the previous night rushed back at her and she forced back more hot tears. It was stressful enough working on animals in an emergency. There was no way she could do Tanner's job on a daily basis.

Standing under the hot spray, she let the water wash the conditioner from her hair and massage the knots in her shoulders. She reached back and rubbed her neck, then sighed and turned the water off. When she was dry, she pulled on her t-shirt and shorts, then gathered her things and walked back to her tent. She was tired. Exhausted, really, even after a few hours of sleep. Then she felt guilty. No, *she* wasn't tired. Bonnie was tired. The poor woman was dead on her feet.

She hung her wet towels over the chair beside her bed and yawned. She debated sitting on the bed but knew if she did, she'd just flop over and go back to sleep. Instead, she slipped her feet into her sandals and walked outside to wait for Connor.

The sky was bright, promising a sunny day.

"Margo, hey." Sarah's voice pulled her attention.

"Hey."

"I didn't get a chance to tell you that you did a wonderful job last night."

Margo gave a half-shrug. "Tanner did all the hard work. I just did what I could to help."

"You're too modest. Tanner didn't save Doug's life by himself."

"He could have."

"But he didn't."

Margo had no answer for that. It was odd to hear Sarah telling her to take some of the credit. Wasn't she glad for her brother to have the whole spotlight? Margo certainly was.

Sarah regarded her for a moment, then smiled. "There's nothing wrong with acknowledging your talents."

"Heh. That's a harder lesson to learn than you think. I was always told it was arrogant to accept a compliment. I guess that kind of got ingrained in my head."

"That's really sad. Why deny something in yourself that you'd admire in someone else? For false modesty?"

"I'm not sure if it's false modesty or plain old low self-esteem." Margo liked Sarah well enough, but this conversation was odd and uncomfortable.

"They do look alike, don't they? You're a wonderful person, Margo, and you helped save Doug's life. You should feel good about yourself."

"Thanks." She shifted. "Have you talked to Tanner? Is he going to the hospital this morning?"

"He's already there. He slept for a couple of hours and went back. He figured you'd visit after you got some rest, too. Did you sleep?"

"A little. It reminds me of when I was interning at a 24-hour emergency clinic. The shifts were insane. We'd go crash on these crappy little cots in the back for a few hours, then be back to work. It was a lot easier when I was ten years younger."

Sarah grunted in agreement. "Wasn't everything!"

Connor waved as he approached them.

"We're going to find some breakfast and go to the hospital."

"Let me know if you need anything," Sarah said as she turned to walk away.

Margo reached for Connor's hand and looked around. "Where's Scout?"

"He went back to bed. Lazy bum."

Margo laughed. "Must have been a long night for him, too, huh?"

"Yeah, he was working hard."

"I'm sure he'd say so."

Connor nodded toward the lodge. "It looks like it's open. Do you want to eat here or the diner?"

"Let's just pop in and make sure they don't need any help."

They walked into the lodge. A young man who was the spitting image of Doug smiled at them. "Can I help you?"

"Hi, I'm Margo. You must be Doug and Bonnie's son."

"Steven." He held out his hand to shake theirs.

"How's your dad? And mom?"

Steven bobbed his head. "Pretty good, considering." He stopped suddenly, his eyes growing large. "Did you say Margo? As in Dr. Margo?"

"Oh."

Connor interrupted. "Yes. She is."

Steven's eyes filled with tears and he rushed around the counter and grabbed her in a hug. "Thank you."

"Oh, gosh." *Please stop hugging me.*

"If you and Dr. Brenneman hadn't been here…" he wiped his eyes. "I don't even want to think about it."

Uncomfortable, Margo nodded and took a step back. "I'm

glad I was here to help. Well, we're going to head to the hospital. Is there anything your mom needs or any messages?"

"Just see if you can help convince her to get some rest."

"I'll do what I can."

She was glad to leave the lodge. Steven's gratitude overwhelmed her.

They took Connor's car to the diner. As Margo looked over the menu, her stomach growled, but her mind recoiled as it tallied the calories.

"Everything looks great."

She nodded but searched the menu for something she would feel comfortable eating. It was exhausting, sometimes being able to eat anything she wanted without those nasty voices taunting her, and sometimes – most times – not.

The waitress came and Connor ordered a Hungry Man's Platter that sounded like it had one – or more – of everything on the menu.

She was almost embarrassed to order her egg white omelet with extra vegetables.

"That sounds good, too."

She glanced up, wondering if he was mocking her. "I didn't want something heavy. I'm tired enough as it is." It didn't feel like he was.

"I'm sure the platter was a mistake, but I'm starving and it sounded great."

The waitress brought them coffee. Margo drank hers black, while Connor dumped sugar and creamer in his.

"Don't judge," he laughed as he poured another spoonful of sugar into the cup.

"No judgment at all, but I'm sure the sugar high followed by the carb crash is going to be wildly entertaining." She tried joking but was too tired to find anything amusing.

"Undoubtedly. After we get back from the hospital, I'm thinking hammock and book."

"The book is going to be pretty pointless, isn't it?" Although laying in the hammock sounded wonderful.

He mocked surprise. "What? Are you suggesting I'm going to fall asleep as soon as I get comfortable?"

"Perish the thought."

Connor laughed a little. "My grandmother used to say that all the time. I think it was the northern version of 'bless your heart' or something."

"Mine, too. She has all kinds of sayings that sound innocent but are pretty cleverly disguised snark."

"It's a lost art."

"It is. Someone should bring it back. Not me, my snark is too obvious."

"We could start a petition. Bring back the art of snark."

For some reason, the idea struck Margo as funny. She started laughing, and the more she laughed, the funnier it got. She imagined Connor carrying around a clipboard, stopping people on the street, asking them to sign his petition. Then she imagined him in an old-timey reporter's cap, with striped pants. She laughed harder, until tears rolled down her cheeks.

Connor was sitting back in the booth, laughing at her laughing. She caught his eye and laughed harder, balling up her napkin and trying in vain to wipe her face.

"Okay, okay, okay. I'm good." She felt the laughter bubbling in her belly again and tried to stop it. She failed, dissolving into another fit of laughter, then taking deep breaths to calm herself.

She managed to compose herself fairly well, the bubbles of laughter finally dissipating.

"You good?"

"Oh, gosh. Wow. The petition thing was so much funnier in my head."

"I'm not the only one taking a nap when we get back."

"Deal."

"I didn't expect you to be so goofy."

"Yeah, well, I'm just full of surprises, aren't I?" She laughed. "Let's stop at Caretti's for caffeine and get to the hospital before I lose my entire freaking mind."

Margo watched the scenery passing by on the ride. She was in that weird state of hyper-alert that comes after a long night with very little sleep, and before an inevitable crash.

At the hospital, she felt guilty for thinking she was tired. Dark circles and bloodshot eyes were the first things she noticed about Bonnie. She sat beside Doug's bed, holding his hand. He was sitting up, looking fresher than his wife.

At the sight of Margo, Bonnie jumped to her feet and grabbed her in a hug.

"Excuse me for not getting up," Doug joked.

Margo swallowed the sudden lump in her throat. "You look great. How are you feeling?"

"Like a million bucks."

She rubbed Bonnie's back. "You need to get some sleep. Steven told us we were supposed to tie you up and drag you home."

Doug nodded. "That's what I've been telling her. I'm fine now, she needs to go home and rest."

Bonnie sighed heavily. She didn't say anything, so Margo knew she must be beyond exhausted.

"Will you please let Margo and Connor take you home? You can come back with Steven."

Margo nodded. "Please."

Bonnie nodded. Her voice was low and raspy. "Okay. I need a shower and change of clothes anyway."

Doug grew somber. "Margo... I'm not sure where to start. 'Thank you' is so inadequate. I don't know how I can ever repay you for... I owe you my *life*."

Margo shifted uncomfortably. "You don't owe me anything. It was mostly Tanner anyway." She smiled at him. "I did what anybody would have done. I'm just glad you're okay now. That's all that matters."

He nodded slightly. "Well. I knew you'd say something along those lines, and you know I need to do something as a token of my – our – gratitude." He glanced at Bonnie. "We can't do a lot, but what we can do is give you free vacations for life. Whenever you want, you have all-expense-paid access to the campground. Fifty-two weeks a year. Forever. That includes any guests you bring with you, forever. Like if you get married or have a dozen kids or whatever."

Margo chuckled. "How about a dozen husbands and no kids?"

"Hey!" Connor objected.

"That's fine. But if they all want to go fishing at the same time, I'd ask that they bring their own gear."

"Thank you. It's really not necessary, though. I mean, this was my first vacation in a thousand years, who knows when or if I'll ever take another one."

A nurse came into the room and checked the machines surrounding Doug. When she left, he grabbed Bonnie's hand and pressed it to his mouth. "Go home. Get some rest. I'm a bit tired myself, so I'm just going to nap. If I can, with all the noise." On cue, the blood pressure cuff began it's automatic process, buzzing and crinkling as it inflated.

Bonnie nodded, kissed him, then let Margo and Connor lead her out of the room. "I feel awful, Margo. Like there's something I should say to you, but I don't even know where to start."

"Please. Don't make a fuss over me." Margo looked at Connor for some support.

He put his arm around Bonnie and steered her toward the elevators. "Let's get you home. You must be hungry. We'll stop and get you something to eat."

She looked up at him. "No, I can't ask you to do any more-"

Connor cut her off. "You aren't asking. Now, where would you like to stop?"

"Any drive-through is fine. Something quick."

Margo knew she must be hungry, exhausted and miserable to let Connor convince her so easily. She hurried to get in the back seat before Bonnie could object to riding in the front.

# Chapter Twenty-Six

Connor felt for Margo. He knew she wasn't a fan of being in the limelight in the first place, but to have people continually fawning over her was probably driving her crazy. He glanced over at Bonnie. "How about Arby's?"

"Perfect. Thank you."

He pulled through the drive-through, ordered Bonnie's food, and handed cash to the kid at the window. A minute later, he handed a paper bag and a soda to Bonnie, then pulled away from the window and out onto the street.

She thanked him, then burst into tears. "I'm so sorry. I didn't even offer to pay."

Connor reached over and squeezed her hand. "Bonnie. It's not a big deal." He turned down the lane to the lodge and found a parking space. He opened her door and helped her out of the car. "Eat. Sleep. We'll check in on you later, okay?"

She wiped her eyes and nodded. "I'm not myself."

Margo put her arm around Bonnie's shoulders. "You will be after you get some rest and eat some curly fries."

Connor nodded. "Curly fries solve a lot of problems."

Bonnie managed a smile as Connor opened the lodge door for her.

Steven rushed from behind the counter. "How'd you get her to come home? Never mind. Mom, let's get you upstairs." He looked back over his shoulder. "Thanks so much."

Connor held the door open for Margo to walk out onto the porch. "Tent or hammock?"

Margo lifted her face to the sky and pulled in a deep breath. "It's too gorgeous to stay inside. I vote for the hammock."

"I was hoping you would."

The walk back to the tent was quiet. Connor could see her mind racing a million miles an hour, no doubt thinking about Bonnie and Doug. They stopped at Margo's tent and picked up her book, then at Connor's for his, then headed toward the river.

Scout dashed up the path toward them, his feet and legs wet.

"Looks like somebody was at the river."

Scout wagged his tail and bounded after them.

It was just after lunchtime, and the hammocks were empty.

Margo smiled. "Good. We have the place to ourselves."

"Great. Now you can drool and snore without disturbing anyone."

She glared. "I don't drool."

"If you say so." He wiped at his shoulder where her head had rested hours earlier. "Still soggy."

"Whatever." She climbed into the hammock, then clutched the edges while Connor got in. They both shuffled and shifted and got situated. Margo let her book rest on her stomach, her hands folded over it. "There's not much point in opening this," she said with a huge yawn.

Connor put his hand on her leg, his fingertips moving in lazy circles. "Probably not." He started reading and awkwardly turned the page with one hand. As he did, he glanced up at Margo. She was already asleep. He watched her for a few moments, pleased she trusted him enough to be close to him and let her guard down enough to sleep. He thought back to the early morning, when she'd curled up next to him and he hadn't moved a muscle so he wouldn't disturb her. He hoped – *really* hoped – it was the first of many such mornings.

In his mind's eye, he went back over the night before, when she'd knelt beside Doug, the life nearly squeezed out of his swollen face, so calm and in control, so confident working in tandem with Tanner. Her hands were steady as she had held Doug's head, helping to clear the place where Tanner had to cut into Doug's neck. He'd never felt so proud of another person as he was watching her work while he did nothing more than hold a flashlight.

He'd also never felt so undeserving. Here was this woman – this beautiful, talented, incredible woman who knelt in the dirt and saved a man's life without hesitation. And here he was, a technically unemployed man avoiding his past who couldn't even do his job well. So why was she stretched out alongside him, relaxed and trusting that she was safe with him?

A sarcastic thought came to him – at least they both had messed up families. Maybe that leveled the playing field a little bit. He sobered. It really was a shame Margo had the family she did. At least he could blame *his* mother's shortcomings on her alcoholism and mental illness. And even when she was drunk, she'd never looked at her sons as anything less than fantastic. Margo's stepmother was just an awful person. He was glad she had her younger sister and her mother.

A fierce wave of sadness welled up. He missed Colin. The one person who'd always had his back, no matter what. Who'd always understood where he came from, and always encouraged him to rise above it and make something of himself.

He tried to quiet the negative voice in his head. Margo saw something in him that made her comfortable with him. What, he had no idea.

At some point, Connor dozed off, too. When he awoke, Margo was stretching.

"You're a genius. I feel so much better after my nap."

He cupped a hand to his ear. "Wait, what was that first part again? I didn't quite catch it."

She rolled her eyes. "You're a genius. A geeeeeeeeenius."

"Why thank you. You're quite perceptive."

"You're quite a goofball."

"Ouch."

"Hang on, I'm getting out of this thing." She inched to the edge and carefully got out of the hammock. When she was on her feet, she stretched again and yawned. "What's on the agenda for this afternoon?"

"How about a leisurely hike?"

"Sounds perfect. Right after I hit the restroom."

"Yeah. I overdid the coffee, so I need to make a pit stop myself."

"Where'd Scout get to?" Margo asked.

Connor whistled and a moment later, Scout bounced out of a bush and ran over to them.

Margo scratched his head. "What trouble were you getting into?"

He wagged his tail harder and doggy-grinned up at her, but didn't answer her question.

After a stop at the restroom, they went back to the tents to leave their books and change shoes. They picked the level trail through massive shade trees. A nice, easy stroll in the cooler woods, holding Margo's hand was just what he needed.

Margo said, "You know, I don't think I ever asked you what your contest question was. We talked about mine, but not yours."

"You'll make fun of me."

"I would never."

"Yes, you will. It's an awesome question, though."

"What was it?"

"An editor bet Dr. Seuss he couldn't write a book using only fifty different words. What book did he win the bet with?"

"Ooh, that is a good one. Was it *One Fish, Two Fish*?"

"Nope."

"*The Cat in the Hat*?"

"Nope."

"*Hop on Pop*?"

"You know a lot of Dr. Seuss books."

"I have a four-year-old niece."

"Good point. You're missing the most obvious one."

"*Green Eggs and Ham*?"

"That's the one."

"Really? I'd think there were more than fifty different words in that one."

"You'd think. The bet was actually from his editor after he wrote *The Cat in the Hat* with only 225 different words. The editor bet him he couldn't write a book using less than that. So he did it with only fifty." Connor continued, "I love trivia. I was tickled I won with a Dr. Seuss question. Did you know Seuss was his mother's maiden name? Or that he never had children of his own?"

"That's some amazing useless trivia."

"Not useless. It won me this trip. And I've gotten more than one free beer with my fount of knowledge."

"Free beer."

"Yup. I was on a trivia team with some work buddies. Trivia Tuesdays were our night to mop up the floor with the competition." He had many fond memories of his work friends, despite the fact they'd all lost touch with him after his move.

"Okay, then, impress me with some other bits of trivia."

"Did you know that a hummingbird is the only bird that can fly backward?"

"I did know that."

"Did you know a single bat can eat up to 10,000 insects in one night?"

"I also knew that."

"No, you didn't."

She raised an eyebrow. "So far, I'm not impressed. I know lots of animal trivia."

"Oh. Yeah. Crap, I guess you would. How about some construction trivia?"

"Okay."

"What's the actual size of a 2x4?"

"It's not two inches by four inches?"

"Nope."

"2 ½ x 3 ¾?"

"Nope. The correct answer is 1 ½ x 3 ½."

"Then why do they call it a 2x4?"

"Beats me. Rounding, I guess. How about this? Did you know that the largest snowflake ever recorded was fifteen inches across?"

"No way."

He nodded vigorously. "Yes way. It was in Montana in the 1800s. Look it up."

"Oh, sure. Tell me to look it up when I don't have my phone with me, and there's zero chance I'll remember later."

He said, "If I was going to make something up, it probably wouldn't have been a giant snowflake. Did you know the world's largest emerald was over eight hundred pounds? It was found in Brazil."

"I like emeralds. They're my favorite color. And, incidentally, my birthstone."

"Really? When's your birthday?"

"May 14. When's yours?"

"February 27."

"Ooh, amethyst."

He raised an eyebrow. "Sure."

"You don't know your birthstone?"

He shrugged. "I never really cared about it one way or the other."

"I suppose it's not much of a guy thing. Unless you're a jeweler."

"Which I am not."

"Or a jewel thief. I'd imagine they're pretty knowledgeable about gemstones."

Connor stepped over a root and squeezed Margo's hand to direct her attention to it. "Hmm, would the actual thief know much about them, or would it be the big faceless bad guy who hired the thief?"

"Maybe the bad guy is really adventurous and does his own stealing. And if not, I would think even the guy doing the actual pilfering would have to have *some* sort of knowledge so he steals the right thing."

"So the plan should probably be a tad more sophisticated than just grabbing all the pretty green stones?"

"Exactly."

"But what if it's part of the strategy?"

"How so?"

Connor bent over and picked up a pebble. "Let's say I hire

you to break into the jewelry store and take all of these." He dropped the pebble into her palm. "All you know is that they're obviously valuable, or I wouldn't want them. But you don't know how valuable or even what they really are. All you care about is getting in, getting the job done, and getting paid. You're not likely to double-cross me and keep them for yourself."

"Because my focus is on the two hundred thousand dollars you're paying me to get the pretty rocks."

"Two hundred thousand? That's kind of steep."

"Hey. I may not know gemstones, but I'm the best in the business, or you wouldn't have hired me to do this important job, right?"

"True."

"My price just went up to two-fifty. You shouldn't have doubted me."

"Ouch. Can we get back to my scenario?"

"Sure, cheapskate. Go on." Margo snickered.

"But if you're a jewelry expert, you might just be using my resources to help you break in, and then you'll keep them for yourself because you know they're worth forty bazillion dollars."

"Forty bazillion, and you're balking about paying me two hundred thousand? You really are cheap. I don't think I'm going to steal jewels for you."

Connor narrowed his eyes. "Are you backing out of our deal?"

Margo stopped walking, dropped his hand, and planted her fists on her hips. "Now who's double-crossing who?"

"Whom."

Margo opened her mouth as though she had a retort but burst out laughing instead. "Wow. So to deflect your treachery, you're resorting to correcting my grammar?"

"Simply using the tools at my disposal."

"Clever."

Connor laughed at her expression, a mix of amusement and plotting a way to one-up him. He reached for her hand, but she pulled it away, then put her palms on his chest and gently pushed him backward. He stepped back and found himself against the trunk of a tree. Margo stepped closer until her body pressed against his and her lips brushed ever so slightly against his.

He looked down into her beautiful brown eyes, waiting for her next move.

She whispered, "You're not planning to double-cross me, are you, Connor?"

His mind had abandoned the jewel thief conversation a while back. He tried to appear nonchalant as he shook his head. "No. It would seem you have an unfair advantage."

"Unfair?" Her expression was all innocence. "I'm simply using the tools at my disposal." Her lips brushed against his throat.

He knew she felt him shudder at her touch. She pulled back an inch and lifted her face to kiss him. He stayed still, content to let her do what she wanted, his hands hanging at his sides, itching to touch her.

"Hey, guys!"

Connor cursed under his breath as Margo jumped back and nervously touched her hair. Her eyes twinkled with amusement. "Busted," she whispered before turning to their unwelcome visitors.

Chandler and Oren held hands, strolling toward them.

"Oh, geez, sorry," Chandler said. She smacked Oren's arm. "We should have gone the other way."

"How was I to know that?"

Chandler rolled her eyes. "We'll let you two get back to your... *hike*."

Margo laughed. "Subtle. Real subtle."

Connor shrugged at Oren's curious expression.

Oren said, "I take it things are going well?"

Connor raised an eyebrow. "Things were going better ninety seconds ago."

Margo blushed adorably. He grabbed her hand and pulled her against him, wrapping his arm around her waist, then heaved a dramatic sigh. "I guess we're done here."

Margo and Chandler looked at each other and giggled.

"Since we already killed the mood, do you have any updates on Doug?" Oren asked.

Margo answered, "He looked really good this morning, and he was in good spirits. We brought Bonnie back home around lunchtime so she could get some rest. We haven't heard anything since, so I assume there's nothing new."

"Did he say how he got into the bees?"

Connor shook his head. "We didn't even think to ask. I think we were both just so relieved to see he was doing well."

Margo nodded in agreement. "Never even crossed my mind. I would like to know, though."

The foursome strolled around the rest of the trail, eventually coming out at the tents.

Steven and Bonnie walked toward the tents from the other direction, as though they were heading from the lodge.

"I wonder what's going on," Oren said, straightening with concern.

Connor shook his head. "They don't look upset, hopefully it's nothing."

They met in the middle of the tent village.

Bonnie reached over and took Margo's hand. "We're heading back to the hospital, but I wanted to thank you."

Connor felt Margo lean slightly closer to him. He could feel her discomfort building, knowing she didn't want any more attention about her role in saving Doug's life.

"I really appreciate you bringing me home. You were right. I feel so much better after getting some sleep."

He felt Margo relax again. She squeezed Bonnie's hand. "No problem. I'm just glad we could help."

Bonnie's hands fluttered, nervous. "I'm afraid there isn't going to be a bonfire tonight. I feel terrible about that, but hopefully tomorrow we'll be able to get one going."

"No one's going to mind," Chandler said.

Steven put his hand on his mom's back. "We should get going."

"Okay. Oh! There won't be any dinner in the banquet room tonight. I'm so sorry." She looked up at Steven. "Maybe we should have pizza brought in or something. I'll call –"

"Mom. They'll be fine. Let's go."

Bonnie fiddled with her necklace. "I know, I just don't want anyone's vacation to be ruined."

All four of them made murmurs of protest until she let Steven steer her away and out of sight.

"Poor Bonnie," Chandler said.

Margo nodded. "I know. She's so worried about everyone else, but she needs to take care of herself, too."

"How about we all go out for dinner?" Oren asked.

Chandler nodded and bounced on her heels. "We could see if Tanner and Sarah want to come, too. A contest winners' night out."

Connor squashed the nugget of jealousy that flared up. "Sounds good."

Chandler grinned. "Yay. We'll go find them and meet you back here in about an hour?" She and Oren left to go find Tanner and Sarah.

"I think I'm going to change into jeans. It's getting a little chilly," Margo said.

Connor watched her disappear into her tent, not expecting to see her again until the group met for dinner. Instead, he had just settled on the bed with Scout when she appeared in his doorway.

# Chapter Twenty-Seven

"Knock, knock."

"That was quick. I didn't think you'd be over until dinnertime."

She raised an eyebrow and offered, "I can leave if you want." She knew he didn't want that at all.

"No." He started to move.

"Don't get up." She went over and crawled across the bed, snuggling herself between him and Scout.

Connor shifted so his arm was under her. "What's up?"

She adjusted her hair, then rested her arm on his chest, her fingertips playing with his beard. "Nothing."

"Just wanted to cuddle?"

Absolutely. "Yup."

He squeezed her and kissed the top of her head. "We can skip dinner."

She smiled into his shirt. "Nah, I'll get cranky. Nobody wants that."

He chuckled. "Note to self. Don't let Margo get hangry."

"It'd be like cuddling with a porcupine."

"Porcupines are awesome."

She yawned. "Until you get stuck with a quill."

"How many porcupines have you treated?"

"One. But lots of animals who had run-ins with them. It's not pretty." She couldn't begin to count the number of dogs she'd taken quills out of.

"I bet."

"Lots of infections and oozing pus. Really gross stuff."

"That sounds horrible."

She nodded against his chest. "It is. The quills are dirty and barbed, so when they puncture the skin, they catch, like a fish hook, and all that dirt gets lodged inside the wound. In the wild, infection is pretty much a given. It's not a nice way to die."

"Most ways aren't."

"I suppose not."

"Tell me about the porcupine you treated."

"It was way back when I was interning. You know that Adventure Safari place?" She paused as he nodded. "They have all kinds of animals. Mostly rescues that can no longer survive in the wild. Anyhow, we got a call to go out because one of the emus got into it with the porcupine."

"Emu?"

"Big giant bird. Like an ostrich."

"Oh yeah. Why would an emu get into a fight with a porcupine?"

She snuggled closer and pulled her leg up across his legs. "The emu was a jerk. It fought with everything. It even killed a sheep."

"Yikes."

"So we had to tranquilize the emu to get the quills out of its face and neck, then we had to treat the porcupine for her injuries. The emu beat the crap out of her, but she ended up okay."

"What happened to the emu?"

"He had to be separated from the other animals. He got his own enclosure after that."

"That's a pretty sweet deal. Beat up a porcupine and get your own place."

"Yup."

"I bet the other emus were jealous."

"I bet the other emus were glad to see him move. He was a jerk."

"Nothing worse than a jerk emu."

"I suppose a jerk ostrich would be worse."

"I thought emus were bigger than ostriches."

Margo shook her head, breathing in his scent. "Nope. Other way around. Ostriches are much bigger."

"You'd think once the porcupine shot him with its quills, it would have backed off."

"Common misconception. Porcupines can't shoot their quills." She raised up on her elbow so she could talk with her hands. "See, the quills lay flat with the fur on its back, but when they're threatened, the quills stand up and rattle against each other as a warning. When they're attacked, the quills pretty much slide right off because the barbs catch under the skin of the attacker."

"Sounds painful."

"That's the point."

"So don't try petting a porcupine."

"I would advise against it."

He laughed. "Where's your sense of adventure?"

"There's a fine line between adventure and stupidity."

He ran his fingers across her back. "I suppose that's true."

Margo reached behind her and scratched Scout's belly. "It's almost time."

Connor groaned and squeezed her close. "Like I said, we can skip it."

She laughed and nuzzled into his neck. "Nope. I'm hungry."

"Fine, we'll get up and go." He made no move.

"If we're getting up, you'll have to actually move."

"No thanks." Instead of getting up, he pulled her head down to meet his mouth.

Okay, so maybe they should skip dinner. Her stomach rumbled, settling the issue.

Scout huffed behind her, then slunk down off the bed and stretched. He meandered out the door and around the corner.

Connor sighed. "I suppose if he can get up, I can, too."

"Exactly." She nudged his side.

"Okay. I'm going."

She laughed at him.

"Don't know why you're laughing. You aren't moving, either."

"I'm waiting for you."

Connor finally sat up and stretched. "I'm up."

Margo scooted off the bed and jumped up, then fluffed her hair. "Perfect." She held out her hand. "Let's see where everyone is."

As they left the tent, Margo saw the other four of their group gathered in front of Tanner's tent. They walked over.

"Where are we going?"

Sarah said, "How about the Roadhouse? I haven't been there in years."

"Sounds good to me."

Everyone nodded in agreement.

Tanner said, "I think that's the fastest I've ever seen a group of people agree on a place to eat."

"Me, too," Connor said.

"How about we head to the parking lot while we ponder this miracle," Sarah added.

"Who's driving?"

"I can take four," Connor said.

Sarah made a "hmmm" sound. "I vote the girls ride together and the guys take a different car. We have some gossip to catch up on."

The plan delighted Margo. It had been forever since she'd made the time to hang out with girlfriends. This was going to be fun. In the parking lot, Chandler and Margo piled into Sarah's car, while the guys got in with Connor.

Chandler sat in the middle back, leaning toward the front seats. "This is fun. So what's up, Sarah? What gossip do you have?"

She tapped the steering wheel and gave a sly smile as she glanced in the rear-view mirror. "Not so much gossip as information that Margo might be interested in."

"Me? What?" Margo sat up straighter, curious.

"Well, I was talking to Tanner. He was really impressed with you the other night."

She sat back against the seat. "Ugh. It was no big deal." She did not want to discuss the Doug situation.

"It was a huge deal. But that's not the point. I haven't heard Tanner talk about a girl since… well, since his last big breakup. That's been a couple of *years*. He swore off women and pretty much threw himself into his work. I think this vacation is helping him to start thinking about things outside the ER again."

Margo's brow creased. "Okay?" *Where is this going?*

"He likes you. I mean, he really likes you."

*Oh, geez, no.*

Chandler said, "Umm, what about Connor?"

*Exactly. Thanks, Chandler.*

Sarah slowed to a stop at a red light. "I know. But you've said several times that you're just friends."

Chandler snorted. "It's pretty obviously not the case."

Sarah shrugged. "I'm just throwing it out there. Giving you something to think about. I know he's my brother, but Tanner's a great guy. He's smart and funny and has a great career, and he's really good looking."

Margo had to laugh.

"Yeah, I know. I'm not saying that in a creepy way."

Margo said,"I know you're not. And I appreciate the fact that you would want me to date your brother." She wanted out of this awkward conversation. "But I'm…"

Chandler huffed in the back. "She's not interested. Just say it, Margo. You're into Connor, and that's that."

Margo wished she had the confidence to just lay it out like that. "Tanner's a great guy. But not for me."

Sarah seemed unconcerned. At the restaurant, she pulled into a parking space and turned the car off. "We'll see."

*No, we won't see.*

When Sarah got out of the car, Chandler muttered, "That was ominous."

Margo made a noncommittal grunt and got out. Sarah was already next to Connor's car. "Yeah, this isn't going to be awkward at all."

Chandler made a noise of agreement. "Did not see that coming."

Margo sidled up to Connor and slid her arm around his waist. He put his arm around her and gave her a questioning glance, which she ignored.

In the restaurant, they only waited a few minutes for a table. When they were seated, Margo was annoyed to see Sarah shuffling around so that Tanner was beside her. She shot Chandler a look across the table.

The words on the menu swam around, escaping her attention. This was ridiculous. They were adults. If Tanner expressed any romantic feelings for her, she'd tell him she wasn't interested and that would be that. There was no need for his sister to be a go-between.

She smiled at the thought. What was next? Sarah passing her a note to circle yes or no? The next thought reinforced the smile. Jean would freak out if she turned Tanner down. She could hear her voice. *Who in their right mind says no to a doctor?*

A *real* doctor. Not a pretend one like Margo. The smile faded. Ugh, why did she let them get under her skin when they weren't even anywhere around?

"And for you?"

Margo startled, not realizing the waiter was ready. "Oh. Sorry. I'll have the grilled chicken salad. House dressing."

The waiter left with their orders. Connor leaned over to her ear, putting his hand on her leg as he asked, "You okay?"

She nodded. "Yeah, just got distracted."

He raised an eyebrow but didn't press.

Placing her hand on his leg, she mirrored his raised eyebrow and tapped his nose. "Really."

"Okay."

Sarah had a mischievous twinkle in her eye. "Are you guys officially dating now?"

Margo's fingers tightened on Connor's leg. "Sarah."

"I was just curious about how serious the competition is."

"Competition?" Connor repeated.

"Oh, didn't you know? Tanner here is quite interested in Margo."

Margo felt her face burn. So much for being good friends with Sarah. No thanks. She knew enough people who didn't know when to quit.

Tanner set his cup down with a thump. "Sarah, knock it off."

"What?" Sarah feigned innocence.

Margo leaned a little closer to Connor, wishing this would just end.

"Sorry, guys. My *sister* is famous for involving herself in things that are none of her business."

"Oh, come on. I'm just putting it out there so everyone has all the facts."

Tanner leaned back in his chair. "The only fact that matters is that Margo and Connor have a thing going."

Chandler's eyes widened. "You *are* interested in Margo. I thought Sarah was talking out her behind."

Margo stepped on Chandler's foot under the table.

Oren put his arm over her shoulders and shook his head. "We need to talk about something else before it gets any more awkward or uncomfortable."

Sarah smirked. "I'm not awkward or uncomfortable."

"That makes exactly one of us," Oren said firmly.

The waiter came with a tray of appetizers and homemade bread. Margo picked at a slice of bread, but never actually put any of it in her mouth. She could feel Connor watching her from the corner of his eye as he ate his deep-fried onion blooms.

"You should tell them the porcupine story," he said mildly, breaking the uncomfortable silence.

Oren said, "What's the porcupine story?"

"It's more about an emu than a porcupine."

Tanner said, "There's an emu? Now you have to tell us."

"It was one of those weird cases I had when I was interning at the emergency animal hospital. We got a call from the Adventure Safari. Their emu was attacking the other animals, and had tangled with a porcupine."

She felt herself relaxing as the mood of the group drifted back into a companionable friendly sort of vibe as they listened to her story.

"So the emu ended up getting his own enclosure because he was such a jerk, and the porcupine recovered and went back home."

The waiter brought their dinners. After he walked away, Tanner said, "How did the emu kill the sheep?"

"Apparently he kicked it, then when the sheep was on the ground, jumped on it, like some kind of gruesome bouncy-house, causing all kinds of internal injuries. Unfortunately, that happened in the middle of the night and nobody saw it so there was no way to help the sheep."

Sarah said, "Tanner, tell us one of your crazy ER stories."

Margo nodded. "I'm sure you have lots of them. People are way crazier than animals."

"People *are* animals," Tanner deadpanned. "Let's see. There was the lady who drove her car through the ER doors because she didn't think she could walk from the sidewalk. She caused something like twenty thousand dollars' worth of damage, and it turned out she was constipated. One suppository later, she felt fine, although I'm sure she didn't feel very good when the police showed up."

"Oh, gosh."

"You'd also be amazed how many people we get who have… various items… um, lodged in the rectum."

Chandler giggled. "Like what?"

"You name it. Candles are *really* popular. We had one guy who ended up needing surgery to remove a battery after it got too far in for him or his wife to retrieve. Word of advice. Don't stick things where they don't belong, and save yourself a trip to the hospital."

"Eeew. That's awful."

Tanner shrugged. "If nothing else, it makes for an interesting shift. Although I think the most interesting one recently was the meth head who tried escaping. Kid couldn't have been more than sixteen, so we were trying to get ahold of his parents and he ended up unattended. Piled stuff up and climbed up the wall into the ceiling. A drop ceiling. He made it about six feet away from where he started when he fell through the tile and ended up breaking his arm in four places and cracking two ribs."

"Ouch."

"Yeah. It's never dull, that's for sure."

Margo swallowed, then said, "Okay, who's next?"

Oren glanced at Chandler before sharing his tale. "I have one. The office building I work in has this courtyard in the middle of the building. Surrounded by one-way glass, so you can see out into the courtyard, but from there, you can't see into the building. There's one conference room against the courtyard. We had this big meeting and there were probably a hundred of us in the conference room, and of course, we're all staring out the window because those meetings suck. Wouldn't you know it, halfway through the meeting, one of our VPs and the vending machine guy walk into the courtyard. So now we're all watching because it's way more interesting than the profit and loss crap."

Margo's mouth dropped open. "What happened?"

"They start making out, so one of the guys gets up and runs down the hallway and bursts into the courtyard and tells them everybody can see them before it gets past being PG. The VP runs into the building and later that day, she resigned."

"That's definitely more interesting than profit and loss reports," Connor said.

"I felt really bad for her. Her husband died like a year

earlier, so I'm sure she was lonely. I don't think she would have had to resign, but I guess she couldn't face anybody."

"There's no way I could keep working there," Margo said. The third-hand mortification was bad enough.

Sarah said, "Didn't she have her own office? Probably should have gone there instead."

Oren nodded. "That's what we all said. There was even a whole floor of empty offices at the time."

They collectively shook their heads.

Chandler said, "My best story was when we had a drug bust back when I was working at McDonald's. It was just a regular day when this woman in the lobby screamed and when we looked, there were cops everywhere, guns drawn, yelling at everyone to get down. So we're all getting down on the ground – which is disgusting, by the way – and the guy on the fry station takes off running and tries to climb out the drive-thru window. Which he was selling drugs through. Unfortunately for him, he got stuck, giving the cops plenty of time to get him."

After another long break in the conversation, Chandler said, "Hey, what were everyone's winning trivia questions? Connor?"

Connor repeated his Dr. Seuss trivia question and answer. "Your turn," he said to Margo.

"What author sent a telegram that read 'Have changed my mind. Send manuscript back.'?"

The question was met with shrugs.

"Margaret Mitchell. She gave the *Gone With the Wind* manuscript to an editor at Macmillan, but later got cold feet and didn't want to publish it."

"No kidding," Sarah said.

Margo managed a small smile then said, "Tanner?"

"What was the original color of Dorothy's shoes in *The Wonderful Wizard of Oz*?"

"Red," Margo and Chandler answered in unison.

"Nope." Tanner shook his head. "Silver."

"I wonder how they turned into ruby slippers?" Connor asked.

Nobody had an answer for that, but Tanner suggested, "Maybe for the movie? Wasn't it one of the first Technicolor movies to be made?"

"It was in the 30s, so it had to be," Margo said.

Connor nodded. "That'd make sense. Red sequins would show up a lot better than silver."

After a beat, Tanner said, "Oren? Chandler? Sorry, I'm not sure which one of you won."

Oren lifted a hand. "I did."

Chandler grinned proudly. "It's a hard one, too."

"Which one of King Lear's daughters was murdered?" Oren asked the group.

"Shakespeare? I'm out." Tanner sat back.

"Me, too," Connor agreed.

Sarah shrugged. "I could probably answer a question about Macbeth, but I have no idea on King Lear."

"Cordelia. And no, I didn't Google it."

Margo said, "I'm impressed."

Murmurs of assent went around the table.

Chandler said, "Oren runs a Shakespeare acting troupe. They did sixteen plays over four years. One of the main actors got pregnant so they took a break, but they'll be performing Othello this November."

Oren blushed all the way to the tips of his ears and mumbled, "Yeah."

"No kidding," Connor said. "Let us know how to get tickets."

"Absolutely," Margo added.

Chandler rummaged in her purse and fished out business cards. "We have a website." She handed them out, beaming, while Oren continued to blush. It was adorable, the way they interacted. Not for the first time, Margo was glad to have met them.

The waiter came and cleared their empty plates.

"Dessert?"

A few minutes later, Margo was taking a second bite of the best strawberry cake she'd ever eaten.

"So Margo," Sarah began.

A tendril of suspicion turned the cake sour. She swallowed and took a sip of water.

"Tanner's done poetry readings."

Tanner scowled. "In college."

"Can you just imagine this deep baritone reading *Lady Chatterley's Lover*?"

Margo felt her face heat as embarrassment and irritation battled for top billing. "I'm pretty sure that's a novel, not poetry. Why don't you tell us about some of your adventures overseas?"

"I'd rather—"

"Sarah!" Tanner gave her a warning glare.

She huffed an annoyed breath and picked at her dessert while everyone else at the table awkwardly pretended nothing was happening.

Margo pushed her ruined cake away. She dreaded the ride back to the campground. She hadn't expected to be ambushed on the way to the restaurant, and she definitely hadn't expected Sarah to make comments at dinner, right in front of Connor.

As the group walked outside, Margo kept hold of Connor's hand. They reached his car and she felt him squeeze her fingers. She leaned over and gave him a quick kiss, then in response to his questioning look, quietly said, "I'll tell you later."

He nodded and let go of her hand.

Back at Sarah's car, she opted to ride in the back seat, giving Chandler the front.

"So? What did you think?" Sarah asked as they pulled out of the parking lot.

"Dinner was delicious," Margo responded.

Sarah was undeterred. "No, what did you think about Tanner? He didn't deny that he's interested in you."

"Can we not?"

Chandler said, "I don't think we need to beat this dead horse."

Sarah shrugged. "I don't see anything wrong with Margo being aware of her options."

Margo sighed and leaned back in her seat. "I'm not sure what they marinated the chicken in, but it was delicious. It might have been a Greek dressing."

Chandler went along with her. "That sounds delicious. My steak was perfectly cooked and the loaded potato was to die for."

"Oh, I see what we're doing. Okay, fine. The ribs were fall off the bone delectable. Can we get back to talking about men now?"

"No," Margo and Chandler said in unison.

Sarah huffed a little, then turned down the lane to the campground.

Margo couldn't wait to be out of the car.

"I'm sorry if I'm coming on a little strong. I just haven't seen my brother interested in anyone in a long time. It would be a shame for you to miss the opportunity to get to know him better. He's a great guy."

"I know that. Connor is also a great guy. There are a lot of great guys in the world."

"At least your family would approve of Tanner," Sarah joked as she parked the car.

Margo's chest constricted and her stomach clenched.

Chandler gasped. "That's super obnoxious."

The car was barely into the parking space before Margo unbuckled herself, pushed the door open, and jumped out. Connor's car was at the end of the lot, cruising toward a parking space. Without a glance back, she hurried out of the lot and to the path that would take her to her tent.

She heard the other car doors closing as she rounded the side of the lodge. Once she cleared the building, she speed-walked as fast as her strappy sandals would allow. The tents were barely in view when Scout spotted her and barreled toward her at a full sprint, his ears bouncing and tongue flapping out the side of his mouth.

She couldn't help but smile. The dog's presence melted some of the tension in her stomach. Hunkering down as Scout reached her, she scratched his ears and rubbed his neck while he licked her face. "Hey, buddy. Who's a good boy? Yes, you're such a good boy, aren't you?"

His tail wagged his whole body.

"I'll have to fill you in later," Margo said as she heard voices on the path behind her. She rose and walked into her tent, Scout on her heels.

She stayed at the nightstand, her back to the door, fiddling with the charger for her phone.

Sarah's voice came from her doorway. "I'm really sorry."

Margo turned. "About which part?" Her voice was steady, surprising herself.

Sarah looked mildly surprised, but her answer was honest. "The crack about your family. I know they're meddling, but I didn't realize it ran a lot deeper than that. My comment was uncalled for, and I apologize."

"It was. I accept your apology."

"I still think you and Tanner would be a good fit."

"You would be wrong. Don't bring it up again."

Sarah hesitated for a moment, then nodded. "Good night."

Margo turned back to the nightstand and plugged her phone in. She heard Sarah's footsteps, and although she knew her comments were mild, she still felt a little shaky. Standing up for herself wasn't exactly second nature.

A moment later, she tensed at more footsteps. Half expecting Sarah to come back and confront her again, she turned slowly. Instead, she came face to face with Chandler.

"You okay?" She sat on the edge of the bed.

Margo joined her. "Yeah. I guess I shouldn't have stomped off like that, but geez."

"No, you were fine. That was totally uncalled for."

"I hate confrontation. No matter how small."

"I've never really minded it." Chandler shrugged.

Margo envied the ability to be bold in the moment. "It's a gift. Be glad you have it."

"That was pretty ballsy, pushing Tanner at you like that. If he was that interested, he could have said something, and you could have politely declined, and both gone on your merry way without anybody knowing. It would have saved a lot of awkwardness. If that was my sister, I'd be livid."

Margo laughed. "That would be just another day for my older sister. Interference is to be gratefully accepted, and of course, followed."

"Of course."

"Because I'm too dumb to get through life on my own." She rolled her eyes.

"Aren't we all? My grandfather is the same way. I'm pretty sure he means well, but it gets old."

Connor appeared in the doorway. "Oh, sorry, I didn't know you had company."

Chandler jumped off the bed. "I was just leaving."

"Don't go on my account. I can come back later." He gave a half-smile. "I live right next door."

Chandler laughed. "I live right across the path." She patted his arm and saluted Margo. "Later, gator."

"After while, crocodile."

When she'd gone, Connor gestured to the edge of the bed. "May I?"

"Of course." Margo settled in near the pillows, one leg tucked under her, the other barely touching the floor. "What's up?"

He flopped onto his side, propping his head on his hand.

Scout jumped onto the bed and promptly curled up directly in the middle.

"Bed hog." Connor scratched his ears.

A moment passed before he spoke again. "What was that all about?"

"Oh, you mean the nightmare dinner?"

"Yeah. I wasn't expecting it to go anything like that."

Margo snorted. "You should have been in the car on the way over. I felt like a hostage."

"What happened?"

"As soon as we got in the car, Sarah started talking about how great Tanner is. I'm like, yeah, okay, and? Then she starts talking about how great it was that we worked so well together with Doug, blah blah blah. Which I didn't really want to talk about, but whatever. I'm guessing that she's hinting at something, and then she just goes all in. Starts telling me she hasn't heard Tanner talk about anyone in so long, but he talks about me."

"Huh." He sounded annoyed.

"Exactly. Chandler, who is so much better at tense conversations than I, told her to get to the point."

Connor chuckled. "That sounds about right."

"Then Sarah says she thinks Tanner and I would make a great couple. And I'm like, ummmm, I appreciate the thought, but no thanks. Then she got even pushier and says it's not like you and I are official or anything, so she doesn't see the problem."

"Nice."

"Yeah. And of course, by this point I'm so uncomfortable I can't think of a response, so I just freeze and clam up. Chandler told her to drop it, and we pulled into the parking lot before it could go any further than that."

"Which takes us to the supremely awkward dinner conversation."

"Yup. And then on the way home, I sat in the back, hoping she'd find something else to talk about. But she started in again right away, and the whole ride was miserable. Then, when we were coming down the lane, she told me to just think about it and I'm like no, not interested, and then she said at least my family would approve of Tanner."

"What?" He sat up. "That was a weird thing to say."

"That's exactly what Chandler said." She sighed, annoyed with herself. "I didn't say anything at all. I just got out of the car and practically ran to the tent. Why can't I speak up for myself? It shouldn't be so freaking hard."

"I don't like confrontation, either."

"She did stop by and apologize for the crack about my family but said she still believed I should talk to Tanner. I was actually so mad that I told her it wasn't going to happen, and not to bring it up again."

"Go you."

"Then I felt like I was going to throw up," she laughed.

"Baby steps."

"I guess so. It sucked. I thought tonight was going to be a fun dinner with some new friends and it ended up being an ambush. I was so uncomfortable all night."

"I think she's right –"

"What?" Margo nearly shrieked.

He held up a hand. " – that Tanner likes you. I've had that impression for a while. But I don't think he was too thrilled with his sister acting like she did at dinner. He doesn't seem like the type to get in the middle of something."

"Something." She raised an eyebrow. "Is that what we're calling it?"

"I don't know what we're calling it."

"But it's something."

He reached over and tucked a strand of hair behind her ear. "It's definitely something."

Margo leaned toward him, put her hands on his face, and pressed her lips to his. Yeah, it was definitely something.

# Chapter Twenty-Eight

Connor could easily spend the night kissing Margo. He could easily imagine plenty of other things, too, but for now, nothing sounded better than stretching out next to her and kissing. All night.

But he didn't want to push her. It was bad enough her family tried pushing Brad at her, and then Sarah – what the heck was *that* – pushing Tanner at her. No, Connor knew if he pushed, she'd end up shutting down and shutting him out. That was the last thing he wanted.

He pulled back and crawled up the bed so he was leaning against the wooden headboard. He held his arm out for Margo to snuggle next to him, which she did.

"I can't believe tomorrow's our last full day," he said.

"I know. I hope Doug's out of the hospital. I'm not sure I'd feel right leaving before he's home." She gave a small groan. "Of course it's not like it's so far away that I couldn't drop by and visit."

"Or call."

She looked up at him. "How pathetic is it that I hadn't thought of that?"

He laughed. "I wouldn't say pathetic."

"What would you say?"

"Hmm, maybe absentminded." To be honest, he had only just thought of it himself.

"That does sound better than pathetic. Although it makes me feel like I should be in a lab coat with wire-rimmed glasses that I can never find."

"A mad scientist?" She'd make a very sexy mad scientist, with a white lab coat buttoned up with nothing underneath, and she'd whip her glasses off and untie her hair and then… *Whoa, hit the brakes there, Skippy.*

"Yes. If I was going to be a scientist, I would definitely be a mad one. I'd have one of those laboratories with the beakers full of green liquids with puffs of smoke and lots of things bubbling."

"I think there's a slight possibility that you watch too much television."

"I hardly watch tv at all."

"I'm pretty sure that at some point in your life, you watched way too much tv."

"College. I always had it on for background noise while I was studying. I probably absorbed a lot of old horror movies. I probably watched Frankenstein a thousand times. The Boris Karloff version, of course."

"I can't say I've ever seen that one."

She pulled back, looking horrified. "Oh, that's something we need to rectify. You need to see it."

"Okay. I'll put it on the list." If she wanted him to sit through seven hours of animal psychic lectures, he'd do it if she was next to him.

"No. No list. You have to see it right away. How about Thursday? We can order a pizza."

"I can make that meatloaf with mac and cheese. No onions."

"Oooh, I forgot you promised me meatloaf. That sounds great. I'll bring the entertainment and the dessert."

He loved the way her face lit up talking about a date. "I hope it's not a VHS tape."

"I have the DVD. Or we can watch it on Netflix."

"That works. I'm not sure I even have a DVD player, and if I do, it's in a box somewhere."

"No problem. What do you want for dessert?"

"I'm not picky."

"There's a cheesecake recipe I've been wanting to try. I might as well do it while I'm still on vacation, right?"

"I love cheesecake."

"I should hope so. That would kind of be a dealbreaker. Only sociopaths don't like cheesecake."

Connor's fingers stroked her shoulder and played with her hair. "What are your other dealbreakers? Remember, I'm technically unemployed and have family issues."

She snorted. "I'd be a total hypocrite if family issues were a dealbreaker."

"But I have a *lot* of family issues."

"Are you trying to talk me out of wanting to spend time with you?" Her tone was light, but he knew the question was serious.

He tried keeping his own tone light. "Just making sure you know what you're getting into."

She squeezed him tighter and planted a quick kiss on his neck. "See, now I have the opposite strategy."

"What's that?"

"My plan was to be so charming and irresistible that you'd be hopelessly stuck by the time you found out all my issues."

She sighed heavily. "And then my family showed up and you saw all my dirty laundry right up front."

He kissed her forehead. "And here I am."

"Here you are. I can't figure out if you're patient and understanding, or some sort of masochistic weirdo who gets off on drama."

He burst out laughing. "Probably somewhere in the middle. Which way I lean depends on the day."

She was laughing, too.

"Should I head back to my own tent?" he asked, not that he was in any hurry to leave.

"Probably." Instead of moving, she lifted her face and kissed him.

"Then you should stop kissing me."

"You want me to stop?"

"Nope." He definitely did not want her to stop kissing him.

"But you think I should?"

Before he could filter his words, he said, "You *should* put your tongue back in my mouth."

She laughed and did exactly that, much to his happy surprise.

Connor pulled her tight against him and let his hands explore her back and arms and neck, while hers tangled in his hair. He had no idea how much time had passed when Scout interrupted them by woofing in his sleep, waking himself up, at which point he decided it was time to jump down and leave the tent.

"I suppose that's my cue to kick you out, huh?"

Connor ran his thumb over her lower lip. "Looks like it." He kissed her again, then reluctantly crawled out of the bed. Instead of leaving, he leaned down and kissed her again.

"You're not leaving."

"You're not helping."

She laughed. "Should I slap you? Call you a scoundrel and order you out of my bedchamber?"

"That's probably overkill."

"Scoundrel."

He chuckled against her mouth. "Okay, okay. I'm going before you slap me."

She pointed to the doorway. "Begone."

"I'm going."

"You're not moving." She drew her arm back and opened her palm. "Don't make me do it."

He sighed and straightened. "Going."

"See you in the morning."

Pausing by the doorway, he turned back and took in her relaxed position, laying on her side with her arm curled under her head, her hair spilled everywhere on the pillow, watching him with a faint smile on her face. "Good night." Walking back to his own tent was *not* what he wanted to do.

She wiggled her fingers at him.

Outside, he took a deep breath and blew it out. Scout bounded out from between the tents and jumped on the bed while Connor zipped the door closed. It was going to be even harder to climb out of Margo's arms when he had to get in his car and leave instead of just walking to the tent next door.

He flopped onto the sliver of bed Scout wasn't hogging, then used his hips to scoot the dog over.

Scout protested, sniffing loudly at the intrusion.

"Oh, hush." Connor reached over and scratched Scout's back.

Scout rolled so his belly was in the air.

Connor scratched his belly, and all was forgiven.

In the morning, Connor was surprised to find Margo's tent already open and empty. He showered and took a few minutes to trim his beard and comb his hair just so. Her tent was still empty.

He waited around for a few minutes, thinking she might be in the shower, but when Chandler came from that direction, she told him Margo wasn't there. He frowned a little, then frowned at himself. She didn't need to be with him twenty-four-seven.

Walking to the lodge, he went into the dining room and spotted her sitting at a table with her dad and Jean, holding a cup of coffee. She saw him and nodded in acknowledgment, but didn't smile.

He hesitated, debating whether to grab a plate and sit with her or find a spot across the room. In the end, he filled his plate and sat with Chandler and Oren.

"What's going on?" Oren asked.

"I have no idea." Connor kept glancing over but couldn't gather any clues from Margo's back.

Chandler raised one shoulder. "Maybe it's a good sign that she's talking to her family? I mean, her dad's finally making an appearance."

"Maybe. Hopefully. The last thing she needs is any more drama." He doubted it was good, whatever it was.

"Those people seem to feed on drama. Like drama vampires. It's where they get their powers."

Connor chuckled. "Very colorful." And accurate.

"What are you guys doing today? Are you doing the triathlon?"

"Are they still having it? I thought it might not happen."

Oren answered, "Yep. I saw Steven this morning. He was getting the canoes set up."

The camp version of a triathlon was a run, followed by a canoe ride, followed by a zombie obstacle course.

Their voices faded into the background as Connor stared

over at Margo. He tried sending a mental message for her to turn around, to look at him, to let him know that she was okay.

Margo's dad leaned over and said something in Jean's ear, then he got up and left, leaving Margo and Jean alone.

Connor itched to go over, but he stayed where he was. His breakfast lost all flavor and he pushed his plate away. Even the orange juice, normally delicious, tasted too sweet and too tangy on his tongue.

Jean looked over and caught him watching. She straightened her shoulders and raised her chin, a triumphant half-smile lifting the corner of her mouth. A moment later, she got up and walked away, leaving Margo alone with a pile of dirty dishes.

"Should I go over?" Connor said, talking mostly to himself.

Chandler put a hand on his arm. "Let me."

He wanted to protest, but said nothing as Chandler got up and walked over. She sat beside Margo and put her hand on her shoulder.

"This is driving me crazy," Connor said.

Oren made a sympathetic noise. "It's a shame."

Connor's eyes cut to his new friend, questioning.

"Her family's so manipulative and crazy. On the upside, they've given me a new appreciation for my family. And Chandler's. Margo's got to be a really strong person to be where she is all on her own."

"She's definitely strong. I wish I knew how to help her."

Oren made a face. "Can't help you there, buddy. Women are a mystery."

"I'm going over."

"You might want to wait a minute."

Connor looked over to see Chandler hugging Margo. He couldn't be sure, but it looked as if Margo's shoulders were shaking like she was crying.

"What did they do this time?" He waited until Chandler sat back in her seat, then got up and walked over, taking the chair on Margo's other side.

Margo's eyes were red and watery.

"What –"

She shook her head. "Not here." She got up, walked over to Chandler to hug her again, and walked fast toward the door.

Connor looked at Chandler with an unspoken question.

"She wouldn't say."

He jumped up and followed her. They walked to the tents in silence, but she did reach over and take his hand. That little gesture reassured him.

When they got to her tent, they sat on the rocking chairs on her little porch.

"What's going on?"

She opened her mouth, then snapped it back shut, her eyes filling with tears. She tried again. "I can't take it anymore. I don't know what to do, I don't understand any of this, I don't know what I ever did to deserve this kind of... I don't even know. I... I can't."

Connor left his chair and gently pushed her knees apart to kneel in front of her, pulling her into his arms. "Hey. It's okay."

She buried her face in his neck, her arms holding him tight. "It's not okay," she whispered. "None of this is okay."

The uneven board cut uncomfortably into his knee, but he wouldn't have moved for anything. He wanted to ask exactly what happened, but he stayed quiet, letting her put it together in her head. She'd tell him when she was ready.

"Can we go down to the river?" Her voice trembled.

"Of course." He stood up and pressed the back of her hand to his lips for a kiss. Scout appeared at her side like he knew where they were headed.

Margo dropped his hand and instead put her arm around

his waist. He draped his arm across her shoulders, glad for the closer contact, but concern gnawed at his insides. This felt like more than the typical stupidness he'd witnessed so far.

They reached the river and Margo led him to the fallen tree they'd been on many times. She settled onto the wood and when he was comfortable, she leaned against him and sighed. It sounded like frustration and resignation.

"They're packing right now. Hopefully, they're gone before lunchtime." She sounded tired.

"For real this time?"

She gave a humorless laugh. "For real."

He waited, wishing he could shoulder some of her load.

"They had a whole new tactic this time. Remember how I told you I paid for college and veterinary school myself?"

"Yeah?" This was starting off in an entirely unexpected direction.

"My dad and Jean offered to cut me a check for all that tuition. *And* a check to pay off the loans I took out to buy into the practice."

"That's a lot of money." His mouth went dry.

She snorted. "A *lot* of money."

"If they have that kind of money, why didn't they help you in the first place?"

"Good question."

"What's the catch?" he asked, although he could guess.

"That's another good question."

He closed his mouth, again waiting for her to put the story together in her own way.

"It's not a gift. It's never a gift. It's a tool to ensure they get what they want. To control me." She took a deep breath and blew it out.

Connor suspected he knew what was coming.

"The catch is that I get back together with Brad."

Whoa. Blindside.

He'd assumed they wanted her to cut contact with him, but actually get back with Brad? He had no idea how to respond, so he stayed quiet, rubbing her back and breathing. In and out.

"That's obviously never going to happen. We're not living in some medieval world where we have to form alliances with opposing houses through marriage. When I said as much, they said Tanner could be an acceptable substitute."

"What?"

"I know, right?"

Connor's mind was spinning. He wanted to punch someone or throw something. Who on earth did these people think they were? Margo was a grown woman. Successful. Smart. No, brilliant. Kind. Loving. Amazing. And they were such fools. Such stupid, short-sighted fools. Did they not understand they were pushing her away? If they didn't stop, they'd lose her for good.

She sniffled. "When I said I wasn't interested in Tanner, either, they agreed for half a second, then let me know that they were just trying to help guide me and that of course I didn't *have* to get back with Brad or date Tanner. I could date whomever I choose."

"As long as it's not me." *Assholes.*

"That's not all." She took another deep breath. "My dad handed me an envelope. The check was in it. I was holding it in my hands. Four hundred thousand dollars. I've never seen so much money at one time."

Connor's heart pounded. That was a life-changing amount of money. And they could just write a check?

"But just in case I was tempted to take the money and not follow through with their terms, they were thoughtful enough to include a contract. Short and sweet."

He swallowed hard. "They didn't." He could barely force the words out.

"Oh, did they ever. The money was mine, as long as I never entered into any kind of relationship with you."

"Margo…"

"No, stop. Whatever sacrificial thing you're about to say, save it. The bottom line is this has nothing to do with you, and everything to do with them wanting to control my life. And before you think I'm some kind of saint, you should know how tempting it was to sign my name and walk away from you."

That stung a little more than he cared to admit, but the truth was, she was right. This wasn't about him at all. If it wasn't him, it would be something else. She could have the money, but never move out of Hickory Hollow. Never dye her hair again. Never get a tattoo. Take out her belly ring. Never drive a Toyota. Whatever. It would hang over her head forever. It was disgusting.

"I handed the envelope back to my dad and told him I wasn't for sale. He called me ungrateful and…" She let out a shuddering breath. "He said I needed to think about whether I wanted a place in this family."

Connor's jaw clenched.

"Why would I want to be part of a family that doesn't want me? Unless I toe the line, of course. I don't understand why they can't accept me for who I am. I don't think I'm all that bad."

He squeezed her close. "You're amazing. You take my breath away, and I wouldn't ever want you to change a thing. I don't understand them, and quite frankly, I don't understand where you get the strength to stand up for yourself. Most people would be more than willing to go along just to keep the peace. I'm in awe of you."

"I don't feel very strong, or like I stand up for myself. In fact, I really just want to curl up under the covers and cry."

He wished she could see herself the way he saw her right now. "Margo, you just walked away from almost half a million dollars. If that's not strong, I don't know what is. Connor didn't have any more words, so he kissed her instead, hopefully letting her see that he was there for her. Her mouth was soft and warm, and after a moment, it was the only thing that existed – or mattered – in the world. Her, clinging to him, letting him see this vulnerable side of her.

Their moment was interrupted by Scout barking at something in the water.

Reluctantly, Connor pulled back. "He's worse than a kid."

Margo chuckled and sat up straight. She called to Scout, "What are you barking at, goofball?"

Scout wagged his tail and ran over, then shook, sending a spray of water droplets over them.

Margo squealed and held her hand up to keep the water from her face. "Thanks."

Connor wiped the water off his arms. "Keep it up, dog, and you'll be in big trouble."

Scout wagged his tail harder, clearly not worried about the idle threat.

"When does the triathlon start?" Margo asked.

"Ten." He looked at his watch. "We should probably head to the starting line. Unless you didn't want..."

"No. No, no, no." She held up a hand. "I want to do a triathlon and stop wallowing in my personal toxic cesspool of ridiculousness."

They got up and he reached for her hand, but Margo was pulling an elastic band off her wrist. She pulled her hair back and tied it while they walked. When she let go, the long pony-tail swung across her back, half a dozen shades of dark brown to light blonde streaks mingling. Connor still couldn't figure out why anyone had a problem with her pretty hair. They were all just nuts and he was sick of spending mental energy on them after a few days. He couldn't begin to imagine how tired Margo was.

The triathlon was set up near the mouth of the walking trail. An inflatable arch marked the official starting line, where thirty-some people were gathered. A grin spread across Connor's face. "Margo, look."

A man occupied a folding chair that was set up next to the inflatable.

"Doug!" Margo jogged over and leaned in to give him a hug.

Connor did the same, clapping his hand on Doug's shoulder. "So glad to see you back. How are you doing?"

"Good." He rolled his eyes and gestured to the activity. "I'm not allowed to help. Bonnie says I'll be allowed to say 'Ready, Set, Go,' but I'm not sure she'll end up letting me. Might be too strenuous," he joked, tapping the bandage on his throat.

Margo said, "It's so great to see you. How are you feeling?"

"Great. The most painful part is the check I have to write to the pest place. They relocated the hornets and searched for other nests."

"Where was it?"

"In the ground, can you believe it? I ran the mower over it and the noise or vibration or something stirred them up and they came blasting out of the hole and attacked me. Bonnie was running the weedwhacker and saw me run. Thank God she was there."

Margo's hand went to her throat. Connor squeezed his shoulder again. Poor guy must have been terrified.

Doug glanced at his watch. "Hey, you guys better get in place."

Bonnie came over and shooed them to the starting line with the other people, including Oren and Chandler and Tanner and Sarah. "Alrighty, folks, we're starting with a half-mile run through this dangerous terrain that comes out at the boat dock. There, you'll put on your life jackets, then take the boat about quarter mile to the marker, dock, leave your life jackets, then go through the obstacle course, where you'll be leaping through flames and battling a horde of hungry zombies. Everybody ready?"

"Ready!"

"Doug?" she said. "Do the honors."

"On your mark! Get set!" He paused for effect. "GO!" He blew a whistle, loud and shrill.

Everyone took off into the woods, not exactly racing, but not hanging back. Margo and Connor settled in the middle of the pack, in an easy jog.

The 'dangerous terrain' was flat and wide. The leaves from the trees shaded the path, making it a nice cool jog. They reached the boats, and Margo hesitated. Connor touched her back. "We don't have to get in the water if you don't want to."

The river was higher and faster than it had been, due to an overnight rain.

"It's okay." Her voice was unsteady.

"I'm serious. We can walk along the bank to the dock and then just do the obstacle course. It's not a big deal."

"No, let's go." She pulled her life jacket over her head.

Connor fastened her straps and kissed her forehead. "It's a really quick trip. Look." He pointed down the river. "They're already getting out."

She looked relieved. "Oh. A quarter-mile sounds a lot farther than that."

Connor held the boat steady while she climbed in the front. He got in and pushed off with his oar. "Here we go."

Margo paddled, stroking her oar in and out, switching sides with every stroke, while Connor steered them from the back.

The water flowed fast, and they quickly arrived at the dock along with two other canoes. Connor steered them to shore and jumped out into water that was knee-deep.

Margo jumped out and grabbed the other side of the boat, pulling it to shore. They took off their jackets and tossed them into the boat, then ran along the flags marking the way to the obstacle course. Once there, they were handed a belt with three tear-off flags, which they fastened around their waists.

The obstacle course was a maze of rope bridges through the woods, coming out to a plank wall, a pit of mud, and a tire and fire run. Instead of jumping over fire, torches blazed beside the tires.

"Ready?"

"Already gone," Margo yelled, climbing up the tree ladder to the first rope bridge.

Connor followed her as she skittered across like a spider monkey. He swayed and tried to keep his balance as he hurried across. Margo was already at the plank wall. She grabbed the rope and walked her feet up the ten-foot wall, threw her leg over the top, and grinned down at him. "Try to keep up," she challenged.

Connor scaled the wall and jumped to the ground below, passing her on the way to the tire run. He ran through, one foot in each tire's center, until a pair of hands grabbed one of the flags on his waist.

Margo shrieked. "Zombies!"

Costumed people growled and swatted at them, trying to grab the rest of their flags.

They dashed out of the tires and toward the mud pit.

"There's a horde!" Margo yelled. "On the left!"

Connor lurched to the right and they reached the mud at the same time. The mud pit was about four yards long and covered by a makeshift chicken wire roof, forcing them to their hands and knees to crawl through sticky mud several inches deep.

"I'm glad these are old shoes," Connor said.

"Go, go, go, they're coming!" Margo pushed his back, ending his hesitation.

He dove into the mud and crawled forward. "Where are you?" he yelled.

Laughing, she answered, "They got me! Save yourself!"

He emerged on the other side and reached back, grabbing her muddy hands and pulling her to her feet. A loud growl at his side startled him and the sound of his second flag being torn from his belt joined it. "Aw, man."

They avoided the next horde, clumps of mud falling off their shoes and clothes as they ran.

"There's the finish line!"

Just before the line, a zombie snagged another flag from Margo. They both crossed the line with one flag left.

"That was awesome!" Margo jumped into his muddy arms.

He lifted her and she wrapped her legs around his waist. Reluctantly, he set her back on her feet, a grin plastered to his face.

Doug manned the finish line, cheering for everyone as they crossed. "Ah, you each have one flag left." He stepped over to the table that was set up with cups of water and reached into a box marked "Survivors." He pulled out two medals on long ribbons, handing one to each of them. "Congratulations, you didn't lose all your flags, thereby becoming infected with the zombie virus."

Connor put his medal over his head and pumped his fist in the air. "Yeah!"

Margo lifted her hands and gave him a double high five. "You can totally be my partner in the apocalypse."

Doug pointed them to a hose so they could spray the mud off.

Oren and Chandler came over. Laughing, Chandler said, "Hey, think I can join you guys when the world ends? Poor Oren isn't going to be much help."

Sheepish, he held up his "Infected" medal. "They got me."

Chandler snorted. "On the first obstacle."

"Ouch," Connor said.

Margo asked, "How many flags did you end up with?"

Chandler grinned. "All three."

"Yeah, she sacrificed me to save herself."

Chandler shrugged. "Alls fair in love and the undead."

"If I ever turn into a zombie for real, I'm biting your sorry ass," Oren grumbled and flicked water at her.

"If you can catch me. I'm guessing I'll be okay," she joked, kissing his cheek.

More cheers pulled their attention back to the finish line, where a couple they didn't recognize crossed and collected their medals.

Sarah joined them, showing off her Survivor medal. Tanner sheepishly held up his Infected medal.

Chandler clucked her tongue. "Oh, Tanner, how disappointing. Your medical skills could have really helped us."

He shrugged. "Sorry, guys. I better start training so I'm ready for the real zombie apocalypse."

Sarah sprayed the mud off her shoes. "That was so much fun."

"It was," the other members of their group agreed.

Connor glanced around at everyone. Comfortable warmth filled his heart. This had been an amazing week, and he was glad to have met these people. Okay, could have lived without

Sarah's nonsense, but aside from that, he liked them all. He wished Shane would have stuck around, too.

Margo put her arm around his waist.

Connor asked, "When's the reporter coming?"

Sarah said, "Six."

"It was really smart, arranging to have the paper come talk to us," Tanner said.

Oren nodded. "I hope the article brings in more business. This is a great place."

In total agreement, they all milled away from the course, heading toward the tents and going their separate ways.

Connor stopped in front of his tent and kissed Margo. "I'm going to hit the showers."

"Me, too. I even got mud in my hair." She laughed, holding up the mud-caked tip of her ponytail.

"You got a spot here, too," Connor said, wiping her cheek.

"I've got it everywhere. *Everywhere.*" She made a face.

Connor had the same sentiment. Which is why he really, really wanted to get in the shower.

A little while later, they met back at Margo's tent, fresh and mud-free. Connor patted his stomach. "Lunch?"

"Yes."

After lunch, they packed in a trip to the river for Scout and a rousing game of mini-golf. Margo won, of course, but only because Connor let her. Well, that's the story he was sticking to.

# Chapter Twenty-Nine

The reporter smiled, asking them to bunch closer together so she could take a picture of the contest winners with Doug and Bonnie. After she took a few photos, she put the camera back into its bag and took out a notebook and a pen.

An hour later, Margo's face and stomach ached from smiling and laughing so much. The reporter had started with some easy questions, then briefly touched on Doug's incident before leading them to talk about all the things Doug and Bonnie wanted to feature about the campground.

"Is there anything else you want to add? Anything I might not have touched on?"

Margo looked around the group, waiting to see if anyone had anything to say. "I just wanted to say that Doug and Bonnie put together a wonderful trip for us. I had an amazing time, and the best part is that I've met some incredible people who will be friends for years." *And some who won't,* she thought as Sarah said something to the reporter.

Chandler nodded and reached over to squeeze Margo's hand. "Ditto. I'm so thankful for this opportunity to have made some wonderful new friends."

Heads nodded all around the group.

The reporter smiled, "Aww, this is such a great story. Infinitely more interesting than the council meeting I covered last night," she joked. "I think I have everything I need, but if you think of anything else you want to add, shoot me an email anytime up until noon tomorrow, okay?" She handed out business cards to everyone and shook hands.

Bonnie hugged her. "Thank you so much. We're glad you came to do the story."

"Thanks for inviting me. We love these kinds of local stories, and my kids will be thrilled to know the mini-golf is open to the public. I'll definitely be bringing the whole family for a few rounds. All the local merchandise in your gift shop is fantastic, so I'll be sure to mention that several times."

Doug nodded and shook her hand. "We'd appreciate it very much."

The reporter was walking back toward her car when a long, distressed, loud howl came from the tent area, followed by frantic barking and something crashing through the brush.

"Scout!" Connor ran toward the sound but had only gotten a few steps when Scout burst out of the bushes, half a football field away from them, alternately running and stopping to rub his face on the ground.

Margo raced toward him, her heart pounding. The poor dog was obviously in distress. She prayed it wasn't serious. Half a second later, the pungent stench reached her.

Behind them, someone yelled, "What's wrong with – oh, crap. Skunk!"

A reeking cloud rolled over the group, stinging everyone's eyes. Retching, everyone except Margo and Connor made a beeline for the far side of the field.

Connor was next to Scout, holding his shirt over his face,

his eyes red and watering. He looked back to Margo, helpless. Scout whined and yelped, drooling excessively.

Covering her own mouth and nose, not that it helped much, she reached the upset dog. "Let's get him to the river and wash off as much as we can."

Scout whined again and swiped at his face with his paw.

"C'mon, Scout." Connor snapped his fingers. "Let's go, boy."

Scout reluctantly got up and followed Connor.

They took off at a steady jog toward the river. Margo followed close behind until they reached the water's edge. Scout wasn't interested in getting in. He whined and lifted his paw.

"C'mon, buddy, we'll at least get you rinsed off," Margo said, grateful he was as obedient as he was. Her eyes stung, and the back of her throat was on fire.

Connor gagged, then asked, "Should I go buy tomato juice?"

Margo waded into the water and coaxed Scout to follow her. He leaned against her leg. She fought the stench and reached down to scoop handfuls of water over his coat. "No. Tomato juice doesn't really work."

"What does?"

She managed to smirk through the smell. "Douche."

"Seriously? It's not *my* fault he got sprayed." Connor coughed.

The pungent stench lost a tiny fraction of its power as the water rinsed some of the oily skunk spray away. "No, feminine douche. The actual women's product."

"You've got to be joking."

"If only."

"You want me to go buy douche."

Margo rolled her stinging, watery eyes. "Yeah, and pick me

up a box of tampons. Quit being a baby and go! It's the best thing to get the oils off the dog."

"What about a shampoo?"

She snapped, "Get whatever you want, just freaking go do it." The stench was attaching itself to her skin and clothes. Not fun.

Connor groaned and took off toward the tents.

The closest store was a quick five-minute drive, so Margo estimated she'd be stuck with the stinking dog for under a half-hour. Her plan was to keep him in the river.

As the water tempered some of the spray, Scout acted more like his normal self, giving Margo the opportunity to get a closer look at him. Her biggest fear was that he'd been sprayed in the eyes, but it appeared he'd taken the hit on his neck and shoulder. "Silly boy, never tangle with a skunk."

It felt like forever until Connor returned with a plastic bag and an armful of towels. "Doug gave me these on my way past," he said.

"Great." Margo was tired of standing in the river. It was starting to get dark, and slimy things brushed against her legs.

Sheepish, he opened the packages of douche and carried the bottles into the river to his dog. "Now what?"

"Just like shampoo."

They scrubbed the dog several times, using all five bottles of douche.

"This is really weird."

Margo laughed at him, standing in the river with empty douche bottles stuck in every pocket of his shorts. "But it's working." The smell was definitely fading.

"I also got shampoo, just in case."

"What, you don't want Scout to smell like a fresh mountain spring?" She rolled her eyes.

"I'm pretty sure that's not what a fresh mountain spring

smells like. And even if it was, why would a woman want to smell like a mountain spring?" He shook his head and blushed bright red. "Pretend I didn't just say that."

Margo cracked up. "Why would I do that? It's a valid question. I suppose that in some corporate office somewhere in the dark ages, men in suits decided that women shouldn't smell like women. Did you know they used to market Lysol as a safe and effective way for ladies to douche?"

"I did not know that." He looked horrified.

She wasn't sure if he was uncomfortable about the cleaning product specifically or talking about douching. Either way, she was having a lot of fun with his blushing. "Personally, I think if your vagina smells like a mountain spring flowing with Lysol, you should probably see a doctor."

Connor snorted and laughed. And laughed.

After a moment, Margo couldn't help but laugh herself.

They stood together, laughing while they rinsed douche off a skunk-sprayed dog.

They led Scout to the shore, where Connor wiped him off with the towels Doug had given him, then gathered all the trash back into the plastic bag. "Here, lemme smell you."

Scout wagged his tail and licked Connor's face. He was clearly feeling better.

"I'm not sure if it's gone, or if I just stopped smelling it."

"I think it's pretty well gone. Skunk is pretty hard to go nose blind to."

Connor shrugged. "I'm going to shampoo him anyway."

"Restore his masculinity?"

"Exactly." Connor took Scout back into the water and shampooed him.

Margo sat on the bank and watched the suds ride the current into the darkness.

A few minutes later, Scout ran over to her. She rubbed him

with a towel while he leaned into her, enjoying the attention. "Who's a good boy? Actually, who's a bad boy? You're lucky it wasn't any worse than it was."

Scout wagged his tail, agreeing with her.

"No more skunks."

Wag, wag.

Margo kissed his nose. "Rotten little beast," she said affectionately.

"Since it's our last night here, I think Scout should have a special treat and sleep with you."

Margo laughed. "No freaking way. Nice try, though."

"Let's get to the bonfire before all the marshmallows are taken."

"Make sure your dog follows you so he doesn't get the bright idea to get into bed while he's still dripping wet."

"I don't mind if he does."

Margo pretended to glare. "Because he'd pick my bed?"

"What? Nooo, that had nothing to do with it." He attempted an innocent look but missed the mark.

"Yeah, okay. If you say so."

They went back to their tents and changed into dry clothes that didn't smell like skunk, then went to the bonfire. She convinced Scout to come along with them. He stretched out on the ground behind their lawn chairs. A few minutes later, Oren and Chandler sat next to them.

A couple of the other campers made jokes about Scout's skunk encounter and Connor's subsequent shopping trip for douche.

"While I'm thinking of it, we need to exchange phone numbers," Chandler said to Margo.

"Definitely. My phone's back at the tent. I don't remember a time I was able to walk out of a room without it and not panic." It was freeing. She hoped she could keep it up at home and not rely so much on having her phone on her at all times.

"Ugh, tell me about it. I'm dreading the idea of having it reattached to my hand once we go back to real life."

Margo let out a happy sigh. "I still have a week of vacation left. They practically forced me to take two full weeks. At first, I was really freaking out, but now I'm looking forward to having the time to just putter around the house and do whatever I feel like doing."

Chandler sighed. "That sounds great. I'm off tomorrow, then it's back to work for both of us. What about you?" She asked Connor.

"I start my new job at Hansen Engineering in about a week and a half."

"Oh, nice. So you get another week to woo our Margo."

Margo giggled and looked at Connor. Was he blushing? "Woo? Did you actually say he could 'woo' me?"

"Woo is a perfectly good word that's fallen out of fashion. I think we should bring it back. Now quit changing the subject."

Connor groaned. "Can we talk about something else?"

"Nope." Chandler shook her head. "Now what's your plan?"

"I have a plan?"

"You need a plan."

Margo put her head in her hand. "Chandler, please."

Chandler ignored her and raised an eyebrow at Connor.

It was funny, watching Chandler back Connor into a corner.

"My 'plan' is to call her and see if she wants to go out while she's still on vacation."

"Out? Out where? To do what? Just going for food isn't going to cut it. And movies are too easy."

"Wow, you just eliminated ninety percent of my options."

Margo reached over and grabbed his hand. "Movies are good. We already have plans for Thursday to watch Frankenstein while Connor makes me dinner."

Chandler grinned. "Oooh, a nice romantic evening at home." She nudged Oren's arm. "You hearing this?"

"Yes, dear."

"What are you making for this dinner?"

Connor answered, "Meatloaf with mac and cheese."

"Meatloaf? That's not very romantic."

Margo shook her head. "Uh-uh. Meatloaf is perfect. Macaroni and cheese is also perfect." She turned to Connor. "Don't listen to her. She probably demands lobster tail and caviar from poor Oren."

Oren piped up. "Exactly."

Chandler laughed. "Okay, okay, you got me. Babe, if you make me meatloaf and mac and cheese, I will be a happy woman."

Oren pretended to write a note on his hand. "I promise to make you meatloaf. But I'm making mashed potatoes."

"Mashed potatoes are my favorite."

He wiggled his eyebrows at his wife. "I know. That's why I picked them."

"You know me so well." She turned her attention back to Margo. "What time are you heading out tomorrow?"

"Sometime in the morning. I'd guess around eight or nine at the latest. I'm not going to bother packing until I get up."

"Please don't leave before we get to exchange phone numbers."

Margo squeezed her new friend's hand. "I won't."

They all lapsed into a comfortable silence, watching the logs glow in the bonfire, each lost in their own thoughts. Margo leaned over and rested her head on Connor's shoulder. It was slightly uncomfortable across the arms of the chairs, but he kissed her head and leaned his cheek against her hair, and she wouldn't have moved for the world.

It could have been an hour or it could have been three by the time the fire started dying down. Connor squeezed her hand and she sat up, ready to go to bed, but not ready for this vacation to be over.

They walked back to the tents, hand in hand, then stopped in front of Margo's. Scout paused, then trotted to Connor's tent and disappeared inside. She wrapped her arms around Connor's waist. "See you in the morning."

Instead of answering, he kissed her, long and sweet and soft. When he finally pulled back, she sighed in protest. He planted another quick kiss on her lips. "Sleep well."

She nodded, then went into her tent and zipped it shut. She changed quickly and fell into bed, asleep in minutes.

She woke with the birds, who were loud and enthusiastic, right outside her tent window. Stretching, she sighed, content. As much as she didn't look forward to packing, or leaving, she did look forward to spending time with Connor out in the real world and seeing where this relationship was headed.

Hefting her suitcase onto the bed, Margo debated packing before or after her shower. She decided to shower and change first, then try to fit everything back into the suitcase.

Not too much later, she stood back in front of the bed, her hands on her hips, a towel wrapped around her wet hair, as she looked around, deciding the best attack strategy.

"Hey!"

She jumped at the voice.

Chandler laughed. "Sorry, I won't keep you from your packing. I just wanted to give you this." She handed Margo a business card with her personal information scrawled on the back.

"Fantastic, hang on. Oh. Crap. My purse is in my car. Let

me see what's in here." Margo found an old receipt in the pocket of her suitcase and wrote her cell number and email on the back.

Chandler made a sad face. "I'll miss this place. We'll do lunch. Soon."

"Absolutely."

Chandler grabbed her in a tight hug. "Take care."

"You, too."

As Chandler left, Margo felt tears pricking the backs of her eyes. In spite of the drama, she was going to miss this trip, these people.

She was *not* going to miss being in such close proximity to her family. She hoped that Elliott made good on his promise that he and Ashley wouldn't be vacationing with the rest of the clan again. She could happily imagine taking trips with her younger sister's family... but not the rest of them. Not with Connor.

It was awfully easy to see future trips with him. Hiking the Appalachian Trail, sitting on a beach somewhere, bundling up in a ski resort before heading down the slopes...

She shook her head. She had no idea what the future held for them. Not even the *near* future. There was no sense in indulging in these fantasies. Not when there was packing that needed her attention.

Resolved, she folded her clothes and put them in the suitcase.

# Chapter Thirty

Connor poked Scout. "Hey. Hey. Hey. Time to get up."

Scout scrooched and snuffed at him.

"Is that annoying? Trust me, it's not as bad as being kicked in the back all night." He poked him again.

Scout shot him a filthy look and slunk down off the bed.

"Oh, now you're offended, huh? Shoulda thought of that when you were kicking me." Connor got up and rubbed his face. "When we get home, I'm not letting you sleep in my bed."

Scout wagged his tail. Rules were made to be broken.

"Whatever. You'll see."

He tossed his duffel bag onto the bed and stuffed clothes into it, then unzipped the tent door.

Scout ran outside and around the back of the tent to do his business.

"Good plan." Connor took his stuff to the shower room, showered, and messed with his hair and beard until he was satisfied.

Back in his tent, he packed the rest of his stuff, then carried the bags to his car, picking up Scout's abandoned tennis balls along the way. After double-checking he'd gotten everything from his tent, he went next door.

"Can I help with your bags?"

Margo greeted him with a brilliant smile. "Absolutely. I'm almost done."

He looked into her suitcase and laughed. "Wow, I just threw everything in my bag. You're way too organized."

"Yeah, but this way I don't have a mess when I get home."

"Yeah, whatever. You keep your crazy logic to yourself. I figure it's all going into the laundry anyway, no point in folding it and making it nice."

"See? You have your own kind of crazy logic. Whatever works."

"Are you always so neat?"

"I'm pretty organized."

"Oh." He scrunched up his face. "Are you OCD, like messes in other people's houses make you crazy to where you start cleaning and putting stuff away?"

"No."

"Well, that's kind of disappointing. I guess I have some work to do before Thursday."

Margo laughed. "As long as you're not on the short-list to star in an episode of Hoarders, it's fine."

"No, nothing like that. But I'm pretty sure I could make a whole new dog from the hair on my couch. I hope that doesn't bother you."

She laughed again and held out her hand to shake his. "Have we met? Hi, I'm Margo. I'm a veterinarian. I spend my days covered in animal hair, fur, saliva, urine, feces, sometimes blood. And the occasional feather. Oh, and skunk spray."

Connor shook her hand and grinned. His house was nothing terrible. And nothing great. He still had moving boxes in nearly every room, and the furniture was all second hand, left by the previous owner. He'd agreed to buy it, to save them the expense of moving it, and himself the expense of buying new stuff. Now he was second-guessing. He hadn't considered that he'd have a woman over that he wanted to impress. Of course, when he'd bought the house, he was pretty sure he'd never want to speak to another woman, let alone impress one.

"Okay, okay. So I won't worry about the dog hair."

"Don't worry about anything. I'm sure your place is nice."

"It's not bad. But it's nothing fancy."

"I'm not a fancy kind of girl." She cocked her head, her eyebrows furrowed. "Connor, I'm serious."

"I know." He cleared his throat. "Is anything ready to take to the car?" He tried pushing the negative thoughts out of his head – the ones reminding him that Brad probably had brand new, state of the art everything, with stainless steel appliances and granite countertops and perfectly clean floors.

Margo handed him one of her bags, and her smile reminded him that even if Brad had a ten thousand square foot house with a butler and a maid and solid gold toilets, it didn't matter. She was standing in front of *him*, making plans with *him*. Brad wasn't on her mind, so why was he on his? Time to let that one go.

"This will just take a second, I'm almost done."

"Okay." Connor watched her fill the suitcase. Two minutes later, she flipped it shut and zipped it.

"That was more than a second."

"Ha, ha."

He lifted it off the bed and set it on the floor. "Ready?"

"Ready." She picked up a small bag and looked around the room. "I'm kind of sad about leaving."

"Me, too. It's been a great vacation."

"Mostly."

He grabbed her hand. "Great vacation. Period."

"Okay."

They took her bags to the parking lot and arranged them in the back of her SUV.

"You said your car was a mess. Looks clean to me."

"Clean? Only the back. And only because I can't pitch to-go containers that far."

Connor laughed. "I did not expect that answer."

"I'm serious." She hit the button to unlock the doors of her SUV, then opened the back door. "See?"

"Wow." He was surprised to see at least half a dozen fast food bags on the floor. "I am shocked. I expected it to be spotless."

"Spotless?" Margo snorted. "I wasn't kidding about my car. Every three months or so, I take it to the car wash and clean it inside and out. That's as close as it ever gets to spotless. I'm much better about cleaning the house, though."

"I feel a lot better now. Even I throw away my take out containers every time I go into the house."

She closed the door and pressed the button to lock the doors. "I guess we should go check out, huh?"

"Did you talk to Chandler?"

"Yes, she stopped by this morning."

Connor nodded. "Good. I should exchange numbers with Oren before we go."

"They're already gone."

"Oh." Connor was disappointed. He didn't meet a lot of guys he'd consider befriending on more than a superficial level, and he could definitely see spending time with Oren. It was especially easy to imagine them hanging out as couples.

He swallowed hard. He was getting ahead of himself, by a *lot*, if he was already thinking of them as a couple.

Margo grabbed his hand. "Let's double-check the tents to make sure we didn't forget anything, and we'll see if they're still here. Did you want to take Scout to the river again, or was last night's skunk river adventure enough?"

He laughed. "That was enough. I don't relish the smell of wet dog in my car."

"It beats fresh skunk."

"Not by much."

She laughed and they walked back to the tents. Margo had left her phone charger plugged in. She rescued it and shoved it into the back pocket of her jean shorts. Connor's tent was bare.

Margo raised her eyebrows. "See? I'm the one who almost left something behind. You want to tell me again how organized I am?"

"You're kind of a hot mess."

She laughed loud. "I tried telling you that."

Tanner and Sarah met them on the path. They exchanged hugs and niceties for a few minutes. They were nice enough, but Connor didn't feel much as they headed away.

"Now I just have to find my dog." Connor stood in the middle of the path and whistled. A moment later, the brush rustled, and Scout bounded through, smiling his happy doggy grin.

"Uh-oh. He looks wet."

"Crap." Connor put his hands on his hips. "Were you in the river?"

Scout trotted over, grinning and furiously wagging his tail. He leaned against Connor's leg and waited for his head to be scratched.

Connor sighed. "Really? I just told Margo I didn't want my car smelling like wet dog. You're in big trouble."

Scout's ears were perked as if he understood every word. And didn't really care.

"C'mon, brat, let's see if we can get a towel for you."

Scout happily followed them back to the lodge and flopped down on the front porch. He yawned and promptly dozed off.

Connor and Margo went inside.

Bonnie rounded the counter and grabbed Margo in a hug. "I hate to see you leave. Promise you'll be back." She let go of Margo and hugged Connor. "Both of you."

"Of course. I hope the article drums up some new business for you." He meant it. They had a wonderful facility, and it should be booked full all season long.

"I'm sure it will. It's been a pleasure, we hope you had a good time."

"The best."

Bonnie looked like she was trying not to cry.

Connor said, "I hate to be a pest, but do you happen to have one of those old towels we used last night for the skunk incident? Scout decided to go swimming, so I'd like to towel him off before we head out. If it's not too much trouble."

"None at all. Just a second." She disappeared into a side room and came back with an old towel and a ratty blanket. "Here, just take them to protect your seat. We have tons. We keep the old stuff when we change out the bedding in the cabins. Comes in handy on occasions just like this."

"Thanks, I really appreciate it."

Doug came in the front door and hugged them both. "Thanks so much for staying with us. We hope you'll be back." He grinned. "Maybe for your honeymoon."

Bonnie elbowed him in the side. "Douglas!"

He shrugged. "Hey, you never know, right? And remember, Margo, your stay will be free."

Margo raised her hands in surrender. "Whatever you say, Doug. Stay away from the bees."

Laughing, they left the lodge. Margo held the blanket while

Connor toweled off the dog. "Yeah, you think this is great, don't you?"

Scout grinned in agreement. Being rubbed with a towel was one of his favorite things ever.

Connor clipped a leash to Scout's collar. "Back to the real world, buddy." They walked to the parking lot, and Margo arranged the blanket across the backseat. Scout jumped in and sat down, waiting for Connor to start the magical window breeze.

Connor shut the door and tapped his key against his palm. "So."

"So."

"It's going to be weird not seeing you this evening." He wasn't looking forward to it.

Margo nodded. "I know."

"I'm not sure if I should ask you to dinner, or if we should do our own thing tonight."

"I know. I was thinking the same thing."

"What did you decide?" Connor hoped she wanted to see him.

"Well… we gotta eat, right?"

"Right."

She crossed her arms and looked toward the sky as if contemplating the situation. "I personally don't have any groceries at home, so I'll need to go out to get something."

"Me, too." He liked where this was going.

"If we just happen to run into each other somewhere, then it doesn't really count as a date, right?"

He pulled her into his arms. "I was thinking I might end up at Gino's Sub Shop around six?"

"Wow, that's such a coincidence. I was probably going to Gino's around six-thirty."

"Now that you mention it, I'll probably run a little later than six. Maybe we'll bump into each other."

She grinned. "Maybe we will."

Connor kissed her. When she pulled back, he said, "I'm looking forward to maybe running into you this evening."

"I might be looking forward to it, too."

Scout barked, his nose already leaving wet marks on the window.

"Gotta go, the chaperone is getting antsy."

# Chapter Thirty-One

Margo turned the radio up and rolled the windows down for the drive home. Stopped at a red light, she belted out the song on the radio, not caring whether anyone could hear her or not. Jean would be mortified.

Suddenly, she felt a wave of pity for her. Did she take joy in *anything*? Certainly not in singing or laughing or doing anything that she deemed embarrassing. What were her passions? Did she have any, or was she so busy being overinvolved in her stepdaughters' lives that she never found anything to enjoy?

The next time they talked, she'd ask. It would undoubtedly end up in some sort of argument or snotty comments, but maybe it would inspire her to find something to do. Something that didn't involve micromanaging anyone. Okay, she knew that was a pipe dream, but she could wish.

One thing was certain. Margo was going to live her life. She loved her job, she loved her patients. This week, she'd rediscovered that she loved being outdoors. She loved being on vacation and not… the thought stopped her short and she nearly braked the car. Glancing in the rearview mirror, she breathed a sigh of relief that no one was behind her.

She loved not micromanaging her staff.

Ouch.

She wouldn't have labeled herself a micromanager until this very moment, but would her staff? That stung. Eew. She scrunched up her face. She'd been doing to her staff what Jean had been doing to her, on a much smaller scale. Not trusting them to do their jobs, because she knew better. She knew the right way to do everything, even better than the people who did the job every day?How arrogant.

Pulling in her driveway, she pushed aside the guilty feelings. Instead of dwelling on how she'd acted in the past, she'd focus on how to stop doing that in the future. Everyone on her staff was capable and reliable. No more telling them how to do their jobs or double-checking that things had been done. Instead, she'd focus that energy on showing them her appreciation and confidence in them.

She felt good about her epiphany as she pulled the suitcase out of the back of the SUV. She set one bag on top of it and carried the other. Keys in hand, she rolled it up to the front door. Inside, she went straight to the laundry room and unpacked directly into the washing machine.

That done, she opened the fridge and made a face. There were a few take out containers full of science experiments that needed to be thrown away. Later. She grabbed a bottle of water and went out to the back porch.

The porch swing swayed invitingly. The porch was picture perfect... and rarely used. She was always too busy to just sit and be. Not today.

Today, she was going to sit on the porch and watch the birds. On cue, a fat robin landed a few feet in front of her. He hopped around a bit, then stabbed his beak toward the ground. He pulled back with a worm who wasn't giving up without a fight. He tugged and tugged, pulling the worm from the ground bit by bit.

Another robin landed right beside him, squawking loudly. The first robin dropped the worm and hopped away. They took off, chasing each other, flying low to the ground.

"Yay, worm. It's your lucky day," Margo said.

She kicked her shoes off and leaned back, enjoying the breeze on her face. Absently, she thought that she might get an ottoman or something to prop her feet on. At some point, she dozed a little, the birds lulling her. The water bottle slipped from her grasp, waking her. She picked it off the floor and took a drink. It didn't get any better than this. Okay, maybe having Connor next to her would be better, but this was pretty darn good.

The shadows stretched and the air cooled just enough to make her get up and go inside. It was almost time to get ready to "accidentally" bump into Connor at Gino's.

She showered and dressed with more care than was necessary for the sub shop, choosing a flowy skirt and nicer tank top with a thin cardigan. She styled her hair, letting it hang in loose waves around her shoulders. Her makeup bag sat, rarely touched as it was. She settled on moisturizer and a swipe of eyeliner and lip gloss, then decided to go crazy and apply some mascara as well.

Feeling like a teenager, she slipped her sandals on and grabbed her purse to "accidentally" meet Connor at six thirty.

At seven thirty, she was still sitting at Gino's with her untouched sub, alone. Her phone was silent, her calls and texts unanswered.

At eight, the waitress gave her a sad smile and wrapped her sub.

At eight twenty, she pulled back into her driveway. True, they'd been half-joking about meeting. Even so, she barely made it into the house before she burst into tears.

At least she wasn't in a prom dress.

# Chapter Thirty-Two

Anger etched Connor's face. "How could you? Why would you throw away all the progress you've made?" His neck was tight and aching.

"I no… dinkig," she slurred.

"You weren't drinking? Really?"

His mother shook her head, listing heavily to the side, about to topple off the kitchen chair.

"What do you take me for?" Connor pinched the bridge of his nose. "Where is it? Where's the booze?"

Her arm hung at her side and her eyes were wide with fear. Probably embarrassed at being caught.

Connor slammed his palms onto the table. "Answer me!"

A thread of drool slid from the corner of her mouth.

Disgusted, Connor threw open the upper cupboards, shoving boxes of food out of the way. Nothing hid behind the plates or cups. He ripped open the cupboards under the sink, his fury sending bottles of cleaning supplies flying. Drawers were emptied, the fridge and freezer investigated.

Finding nothing, he stormed out of the kitchen, ignoring

his mother's tears. He tore through the linen closet and the bathroom cupboard, checking all her old hiding places.

There were no bottles anywhere. Suddenly inspired, he ran outside to the trash, tearing bags open and finding nothing more than old newspapers and rotting food. In the garage, there were no bottles in the car or any of the cupboards. Nothing in any of the accessible plastic totes.

Confusion tempered his anger. Back in the kitchen, he faced his mother again. "Mom. I need you to tell me the truth."

She said something, her words slurred and unintelligible.

Fear spiked through the anger and confusion. "Mom?"

The side of her face was slack. He'd seen her drunk a thousand times, and a thousand times she'd been talking and gesturing and lively, with bright, shining eyes and loud laughter until she'd pass out. Not like this. He'd never seen her like this. She'd never been that careful with her bottles. The only thing he smelled on her now was dish detergent.

Part of her mouth moved again, but the words made no sense.

He began to shake.

"Mom? Hang on, Mom." Connor yanked his phone out of his pocket and called 9-1-1.

He stayed on the line until he heard the sirens, then ran outside to flag them to her. His heart pounded as the EMTs rolled the stretcher up her cracked sidewalk and into the house. Neighbors poked out of their houses, drawn to the flashing lights like flies to poop.

He had the foresight to grab his mother's purse. Hopefully, her insurance card was handy.

The EMTs quickly and efficiently got his mother loaded into the back of the ambulance while asking him direct questions about her symptoms. Time lost all meaning as it both stretched and sped by. The ambulance door slammed shut, leaving Connor alone on the sidewalk.

He blinked back tears, then ran inside to lock up the house and grab his keys. He took a moment to compose himself before starting the car. It wouldn't do him any good to arrive in an ambulance after hers.

Hyper aware of his speeding, Connor drove to the hospital, twenty minutes away.

The hospital loomed up ahead, the ambulance parked at the doors, the back open, with no one inside. Connor parked his car and jogged inside. At the counter, he was given a stack of forms to fill out, but no answers. He filled in as much as he could and handed over the insurance cards he found in her wallet. "I don't know what's valid."

The woman at the counter rolled her eyes as she took the cards. "We'll figure it out," she snapped.

"Do you know what's going on? When can I see my mom?"

The woman fixed him with a glare. "I obviously don't have any information. Wait over there and someone will come out when they can." She looked down, dismissing him.

Connor's jaw clenched. He wanted to reach across the counter and shake her until she told him what was happening. Instead, he took a deep breath and sat at the edge of a plastic chair, leaning forward with his elbows on his knees, his hands clasped in a fervent prayer.

When he'd finished pleading for his mother's life – and her forgiveness – he pulled his phone out of his pocket.

"Oh no." He ran a hand over his face, guilt over Margo's missed calls piling onto his guilt over his mother. He dialed her number. After a few rings, it went to voicemail. He hung up and tried again. On the third ring, she picked up.

"Yes?" Her voice was thick. Cautious.

He didn't bother with niceties. "I'm at the hospital."

"Are you okay?" Her concern was immediate.

"I'm fine. It's my mom. I don't know what's happening." The words jumbled, rushed together as his throat constricted. "Nobody's telling me anything."

"I'm on my way. Do you need anything?"

He shook his head, then realized she couldn't hear that. "No. You don't have to come," he began lamely.

"I'll be there in twenty."

"Okay." His voice was barely a whisper.

The call disconnected.

The minutes stretched out, torturing him. His leg bounced with the nervous energy he couldn't find another outlet for.

He walked over to the counter. "It's been almost an hour, can you tell me anything?"

"I *still* have no information for you," she said without a shred of humanity.

Connor bit back a comment and turned back to his seat.

True to her word, twenty minutes later, Margo came into the room and hurried over to him, concern etched across her face. "Have you heard anything?"

He stood and grabbed her in a hug. "No. Nobody's even come through for me to ask."

"They can't tell you anything at the counter?"

"Won't. Not the friendly, cooperative type."

An hour and a half later, Connor's nerves were frayed to the point of breaking. "I need to know something. Why hasn't anyone come out?" He watched the doors that separated the waiting room from the patient area. They opened and he was on his feet.

A nurse came out and walked over to the counter, exchanged a few words with the unpleasant woman, then walked back to the doors.

"Wait!" Connor rushed over. "Can you tell me anything about my mother?"

The nurse gave a blank look. "I'm sorry…?"

"Angie Anderson. She came in almost three hours ago."

The nurse reached out and touched his arm. "I'm so sorry, we didn't realize there was family here for her."

His blood boiled. Pushing the feeling aside, he said, "Is she okay? Can I see her?"

"Sure. Right this way."

Connor followed the nurse through the doors. It wasn't until they closed behind him that he thought to say something to Margo, but it was too late.

The nurse walked too fast for him to linger with his thoughts. She turned a corner and pulled a curtain back. "Here she is."

Connor swallowed hard. She looked so weak and pale and tiny against the stark white of the hospital pillow. Her eyes were closed. Tubes connected her arm to various machines and bags of fluid.

"Is she… Will she be… What's wrong with her?"

The nurse smiled kindly. "She had a mild stroke. There may be some lingering effects, but she'll be fine. You'll get more information when she's moved to her floor." A chime sounded and her eyes flicked to the direction of the sound. "Gotta go. You can sit with her."

"Thanks." Connor was talking to her back as she sped away.

He turned from the flurry of activity surrounding them and sat on a hard chair beside her bed. He took her hand. It was cold. "Mom? Hey, I'm here."

Her eyelids fluttered.

"The nurse says you're going to be fine. Hopefully, we'll get you out of here so you can rest at home. Maybe Scout and I will stay with you. You could stay with us but you'd probably be more comfortable in your own bed. I know I am. Can't get a good night's sleep in a strange bed." He knew he was rambling.

The machines flashed numbers and beeped at random intervals. There were so many things demanding attention he wondered how anything got noticed through all the visual noise. Commotion in the hallway pulled his gaze. Nurses pushed a bed, running down the aisle, while another nurse rode on it, kneeling beside the patient, administering CPR. They were gone in a second, the noise trailing behind them after they turned down another hallway.

"That didn't look good, did it? I hope it turns out okay."

His mother groaned slightly and turned her head.

"You okay?"

Her eyes fluttered again, then opened slightly.

He could tell when her eyes focused and she recognized him. Her shoulders relaxed and her hand slid across the crisp sheet, searching for his. He grabbed her hand and gently squeezed. "Hey."

She smiled slightly and her eyes drifted back shut.

"Excuse me, sir?"

He jumped to his feet. "Yes?"

"We're taking her up to her room now. She'll be in 903. Give us a little bit to get her situated, then you can come up there, okay?"

"Thanks." He looked around. "Um, how do I get back to the waiting room?"

A young girl, probably a student or volunteer, grinned. "I'll show you. It's kind of a maze in here, isn't it?"

Before he could answer, she was off. Apparently, all the nurses only operated on one speed. *Fast.*

She led him back to the doors to the waiting room and gave

him a perky, "See ya!" before trotting back into the fray.

Margo was sitting on one of the chairs, her feet propped up on another. She stared intently at her phone.

"You're still here." Even he could hear the relief in his voice. "I'm sorry I didn't say anything before they took me back."

She waved her hand, dismissing his apology. "Connor, stop. How is she?"

"They're moving her upstairs to her room. 903. They said to give them a little bit and then I can go up. She was really pale. The nurse said it was a mild stroke, but she'll be okay. I hope she knew what she was talking about."

"I'm sure she wouldn't have said anything unless she was sure."

"You're probably right."

She sat up, putting her feet on the floor.

"You don't have to stay…" he trailed off. It was awkward, it was boring, it was late and dark, but he really did want her to stay.

Margo stood and wrapped her arms around his waist. "I have nowhere else to be. Let's head up to see if your mom's in her room yet."

"Are you sure you don't mind?"

She simply raised an eyebrow and slung her purse over her shoulder, then held out her hand to his and walked over to the bank of elevators.

"I really appreciate you coming. I'm sorry I didn't call sooner."

The doors slid open. They stepped inside and Connor pressed button number nine.

Nine. That had to be a good sign, right?

"It's okay. I was having flashbacks but then you came through, so it's all good."

He grimaced. "I know. I thought of that when you didn't

pick up the first time I called. I'm glad you picked up the second time."

"I debated. But I figured if you were going to ghost, you wouldn't have called at all."

"I wouldn't ghost you."

"I know." She squeezed his hand. "Okay, I admit I wasn't so sure earlier."

Connor let go of her hand to put his arm around her back. "I'm glad you're here."

Her arm settled around his waist as she leaned into his shoulder. "Me, too."

"I've never had to deal with anything like this alone. Colin was always the one who handled this stuff." His throat tightened. "I'm scared. I just buried my brother, I can't lose my mom, too."

"Hey." Her voice was gentle. "It's okay. She's going to be okay."

The elevator rolled to a stop and the doors slid open. They stepped out onto a quiet floor and quickly found the waiting room just down the hallway.

Margo stood in front of Connor, facing him. Her hands were on his sides, her eyes holding his captive. "It's going to be okay."

He wanted to believe her.

"If she was in immediate danger, they wouldn't have moved her to a room."

Good point. He took a deep breath and let it out slowly, pulling Margo against his chest. "Okay. You're right." Another deep breath. "I'm going to go see if they'll let me see her. You're okay here?"

Margo held up her phone. "Ebooks. They're a thing of beauty."

"So are you." He gave a small chuckle.

# Chapter Thirty-Three

Margo watched him walk down the hallway. It was after midnight, but she wasn't tired. She stared out the wall of windows for a while, watching lights from the occasional car enter or leave the parking lot far below where she stood. On a roof below her, the air conditioning unit fan periodically swirled, then rolled to a stop, only to start again a minute later. "That can't be efficient," she muttered.

The lights behind her reflected against the glass, too bright for her to make out the stars. When she got bored of the dark scenery, she settled onto a barely cushioned chair and propped her feet up. She swiped at her phone until her book reappeared, then read until her mind drifted.

Not for the first time, she was glad she'd answered the phone. It had been so tempting to ignore his call after she'd left him voicemails and text messages that had gone unanswered for hours.

She hoped his mom wouldn't have any long-term ill-effects. She'd been sitting alone for almost two hours and was engrossed in her book again when Connor appeared in the doorway.

"She's asleep, they told me she'll probably be out of it for a while and I should go home."

Margo shoved her feet into the shoes she'd abandoned and closed her ebook app. "Hungry?"

He looked unsure for a moment, then his stomach growled. "Starving."

"Me, too. I was too pissed off to eat earlier." She smiled and nudged his side.

"The only place open is the diner."

"That's perfect. Nothing better than a massive breakfast at three a.m."

Connor smiled and took her hand. "That sounds amazing."

They drove separately, meeting in the diner's empty parking lot. Inside, they took a corner booth and both ordered "Deluxe Hungryman" breakfast platters. The waitress was far more enthusiastic than any person had reason to be at that hour.

Their platters arrived a few minutes later, and they dug into the food without much conversation. Eventually, they pushed back empty plates.

"Oh, crap." Margo leaned back in her booth. "I don't think I've ever eaten that much." A barrage of thoughts rained through her mind, all those old criticisms and self-loathing phrases that plagued her younger years. She pushed them away. One huge breakfast was not the first step into back-sliding into her heavier self. Even if it was, so what. There were worse things to be than heavy. It was time to pack that particular baggage away.

Connor rubbed his belly. "I'm going to sleep for a week."

"Better get home first."

"Ugh. Maybe I'll just sleep in my car."

Margo laughed. "Let's roll you out of here."

Connor paid the check and they walked to the parking lot.

He paused by her car. "Thanks again, Margo. It means a lot that you came."

"You're welcome. Just don't call me before noon tomorrow." She planted a kiss on his lips, then quickly added, "Unless it's important. Of course."

He nodded. "I'll talk to you tomorrow. No, that's today. Later today."

"Drive safe."

"You, too." He pulled her into a tight hug and kissed her before walking to his own car.

Margo pulled out and drove home, glad it wasn't far. The lack of sleep and giant breakfast were conspiring against her, trying to lull her to sleep. She pulled into her driveway and hurried into the house. She locked the door behind her, not bothering to turn on any lights, then crawled directly into bed, stopping only to plug her phone in to charge.

Morning came faster than she would have liked. The sun streamed through a crack in the curtains. *Rude.* She was already in the shower when she groaned and realized she didn't *have* to get up. She could have stayed in bed. Rinsing the conditioner from her hair, she muttered, "Figures."

Since she didn't sleep late, she lingered in the shower, enjoying the hot water instead of jumping out to get on to the next task.

When she was fully pruned, she stepped out and wrapped herself in her favorite fluffy towels, one around her body and one wrapped around her hair.

She checked her phone to make sure Connor hadn't messaged her. He hadn't. She hoped his mother was doing better today.

When she'd dressed, she did a few chores around the house. She waited until ten, then messaged Connor. His reply was immediate.

*Heading to the hospital now. Will call you later.*

She replied with: *LMK if you need anything.* Then she put the phone into her back pocket and thought about how to spend her day. A whole day with nothing on the agenda. The thought made her giddy.

*Chapter Thirty-Four*

Connor arrived at the hospital to find his mother's room empty. He was debating how long to stay when a nurse wheeled his mother back into the room in a wheelchair.

"Mom. You look so much better." He leaned down to give her a hug.

"I feel a lot better." Her speech was almost normal, although he did notice one side of her face drooped.

"When can she go home?"

The nurse answered, "In a couple of days. We need to run more tests and see if we can get that blood pressure under control."

Connor looked at his mother. "Haven't you been taking your medication?"

"I ran out and I felt fine, so I never bothered getting it refilled."

The nurse clucked her tongue. "You can't be doing that."

"Believe me, I've learned my lesson."

"Mom, you could have died! You have to take better care of yourself."

Angie put her hand on his cheek. "Connor. It won't happen

again. They've already set up an appointment next week with my regular doctor."

"Is it a money thing? If it's too expensive, I'll help. You can't go without your medication."

"Nope, it's just because I felt fine. I know better now. I promise."

"Mom," his voice held a warning.

"Don't 'Mom' me. Talk about something else."

The nurse helped her back into the bed, then left for her other rounds.

Connor felt the heat in his face. "What do you want to talk about?" He avoided her eyes, opting to stand and look out the window.

"What would *you* like to talk about? Looks like there's something on your mind."

He shoved his hands deep in the pockets of his jeans. "I met someone."

Her eyebrows rose. "You did? On your camping trip?"

"Yep."

Silence hung for a minute.

"Well? Are you going to tell me anything else?" He heard the impatience and excitement in her voice.

"I'm not sure where to start."

"What's her name? Where's she from? Is she nice? Does she like you, too? Are you seeing her again? Pick one of those to start with."

"She's from Hickory Hollow. She's very nice. She likes me. I'm seeing her this evening. Her name is Margo."

Angie grinned, half of her face not quite cooperating.

"What?"

"Your face. You really like this girl."

"I do."

"Margo." Her brow creased as if she was trying to remember. "The Lewis girl? I thought she was married and had a little girl."

"That's her younger sister, Ashley."

"Oh, that's right." Her eyes widened. "Ooooh, you're dating the doctor."

"Veterinarian."

"Animal doctor. That counts."

The words of her family came back to him. All the snide comments about her not being a "real" doctor.

"What?" she asked.

"Her family kind of sucks."

"Don't say that. You can't really know unless you've seen it for yourself."

"No, I did." At her confused expression, he went on. "They were at the campground. Her dad, stepmom, and her sisters with their families. Her younger sister and her husband are great. In fact, I'm going to be working with him – Elliott – at Hansen. But the rest of them are awful."

"How so?"

How not so? "She saved a man's life. There was a doctor there – a people doctor – and the two of them worked on him and saved his life. Her stepmother said Margo was probably in the way. I was there, Mom. She was incredible. Before that, though, they invited her ex-fiance along on the camping trip and kept trying to force them together. They actually expected her to be a trophy wife for this moron instead of doing what she wanted to do."

"What did she think of all this?"

"She hated it. And her family hated me." He was starting to take it as a compliment. They liked Brad, and look what a jerk he was.

"Why would anyone hate you?"

"I know about the wedding crasher."

She chuckled. "Ah. Yeah, well, that was a long time ago."

"Not long enough, apparently. Her family was so against her having anything to do with me that they tried paying her off."

"What?"

His frustrated words tumbled out. If he hadn't witnessed it himself, he would have thought the story was exaggerated. "Margo paid for all her schooling herself. She worked and got grants and loans and scholarships. Her dad wrote her a check to cover all the tuition she paid, plus all the money she just took out to buy into the veterinary practice. On the condition that she stop seeing me."

"And she refused." His mom didn't seem surprised.

"Yep." He sat on the bed and took her hand. "Not because of me."

"Of course not. Because she's not for sale." Angie echoed Margo's words.

"Exactly."

She squeezed his hand, hard. "You best not let this one go, Connor."

"It doesn't bother you that you might have to interact with Jean at some point?"

"Oh, please. I haven't spared that woman a thought in twenty years. Your father loved me, and I loved him." She shook her head sadly. "He would have been better off with someone else, I know that. I put that man through the ringer time and time again. But I loved him so much. I still do."

"He loved you too, Mom."

"I know. Anyway, I certainly don't have a problem with Margo just because she's Jean's stepdaughter. When do I get to meet her?"

"We just started seeing each other. Soon, though."

"After I'm out of here. I look like death warmed over. Don't want to meet her like this." She laughed and tugged at the hospital gown.

Connor reached over and grabbed her in a hug.

"What's that for?"

"I'm glad you're okay. I was scared." He downplayed it. He wasn't just scared, he was terrified.

She rubbed his back. "Me, too."

"And I'm sorry."

"You don't have to be sorry."

Black guilt flooded his heart. "I do. I wasted so much time accusing you of drinking when I should have been calling 9-1-1. I'm sorry."

"Stop. You don't need to apologize."

"Yes, I do. You've been sober for years, and I immediately jumped to conclusions."

"Look at me." She gently grabbed his beard. "I don't blame you, so stop blaming yourself. I did a lot of damage over the years, and you're not wrong to be suspicious. Even after all this time. I'll always be an alcoholic."

"If I had waited a few more minutes…"

"You didn't. I'm here and I'm going to be fine." She kissed his forehead. "You should go home and take a nap. Eat something. You look like death warmed over." She patted his cheek.

He chuckled. "Thanks, Mom. You always say the sweetest things."

"Go see if your girl wants to have lunch or something."

Hugging her again, he nodded. "That's a great idea. I'll come back this afternoon."

"Nope."

"What?"

"Tomorrow. Come see me tomorrow. Ginny is coming to visit this afternoon, and she's bringing me some books and my iPad. If you don't mind, bring me a change of clothes so I can bust out of here."

"Alrighty then, I'll see you tomorrow around this time."

"Perfect." She patted his cheek again. "You're a great son, Connor. I love you."

"Love you, too."

In the parking lot, he slid into his car and dialed Margo's number.

"How's your mom?"

"Great. She looks great today. They said she'll be able to come home either Friday or Saturday." The relief sent a lump to his throat. He squeezed his eyes shut against stinging tears.

"That's wonderful news."

He took a minute to get himself back under control. "Did you have lunch yet?"

"Nope. I just finished making a grocery list."

"Want to meet at the store? I need to get stuff for tomorrow night's dinner."

"Sure. When?"

"I'm just leaving the hospital, so twenty minutes?"

"Perfect. I'll see you there."

They hung up and Connor let out a long breath. His mother was going to be fine. He and Margo were doing fine. The major crises of the past days were all under control.

It was ridiculous how much he was looking forward to grocery shopping with Margo. Something so mundane and domestic, and he was as excited as if they were going to be walking a red carpet. More, probably. He craved normal. With her. Meatloaf for dinner and curling up on the couch with a movie. For the life of him, he couldn't imagine anything better in the world.

# Chapter Thirty-Five

Margo waited on the sidewalk, checking her phone as she leaned on the cart.

"I hear this is a great place to pick up women. You interested?"

She stood up straight and pointedly looked him up and down. "Sure thing, cowboy."

Connor snickered, calling her attention to a horrified-looking woman who was openly staring at them with disapproval. Margo covered her mouth and laughed, then pushed the cart toward the doors.

When they were inside, they stood in front of the oranges and laughed.

"That poor woman."

Connor shook his head. "She was probably getting ideas. Thinking about how many eligible bachelors she runs into in the pharmacy line."

"That's awful."

Margo pushed the cart up and down the aisles, picking stuff from her list while Connor added items from his.

"We should get a box of spaghetti or something to use as a divider."

"If you don't take the corners like a NASCAR driver, the stuff will stay where it belongs."

Margo whipped the cart to the side. "You mean like this?"

"Exactly. Now I need different celery. You made that one seasick."

"That's the first time I've ever heard of seasick celery."

"That's because you don't travel in the same culinary circles as I do."

"Culinary circles? Is that a Portland thing?"

He used a snooty voice. "Psht. It's a global thing. Hickory Hollow excluded, apparently."

"Okay, Gordon Ramsay, can we move on?"

"As long as you don't upset any more of my food."

"Now it's upset?"

"You'd be upset if *you* were seasick."

"Touché. Can you grab me that bag of carrots?" She pointed.

"Baby or adult?"

"Baby."

He set the carrots in the cart. "What did you decide on for dessert?"

"I found a recipe for pumpkin cheesecake. I'm going to try it. If it doesn't work, I'll go with Plan B." There was no Plan B.

"Which is?"

*Crap. Gotta think of a Plan B.* "Stop and buy something on the way to your place tomorrow night. Like Oreos."

"Perfect. I love Oreos."

"Now you're going to be disappointed if the cheesecake turns out, aren't you?"

"A little." He paused in front of the meat case and made his selections.

"Maybe I'll see if I can find a recipe for Oreo cheesecake."

"I'm getting hungry."

Margo laughed. "You're always hungry."

"Not *always*. Sometimes I sleep."

"What else do we need?"

"Cheese."

She held her arm out and pointed. "To the cheese!"

When they finished buying the groceries, Connor pushed the cart to the parking lot. He loaded Margo's purchases into her car. "I'm over there." He gestured to his car, on the other side of the cart park.

"Are we going to your place or mine? I didn't get anything that needs to go in the fridge."

"Then my place it is."

Margo followed Connor to his house and parked beside his car. She could hear Scout's excited barking from inside the house. Grabbing some of the bags from Connor's trunk, she followed him to the front door.

"Careful, Scout'll probably try to knock you over."

As soon as the door opened, Scout barreled out and danced around Margo. He held a mangled stuffed frog in his mouth.

"Hey, sweetie. Let's go set these bags down and I'll pet you, okay?"

Scout wound his way around her legs, his tail working overtime, wagging his entire body.

They made their way into the kitchen, where she set the bags on the counter, then leaned down. "Okay, buddy, here we go." She scratched his ears and back. "I missed you, too, oh yes I did." He dropped the toy on the floor and grinned up at her.

When Scout calmed down enough to walk over to Connor, Margo looked around the kitchen. "This is really nice." It looked like it had been updated recently.

"Thanks. I can't take any credit. The people I bought it from did a lot of remodeling."

"They did a nice job. Why'd they leave?"

"The real estate agent said they were moving overseas. They also wanted a quick sale, so I got a great deal."

"Nice." Margo ran her hand over the dark granite countertops. "If I was designing a kitchen, this is exactly what I'd do." In the house she'd recently bought, she'd started by remodeling the master bathroom. The kitchen upgrade would be next.

"If I was designing a kitchen it would look like crap. I'm really glad I don't have to. I'll give you the grand tour."

"Fabulous."

Connor led her through the house. It wasn't big, but everything had been updated. "I even like the colors they used, so I won't even have to paint for a few years. Unless a certain dog gets out of hand and decides to chew something."

Scout's ears perked up.

"Yes, I'm talking about you."

"Oh, that doesn't sound like something he would do." Margo winked at Scout like they were sharing a secret.

"Nah, he's a good boy."

Scout boofed in agreement.

Connor laughed. "Mostly. I remember Colin telling me he went through a sock phase when he was a pup. He'd steal socks out of the laundry and eat them."

No surprise. Margo had operated on more than one dog to find a stomach full of socks. Or underwear. "That's pretty common. I don't know what the fascination is, but labs love eating socks. Well, they love eating in general."

"I can relate."

"This is a great closet."

"My mom was all about the closets, too. Wait until you see the one in the bedroom."

"Lead on." She may or may not have been super curious to see his bedroom.

Connor walked into the bedroom and reached over to pull the comforter to the edge of the bed. "Yeah, so I obviously don't make my bed every day."

She swallowed hard at the rumpled bed, trying not to imagine ways they could mess it up even more. Connor's clean masculine scent hanging in the air wasn't helping matters. "That's the one thing I do every single day. No matter what, as soon as I get up, I make the bed. And every night, I'm glad I come home to a neat bed."

"Huh. That makes sense. And over here is the closet. Ignore the boxes." He pulled the closet door open.

"Holy cow. You could put an entire bathroom in here."

"Bathroom's next door."

Margo followed him to the master bathroom. "Ooh, separate walk-in shower. Those are amazing. It was number one on my list for my master bath remodel."

"That concludes this portion of the grand tour. Unless you want to see the attic crawlspace."

"Let's save that for tomorrow."

"Perfect."

They went back to the kitchen, where Connor motioned for her to sit on a stool at the island while he made sandwiches.

"Are you visiting your mom this afternoon?" Margo bit into the ham sandwich.

"Nope, she told me not to. Her friend is visiting and taking her some books and her iPad. I hope she naps, though. She seemed really tired."

"It's hard to rest in the hospital. All the noise and constant poking and prodding."

"I told her I'd stay at her place for a few days when she comes home. She could stay here, but I figured she'd get more rest in her own bed."

"I would think so."

"And Scout's familiar with her place, so it works out. I don't have to worry about him getting into anything he shouldn't."

They finished their sandwiches and Margo stood. "Thanks for lunch, but I should get my groceries home."

"You don't want your carrots getting upset."

"Exactly. Let me know what time I should come over tomorrow."

"I'll text you."

"Great." Margo walked into his open arms and turned her face up for his kiss. Several long minutes later, she was breathless. She pushed back against his chest. "I'm going now."

"See you tomorrow." He kissed her again.

She pried herself away, paused to scratch Scout, then left.

She was nearly home when her phone rang. She pushed the button on her steering wheel that connected the call through the car. "Hello, Jean."

"What are you doing?" She made the question sound like an accusation.

"Driving home."

"Oh, where were you?"

"Connor's place."

There was a significant pause. "Oh."

"What's up?"

"I'm calling to invite you over for dinner tomorrow night."

"I can't. I have a date tomorrow night."

"With *Connor*, I suppose."

"Yes. With Connor."

"And you won't reschedule to spend time with your family."

"No."

Margo could feel the annoyance in the silence. She pulled into her driveway and waited for the garage door to raise. "Are you going to say anything else, or just be mad at me because I won't change plans I already had?"

"I'm not mad. Just disappointed. I should be used to that by now, shouldn't I?"

Margo pulled the car into the garage. "Okay."

"I was going to make that grilled chicken you like."

"Why?"

"I'm not sure what you mean."

"I mean why? Why are you inviting me to dinner and why are you making the chicken I like? What's the agenda?"

"I don't know why you have to assume there's an ulterior motive every time I do something nice for you."

"Maybe because you don't do anything nice for me unless there's an ulterior motive?"

Jean sighed. "Really, Margo?"

"Can you just tell me what you want?" The night at the hospital and lack of sleep suddenly caught up with her, and she just wanted to crawl into bed.

"Your father and I wanted to talk to you."

"Why?" She wanted to scream.

"We don't talk. We just wanted to sit down and find out what's going on in your life."

"Simple. I'm dating Connor. It looks like it could get serious. I'm very happy."

"Margo, he's –"

"Stop. Right there, just stop. I'm not going to listen to you say negative things about him." She bit her tongue before announcing she knew about the wedding.

"You can do better."

Well, that didn't have to mean just men, did it? Margo hung

up the phone. With a heavy sigh, she got out of the car and went around the back to get her groceries.

Her phone vibrated with an incoming call from Jean, but she ignored it. She was in no mood to listen to any more criticism, or harsh words because she dared to hang up. She put the groceries away, then curled up on the couch with the remote and a magazine, neither of which she touched. Instead, she dozed off.

# Chapter Thirty-Six

Connor spent the rest of Wednesday unpacking the last of the boxes he'd been neglecting, and playing in the yard with Scout. Eventually, he threw a tennis ball and Scout watched it sail past him, then dropped to the ground and rolled around on his back.

"I guess we're done, huh?"

Scout made a groaning gurgling noise as he rolled.

"Good. My arm was getting tired." He leaned back on the porch swing. His thoughts wandered between the new job he'd be starting next week, his mom, and tomorrow's date with Margo. He still wasn't sure how their relationship was going to work now that they were in the real world. Mostly. It would be really real when they were both back to work. He wondered how their schedules would line up, or *if* they would.

He sighed. He didn't want to think about all the obstacles that would soon be rearing their ugly heads.

Scout came onto the porch and lay at his feet.

The afternoon bled into the evening as Connor relaxed. Fireflies dotted the darkening yard, sending Scout into a frenzy of trying to eat them.

Connor whistled for the dog and went inside. "Quit eating bugs. You're going to give yourself a bellyache."

Scout wagged his tail, but Connor knew he wouldn't alter his snacking habits.

Connor cleaned the already-clean kitchen and vacuumed the living room, then dusted the television. When he was satisfied everything was acceptable, he flipped the tv on and scrolled around to connect to Netflix, then added Frankenstein to his playlist. He raised an eyebrow at the description, but if that's what Margo wanted to watch, that's what they'd watch.

Eventually, he went to bed and slept soundly. Mostly. Scout's snoring didn't really lend itself to a full night of restful sleep.

Thursday came bright and hot and humid. He turned the air conditioning up before going to the hospital.

His mother was sitting up, swiping across the screen of her iPad. Her face mostly matched today, the stiffness fading from half her face.

He leaned over and kissed her cheek. "How's it going?"

"Good. They said I can go home tomorrow. They ran about a million tests and everything's coming back good."

"That's great."

"What are you up to today?"

"Visiting my favorite lady."

She chuckled. "Then what?"

"Then probably some lunch. I was going to take Scout to the park, but it's too hot. Then tonight I'm making dinner for Margo."

"Ooh, what are you making?"

"Meatloaf and macaroni and cheese."

"Dessert?"

"She's making dessert."

"Sounds like you two really like each other."

He couldn't keep from grinning. "We do. There's one pretty big obstacle, though."

"What's that?"

"She doesn't like onions. So I'm making the meatloaf without onion."

Angie set her iPad down and sighed. "I'm not sure I can approve of her now. You really should have told me this sooner."

"Sorry."

"Do you really want an onionless future?"

"I'll still have onions."

Angie laughed."Just imagining you sitting in the closet eating an onion on the sly."

"I don't think I'm going to have to eat onions in secret."

"It's a fun image, though."

"You're weird."

"It's part of my charm."

Connor laughed. "What are you reading?"

They spent the next hour talking about books they'd read recently until Angie yawned. "They'll be bringing my lunch soon, then hopefully I can take a nap."

"You're still not feeling good?"

"I feel fine, but the whole episode made me kind of weak. They said it's normal. I did some reading on the Internet about strokes, and if the worst I've got is some weakness and stiffness, I'm not going to complain at all. I read some really scary stuff."

"Don't get your medical information from the Internet."

"I know it's no substitute, but no one seems to have much time to answer questions, and I can't think of any when they flit into the room."

"Make a list for your follow up appointment."

"Yes, boss." She punctuated the words with an exaggerated sigh.

A pleasant guy in white scrubs pushed a cart into the room and set a tray of food on her bedside table. "Here's your lunch, Angie."

"Thank you," she said.

When he left, she pulled the cover off the plate and made a face. "Bleh. They put me on the no salt, no taste diet."

"It doesn't look bad."

She raised an eyebrow. "It looks like prison food."

"How many times have you had prison food?"

"I can imagine."

He studied the bland plate. "Yeah, I'm guessing that's pretty close."

She made a noise of disgust. "When you spring me out of here tomorrow, we're stopping for real food. Or even better, save me some of your leftover meatloaf."

Connor kissed her forehead. "I will. Enjoy your lunch."

She eyed him suspiciously. "What are *you* having for lunch?"

"Lettuce. No dressing. Definitely no salt." He grinned and backed out the door. "Love you!"

"Love you, too, brat."

Connor got into his car smiling. He still felt bad about accusing his mother of drinking, but, true to her word, she didn't seem to be holding it against him.

He stopped at a drive-thru and felt a pang of guilt as he ordered his salt- and fat-laden lunch topped off with a sugary drink. The feeling passed as the smell of fresh French fries filled the car.

At home, he shared the fries with Scout, with a warning not to tell Margo. He spent the afternoon recleaning what was already clean, then rearranged the furniture, only to put it back where he'd started. Followed by a few dozen pushups to burn off some of his nervous energy. This was ridiculous. Margo had already seen his house. All of it. Including his unmade bed. Which, incidentally, he'd made when he got up this morning. She was right. Walking into the bedroom and seeing the bed already made was a good feeling. Although messing up the bed with Margo would be a pretty good feeling, too.

The minutes ticked by slowly, dragging the afternoon on and on.

He watched some bad talk shows, then a riveting episode of Dr. Phil. Shaking his head and feeling much better about his own life, he finally flipped the television off and went into the kitchen to mix up the meatloaf.

Scout sat by his side, watching and waiting for something to fall off the island that he could devour.

"Sorry, buddy, you can't eat raw meat."

Scout cocked his head, his ears perked.

"Meat? That's all you heard, isn't it? No raw meat for you. How about a carrot?" He dropped a chunk of carrot onto the floor.

Scout grabbed the carrot and ran into the living room.

Connor called after him, "Don't you spit that on the carpet!"

A second later, Scout reappeared and took up his station at Connor's side.

"You didn't eat that carrot, did you?"

Scout wagged his tail.

"Do you have to pee?"

Scout stood and glanced at the sliding doors, then back up at the counter.

Connor walked over and slid the door open. A wall of heat pushed back the cool air of the kitchen.

Scout trotted across the yard to do his business, then ran back inside, panting.

"I know. That's freaking hot, isn't it?" Connor went back to his meatloaf. "Great idea to make a dinner that uses the oven, huh? I probably should have grilled steaks or something more seasonal. Oh, well."

He grated the three different kinds of cheese while the macaroni boiled on the stove. "Yes, I know I could have bought pre-shredded cheese, but it's not as good." He dropped a small hunk of cheese on the floor. Scout practically inhaled it and waited for more.

When the food was in the oven, Connor set the table. "Okay, now we can relax." He walked into the living room, put his hand on his hip, and pointed. "What is that?"

Scout flopped on the floor, covering his snout with his paw.

"That wouldn't be the carrot I told you not to drop, would it?"

Scout pretended to be asleep.

Connor picked up the carrot and waited.

Scout opened one eye, then quickly closed it again.

"Yeah, you sneaky little bugger."

The tip of Scout's tail moved.

"I know you're not asleep." Connor carried the carrot into the kitchen and threw it in the trash. When he went back to the living room, Scout was on the couch.

Connor checked his phone and saw a text from Margo. His heart dropped, assuming she wasn't able to come, until he actually read the message.

Cheesecake disaster. Going with Plan E.

He texted back,

What happened to Plans B – D?

They all melted.

She punctuated the text with a winking emoji.

Tragic.

I'll be there in about 30?

Perfect. See you soon.

He hesitated, then added a smiley face. Before he could change his mind, he hit the button to send the message. He sighed and looked at Scout. "I just texted a freaking smiley face emoji."

Scout wagged his approval. If he could text, he'd send all the emojis.

"I might have to turn in my man card."

More tail wagging.

"You don't care, do you?"

Scout flopped onto his side and stretched his toes.

"That's what I thought."

He checked his phone every two minutes until Scout leaped off the couch and ran to the window, barking his head off. Connor jumped up and watched Margo get out of her car and walk up the sidewalk with a bag. As he pulled open the door and took in her springy sundress and strappy sandals, he second-guessed his own khaki shorts and plain blue t-shirt. She was already on the porch, he didn't have time to change.

She smiled at him and his clothes were forgotten.

"Hi. So this is Plan E?" He reached out to take the insulated bag she was carrying.

"I think it's J, actually."

He stepped aside and let her in, then closed the door and

led her to the kitchen. "I hope these weren't all actual disasters."

"Only one. The rest never made it past the idea stage."

"Good. I was imagining a kitchen full of dirty dishes and ruined ingredients." He set her bag on the island.

She reached inside and pulled out a glass dish. "This will need to go in the fridge."

He put it in for her.

"And this is what's left of Plan A." She pulled out a round dish and lifted the foil off.

Connor tried not to laugh at the chunks of cheesecake.

"Go ahead. Laugh. It's awful."

It did look awful. But it smelled delicious. "What happened to it?"

"I tried to take it out of the springform pan before it was cool. It didn't like that."

"It's probably still good. Your graham cracker crust looks good."

"Yeah," she sighed. "I was really proud of that."

Connor chuckled and set the cheesecake in the fridge. "It's the perfect dessert for watching Frankenstein."

"It *is* a monster."

"It smells good."

"So does dinner."

"It's almost ready."

"Fantastic. I just had a sad little salad for lunch so I'd be hungry."

"Yikes, no pressure, right?"

She laughed. "No pressure."

"After I started the oven, I realized I should have made something a little more heatwave-friendly."

"Yeah, it's awful out there. My clothes were sticking to me as soon as I walked outside."

He made a conscious effort to not ogle the places her dress had probably been sticking. It wasn't easy. Giving undue attention to putting on his oven mitt, he said, "Yeah, even Scout didn't want to stay outside. Usually, he doesn't want to come back in, but not today."

"I'm really glad we didn't have this heat-wave while we were camping. That would have been miserable."

He pulled the dishes out of the oven and set them on the stove. "I'll get you a drink while these cool. What would you like?"

"What are my options?"

He opened the fridge and said, "Water, wine, beer, iced tea, expired orange juice, and milk. Also expired."

"Iced tea, please."

"Good choice. I hope you don't mind mint?"

"Love it."

"Great." He filled two tall glasses with ice, then poured tea into them.

Margo took a sip. "This is really good. What kind of mint is in it?"

"Peppermint, wintergreen, and spearmint."

"Ooh, fancy."

Connor admitted, "It comes in a bottle already mixed together."

"You didn't have to tell me that. I would have been really impressed."

"Yeah, but the truth would come out eventually. It's better to be up-front about my mint mixing skills."

"Then I'll just be impressed with your foresight and wisdom in choosing that particular mint blend."

He lifted his glass and clinked it against hers. "Excellent. Shall we fill our plates at the stove, or would you prefer I bring the food to the table?"

Margo stood. "No, that's too much trouble."

They filled their plates at the stove and sat down at the table.

"I like the tall table."

Connor nodded. "I got the bar height table so *someone* can't put his face on the table while I'm eating."

Margo chuckled and looked down at Scout, who patiently waited for a morsel to fall to the floor. "He wouldn't be talking about you, would he?"

Scout's tail wagged furiously.

They ate in silence for a few minutes.

"Thank you for dinner. This is really good."

"Glad you like it."

"I have to admit, you were right."

"Awesome."

Margo laughed. "Don't you want to know what about?"

"Doesn't matter. I'll take it. But if you insist, what was I right about?"

"Your meatloaf. It really is the best meatloaf ever."

"Ah, that. Yes. I thought maybe you were going to tell me I was right about being ridiculously handsome and irresistible."

Margo rolled her eyes. "That goes without saying."

He laughed. "Good comeback."

"Thought you might like that."

"I'm glad you like the meatloaf. The secret is..." he looked around suspiciously and lowered his voice. "Cheese."

"Cheese?"

"Shh! I shouldn't even tell you this. But the secret is to add cheese to the meat mixture. Gives it moisture and extra flavor."

"Hmm. I thought the secret was some obscure spice."

"Perhaps the meatloaf has many secrets."

"I'm starting to think I shouldn't have eaten it. It seems awfully mystical for a hunk of ground-up meat."

"We haven't even talked about the secrets in the macaroni and cheese."

"More cheese secrets, I would assume?"

"You would be wrong."

"Of course."

"The secret in the mac and cheese is garlic."

"Garlic?"

"Garlic powder, specifically. I add a variety of spices to it to give it an extra kick."

"Well, whatever you did worked. But I'm not asking any questions. I don't want to stumble into a world I should know nothing about."

Connor grinned. "Your dessert probably has some secrets."

"Yeah. Which they didn't reveal to me at all. If I knew the cheesecake's secrets, it wouldn't be a crumbled mess."

"Patience, grasshopper. You will learn the secrets when they are ready to be learned." He bowed his head toward her.

"Next time, the secret will be to *buy* a cheesecake. Voilà. Problem solved."

Connor shook his head. "Speaking of cheesecake, I'll clear the dishes and we can get the movie started."

"I can help."

"Another secret – I'm just throwing them in the dishwasher for now."

"You're just full of secrets, aren't you?"

He wiggled his eyebrows. "You have *no* idea."

"What does that even mean?"

"I have *no* idea."

They both laughed as Connor loaded their dishes into the dishwasher. He handed her two forks and a stack of napkins, then grabbed both desserts from the fridge. He arranged them on the coffee table, then went back into the kitchen to grab glasses and the pitcher of iced tea.

"Now we won't have to get up."

Margo nodded approvingly. "Good thinking."

He clicked the television on and loaded Netflix. "Okay, I had it queued up earlier." After some technical difficulty, he got the movie started.

"I hope you like it," Margo said. "It's my favorite."

"I'm not really into horror movies, but I'll give it a shot."

She tucked her legs under her, to the side, and grinned. "It's awful, it really is. But I love it."

He raised an eyebrow. "I can hardly wait."

They ate through the desserts while the movie played. Scout lay on the floor in front of the couch, snoozing while Frankenstein's monster terrorized people.

When it was over, Connor nodded. "Yes."

"Yes?"

"Yes, that was awful. But it was fun awful. I liked it."

"You're not just saying that?"

"Nope, two thumbs up for extreme cheese and awfulness."

"It doesn't follow the book very well."

"I was trying not to compare."

"Really?"

"No. I haven't read the book since high school."

She swatted his arm.

"In fact, I don't remember much about it except the big debate about the monster's name."

"Ah, yes."

Connor grinned, thinking back to high school. "There was this huge discussion that ended up with a couple of kids getting detention. One girl was really worked up and yelling about how the monster's name isn't Frankenstein, and a couple of the guys thought it was funny, so they kept taunting her. Eventually, she ended up in tears and the guys got detention."

"Too funny. It annoys me when people get it wrong, but I don't think I've ever gotten that upset about it."

"Seems pointless to get upset about it when it's such a widely held misconception."

"Although it being a widely held misconception is no reason to contribute to the inaccuracy."

"True." He stretched and grabbed the remote. "It's still early. What else should we watch?"

"Your turn to pick."

He scrolled through his list. "How about this one?"

Margo laughed. "*You've Got Mail*? I love that movie."

"Me, too."

While the opening credits rolled, he finished his plate of desserts. "What was in this?"

"Angel food cake, vanilla pudding, Cool Whip, pineapple, and strawberries."

"It's delicious."

"It's one of my favorites."

"The cheesecake is great, too."

Margo leaned back against the couch and smiled. "In spite of its Frankensteinish appearance?"

"With enough Cool Whip, it doesn't look bad at all."

"Can you pause that for a minute? Potty break."

Connor grabbed the remote and paused the movie. "Good idea. I'll take these back to the fridge before I eat it all."

Margo walked down the hall while he took the dirty plates into the kitchen and put them in the dishwasher. He let Scout out to do his business and put the desserts in the fridge.

# Chapter Thirty-Seven

Margo washed her hands and sat on the couch. Before settling in, she poured herself another glass of tea. Connor came back into the living room and sat beside her. She shifted closer to him as his arm snaked around her back.

He restarted the movie and they watched in relative silence, their comments mostly relating to what was happening on the screen.

She half-wondered if he could feel how her heart pounded, being so close to him. She was hyper-aware of his fingertips tracing a slow path back and forth across her bare shoulder, and the taut muscle of his leg as her hand rested on his thigh.

"So, why is he –" he began.

Margo turned her head to look at him and suddenly their mouths were together. She had no idea if she kissed him or if he'd kissed her, nor did she care. Turning toward him, she wrapped her arms around his neck. His hand wound into her hair and his other rested on her knee.

At some point, they moved, and she ended up on his lap, his hand inching higher on her leg as their tongues tangled together.

The volume of the television blared suddenly, startling Scout into a barking frenzy.

They pulled apart, momentarily confused. Margo slid back to her spot and fixed her skirt.

"Remote." Connor pulled the remote control from between the couch cushions and turned the volume down. "We must have sat on it."

"I can't believe Tom Hanks shouted at us like that."

"I know. Rude." He ran a hand through his hair.

"I should probably go."

"You don't have to. If that wasn't okay…"

"No, no. It was okay. Very okay. But I should probably go before it goes too much farther where I'm not sure if it's as okay."

He looked a little confused. "Sure. I don't want to do anything if you don't."

"It's not that it wouldn't be okay." She let out a sigh. "And it's *definitely* not that I don't want to stay." She fiddled with the hem of her skirt. "Because I do. I just don't want to go too far down this road until we decide where this is going."

"Yeah. That's good. We need to talk about what we want."

Margo nodded. She felt awkward. Her only "real" relationship had been with Brad, and they'd never had one real, honest conversation. He told her how he felt, then told her how she felt, and she'd gone along with it. She didn't want that again, and she certainly didn't want anything like that with Connor. She took a deep breath. "Sorry, this is really awkward. I'm not good at thinking a lot about what I want, let alone *talking* about it."

Connor gave a laugh and sat back against the couch. "I get it. It's not exactly one of my strong suits, either." He held out his arm and she leaned back into him.

She took a deep breath. Might as well just lay it out there. "Okay. So. I'm not interested in anything casual. I'm not interested in rushing into marriage or anything like that, but if we're going to have a relationship, I would expect it to be exclusive and monogamous." She frowned and shook her head. "No, not just expect. It would *have* to be exclusive and monogamous. That's a dealbreaker."

"Agreed."

"Really?" She wasn't sure why she was surprised.

"Of course. I've never been interested in playing the field. I want to be with someone who wants to be with me. Simple as that."

"What are your dealbreakers?"

"Cheating, which we've already established. Lying. All that underhanded, toxic stuff. Disrespect. Fighting dirty. Name-calling and stuff like that. I won't live with that again."

"Agreed."

He asked, "What else?"

"Being fair. Like splitting chores and stuff like that. I barely clean up after myself, I'm certainly not cleaning up after someone else."

"Definitely. I'll cook and you help with the dishes."

"Deal. And don't expect me to cook very often. I survive on takeout and I'm quite happy with that." The more she said out loud, the more comfortable she got with expressing her needs.

He said, "You'll have to go to sporting events with me. I love going to watch baseball and football."

"I'm so in. I love sports. You have to give me flowers every once in a while. Or leave notes in my car. Random things like that, just to make me feel special. Like you're thinking of me."

"Absolutely."

Margo turned and hugged him, tight.

"One more thing. Huge dealbreaker."

She pulled back and looked at him. "What?"

"You have to keep your belly ring, because it's freaking hot."

She kissed him. Against his mouth, she smiled and said, "I can do that."

*Epilogue*

One Year Later


"By the power vested in me by Become Ordained Today dot com, which is miraculously recognized by the Commonwealth of Pennsylvania, I now pronounce you husband and wife. You may kiss your groom." Doug beamed as the small crowd cheered and Margo kissed her groom.

Scout barked his approval and danced around their legs. He was joined by his new sister, Daisy, a yellow lab mix they'd adopted two months earlier.

Laughing with pure joy, Margo finally pulled away from Connor and they faced their audience.

They married in the gazebo Bonnie had decorated with swaths of white tulle garland and twinkling white lights. The sun contributed a spectacular splash of pinks and reds as it set.

The reception was about twenty feet away in the pavilion Bonnie had also decorated. Margo's friend, Megan Caretti, snapped pictures of every moment.

Their families and closest friends surrounded them,

covering them with love, smothering them with hugs, kisses, and well wishes.

Music played while servers set out the buffet.

Margo smoothed her simple white dress. The evening was pure perfection. She felt Connor's arm around her as she surveyed their loved ones. Ashley and Chandler were both pregnant and thrilled. Olivia sat on Elliott's lap, playing patty-cake.

Heidi wrangled her boys. It had taken a while, but she'd come around. In fact, she and Margo were getting along better now than they ever had.

Connor's mom, Angie, sat beside Margo's mom, Diana, showing each other pictures on their phones.

John and Jean had declined to attend. Margo was deeply disappointed, but not surprised.

Laughter filled the evening air as Margo and Connor claimed their seats.

Connor's breath was warm on her neck. "You are so beautiful."

Margo nearly cried at the pure love in his voice. Her eyes drifted closed and she turned to rest her forehead against his.

Bonnie directed the servers to pour champagne. When everyone had a glass, Oren, their best man, stood and held his glass aloft until everyone quieted.

In the silence, someone gasped. Scout and Daisy casually stood behind the cake table until Bonnie frantically shooed them away. Both of them had frosting on their whiskers and not an ounce of regret between them. Margo covered her mouth, laughing. "Don't worry," she told their guests. "There are sheetcakes in the kitchen, so your piece won't be contaminated by tongueprints."

Oren laughed. "I had this whole long, touching speech prepared, complete with Shakespeare quotes. But that kind of feels like overkill after being upstaged by a couple of cake thieves."

Everyone chuckled.

"I think I'll just say this: Fate knew what it was doing when it threw you two together." He lifted his glass. "To Connor. To Margo. And to being caller number nine."

---

Enjoyed this trip to Hickory Hollow? Keep those warm fuzzy feelings going and dive straight into Book 3 in the Hickory Hollow series, The Boy Next Door.

*When Kim Donahue takes in her orphaned nephew, she puts her dreams on hold for his protection – until a former superstar moves in next door who might be good for both of them.*

Hickory Hollow. Get comfy, stay a while!

You don't want to miss news of upcoming books, events, and behind-the-scenes sneak peeks! Sign up for my newsletter today at carriejacobs.com!

# Acknowledgments

As far as fun day jobs go, being a writer has to be near the top of the list. I get to sit in my house all day, playing with my imaginary friends, and we have a blast. I even get to say things like that out loud and no one gets concerned because... "writer."

I also get to take a little creative license with reality. In the book, Scout runs off-leash and unattended. In real life, I'm a big fan of dogs being under their owner's control.

One thing I did *not* make up is that beginning in the 1920s, Lysol was advertised for feminine hygiene. Yes, the cleaning product. Google it, I'll wait. *shudder*

Writing a book involves a lot of people, many of whom don't even know they're part of the process.

I'd first like to thank our incredible veterinarian, Dr. Deb Deppen, DVM. She not only takes wonderful care of our animals, she also never batted an eyelash when I asked her if she'd perform an emergency tracheotomy on a human (she would), or when I questioned her about using feminine douche as a remedy for skunk spray (sure, as long as it's non-toxic).

A huge thank you to Beth Brown of Recensere Editing. She did an amazing job of helping me to make this a better book. https://recensereediting.com/

Thank you to Michelle Haring of Cupboard Maker Books for being not only a great friend, but also an amazing supporter of local authors. If you're ever in central Pennsylvania, you *must* stop by Cupboard Maker Books, the most awesome indie bookstore ever. There are rows and rows and rows of books, and to sweeten the deal, there are also cats. https://cupboardmaker.com

My 4th Wednesday Critique Group – I seriously love you guys. I couldn't ask for a better group of colleagues. I always look forward to your comments and critiques, because you always point out things I need to see. This group is such a big part of my journey, and I am grateful.

To my bestie writer friends who get me, I can't thank you enough for your support and encouragement. You know who you are.

To my non-writer friends who get me, thank you so much for your support and enthusiasm! I love you bunches. You also know who you are.

To my sworn enemies… one day, sweet vengeance will be mine. You don't know who you are. (But you will. Muwahaha…)

I have to give a shout out to Molly Jane, the goodest girl ever. Molly is our yellow Labrador, who provided the inspiration for Scout. Like Scout, she loves playing in water and dirt and mud, and she never passes up an opportunity for a nap. She thinks every day is the best day ever. I should follow her lead on that.

I guess now I also have to shout out Cersei and Emma, our furry feline fixtures. They sit in my office and judge me as I work. Thanks, I guess?

Mom & Dad – thanks for everything. Especially the free proofreading. (That would be Mom. Definitely not Dad, who doesn't even have an opinion on the Oxford Comma. Can you believe such people exist?!)

Austin – keep doing what you're doing, Child O' Mine, you're doing great and I'm proud of you.

Saving the best for last, thank you Scott. My dreams are only coming true because of your support. I love you.

# About the Author

Carrie's love of storytelling began in early childhood and never wavered as time marched onward. She reads in pretty much every genre imaginable, but found her writing happy place in small town contemporary romance and romantic comedy.

From that love came Hickory Hollow, a mashup of her hometown and places she's either visited or would like to. Her favorite part of Hickory Hollow? The residents don't have to drive an hour to get to Target, like she does in real life.

Carrie lives in beautiful central Pennsylvania with her family and very spoiled furry editorial assistants.

Connect with Carrie through her newsletter or social media!

Website: carriejacobs.com

facebook.com/writercarriejacobs

instagram.com/carriejacobsauthor

goodreads.com/carriejacobs

www.ingramcontent.com/pod-product-compliance
Lightning Source LLC
Chambersburg PA
CBHW030830110726
47900CB00006B/1829